I0745486

The Merciful

Also by Jon Sealy

The Whiskey Baron
The Edge of America
So You Want to Be a Novelist

The Merciful

a novel

Jon Sealy

Haywire Books
Richmond
Virginia

HAYWIRE BOOKS

Copyright © 2021 by Jon Sealy

This is a work of fiction. The names, characters, places, and incidents are either the product of the author's imagination or are used fictitiously, and any resemblance to actual persons living or dead, events, or locales is entirely coincidental.

All rights reserved. No part of this book may be reproduced in any form or by any electronic means, including information storage and retrieval systems, without permission in writing from the publisher, except by a reviewer, who may quote brief passages in a review.

ISBN: 978-1-950182-07-7
Library of Congress Control Number: 2020942603

Cover Design: Baxton Baylor
Proofreader: Benjamin Kolp
Author Photo: Casey Templeton

For my daughters,
Helen Ann & Lydia

All art is a kind of confession, more or less oblique.

— James Baldwin

OVERLOOK

I know it well: the height of summer in the Lowcountry. The maddening swelter that in less civilized eras drove men to murder their wives and light out for the territories. Fortunately for the women of Overlook, those days were long gone. There were rules to abide by. The west had been tamed. There was nowhere for a man to go, which meant couples all over town had opened their Friday newspapers together to read about the hit and run, how the girl was riding her bicycle home from work when she was dragged a hundred feet down an unlit highway by an unknown motorist. The *Island Packet* out of Hilton Head spared no morbid detail, withheld no judgment for the culprit, and readied the mob with salacious photographs of police tape and roadside foliage, the body just outside the frame. Because this was the region's first juicy news all summer, even the *Post and Courier* up in Charleston carried the story in its Sunday A section: "Search Continues for Driver of Vehicle." A spokesperson for the local police department said they were following several lines of investigation. Justice would be served.

Her name was Samantha James—Sam—and she was a student home for the summer before her sophomore year at the

University of South Carolina. She worked at a Japanese restaurant off the boulevard in the old town of Overlook, a quirky assortment of shops run by the wives of wealthy retirees: seashell jewelry, chic clothing, a children's bookstore, and a mess of art galleries and second-hand antiques. Most of these businesses had to be losing money, especially after the downturn, the recovery that never was, but they gave the business owners something to do and added a certain civic pride to a town unknown outside the region. Locals liked to think of themselves as the Bohemian second cousins of Hilton Head, plenty of inlets and golf courses but no beaches or out-of-state tourists, merely a laid-back lifestyle that catered to upscale Baby Boomers and the companies that developed their gated communities.

Sam was nineteen years old and the eldest daughter of an insurance executive who spent four days a week on the road, the price of living in a funky coastal town with no industry beyond land development. She waited tables Thursday to Sunday nights, and she'd just returned from a trip to Michigan with her mother to visit her grandparents in Farmington Hills. She was still dating her boyfriend from high school, a used car salesman who had not been invited to Michigan, and she'd not seen him in more than a week, when he'd invited her over for a pitiful dinner that may have been a last-ditch effort to salvage their relationship. She'd texted him when she and her mother landed in Savannah Thursday morning, equivocally arranged to meet him after she got off work, and rode her bicycle to the restaurant.

The restaurant, Tokyo, closed at ten, and then Sam had after-hours duties: rolling napkins and silverware, refilling the salt and pepper shakers, vacuuming the dining room, tipping out the cooks and bartenders. She clocked out a few minutes after ten, when the manager was counting the nightly till and the dishwasher was drying the last of the dishes and the cooks were having a cigarette break by the dumpsters before they hosed off the kitchen mats. According to newspaper reports, none of the Tokyo staff remembered seeing her leave, for it had been a surprisingly busy night and everyone went home, blinkered and bone-weary. There was a missing hour in her life, based on when she clocked out and the estimated time of death, that no one on staff could account for. It was generally agreed that after she completed her duties, Sam would have unlocked her bicycle from the lamppost in front of the restaurant, fastened her helmet and turned on her blinking light, and headed home. There was no reason for her to stay much later than ten, and there was nothing in the area around the restaurant for her to do. Old Town Overlook would have been well lit, and perhaps a few kids would have been out, on their way to one of the town's few bars. Overlook was safe at night, more or less, the few very real threats kept indoors, in dark corners, away from the public's view.

Everything that happened in the life of Samantha James after ten o'clock would forever remain conjecture. Perhaps she took a detour to one of the bars, but no witness could verify it and there were no charges on her debit card. At midnight, her mother asleep at their home on Gardenia Drive and her father asleep in a rental house in Charlotte, Sam's boyfriend—a rangy, pimple-faced, self-loathing young man named Gibbs—looked up from his pitiful life and saw his girlfriend had not shown up. It was late. Had she forsaken him? You can say this for Gibbs: he'd somewhat moved out of his mother's house after high school and rented a room from her above their garage, a detached apartment complete with its own bathroom and kitchenette. He nevertheless regularly helped himself to the contents of his mother's refrigerator, which is precisely what he did after realizing how late his girlfriend was. He was hungry. She had promised him Tokyo leftovers. He made himself a ham and cheese sandwich in his mother's kitchen and turned on the television, keeping the volume low so as not to wake her. Then, sated by the sandwich, he stepped into the night to light a cigarette and call Sam. Her phone went straight to voicemail. He called the restaurant but no one answered. Curious but not yet anxious, he thought about calling her mother, but decided against it. Finally, after much hemming and hawing, he got in his old Jetta and drove out to look for her.

To get from the restaurant to Gibbs's house—assuming she went straight there—Sam would have ridden west on Reedy

Road two miles from Old Town to Highway 278, which led into Hilton Head. She would have crossed the highway, six lanes without a median, and made her way into his neighborhood. No guard and no gatehouse at the front of Gibbs's neighborhood. His parents were indigenous to the Carolinas and therefore did not share the pretensions of carpetbaggers such as the Jameses. She could have ridden her bicycle straight in, propped it against the side of the garage, and skipped up the steps to Gibbs's apartment with the sushi deluxe dinner in her hand and a smile on her face. But no, he thought, as he maneuvered the whiny Volkswagen out of the neighborhood, she must have gotten tired, or developed a migraine, or decided to run off with one of her fellow servers. The darkest possibilities had not entered his mind then, not yet.

The two-mile strip of Reedy Road between Old Town and 278 was unlit, but the road was a straight shot except for one dangerous curve. Here at the end of July, the roadside foliage—scrub brush and honeysuckle and trumpet creepers and a thicket of trees, from live oaks and maples to dogwood and mimosas—was overgrown so that even under the best of circumstances, a bicyclist needed to remain vigilant. Despite the recklessness of the ride between the restaurant and her boyfriend's house—to say nothing of the equally reckless trip between the restaurant and her parents' house—Sam insisted on riding her bicycle, both for eco-friendliness and so she would not have to contend with the upkeep and insurance and gasoline required by a car. Gibbs had always put up with her quirkiness, was in fact endeared to it, but he would never forgive himself for his complacency.

As he drove east along Reedy Road, he kept an eye out for Sam, still thinking perhaps she'd merely gotten a flat tire and needed a lift. He reached the notorious curve and slowed to a crawl, put on his hazard lights, and coasted into the grass. Rubber scuff marks slashed across the westbound lane like brush strokes in a child's clumsy painting. A scattering of metal debris in the road created a trail that led to Sam's bicycle, in the weeds, wrecked nearly beyond recognition. Gibbs pulled a flashlight out of the glove box and yelled, "Sam!" into the night. He paced the road up and down several times before he found her body lying face-down in a ditch. Although he couldn't tell for sure, he believed immediately that she was dead, a belief paramedics confirmed twenty minutes later. In the interim, Gibbs dialed 911 and stuttered through, holding Sam's lifeless hand and feeling lightheaded from the unreality of it all until, finally, the police and EMS arrived to relieve him of his vigil.

The article just made the front page of the *Island Packet* Friday morning, although it meant holding up the presses for a hastily written rail of *no comment* and *all we know at this point*. But on Saturday, Sunday, Monday, all the regional papers splashed the feature on A1, included photos and sidebars about the outraged cycling community. The mood across the region soured as the mystery lingered and the TV vultures crowded the scene of the accident, made sure to capture the police tape, scoured for blood they could film. Sam's Facebook photograph—which showed an attractive, clear-eyed young woman who looked like she might have a bright future in public relations, smiling into the camera from some outdoorsy excursion, trees and sky behind her—was plastered everywhere but the local milk cartons, always raising the same questions: Who was the driver? Had he been drinking? Did anyone see anything? And where was Sam during the missing hour between clocking out and the accident?

Authorities asked witnesses to come forward. A hotline was set up for anyone with information. Anything at all. Then on Tuesday, the news media reported that a person of interest had come forward, that police were examining a damaged vehicle. The police spokesperson said they were taking the investigation seriously. No arrests had been made. Yet. Information would be forthcoming. On Friday, a week after the first news reports, the information came forth.

My old roommate, Daniel Hayward, was the person of interest.

THERE BUT FOR THE GRACE OF GOD

1

Sometimes you have to shatter your life.

Daniel Hayward told me this years ago over a bottle of Wild Turkey by a campfire on the banks of the Chattooga River. He and I had recently graduated from the College of Charleston and were on a rafting trip with a group of guys before we all scattered across the American empire. It had been an exhilarating day on the river, enough rapids to give us a few jolts in our raft but plenty of long stretches where the river was like glass and we cracked open beers, no sound more satisfying under a Carolina sun than the pop and hiss of a can of cold lager. A few hours before making camp, we hit a rock and went over Second Ledge backward. The most experienced river rat among us, who was in the other boat, said the rapid was easy to contend with, hit it straight on and it would be no problem. Until it was a problem: an unexpected rock, hidden beneath the water, sent us off course. I vividly remember, all these years later, the sound of the raft as it lurched sideways and how I, on the starboard side of the raft, peered over the drop and into water boiling in an eddy below.

Then we were over and somehow bobbing down the river, cries of *Whoo!* and *We styled that!* belying our relief from not spilling out. Although I grew up less than twenty miles from the coast and knew the breathtaking expanse of water, taking a raft down this wild and scenic river was an almost mystical experience. The guys and I talked about it—about what it meant to be a man in the twenty-first century, about the primeval experience of getting out into the woods, about humans' innate fascination with fire and water, and about our past experiences of roughing it with our friends, our fathers, our brothers. We talked about Second Ledge and how people died on this river, and how we had the Bull Sluice to navigate the next day.

Then night settled in and the fire smoldered and Daniel and I were the last men standing, passing the whiskey between us, our minds thick with a slurry of booze and mesmerized by the crackle and flames. "I've been swimming in the Lowcountry rivers, but this is a whole different experience," I said. "I don't know if it's the rapids or the fact that we're on our own out here, you know? I mean, if something happened to us, if one of us caught a finger with that ax or got bit by a copperhead, we'd have to hike how many miles to get out? A bad enough injury, you wouldn't get out at all."

Daniel took a sip of the Wild Turkey, held the liquor in his mouth for a moment before swallowing, and said, "Sometimes you have to shatter your life."

I thought about this one Friday evening more than a decade later, when I found out my old friend—who had married the mystery girl and moved down to the coast to sell data-mining software and play golf in my hometown of Overlook, South Carolina—was arrested for the hit and run killing of a college girl on a bicycle, the incident alleged to have happened after a business dinner with an attractive client. The client, Karen Sinclair, was a formidable businesswoman pushing forty, divorced, sultry, mysterious in a way only certain women allowed themselves to be after the age of twenty-five. Daniel had been married seven years and had no business at a late-evening one-on-one with such a woman. Shatter your life, indeed. This was merely the first of many such compromises I would have to reconcile with the man I knew from college.

Daniel Hayward was brilliant but lazy. He came to Charleston from Ohio for the girls and the beach. The son of a Cleveland hospital executive and fundraising socialite, he entered college knowing how to work a crowd, how to make people feel good about themselves in his presence, and how to get what he wanted without appearing like a politician. He never would have made it in politics, I believed, because he had a moral center. *I'm an asshole,* he once confided to me during one of those drunken truth-sessions indulged in by the young. I tried to tell him, *No, no, you're a good guy,* but he replied with, *Whenever there's a choice between doing the right thing and doing what's best for me, I do what's best for me every time.* Another line I chewed over after the arrest. I'd studied enough philosophy in college to have definite opinions about intentions versus consequences, and about Daniel Hayward I'd concluded this: we all have mixed intentions and mixed results in life, which by any measure makes us less than noble creatures, yet goodness stems, in part, from accountability. The Daniel I'd known had always taken responsibility for his life and his actions, which should have been enough.

And yet.

We came of age in a different era, and I'd known him in a different life. By the summer of his arrest, America had become arrested by politics, and when the news of his broke, I was working as a business consultant for a firm that offered strategic communications—a once-aspiring novelist who now worked with 20th century corporations struggling to find a profit in the 21st century—and I looked up at a world transformed, a world where context and nuance no longer seemed welcome. Like the corporate clients I worked with, I'd somehow become part of the system and was struggling to keep up even as another recession loomed in our economy. Daniel Hayward's arrest gave me my first occasion, in early middle age, to look backward, and I realized just how much and how quickly the world had changed. The criteria by which I might evaluate my friend had changed, so did I even really know him? Had I ever known him? Did I know myself?

2

A story must begin somewhere, and for me it starts when Daniel Hayward first met his wife. We were freshmen in college, single, uncertain yet headstrong, ambitious and impossibly stupid, when one afternoon Daniel returned to Craig Hall grinning like some smitten Lysander or Demetrius, and said, "I've met her."

"Who?" I'd been sitting on my bed, strumming a guitar, and ignoring the unreadable orthography of *The Canterbury Tales* in its original Middle English.

"Francine."

"Francine, huh." I set the guitar down. "I suppose Fran and Dan has a nice ring to it."

"No, Jay. Francine."

I'd only known Daniel a few months at that point, but in the way of young friendships, I felt I knew him well enough to recognize something had shifted in his life. Like scaffolding stripped from a renovation to reveal something beautiful, Daniel seemed to have transformed into the man he would be for the rest of his life. Meanwhile, still in my late adolescent cocoon—rawboned, mop-headed, acned—I'd never seen my friend so elated, nor seen a man with a literal twinkle in his eyes, a man in love in the spring and ready to sally forth with an ode of praise for his Venus's eyes and mouth and skin and breasts, an ode to time and the value of human life. Carpe diem. Tempus fugit.

Daniel Hayward had been struck.

"Who is she?" I asked.

"A girl I saw, walking down the street."

"You get her number?"

"No, but I followed her to the gym and saw her sign in. I got her name."

"You didn't talk to her?"

"What would I have said?"

"I don't know. 'Hi'?"

"No, Jay, you have to understand, you can't just go up and talk to a girl this beautiful, this perfect. You have to have a reason."

"You couldn't make something up? It's a little sketchy, following her like that. Don't you think? A little stalker-ish?"

"Not if we're perfect for each other." And here he launched into it. "Her eyes, Jay, green as emeralds, her skin lightly tanned." His eyebrows shot up as he leaned in and lowered his voice. "And she's blonde."

I was a South Carolinian, where blonde women abound. Half the women in my family were blonde, by bleach if not birth: frost, highlights, whatever miracle the hairdressers pulled off. But for Daniel, raised in the slush of industrial Cleveland, blonde was apparently something exotic, something to celebrate along with blue skies and barbecue after Labor Day.

For a Midwestern boy new to the South, blonde was *blonde*.

"What are you going to do?"

"I have to find her," he said, and he lay on his bed, crossed his arms behind his head, and closed his eyes to dream of his Francine, his Helen of Troy.

Find her he did. The College of Charleston was a small campus, yet it nonetheless took him into the next semester to track her down. He attended every party from every sub-group he could think of: the keggers in historic houses up Coming Street, where two hundred strangers would show up to drink in alleys between the shotgun houses; the rugby team house parties, where girls would link arms and sing the unofficial college anthem (*It's a damn fine college but we didn't come for knowledge*); the subterranean raves in the catacombs hidden by King Street storefronts, apartment complexes that wended into a leaky wonderland far removed from sunlight. He finally found her at a philosophy club-slash-religious studies oyster roast out on Sullivan's Island. There was a Zen koan in there somewhere, for the mixer was my idea to give him a break from the Natural Light beer and the smoky Confederate living rooms of the college's business class. He came with me to the mixer without expectations, yet there she was, in a yellow Billabong shirt and Daisy Dukes. I couldn't say how Daniel approached her, or what he said to win her over. What I know ends with him pointing her out and saying, "There she is!" before taking off. I never even met her, simply watched the two of them siphon away from the crowd and proceed to spend the next three hours on the beach. Occasionally, I would glance over at them, see them smiling and laughing, and wish Daniel well.

Myself, I bounced among a handful of philosophy majors, mostly upperclassmen holding forth on Heidegger and the difference between *Being* and *being*. As a college freshman raised two hours south in Overlook, I felt behind in my intellectual life, cowed by urban scholars who had done more than ride a skateboard and play music through high school. I entered college knowing next to nothing of human nature and with a near-total inability to navigate human interaction. I was looking for an invitation to a party I assumed existed beyond the limits of my knowledge, and spent my college years trying to catch up. Yet it was clear even tonight, amid loud and opinionated upper classmen, that I would never be cut out for the philosophy crowd. I understood myself as a *being* among *beings* in the greater *Being* of the universe, but ascribed instead to what William Carlos Williams called the poetry of *no ideas but in things*: the sycamore branches growing wild in the gloaming, the crackling sparks from the fire near the beach, the long stretch of cooling sand, the freighter moored in the distance nothing more than a blue blur on the vanishing horizon.

While Daniel made his first stuttering step in a long courtship of Francine, I listened to a heated dialogue about existence and inter-subjectivity and then made my way to the oyster roast. There, I passed a few awkward words with an environmental studies professor named Ned, who stood hunched over and shoveled oysters into his mouth like a man coming off a three-day hike on the Appalachian Trail. I had taken the professor for a vegetarian, just another way I'd misread someone, more proof I had much to learn. Ned looked up sheepishly and said, "Mm, hungry." Then he said, "Are you a philosophy major?" Then he said, "Which section are you in?" Then he said, "How are you finding the course?" Then he said, "Well, I'll see you Monday."

At the end of the night, Francine's boyfriend drove his hand-me-down Jaguar out to the island, picked her up, and took her home. Daniel found me leaning against a live oak, placidly watching the crowd disperse in the April dark, and he said, simply, "Well, damn."

"Sorry, man," I said.

"Any luck on your end?"

I shook my head. I'd long since given up on finding a home in the philosophy club and an identity as a deep thinker. I felt dumb and at sea around this crowd.

We got into my truck and drove back to the peninsula while Daniel filled me in on his Francine. That's how he would refer to her, even in the many years to come when they were not together: *his* Francine, as though he knew even at nineteen that fate was not something to be trifled with. His Francine, it turned out, was Francine Glass, the daughter of a pair of Israeli-Americans of German descent. Her grandparents moved to the U.S. between the wars and then immigrated to Israel in 1949. Her parents returned to live in Myrtle Beach after their wedding, where her father owned a chain of Wings beach supply stores. Although she was beautiful back then, Francine later became a kind of bombshell in her thirties, with provocative curves and a fierce wit, and she appeared to be living a most comfortable life in Overlook, all yoga pants and Target and enough freelance public relations work to appear the image of success.

But all of that was to come. Daniel may have believed the two of them would be perfect together, but that night in April, he could not have fathomed what was in store for him. Instead, he knew only that Francine was a philosophy major minoring in Jewish Studies, that she had an interest in creative writing, and that she shared enough interests with Daniel—music playlists, top-five movies, all the things college students worried about, at least in those days—that he found himself truly smitten. As we pulled into the parking garage across from the dorm, he said, "It won't last between them."

"She tell you she had a boyfriend?"

"They always slip it in, don't they? But no, she called him 'her ride.' It won't last."

"What makes you so sure?"

"We're fated to be together," he said.

3

I first heard the news from Facebook. A mutual friend shared a link to the *Post and Courier* article describing the hit and run.

Daniel! No! she wrote on her wall, yet the article was damning in its details. The photos alone—Daniel's Durango with a shattered windshield and a crumpled bumper, his unsmiling mug shot, the crime scene with tape wrapped around roadside trees, blue lights flashing in the background, a mangled bicycle—would convince most of the state of his guilt before his arraignment. The article was even less kind than the photography. Samantha James had been dead three days before Daniel offered himself up as the (alleged) culprit.

Commentary beneath the article was less kind still. *Murderer. Coward. This man deserves to rot in the deepest pit of hell.*

How to reconcile the acrimony today with the Daniel Hayward I'd known in college, more than a decade ago? The man who, upon finding the love of his life had a boyfriend, returned to me at the oyster roast and said, *We're fated to be together,* and then proceeded to date casually and hold out hope until the year after graduation, when he met Francine again by chance and courted her and married her? Such patience, such respect, such grace. I read and reread the news article with a heavy heart, and tried to remember my old friend and draw out some psychological explanation to help me process the news. We'd had a falling out after college, so a few brief memories offer the lone insight I had into the truth of his life, the one clue to his character that might make sense of his decision one evening to go out with a woman, get in the car after he'd had too much to drink, drive off from hitting a bicyclist, and wait several days to come forward as the guilty party. Was he a coward? Did he feel remorse? Everyone in town seemed to have an answer, but I was baffled. Time does a number on all of us, yet I still believed, from knowing Daniel in those brief, halcyon days, that he was not a bad man. He was a romantic at heart, yet he'd made a fatal mistake, his tragic error.

I said nothing to my wife at first. Kate and I lived a decently hermetic life in those days. After college, I'd given up on the great American novel, went to business school at Purdue, and took a job as a marketing analyst at a small consultancy in Virginia. Kate had traveled there for an ill-advised graduate school program and then taken a job in records management for the state. By the time

I'd joined her and embarked on my own career, she was ready for a life like her parents': a house in the suburbs, church bake sales, children, and the long slow slide of middle age, whereas I'd still felt cavalier about life and would have been at the bars every night if she would have come with me. Instead, we were settled in a slapped-together townhouse and trying to plot out what the rest of our lives might look like. We'd recently faced disaster and were now at something of a crossroads. To escape the big questions, we stayed in and binge-watched old TV shows on Netflix and allowed one month to bleed into the next, one year to another. I still had half a novel on my hard drive, a Pat Conroy kind of story about growing up in the Lowcountry, but the problem with the book was that I had nothing to say. At twenty-two, I'd assumed I would keep at it, but then a few months off became a few years off, and here I was, time accelerating in a hemorrhage rather than a bleed.

After hearing the news about Daniel, I retreated to my home office on the pretext of working, opened a bottle of wine, and proceeded to get drunk while reading everything published about my old roommate and the accident. The news outlets had little else to say, but the vitriol in the comments was limitless. A mob had determined Daniel's guilt—drunk, no doubt—and sentenced him to a slew of punishments reminiscent of the Spanish Inquisition. Having grown up in Overlook, I knew the dynamics of life in a small town, yet I was still surprised to see the sheer creativity of these anonymous trolls. One poor soul had the temerity to defend Daniel, only to be attacked herself.

If you only knew Daniel, you'd know he'd give you the shirt off his back.

How can you defend him? The man's evil and needs to be locked up.

I hope you get hit by a car.

I hope you die.

Daniel had come forward this week and allowed the police to examine his vehicle. His name was kept out of the news for a few days, but now the story had been unleashed. He told authorities he believed he'd hit a deer and felt terrible. He was cooperating, and while the police had confirmed his Durango had struck

Samantha—blood and hair were found on his bumper—he had been neither formally charged nor arrested.

The man has connections. What about poor Samantha?

The police are idiots or corrupt or both. If this were any ordinary investigation, he'd be behind bars right now.

The prosecutor's office released a statement that said they were continuing their investigations. I was surprised to see the prosecutor was a young woman named Claire Fields, a few years my junior in high school. She kept a low profile online, but I recognized her from her employment profile on the county website. She had fiery hair and green eyes and a far-off look I understood immediately. I felt a stirring in my blood that I hadn't sensed in months, maybe years. I was struck by how much different she looked, how much more grown up. At thirty-three, I still felt like a young man waiting for life to arrive, so it always shocked me to see someone my age who had embarked on their life's work in earnest. Landed a director or vice-president level job, or traveled into a war zone, or made a killing in a business venture. Yet here was Claire Fields, thirty-one years old and in charge of my friend's fate. She was ready to walk into a court-room and pronounce Daniel guilty, stack up the evidence, and send him to jail, assuring the press that her office believed Daniel did not represent a flight risk and that he was cooperating. "We ask for patience as we continue working with law enforcement," she said in a statement. "Justice will be served."

Had it not been for the phone call, I might have ended my night with a few glasses of wine and let thoughts of Daniel Hayward slide away, an unfortunate turn of events for someone I'd known long ago. The first of many a downfall heading toward my generation. When my cell buzzed with a private number, I meant to hit Ignore but instead slid my finger the wrong direction and inadvertently answered.

I stared at the blinking green light and then said hello.

"Hi, Jay?" said a woman's voice. She sounded tinny and young and far away.

"Who is this?"

"This is Francine Hayward," she said.

I leaned back in my chair and picked up the bottle of wine and poured the final glass.

"Hi, Francine. I just heard about Daniel." I kept my voice low. Kate was already asleep, but all the same. I didn't want her asking questions.

"He talked about you, on occasion," she said. "I think he always regretted that you didn't stay close."

I wanted to ask if he'd explained our falling out, if she knew what I'd said at their wedding, but there was no reason to dredge it up. It was a harmless comment, uttered after too many whiskey shots, and given Daniel's current circumstances, everything that happened in the past was mere prologue. I presumed she had called me now for a voice of reason to say Daniel was still the man she married, that she'd not made some damning error of judgment years ago.

"He always says you were a stand-up guy, one of the most trustworthy people he knew," she went on.

"That's nice to hear," I said. "We always had a good time, but I don't know about all that."

"You're not trustworthy?"

"I like to think I am, or at least I can be. Just not sure that's the first thing I'd say about myself."

"Daniel still thinks highly of you."

I took another sip of the wine. Gulp, really. "How's he doing?" I asked, stupidly.

"How do you think?"

For the first time, she had an edge in her voice that made me think she wasn't just looking for someone to talk with who could reassure her that her husband was a decent guy despite all that had happened.

"I'm sure it's a tough time," I said. "It's an awful situation, for everyone involved."

"You can't imagine it," she said.

"No, but I do think Daniel's got a good heart. The things people are saying online, I know they're not true, and you've got my sympathies."

"Thanks," she said.

I believed I was well on my way to reassuring Francine that her husband was still the man she thought he was. The online comments were vulgar and atrocious, and I could easily see how you'd become unmoored in her position. You'd begin to question your own sense of morality, and ask how well you knew your husband after all. Daniel and I hadn't spoken since his wedding seven years ago, but I still thought of myself as his friend, and was unmoored myself. "I'm sure everything will work out," I said in an effort to close this conversation down.

"I'm sure it won't," she said.

"You don't know that. It sounds like an accident, after all."

"I need someone to take care of Daniel," she said. Like your boss sending a weekend-killing email at four-thirty on Friday afternoon, I understood that Francine and I were settling into something longer than it would take for me to finish the glass of wine.

"How so?" I asked.

"Things have always gone Daniel's way. I have no doubt he's guilty—of hitting the girl, of killing her—but it wasn't like people say. He's not a coward. He's not a bad man."

I imagined my own indiscretions behind the wheel. Younger days, for sure, but I knew how it could happen. "I know it," I said. "It's easy to get into an accident like that. You get a phone call, you look away for a second. Could happen to any of us."

"But it didn't happen to any of us. It happened to my husband, and I need someone to take care of him."

"Hold on a sec," I said.

I drained the wineglass and headed downstairs. My office was across the hall from the master bedroom, where my wife slept, and this conversation was taking a turn I could only handle in the parking lot of our townhouse community. There are times when you have more privacy in public than in your own home.

"So," I said as I slid out the front door. "Why are you calling me?"

"Would you drive down here and talk with him?"

"With Daniel?"

"They're going to arrest him in the next few days."

"Why the delay?"

"He's come forward. They've let him know they're going to charge him, and said they'll let him know the official day over the weekend. If he doesn't turn himself in voluntarily, they'll issue a warrant and come after him."

"I don't know what I'd say or how I could help," I said. "I'm not a lawyer, you know."

"He has a lawyer," she said, "and he should be out on bond the same afternoon. But whatever happens, his life is ruined."

"It might be a bit premature to say that," I said. "This might turn out fine."

"How's he going to come back from this?" she asked. "Even if the hit and run was purely an accident, he's killed someone. He'll always have to go through life with that knowledge. And if he is convicted? He could get twenty-five years."

"Jesus."

"South Carolina doesn't mess around. You know this state. I'm surprised they don't already have a militia lined up a firing squad. Daniel needs someone who knows he's not a monster. Just to reassure him he'll make it through this, wherever it leads."

"And you're not that person?"

She let that comment go unanswered.

I was walking slowly around the neighborhood and paused near the front. I watched a couple of kids hanging out on top of the electrical transformer. One of them was hunched over in the street. I held the phone away from me and stared at it for a moment. When I started walking again, the kids slunk off into the shadows behind a row of townhouses.

I asked Francine, "How did you get this number anyway?"

"Oh, I have my ways," she said, and it made me uncomfortable to hear the flirtatiousness in her voice.

"My cell's unlisted," I said, leaning over to see what the kid had been doing in the street. A thumbtack from the community bulletin board was in the road, poking up and ready to be run over.

"So you'll help Daniel?" she said.

Perhaps I was distracted by the neighborhood kids, because it didn't occur to me to ask where she was calling from. Daniel hadn't been arrested yet, so where was he at this moment? Was

Francine already cutting bait, trying to muster the courage to leave her husband drowning?

"I'll think about it," I said.

"Thank you."

She got off the phone quickly then, before I could change my mind or think to ask for Daniel's contact information. Perhaps he had the same cell number from college, but otherwise what could I do?

I looked around but didn't see where the kids had gone. They were always out in the street, and it had become a problem this summer. One neighbor on the HOA board always had a story to tell about small-time vandalism, and I suspected our community would never be the kind of leafy suburban development where the upwardly mobile wanted to raise their children. Assuming raising a child was still in the cards for Kate and me. Things were presently in doubt.

On my walk back, I tried to recall what I knew about Francine Hayward. She'd been a philosophy major at the College of Charleston, but our paths had never crossed. Daniel had continued his search for her all through college and found her in the summer after our senior year and married her a few years later. I'd gleaned a few snippets about her but had only met her once, at the wedding. She'd clearly loved him, and I thought now how painful it must be to see the one you loved, the one you'd staked your life on, reduced to—what? A mortal man who made mistakes?

The thing I was learning about regret was that it snuck up on you. A little pressure at the wrong moment could re-frame your entire existence. I knew this, but lacked the heart, on the phone with Francine, to say there wasn't a thing I could do to save her or Daniel from his mistake. If he weren't guilty, the law would figure it out. It wasn't like the old days where you gathered testimony and all it took was one damning witness to put you away. The online trolls could fire off their nasty comments, but the law had DNA testing and everything else to convict or clear a person. Claire Fields may have been young, but the prosecutor was still bound by the limits of evidence and the letter of the law.

And if Daniel was guilty? That was territory I could only imagine, and had no counsel for Francine.

When I finally returned home and climbed into bed, I thought about Daniel and what his morning-after must have been like. He would have woken with cobwebs and a few patchy images of the night before. Drunks know those mornings well, the moment you snap into consciousness and realize there are missing hours when the devil could have done his mischief. Most of those mornings end with a vomit and a chaser of shame—once more into the breach, a loss of control—but if you carried on long enough you eventually ran up against something sinister: a missing tooth, a damaged car, a stranger in your bed. It had been years since my own reckless days, but I'd been lucky more times than I cared to face.

Perhaps certain images blurred in Daniel's dreams that night, so he would have woken to the memory of the thump from hitting something on his way home. A loud bang that jolted the vehicle out of its lane. A deer? A pothole? And he'd kept going, parked, stumbled into bed. Those last moments before bed were the first you forgot, so more and more images would have returned to him, and the memory of that collision would have been like a stone in his chest, increasing in weight, pressing against his lungs. In the light of day, his head aching from dehydration, he would have gone out to see the damage to his car and realized it had been no dream. He'd hit something in the night. With the newspaper reports that followed, he would have known exactly what he'd done, who he'd hit. It was the moment you sliced into your skin while chopping vegetables and saw the red trickle of blood before you felt the pain. This was the moment you didn't come back from, the curtain that choreographed your life into before and after. And at that point, I could only imagine his dual feelings of remorse and the desire to get away, to undo what he'd done and forget about it. Move to some isolated western state and start over.

Wake from the nightmare that had become his life.

4

The day after Francine called, I had a business meeting with one of our clients, an envelope manufacturing firm that had recently woken up and realized their core business was stuck in the last century. Email had killed the personal letter-writing business twenty years ago, so our client was actually in the marketing business and was only now figuring that out. My job was consulting 101: Know your business. Know your customer. Know your customer's business. The firm I worked for specialized in helping companies transform from a dying industry into something more profitable, but I was really something of a business therapist. My job was to show up in meetings and listen to clients spout their buzzwords—innovation, big data, responsiveness, accelerate, creativity, digital, diversity, unconscious bias—synthesize what they really meant to say, and package it in a format that made sense for them. I imagine it's like a counselor explaining to someone how they're enabling their partner's bad habits: You give them the language to recognize and accept what they already know, and then there's maybe a fifty-fifty chance they'll take your advice and correct course. Companies love the word *innovation*, and as an outsider I found it bemusing that all my clients positioned themselves like they were Bell Labs changing the world, when all they really wanted was to find a way to do the same thing for less money so they could keep the stock price going up.

Because I'd heard it all before, I zoned out as soon as the envelope executive began talking about *transforming for the future* and their *accelerated digital-first strategy* and instead thought about Daniel Hayward. I knew a hit and run was a serious offense, but I didn't know they could put you away for twenty-five years. I'd had a few high school friends wind up in a holding cell for vandalism, and I had an uncle who occasionally spent the night in a drunk tank, but I'd never known anyone go away for such a long stint.

"What do you think, Jay?" asked one of my colleagues. "Could we turn a proposal around tomorrow for a culture campaign?"

"I don't see why not," I said, snapping back into it. "Uh, we've got the usual channels to reach employees. The intranet, the e-newsletter—do we want to do anything different? Maybe some guerrilla pop-ups around the manufacturing facility?"

"I love it," said my colleague. "We can show you some mock-ups of a few disruptors we pulled together last year for another client."

"As long as you stay within our safety regulations," our client cut in.

"Oh absolutely. We can work with facilities on something, maybe that hangs from the ceiling so we don't create any tripping hazards."

Our client's eyes lit up, and I recognized the look of a woman as bored in her job as I was with mine. The metrics almost didn't matter. Our job was to make something fun, to make corporate life tolerable.

That night in bed, I told Kate what was happening with Daniel.

"Oh, God," she said.

"I know."

"Do you think he hit her?"

"Probably. He says he thought he hit a deer."

"Uh huh." Kate was a bureaucrat now, and had little truck with rule breakers.

"You know how the roads are down there," I said. "It's not a bad assumption."

Like our Richmond suburb, Hilton Head Island was perennially lit in a sodium haze, like a Wal-Mart parking lot. But across the sound in Overlook, the developers were only beginning the work of turning the mainland into a Lowcountry theme park, which meant you could still find true dark, where the deer were lit like ghosts in the starlight.

I ranted about the online commentary, how everyone had found him guilty without knowing a thing about him, and how maybe I didn't know my old friend either, and how life seemed so unpredictable. "You make one mistake," I said, "and wham! You can forget about happiness."

She waited a moment before responding, as though trying to find the subtext in this conversation. The longer we were married, the less it mattered what we actually said. We already knew each other and could gather the gist of each other's days. Instead, the day-to-day shuffle of our marriage hinged on what was left out. She said, "You haven't seen Daniel in a long time. Do you think you'd want to go see him?"

"What, in jail?"

"He might want a friend."

"I don't know that he'd want to see me," I said, though in truth I was feeling complacent. It had been a shock to my system, for sure, but seeing Daniel in the flesh would be a mistake. It would confirm that I didn't know him, and possibly suggest I'd never known him, and that the entire world as I understood it was a sham. I believed it might be better to search for the Truth within my memories and imagination, to find Being in what Wallace Stevens called *the palm at the end of the mind*.

I knew Kate could sense there was more to my interest in Daniel than I was letting on, that some fissure had erupted inside me. Friends inevitably let you down, but when something takes hold of your spirit the way Daniel's hit and run had taken hold of mine, it's a sign that something else lurks below the surface. Kate had better intuition than I did, so perhaps she already suspected we were approaching an inflection point in our marriage, and that I was steering us into dangerous waters. We had a fine marriage, by many standards, but we'd had enough roadblocks that I believed we were both wary of the future.

"I mean, I haven't seen him since college," I went on. "That's a long time ago."

"It doesn't seem it." She snuggled closer and touched my foot with hers.

"Ten years last spring."

"Hard to believe."

I was silent for a moment, because I could sense nostalgia creeping in and could feel her edging into territory I wasn't ready to confront. Namely, the prospect of trying again for a baby. When you're young, no one tells you pregnancy becomes a challenge in your thirties, yet we'd heard about friends who had been trying for years, who had gone through treatments and taken drugs and looked into surrogacy. Those were heavy life questions, and had crept up on us. A coherent story of our marriage was one of the few lifelines we had left. Kate had gone to graduate school for theater, given up that life as impractical and taken a mind-numbing job for the state. She had student loans in the mid-five figures and no way to pay them. We were in our early thirties, and like a light switch Kate had decided she was ready for children. I'd been skeptical, with our debt, but she'd insisted. One morning she'd woken up with her biological clock screaming at her, and she'd sold me with horror stories about the cliff of age thirty-five and what that meant about possible birth defects. She'd gone off birth control without preparing me for what was to come. Month after month, she'd dropped the negative pregnancy test in the trash with a thump, brushed past me in the bedroom and busied herself in her office, the room that might one day become a nursery. All of that was nothing compared to the miscarriage. In the spring, she'd taken a positive test at six weeks and cried with joy with her arms around me. At eight weeks, after the bleeding came and went, she cried alone in the bedroom while I paced the house. Now she was ready to start again, and I was nudging my foot out the door, uncertain whether I could go through all of that again. I feel women are stronger than men in many respects, and I know my wife is stronger than I am when it comes to matters of the heart.

All of this is to say that you could feel the strain behind every conversation. No, college did not seem all that long ago, but it was. We were in the thick of life and only beginning to recognize it.

"She's just such an abstraction," I said.

"Who?"

"The girl, the bicyclist. I keep reading the news. There's one photo of her floating around, a kind of grainy cutout of her with a group of friends. I can't imagine how vicious it must be to find out your daughter's been killed in a hit-and-run, and if it were you, I'd be ready to kill someone."

Kate shifted her feet again, and I pulled away.

"But I know Daniel," I went on. "Or knew him, anyway. He wasn't like all that online commentary says. He's a good guy, the kind of guy you'd call if you got in a jam. A little self-centered, but we all were in college. He was a hard worker, and had more focus than I ever did. Maybe it was because he was from Ohio and came all that way to college. I don't know, maybe he felt like he needed to earn a four-year vacation at the beach. Or maybe it's a Midwestern thing. Your family's industrious. Is that how everyone is up there?"

"Only if you're of German heritage."

"Well, anyway, he's screwed now," I said. "He had his life before he hit the girl and he has his life after he hit the girl. Even if he gets off, or ends up with a community service sentence, this is going to be the moment that defines him. Everything in his life will come back to this one moment. Everything he ever is or does, this will be in his background."

"That's a sad thought," Kate mumbled, already drifting away.

"What really frightens me," I said, "is that we've all been there. We've all done something we're not proud of, made some bad decision in the spur of the moment. It's a 'there but for the grace of God' moment. We've just been lucky."

She said nothing, and I couldn't tell if she was asleep, or just didn't care for this line of thought. But it was true. I'm not an overtly religious man, but I was raised Baptist and knew my bible. *He that is without sin among you, let him first cast a stone at her.*

I lay awake for a long time, thinking about my life and my dislocation. When I was younger, I would have said, yes we're all sinners, but grace is just around the corner. That made a nice story, the fall and redemption, but now everything felt flat and one-dimensional. The thing about stories is that they are inherently dishonest. They put a frame around the world to create meaning, but I knew from my consulting business that you could frame the narrative however you wanted. A story was manipulation, and right now, the media was creating one version of events around Daniel Hayward. Claire Fields and the DA's office had another story. Daniel and the defense attorney had their own angle, and it would be left to a judge to sort out the truth. Everyone has their own side, and if life had taught me nothing else, it was that there were very real limits to what we could know about another human being.

As for myself, I'd framed my own life a certain way, but now circumstances had broken the frame and forced me to reevaluate. I wondered what it would be like if I pulled up stakes, moved back home to South Carolina, and tried to start over. Kate and I had no children, so while a divorce would take an emotional toll, life would go on. Perhaps that was crazy, but for all I knew, Kate was lying awake thinking the same things, searching for a way out, a way to rewrite her own story. Was this how a marriage ended? Not with a hot-blooded argument or an affair, but instead with the gradual cooling of entropy?

Shatter your life indeed.

Before I fell asleep, a memory from graduate school surfaced unexpectedly. One gloomy night in February, in the trough of winter, I lost control of my life in a way I never had before or since. My cohorts and I were drinking in a bar called Nine Irish Brothers, a dim and dark-wooded establishment with mirrors on the walls and old-timey glassware. Here you would find, on any given night, a dozen or more graduate students from the business school drinking everything from Bud Light to White Russians, some at the bar, at tables in the back, hidden in the low lighting and amid the fog of cigarette smoke in the days when you could do such things.

I was dating Kate long-distance, so I was unaffected by the romantic shuffle in my program. Much of life in an MBA program was a game of one-upmanship, showing off by getting up earlier or working through lunch on a brief, interjecting in class to get a word in—the same skills we would need to succeed in client meetings in a couple of years—but at the end of those long, competitive days, we drank. Even if you were part of the 6 a.m. crowd, it wasn't couth to ghost out of the bar before midnight. When it was late enough, everyone cozy-drunk to the point of congratulating themselves on how great they all were and how they would soon be running the world, I slunk into the gloomy Midwestern night. The chill bit into my bones and sucked the air out of me, and though I'd left my coat in the bar, I was drunk enough to shrug it off as lost forever. There was no going back, into the noise and the smoke and the drunken good cheer that could grow dangerous in a flash. Instead, I jammed my hands into my pockets and tick-tocked left and right across the parking lot to my truck, where I paused a moment and then peed on the front tire. What the hell, no one was around.

While I waited for my truck to warm up, I called Kate, who was certainly in bed already. This I remember. The rest of the evening exists in mere fragments, each snippet more distressing than the last.

When she picked up, I slurred about how was her day.

"It was fine," she said coldly. "Where are you?"

"Oh, here and there."

"You staying safe?"

"Nice and warm. I got a bottle of something at the house. You want to crack open some wine?"

"It's after midnight."

"I miss you," I said. "I'm lonesome."

"You miss me because you're lonesome?"

"No, that's not what I meant."

As I struggled to make myself clear, I put the truck in gear and headed onto the highway and across the river, pinning the phone with my shoulder as I shifted gears. At Fifth, I looked over and saw the lights spilling out of the Knickerbocker and thought briefly of having another drink. Then I ran a stop sign at Seventh.

When I hung up, I folded the phone in half and saw that I'd missed my street. I tapped the brakes and swung a U-turn but didn't make it. My truck hopped the opposite sidewalk with a whoomp and I slammed on the brakes and came to a stop in someone's front yard, banged up and disoriented.

My ears rang from the noise of the car scraping against the concrete, and my first thought was that I had to get out of there. I looked out the window and saw no one. No pedestrians, no bicyclists, no other cars. The front yard was demolished. A light clicked on in the house.

My truck had stalled out, so I pressed the clutch and was able to turn over the engine. I put it in first and rolled off the yard, onto the sidewalk. The muffler scraped against the curb as I dropped it onto the street, a noise loud enough to wake the devil. Then I somehow managed to navigate back to my house and tuck the car in a space in the back alley, away from the eyes of any patrolling officers.

First thing I did when I got out of the Ranger was lean over and throw up. Then I peed on the backyard fence and scuttled inside. I poured a glass of water and rubbed my shoulder where the seatbelt had caught me. My roommates were still out at the bar, but our dogs swirled around the living room, sniped at each other while I studiously ignored them. I sat in a chair and leaned back with the glass of water in my hand and closed my eyes. The room spun. I drained the water and put the glass on the coffee table, leaned back in the chair, and drifted off, feeling a chill in my breast with the knowledge of how easily it would have been to hit someone—how quickly those accidents happen, how irrevocable. Your rational brain shut off as fight-or-flight kicked in.

My heart thrummed in my chest as the room continued to spin, warm air blowing through a vent in the ceiling, the house creaking as it settled, the menace of the world at bay, for now, beyond the darkened windows.

5

Richmond is a landlocked city in the Piedmont, but I imagined a ship off the coast of South Carolina, the sea like glass reflecting the starlight, waves lapping the coast. I ventured there in my mind, the straight shot down I-95, piercing into the heart of South Carolina and the forests of the Pee Dee River Region. Farther still, the piney woods fell away, replaced by open country punctuated with live oaks and Spanish moss. Near the Georgia border, the marshes of the coastal plains took over, with lush grasses and flora so green it seemed electric, the region an elegant merging of swamplands and golf courses.

The Carolina Lowcountry was known for several things: the romance of Charleston, moonlight and magnolias, beaches and marshes, crawfish and Pat Conroy, the Piggly Wiggly, Parris Island, Fort Sumter, golf, Gullah culture, sweet tea, and gentility unlike anywhere else on earth. It's an easy place to grow nostalgic for, and to remember fondly if you've lived there and left. Maybe the locals do, but visitors seldom confront the heat and horseshit of Charleston, the stench of pluff mud and paper mills, the conservative legislators who preach family values while shrugging off brazen affairs (*hiking the Appalachian trail,* said one former governor), the class structure of poor blacks and white developers and the old-money society hidden in plain sight. The romance was one big facade, I thought, the emperor's new clothes.

The town name of Overlook was something of a misnomer, as you wouldn't say it looked over anything in particular. In grade school, they told us the town was built on a slight bluff and that from an old watchtower, Colonial guards could look out over the major inlets and waterways to stave off a threat from the sea. Nothing but a country crossroads until recently, when the developers came in and cleared the palmettos and filled in the swamps and graded the roads and sidewalks and fashioned a storm system for a thousand-home retirement community called Sunset Bluffs. Today the town gives Hilton Head a run for its money for curb appeal and golf courses, and it one-ups the island for sheer local character. The coastal plains are remarkably flat, all the buildings low and seemingly somehow built into the land so that the geography still takes precedence. The developers had done a nice job of preserving—or creating—a false sense of paradise here, which allowed retirees from elsewhere to soak up the sunshine, watch Big 10 sports, and while away their time on the pedantic issues of their homeowners boards.

Two mornings after Francine's call, I woke to the sound of sprinklers before five. The gray light of dawn was still an hour away, what they called nautical twilight for the way that stars still winked in the sky, allowing navigation on the open seas. I pictured Daniel Hayward, alone in a house in a gated community, his wife staying with a friend. Perhaps he was awake now, ruminating on his wrecked life and worrying about how he would get through the day. I could see his house, or what might be his house: a gray craftsman home with abundant stonework and a circular driveway, a three-car garage and a pair of lemon trees near the front porch. This was what Daniel had aspired to: his Carolina blonde wife and his golf course home. From the street, you'd never know about the cracks in the dam, the trickle of water that was about to drown out their happy life. I lay in bed for a long time, listening to the birds as the window glowed from the emerging light. When it was clear I could not go back to sleep, I crept to my office to search for any updates on the hit and run.

A clip from the local TV station showed Daniel on his perp walk for the arraignment, solemnly walking into the courtroom, dutifully ignoring the questions called out to him by reporters. The attorney accompanying him was a white-haired Charlestonian named Henry Somerville, a man of the old school and old money. A gentleman lawyer with connections to the city's power brokers. I'd met several attorneys like him through my consulting work, men with assertive personalities who had the type of confidence you had to pay for, the kind of men who might do a fine job running a company—or a country—into the ground. The alpha wolf. Plenty of men slid into that persona. Lawyers, financial officers, salesmen: these careers fed the animal in men. My generation was marked by the War on Terror and the 2008 financial collapse, both events byproducts of overconfident men like this attorney, men who believed themselves warriors and who made snap but firm decisions, decisions that brought down countries, foreign and domestic. I mistrusted such a personality, but also admired it in a perverse way, its will to power. If you could give up your belief in Jesus and human kindness and altruism—which I could not, in those days—you could go far in life and make a fine living and attain ranks of respect and freedom only personality could buy. Men like Henry Somerville seemed to intuit this without articulating it, which is how they were able to carry on. They'd faced the music of nihilism and continued to dance.

One final player in the drama was the judge, Kenneth Rhodes, one of only a handful of black judges in South Carolina since Reconstruction. When Claire Fields and Henry Somerville built their stories of what happened the night of the hit and run,

Judge Rhodes would be the final arbiter, the man with the vision to see beyond the frame of a story and find the Truth. I thought about what it must have taken him to get where he was, and the challenges he must have faced, and knew that beyond the clichés and easy answers, Judge Rhodes must have been a man of grit, a man with texture. Reading about him, I felt my entire life thrown into relief: my drunk driving accident in graduate school, my marriage to Kate, the aborted dreams of my younger self, the drudgery of early middle age. It struck me that perhaps I'd never really known anything, as if I'd been living in shadows, seeing the shape of things but not the finer details, and now the details were coming into focus. While the world dawned around me, I opened a blank document and stared at the page. I thought about Daniel Hayward, and Claire Fields, and Henry Somerville, and the poor girl who'd been struck and killed on the highway. There was more to the story than the newspaper headlines and the commentary on Facebook. I thought about Kate, and the trouble we'd had, and I set out to discover something about this world and our place in it.

I thought about my old novel in the drawer, and how I had nothing to say about my own life, and I remembered a line I once read from James Baldwin: "People pay for what they do, and still more for what they have allowed themselves to become, and they pay for it very simply: by the lives they lead." Years ago, when I still thought I might one day make it as a novelist, I'd written this line on a neon green three-by-five card and taped it to my wall. What had I allowed myself to become? I was a corporate consultant who hid behind what has rightly been called the garbage language of business—innovation, disruption, consumer-centricity—while the rift widened between my wife and me and the stakes were growing serious for my friends. Francine had asked me to help Daniel, yet there was nothing I could do beyond serving as a witness to the unfurling tragedy. I doubted I would ever be able to put words to what it all meant—possibly nothing—but simply understanding the pieces well enough to ask the question. That must suffice.

This was no mistake of fact, I began.

THIS WAS NO MISTAKE
OF FACT

1

Women without children can grow cagey in their early thirties. Perhaps it's because, at least in middle America, the world still watches young women with expectation, and then suspicion, and then acceptance, and perhaps this process trains women to put up their defenses. Men have it easier: a shrugging of the shoulders at their youthful sallies, and then acceptance as they find their places in the world, and then respect as they take on some mantle of leadership.

As a childless—and husband-less—woman of thirty-one, Claire Fields was acutely aware of this dynamic, and she felt a never-ending yet mild anxiety about the direction of her life: one disastrous year at Fordham followed by three ruthlessly successful years at the University of South Carolina, law school, a two-year clerkship in Charleston, and a position back home in the Bayard County solicitor's office. Maybe not a dream career for a woman, or a man, wanting to get out into the world, but it is stable, predictable work. A job she could do with pride and leave the work at the office. Her personal life, however, was in shambles when her office held its summer picnic at a state park along the banks of the May River. It was a beautiful Saturday afternoon there beneath the shade of the live oaks, with their strings of Spanish moss. The loamy soil, the marsh grasses that swayed in the wind, the mystery of the slow-moving river that seemed to still time. Claire felt generally at home here in Overlook but dreaded the time with her co-workers. She'd recently botched a case and created something of a scandal in her office, so she felt sick at the thought of her colleagues gossiping about her. Furtive glances and speculation.

She arrived an hour after the scheduled start of the picnic, where thirty of her colleagues and their families had already set up camp. Someone's husband had the grill going, with burgers and dogs, a buffet of buns and condiments on the picnic table beside him. At the end of the table, an explosion of juice boxes had attracted a fallout of yellowjackets, their nasty little legs quivering across the sticky surfaces. Her paralegal, Susan, stood outside a bounce castle, hands sternly on her hips, eyes hidden behind Ray Bans, and watched half a dozen ruddy, leaky children scramble and bounce off walls and scream bloody murder.

No sign of her boss, Chuck.

The attorneys mingled in their clique, outnumbered by the secretaries and paralegals who dressed more casually and appeared more genial and at ease. A group of secretaries sat in captain's chairs in a clearing beneath a live oak. Jackie Stone and her husband—Will?—sat alone at a picnic table.

Jackie was a few years older than Claire and the only other female attorney in the office, which meant Claire found in her both a rival and a support system. Claire liked that her colleague was professional and well respected even among the male attorneys, but in truth Claire found her a little too quick to cast judgment on other women. Jackie seemed to appreciate her for being an upwardly mobile professional without children, but she sensed the woman wouldn't hesitate to snatch back her approval should Claire do something rash—fall for the wrong man, join the ranks of motherhood, express the wrong political belief.

Meanwhile, Claire judged the woman herself for wearing clothing that was a little too tight for her age.

"Welcome to the jungle," Jackie's husband said.

"Thanks. Good to see you again."

He took a swig of Bud Light.

Jackie glanced over and said, "We were watching Susan with the kids and thinking how noble it was for her to take over as babysitter."

"Moms seem to fall into that role," Claire said.

"I know, right?" Jackie put her chin in her hands. Today she wore a loose-fitting shirt that revealed too much of her shoulders and a maxi-skirt that hugged her hips too tight.

Will—definitely Will—asked how she was doing.

"Fine," Claire said, and she wondered if he knew anything about her recent trouble at the office. She suspected married couples told each other everything, but Jackie and Will seemed to have an unusual marriage. "You?"

He shook his head. "Can't complain. Glad it's a cool day." The man was big as a doorway and had the kind of head that looked like it had been in a few boxing rings. You could almost hear the gloves bouncing off the side of his head—*doof, doof, doof*—squaring it off and jostling loose whatever rattled around between his ears. Which was not much, Claire believed.

"Chuck here yet?" she asked, resisting the urge to look at her watch. She'd been here all of five minutes, and would have to stay at least an hour to be polite.

Jackie craned her neck and said, "He was a minute ago."

"You know how he likes to mingle," Will said. "He'll be back over here soon so you can get your gold star and take off." He winked and took another swig of his beer.

Claire stuttered.

"Oh honey, we're all thinking the same thing," Jackie said. "He's got to have a team-building picnic so he has something to put in the newsletter for voters."

"Fostering collaboration," Claire said.

"You got it."

Their boss, Chuck Goodall, was a stately, old-money country lawyer who'd owned a small but successful family law practice before running for county solicitor. A couple years into his first term, he'd found a new wave of energy, vigor, and potency, which likely meant he was still several years from retiring to glasses of bourbon and the company of former judges and senators who lived in unlisted homes in tucked-away neighborhoods throughout the region.

"So what's going on?" Claire asked.

"Everyone's talking about the hit and run," Will said.

"Wasn't it awful?" Claire said. Police were still gathering evidence and sending out press releases asking for anyone with information to step forward.

"We've been to that restaurant a few times," Jackie said. "I keep trying to place her."

"We've probably had her," Will said. "We go there often enough. But I have to say, I'm not sure I'd want to be riding a bicycle home at night like that. Seems like a stupid thing to do."

"So what you're saying is it's her fault she got run over?" Jackie asked.

"No, of course not."

"What are you saying then?" Jackie leaned away from him like he was confessing to child molestation or something.

"I'm saying, nothing, I don't know. I just think, why you got to ride your bike along some dark road in the middle of the night? And what was she even doing out that late? The news said she clocked out an hour earlier."

"So she was asking for some drunk to come along and run her over, you're saying."

"No, I'm saying I'd worry about hitting her even if I were sober, and I'm a good driver. These bicyclists that have this 'share the road' attitude, they don't realize how dangerous it is what they're doing. You just come up on them and if you're not vigilant—wham! You knock one to the side of the road."

"Personal experience?" Claire asked.

"Almost. I can't tell you how many times I've *almost* hit a bicyclist. And this was driving the speed limit in the day time, mind you. Driving at night? Forget about it."

"They say she had a proper light," Claire said.

"That's right," Jackie added, "and it's not like it was some windy mountain road. It's a pretty straight shot through there."

"And why wouldn't the person stop unless they'd been drinking and were afraid to get caught?"

"Maybe he thought he hit a deer," Will said.

"He?" Jackie lowered her chin and leered at him.

"You think a woman hit her?"

"I don't know who hit her."

"It was a dude," Will said. "A woman would have turned herself in by now."

"We're not tough enough to take the heat?" Claire asked.

"I don't believe so."

"You'd be surprised," Jackie said, and Claire laughed.

"What?"

"With as little as you understand about women, it's amazing you managed to ever get married," Claire said.

"He must have drugged me," Jackie said. "I never heard such idiocy when we were dating."

"You could sue him for misrepresentation."

"False pretenses."

"Malicious intent."

While the women chuckled at their cleverness, Will looked away, poor man. Just another over-thirty dude set in his ways. He liked a healthy serving of meat with his dinner and believed women were not good drivers but took responsibility for their actions, whereas men were good drivers who made careless decisions, on the road as well as life in general. Claire could see the wheels turning in his head, and though she hated to admit it, part of her agreed with him about the hit and run: Indignation was one thing, but the girl was being foolhardy out on the road at night, and it made Claire angry.

She clasped the first two fingers of her right hand with her left, squeezed, and tried to shut out these thoughts. A young woman—a beautiful young woman—had been killed, and eventually, she knew, the investigation would turn up something and a case would make its way to the solicitor's office. One of them would be tasked with delivering justice, which meant siding completely with the victim.

Jackie had shifted her attention toward the grill and the bounce castle, and now had her eyes set on Chuck who was making the rounds. Something about her gaze seemed off to Claire. Here was Jackie, wearing clothing that hugged her provocative curves, leaning forward over the picnic table so that her breasts, smashed together between her arms, flashed cleavage like a beacon. It was a quick glance toward their boss, but it made Claire wonder. Meanwhile, Will was in his own world, staring at the dirt and likely thinking of some accounts payable or cyber-security problem with his own work, some audit he needed to conduct on Monday.

Claire wouldn't necessarily blame Jackie for trying to make her own fun—and she was in no position to judge after her most recent fiasco with Detective Barry Dewitt—but with Chuck? Chuck Goodall was a thick-faced man with silver hair and a chin that jutted into a room like a spear. He carried himself as a man's man and took over a room when he entered, dominated meetings. Even leaning back in his chair, he maintained a *presence*, but most of the time he hunched forward by nature, a bit like a gorilla. The weathered flesh, the bushy eyebrows, the red skin, the muscles in his neck and shoulders, the broad chest, the way he knocked his thick knuckles on a conference table: you paid attention to him. He was also married to a woman who had been depressed since the mid-nineties, who never came out to these events. In a way, you expected him to be involved in some clandestine affair, although maybe not one as humdrum as someone at the office.

She got up from the table as Chuck came over and brazenly said hello to Jackie and Will. No flinching, no furtive eye contact, no flushed faces that would suggest he and Jackie were embroiled in a flirtation much less a downright affair. Perhaps Claire had imagined what she saw. She hoped so, for she was not interested in learning about the illicit activities of her co-workers, and wanted only to leave as her boss made small talk with Jackie's husband.

"How's the boating business?" Chuck asked.

"People are still sailing," Will said.

"You seeing any uptick these days?"

"Oh yeah. We've been booming for a few years. Depending on how this summer goes, we might try to open a few new stores."

"Good, good. Glad to hear it. Y'all have any retail stores in the Charleston market?"

"We do, out in Mount Pleasant."

"Really? Where at?"

"Off Coleman Boulevard, right across Shem Creek. You can see the water from the parking lot."

"I think I know where you're talking about. I've got a cousin with a shrimp boat. Been thinking about investing in one myself."

"It's a nice hobby."

"And Jackie," Chuck said, "what's new in your world?"

She threw up her hands, perhaps not trusting herself to speak without giving something away.

"Got a couple new cases for you," he said. "Let's grab lunch this week. You too, Claire," he added.

Chuck sat down and began drumming the picnic table with his thumb, and Claire scurried away before he said anything more.

She said hello to her paralegal, Susan, who was still lifeguarding the bounce castle.

"Hello!" Susan said as Claire neared, "and how are you?"

"Fine, thanks."

"Come to hang out with the kids?"

"Why not?"

"You remember Maddy and Joe?"

"Of course."

"I'd call them out here to say hello, but…"

"No need. They seem to be having fun."

"Those're Jeremy's twins. And I'm not sure who the little girl belongs to."

"I see you're on babysitting duty."

"I don't mind it. I'd rather not be talking to the adults. You're fine," Susan said, placing a hand on Claire's forearm, "but it's all real estate and work talk from the men. Such a bore. And the women are no different. Grocery stores and private schools. And their dogs—always their dogs. What is it about people that they can't have an interesting conversation about something other than their dog shedding more than usual?" She snapped her fingers at one of the children and said, "That's enough!" After a moment of silence she continued to Claire, "I suppose I'm no different. All I want to talk about is my kids. That's all a work picnic is, right? A place to show them off. What do you do all day without kids to take care of?"

"Oh, this and that," Claire said. That kind of question from anyone else would raise her hackles, but Susan was exempt, perhaps because she always seemed a bit unhinged. Claire liked that someone could be so unabashedly obtuse, and how it made her embarrassingly honest.

Yet Susan for once seemed to recognize the faux pas and quickly tried to cover it up.

"It's fine," Claire said.

"See, this is why I'm watching the kids."

"I don't blame you. I'm going to sneak out of here in a few minutes myself. Just wanted to put in an appearance."

Beyond them, the lazy May River swayed by in true Lowcountry fashion. Nowhere to be, nothing to do. If you looked at the scene through the eyes of a bird overhead, you wouldn't see the people on the ground through the canopy of live oaks, with their drama and peccadilloes. Instead, you would see the curves of the brown water, the leafy branches of live oaks, the porter's lodge at the edge of the park and the roofs of houses in gated neighborhoods in the distance.

2

That evening, when she returned to her townhouse, she turned on the television while she watched dinner. The news carried the story of the hit and run, with authorities asking anyone with information to come forward. Samantha James's coworkers at the restaurant had all agreed she clocked out like usual and rode her bicycle home. No one had seen her in Old Town, so police were looking for anyone who may have been driving Reedy Road between ten and midnight Thursday. The newscaster stood on the side of the road, with yellow crime tape behind her wrapping around the trunks of roadside trees. The ground behind her was carved up, where clearly something ugly had gone down. The newscaster enunciated clearly and spoke dispassionately.

This quiet strip of Reedy Road.

Authorities are asking for your help.

Thank you, Jim.

The studio anchor transitioned them to an interview with the family from earlier today. Gary and Beth James stood grimly in front of the police station. Gary held his arm around his wife, who said nothing. *I just don't understand,* he said. *My daughter was extremely cautious. She always rode with a flashing light so you couldn't miss her on that stretch of road.* He paused and could say nothing more, rescued by the newscaster who repeated what her counterpart on Reedy Road had said.

Anyone who knows anything.

Claire was mesmerized by the news. From the photo, Samantha James could have been anyone she knew. It could have been her at nineteen. Slender. Pretty. Joyful. Claire knew the case would likely end up in her office, perhaps on her desk, and seeing the innocent young girl and watching the wrecked family struggle to find the words, she felt anger boil inside her. She thought about her own life, how she and her friends used to roam around Columbia during her time at USC. With a one-semester exception, she seldom got drunk in college, was not a partier, but the streets at night were never completely safe. Any of them could have been hit by a speeding car. Her mother had passed away her freshman year, so she thought about what it would have done to her father to lose his only daughter soon after losing his wife. It made her heart hurt to imagine him at her funeral, and she thought it was but a small mercy that Gary and Beth James had each other. She didn't know when Samantha's funeral would be, but she knew it would only be the beginning for this family.

The news cut to a commercial, and the TV blared about a good deal on a Mazda, a Ford, a Hyundai. *Cars, trucks, vans!* the dealer said with arms wide open. *We've got it all at Davis Brothers Auto-Max!* Claire didn't know if this man was one of the Davis brothers, or if there even were Davis brothers, but she knew he was ready for her business. He smiled widely, oblivious to the fact that his commercial had been preceded by news of a gruesome hit and run.

3

Three days after the office picnic, on Tuesday morning, Chuck came into her office with a file folder, sat down, put his feet up on her desk, and assigned her the task of charging Daniel Hayward with the killing of Samantha James. A hit and run for sure, he said as he set the case files on her desk, with manslaughter on the table. "He's at home right now, but he's been cooperating with the police."

"He's not been arrested yet?"

"Not yet. They want to make sure the evidence is there."

"Is it?"

"He's giving the I-thought-I-hit-a-deer story but"—Chuck held up a hand to assure her—"he will be arrested. Matter of fact, he'll probably turn himself in later this week."

"And the girl's family?"

"We've kept them informed."

Chuck gave her a look that said, Do I even need to say it? We've got a delicate balance here, the same delicate balance everywhere in America, privacy and due process on the one hand and justice and law and order on the other, and there is no consistency, not among people, the press, the citizenry. Of course we've assured them we're doing everything within our power to ensure they receive justice, and that to be too aggressive might kill their case before it begins. The James family understands as well as anyone that justice works in this country but it works slowly. Meanwhile, we've got a job to do, so let's carry on.

Chuck did not have to say any of this, of course. A flash of weariness in his eyes, a modest upturn to the corners of his mouth said it all. Claire was sharp enough to understand the situation without having to be told, and Chuck knew it, and she knew he knew it, and on and on.

Nonetheless, she could not resist needling him one last time.

"I suppose it doesn't matter," she said. "If we screw up this case, the entire town will be after us."

"Ah. That's where you come in."

"Right."

"You're up for it, after—"

"Only thing you can do is get back on the horse," she said.

"That's why I hired you," he said, and she felt an edge to his voice. If she screwed up another case, would he give her a third chance to redeem herself? "You've already mentioned the stakes here," he was saying. "We'll have our usual strategy meeting in a few days, once Daniel's been arraigned. I'm sure you already know this, but I should warn you it's not going to be the easiest conviction."

"I know it."

"The girl clocked out of her job at ten and was struck around eleven."

"And in the interim?"

"Nobody knows."

"Awesome."

"And," Chuck went on, "unless we can find several witnesses, it's going to be tough to prove Hayward was intoxicated. The one thing we have in our favor right now is that his vehicle is apparently in abysmal shape. I haven't seen it yet, but the detective tells me there's no way he'll be able to claim he didn't know he hit something. See what you can dig up on deer impacts. Maybe talk to some body shop owners."

"Does he have a lawyer yet?"

"Henry Somerville, down from Charleston."

She cursed.

"That sends a signal though, doesn't it?" he said.

"That he's put up the money to play offense."

"Precisely what you'd expect from a guilty man."

"We know that, but the jury won't."

"I'm putting together a statement for the press this afternoon. They're already on our side. Haven't you been reading the papers?"

Indeed she had, with the same gross curiosity as everyone else in the community. A heart-wrenching story, complete with a mystery, a victim, a villain, and an inquiry into the inner workings of the human heart. How could a man leave another human being to die on the side of the road? The two simplest explanations were that he had been drinking, which is usually what happens when someone drives off, or, Claire supposed, it was possible Hayward was telling the truth, that he legitimately thought he'd struck a deer. Overlook was considerably less developed than its neighboring Hilton Head, which meant the roads were implacably dark at night. Overhead branches from old-growth oaks meant not even light from the full moon could penetrate certain stretches of the road. Deer were plentiful. If that were a cover-up story, concocted by Henry Somerville, then it was a good one for its sheer plausibility.

"Start with the facts," Chuck said. "From the preliminary investigation, it looks like we've got a great case. With any luck, we'll be the town heroes by Thanksgiving."

And you'll have a headline for your direct mailers come election time, Claire thought. *And I'll still have my job,* she reminded herself.

When Chuck had left her office, she made a list of everything she needed to do: familiarize herself with the facts of the case, read the police reports, meet with the lead detective, the defense attorney, and the family—all this before she would be ready to start drafting a strategy. She made a note to drive the route Samantha would have taken on Thursday evening, to stop and see what the accident site looked like, smelled like, felt like at eleven o'clock. Only by going inside the minds of Samantha and Hayward would she begin to see with clarity the framework for what happened and how it fit within the letter of the law. She also needed to figure out what Samantha was doing for the missing hour after she clocked out. Nothing would excuse Hayward, but she knew the defense attorney well enough to know he would drop a few bombshells. When he handed her the case file, Chuck hadn't said, *Don't screw this up.* She was a grown-up and knew the stakes perfectly well.

Neither Chuck's office—nor Claire—could afford for this case to go south. Not in this town.

4

Get back on the horse. Claire Fields had been telling herself this for two months now, two months in which she'd remained out of the solicitor's office limelight, negotiating plea deals and trying petty crime—clear-cut larceny, a case of arson, embezzlement— crimes barely above the level of a part-time magistrate. This was where she preferred to stay, ever since the incident with Michael Baldwin. Everyone, in every career, eventually runs into such a case. The world allows one grand mistake, and this mistake may even be necessary for us to move forward in our lives. Adversity. Failure. Recovery. Perhaps these are the core tenets of success. At least Claire hoped so. If she could face down Henry Somerville, the Daniel Hayward trial would be her comeback.

Michael Baldwin had been a career criminal in and out of the county lockup his entire life, all twenty-three years, and everyone in the solicitor's office knew it was just a matter of time before he landed in the state penitentiary. That time came at the beginning of the year when he robbed a bank and shot the teller. Claire prosecuted him for grand larceny, first-degree murder, and a host of other crimes. After a quick conviction, the jury recommended Baldwin serve forty-five years with no parole. Before the formal sentencing, the defense objected on the grounds that the solicitor's office had withheld evidence. True, Claire should have disclosed that she'd had a relationship with the investigating officer. True, she should have seen the DNA evidence had been procured without a proper search warrant. But these facts did not change the core of the situation, that Baldwin had walked into the bank with the intention of taking a life and making off with a duffel bag full of cash. Did Claire's mistakes, her ineptitude, her inexperience, mean Baldwin was any less guilty? No, but Chuck stepped in and, after much negotiation, wheeling, dealing, and whatever else went on in the old boys' club of the judge's chambers, forty-one years of Baldwin's sentence were suspended. He would serve four years with no parole. Everyone knew this meant he would return to the streets at twenty-seven, with no more job skills than he had now and zero rehabilitation, but with fresh bitterness and fury to take another life.

This was a mistake—a big one, Chuck had acknowledged to the press. "We're doing everything we can to ensure nothing of this magnitude ever happens again," he said.

Inside the solicitor's office, the mood had been tense for a few hours, but business went on. Cases came in. Chuck motored in and out of the office, and when he was in, his office door was closed. Without it having to be mandated, Claire began taking on lower-level cases. The victim's husband came into the office twice, and neither time did he confront Claire, if he even knew who she was. Of course he would have known her name, because her name was all over the newspapers: *Claire Fields, the prosecutor who tried the case, could not be reached for comment. Chuck Goodall released an apology to the victim's family.* Broadcasters aired quick snippets, and while most of Claire's grade-school friends had moved on, their parents were still here and paid close attention to the small-town rumor mill.

No mention was made as to whether the victim's family accepted Chuck's apology. Claire would not have. That was the kicker, her own sense of atonement.

After two days of media scrutiny and prosecutor stonewalling, Chuck came into her office, sat down, put one foot on her desk, and said, "You busy?"

"What can I do for you?"

He put his other foot up and crossed his legs at the ankle. "Michael Baldwin," he said.

She took a breath.

"Easy mistake to make," he said.

"Tell that to the victim's family."

"I did. Her husband's come to see me twice now, and both times I've explained as much as I can. You can't explain away bad luck."

"It wasn't all bad luck," she said.

"No," he agreed, "but the case was shaky from the start. I didn't tell you that, because I didn't think it would matter. We could retry the whole thing, but the character witnesses, they're not the most reliable. Who knows what kind of sentence we'd come up with a second time?"

"There shouldn't have to be a second time."

"Can't argue with you, but it is what it is. There won't be a next one, right?"

She shook her head, and he let the silence hang for a moment, long enough to say everything he wasn't saying, about how stupid she'd been, how naive. She felt like he no longer respected her, if he ever did, and had chalked the affair and the screw-up to her being a woman.

Before he left, he got in one more dig and asked, "Are there going to be any other reports in the paper? Anything more to the story with you and Detective Dewitt?"

"That's over."

"Because if there were anything—"

"There's not," she said, her humiliation complete.

"Okay, fair enough. Well, take yourself out this weekend, have some drinks, do whatever you do to relax. We'll move on."

She thanked him warily, still expecting another shoe to drop. Another dig at her romantic life, a comment about damage control and the newspapers. But he must have understood that the forty-one years off Baldwin's sentence, the grief, the embarrassment, were all enough to ensure she took care. Plus, she understood he could fire her whenever he wanted now, but she also suspected he enjoyed having that power. He wasn't up for reelection until next year, plenty of time for a few major wins. Of course the wins would not come from Claire, but she nonetheless had her career, for now. A lever and a place to stand, as Archimedes had said. That was all a person needed to move the world.

Although she traditionally was neither self-pitying nor one for shopping therapy, she took herself to the Tanger Outlets after her come-to-Jesus with Chuck, still feeling skittish about her career prospects after the screw-up, embarrassed and, truthfully, a little lonesome in the wake of the affair. They'd known each other in school, and now he was unhappily married and on the prowl. The relationship was short-lived, a few late-night meetings about the case, an invitation to Claire's place for takeout dinners. She'd never intended for more, knew he was married, and didn't even feel the old flutters of chemistry between them. He was a friendly face, she was in need of a friend, and one night after a bottle of wine—

"Claire? Is that you?"

A woman was looking at her sideways on the sidewalk in front of the Banana Republic. The woman was pushing a stroller, and had two young children scampering at her feet. She smiled, and said, "It's me, Wendy."

"Oh, hi!"

Claire gave Wendy from high school an awkward hug. Lithe as ever, Wendy wore snug yoga pants, a shell necklace and a face of carefully applied makeup.

"It's so good to see you," Wendy said. "How are you?"

"I'm doing well. How about you?"

"Oh, you know." Wendy from high school waved at the kids with pride as though that said everything. "What have you been up to? Are you in town?"

"I am. I work for the solicitor's office."

"As a lawyer?"

"That's right," Claire said, wondering if Wendy from high school was playing dumb or if she'd somehow missed all the news of the past few weeks, in which Claire's name was all over the papers.

"That's wonderful," Wendy from high school said.

"What about you?" Claire asked. "What are you up to?"

Wendy blinked a few times. "Oh, staying busy. These guys keep me running twenty-four hours a day."

Claire gave a nervous laugh. She had no concept for judging ages, but Wendy's walking children couldn't have been more than three or four. The boy and the girl chased themselves in circles around Wendy and the baby stroller, in which an infant slept peacefully. Wendy seemed to bask in her motherhood, and Claire thought—admittedly without mercy—that Wendy from high school brought the children to the outlets simply to show them off to the world. Her career mess aside, Claire's life was a success. She had an enviable job with more than enough prospects, but with other women there was often an unspoken competition around hearth and home. It was a game Claire did not want to be playing, but she was in it now, and Wendy had clearly won.

Wendy sighed and said, "Well, it was good to see you!"

"Yes, you too."

"I'm sure we'll see you around."

And with that, Wendy from high school and her three children moved on to find someone else to vanquish.

Claire ducked into a restroom to compose herself.

5

Did she ever want a life like Wendy from high school had? Did she ever want children? She couldn't say, but she knew when her life had gone off the rails. She was born to a modest family who filled the house with books and encouraged her to dream big. Her parents were introverted and kind, and somehow mustered up enough lust to make a baby before deciding to sleep in separate bedrooms. When her mother died during Claire's freshman year at Fordham, it was all her father could do to persuade her to remain in school.

"Enroll at USC if you have to, but don't take time off," he told her. "I'll be fine," he added, but she didn't believe him.

She enrolled in the Beaufort campus, moved home with her father and helped with the grocery shopping. After a year, she transferred to the main campus in Columbia and roomed with some girlfriends from high school who had forgotten everything they'd crammed into their heads for the SATs. She drove home to meet her father once or twice a month for Sunday lunch at a now-defunct sandwich joint that blasted country music radio and made their own Cajun-style spice mix. Lazy fans blew hot air around the dining room.

When she was a child, her parents half-heartedly took her to the local Methodist church, but they never marshaled enough enthusiasm to make it a habit. One weekend they stopped going to the Sunday service—perhaps they had plans, perhaps they were out of town, or perhaps weather had swayed them to stay in—and they'd never gone back. Claire had an aborted relationship with Catholicism while she was at Fordham. How she ended up at that university, she still didn't know, and she never felt pressure from anyone there to reconsider her faith. But the ritual, the iconography, the community all called to her at a time when she was looking for answers. She never went so far as to convert officially, so she never took a mass, and never truly understood the alien nature of transubstantiation, but she did appreciate having somewhere to go, those moments of solace, the work done to repair what she believed to be her damaged soul. These days, she had no religion in her life, and didn't feel its absence.

New York City: when she thought about it now, that year—nine months, really—was like a dream, an interlude between the long line of reality that was her life. At thirty-one, she'd grown into herself as a woman, medium height with straight but thick hair she kept in a neat press, an attractively full figure she kept hidden behind conservative, professional suits, and green eyes you rarely took note of unless you were in an intimate conversation with her, which was unlikely. She kept herself to herself. Friendly, affable, amiable, but not intimate with many people, and hardly anyone she worked with. She deleted her Facebook account when she took the job as a prosecutor, but before she did, she'd had her privacy settings as rigid as she could make them. In every photograph, she wore sunglasses—aviators—without which she never left the house. She would prop them on top of her head indoors. She blamed the Lowcountry light, the blinding flash of it, but she also appreciated the barrier between herself and the rest of the world, like a drink in hand that serves to distract from the wounds that lay hidden deep.

Oh, she had fun. She was no hermit, no downer. Her friends would describe her as warm-hearted and kind yet she was extremely introverted. She needed to be alone to recharge, and drew her energy from solitude. There was a difference between solitude and lonesomeness, and the world was filled with such people who know the difference, but the domineering, the assertive, the aggressive, the salespeople shuttered them out. Claire was never a salesperson, even before her mother died, a hard-wired literalist. She appreciated rules, and so long as she knew the parameters of a given situation, she thrived. The trouble was that sales—and the complementary modes of living—relied on subtext, hidden meanings, instinct, working by feel. She was not one to work by feel. She dealt in facts, in analysis, in judgment. She was perfect for life in the law. Black and white. This side against that side. Here are the facts. Whose case is stronger? In most cases, the outcome was already certain, but like the final moves in a close chess game, the players finished out or negotiated a draw. The older ones operated out of boredom. They drank and bent the ethical rules and flirted with danger, rediscovering the thrill of the unknown. Claire was not there yet, and likely never would be.

In fact, one of her biggest fears was to be caught in the wrong place at the wrong time doing something she shouldn't have been doing, her hand in the cookie jar. She had done very few things in life to warrant such a fear, which might explain the fear's continued existence, having never been faced down by experience. In reverse-chronological order:

(1) She heard a rumor of cheating on an exam in law school. Nothing confirmed, and she didn't really know the person who allegedly hacked into the professor's account on the server and printed off test questions ahead of time. In the corporate world, Claire thought, such a person would be considered next in line for a promotion (for no matter what the corporate mission statements said about ethics, rule-breaking was the way to get ahead; the only place worse, she'd discovered, was in working for the government). And what did Claire do wrong? Why, she simply never reported her classmate, never filled out an anonymous tip to the honor board, never encouraged an investigation. She talked it over with a boyfriend, who persuaded her it was none of her business, but that wasn't true, she could see now. One cheater meant the entire curve could be thrown for that class, to say nothing of the complete breakdown of law and

order. She still believed she was as guilty as the computer hacker, even if she didn't know for a fact that cheating had occurred. She'd kept silent, which was as bad as the crime itself.

(2) In college, she'd lied to her father about having a quasi-live-in boyfriend for several months during her junior year. This was her first year at USC, when she was still trying to wrap her head around adult life and life without a mother. She went out nearly every night and stumbled home to her apartment, her breath reeking of gin and her eyes puffy and her brain eerily calm. She received pitying looks from the girls she lived with, but that never bothered her at the time. She merely shuffled to bed, slept in her clothes, and avoided those girls during the day. She'd found a crowd she got on with, a few kids who went to her high school whom she'd not known during school but whose company she enjoyed. She began casually sleeping with one of those boys, Joe, a pudgy and brilliant engineering student of partially Middle Eastern descent. Syrian, maybe. That summer, she moved into her own apartment, and Joe more or less moved in with her—fine, except that she'd not told her father she was dating anyone, and had no interest in explaining herself. How many times had her father called while she lounged in bed with the boy? How many times had she covered her tracks and said, "No, Dad, I'm not seeing anyone right now"? And how much had she actually fooled her father versus merely fooling herself? Tough to say, but that period was not one of her proudest moments. In fact, that year probably held the distinction of being her biggest regret, the booze and the boy and the treating her body like a dumpster. She'd put on weight. She'd taken up smoking and lost the weight. She'd been lucky to avoid birth control accidents. She shuddered to think, now, what one burst condom might have cost her then. Fortunately, she made it through that period in one piece. The boy, Joe, moved on as boys do, and she mostly sobered to begin her senior year.

(3) That same year, before she sobered, she smoked several bowls of marijuana with the boy. The drug did nothing for her, and it was hardly the worst thing people were into—crystal meth was on the rise but had not yet become a national crisis; many of her fellow students routinely took Adderall for help concentrating; all of this to say nothing of the legal pharmaceuticals people pumped into their systems: Ritalin, Paxil, Xanax, Valium, Lortabs, Oxycontin. Some boys she knew experimented regularly with Viagra. What harm was there in smoking a little weed? Yet she looked back at that time and, again, saw herself making poor life choices, breaking laws, letting down her future self.

Before college, there was the usual litany of wrongdoing that every child experiences, the massaging of the truth, cutting up in class, speeding down the highway, backstabbing friends, cursing, and the like—all the experiences of someone in the late 20th century coming of age in a relatively sheltered home.

Although she had not seen her father much after college—the blue-moon weekend during law school, and about twice a month now that she was back in Overlook—she still kept a photograph of the two of them on her desk. A visitor to her office might look at the picture and see a sad-eyed girl standing next to a proud old man. First impressions: the man's bizarre outfit (a faded navy button-down, beige cargo pants, a beige vest, a black plastic Timex) that made him look like some kind of fly fisherman. He had curly gray hair and a wry smile masked behind a gray beard, his head cocked rakishly to the side, squinting into the camera even though it was a gray day, cool for the summer, perhaps sixty-five degrees, mist in the air. They stood in the backyard, the grass and soil soft at their feet, like plush carpet. Claire remembered that, and the way her thin arm brushed against her father's much thicker arm, their hands nearly touching, that awkward space of near-independence, when all she'd wanted was to give her father a hug. You could see it by the expression on her face. She was ten years younger than she was today, her face unlined, her bones smaller, her neck long and thin like a swan's. She had a redhead's pale skin, pink now for the summer, a constellation of freckles. Rather than a girl's bright smile and clear eyes, she squinted, like her father, the man who called her Claire Bear and tucked her into bed—*Bedtime for Claire Bear*—her eyes recessed. She held a very real but very slight smile, her lips pressed together, so that one could easily believe she was on the verge of crying. They stood there in symmetry, father and daughter, the old man and the girl. No, not a girl, a college graduate and a full-fledged adult, with all the accompanying responsibility and sadness. The brilliant green foliage behind them, the somber sky, waiting.

6

Claire's office was adjacent to the courthouse, a newish nondescript government building a few miles from Old Town. Primarily traffic and juvenile cases, some every fifteen minutes, a dull exercise for any observer hoping for Hollywood-style courtroom theatrics. Sure, there were plenty of criminal cases—robbery, drug offenses, even the occasional murder—but most of them settled out of court. The police in Overlook didn't go around arresting people who weren't guilty of something close to what they were charged with, so for the sake of expedience most defendants settled out of court. Claire nevertheless found the courtroom exhilarating. Nothing was more interesting to her than to plan a day's work. What the general public never knew was that managing a prosecutor's caseload was an art form because you had to change gears so quickly, and to see a skilled prosecutor in the flow was something to behold. That kind of drama, however, didn't make for good television, which meant the public was still stuck with a *Law & Order* and *CSI* understanding of criminal procedure. Not that those shows weren't entertaining, but they had almost nothing to do with life in the courtroom. Or life in general, for that matter.

On Tuesday morning, after Chuck assigned her the Daniel Hayward case, she walked down to the police station to meet with the lead detectives who would be on their way to arrest Hayward that afternoon. The first, a veteran lieutenant named Hollings, was a bullet-shaped man in his fifties who looked like he'd spent the past thirty years eating nothing but fast food. He was losing his hair, had plenty of flesh in his jowls, and kept his hands folded femininely in front of him. Claire knew him to be a country boy at heart, from up in Walterboro. He likely fancied deer hunting and Long John Silvers and cars with big-block engines, all talk of hemis and 454s. Although he had the beady-eyed look of a numbskull, Claire knew he didn't miss much. He could tell you what color shoelaces he'd seen on people that morning and what it meant about developing gang activity. Not that there was any real gang activity in Overlook, but drug mules passed through along the nearby I-95, heading from Florida to New Jersey, and every once in a while someone stopped over to visit the beach. Not with drugs, mind you, but on the return trip south. Their shoelaces gave them away.

The detective in charge of the investigation was a younger man named Blake, about thirty, ex-military, who looked like he woke at five a.m. daily to lift weights. He was smaller than Hollings, maybe five-nine, muscular, a guy who could handle himself in a bar brawl. In plain clothes—a blue Oxford shirt and khakis—he appeared relaxed and in control of himself. He had close-cut sandy hair with a bit of curly wave on top, bright blue eyes. Although his shirt covered them up, he wore several tattoos, a blue star on the back of his right arm and some kind of hieroglyphics on his thigh. Off-duty, he would wear t-shirts and long gray shorts and tan loafers with no socks, which revealed these tattoos and tanned skin with a slight burn. Give him a beer on a Sunday afternoon, he was your neighbor out tending the grill.

But here he was, in uniform and ready to arrest Daniel Hayward, and the first thing he said to Claire was, "I might just kill this guy when I get him into a room."

"Is that what you'll do," she said.

"Detective," his lieutenant said from across the room.

"I'm serious. I saw the girl's body. He dragged her a hundred feet. No way he thought he hit a deer. No, he knew he hit someone and he drove off. You don't do that, you just don't."

"So, what? You're going to beat him up? Knock him around a bit?"

Blake cracked his knuckles. "I just might."

"You do, you don't need me. I can't prosecute after that."

"Make me feel better though, give him the same kind of treatment he gave her."

"Blake," Hollings said.

"What? You don't want to take him out somewhere, some night?"

"I didn't say that, but that's not our job."

"Right, our job," Blake sneered.

"You done?" Claire asked him. "I appreciate where you're coming from, but that's not what I need from you. What I need from you is to get a confession out of him. See what he'll tell you."

"I hit a deer, is what he's going to say. If he says anything, now that he's got that lawyer coming down."

"Well, see if you can get him to say something before he lawyers up."

"Oh, I'll get him to talk." When Blake stretched his back and ran his tongue along the inside of his mouth, she thought she wouldn't want to be on the wrong side of the interrogation table from him. *Daniel, I understand. It's easy to do, you're out all night you look away to answer your cell phone—boom! It's late. You're tired. It could be a deer, right? That wasn't a bicycle you saw, right? People make mistakes. Good people. Let us help you.*

"Lieutenant?" she asked.

"We'll nail him," Hollings said. "We get a confession out of him, what's the worst you can charge him with?"

"Depends. Vehicular homicide, manslaughter, hit and run. Could just be a reckless driving charge. Slap on the wrist. The higher the charge, the harder to prove."

"You want to charge him with reckless driving?"

"No, I don't," Claire said. "I think he knows he's guilty of something big. Get him to confess, maybe we can settle for something in the middle with guaranteed jail time. You get in front of a jury, no telling how it'll go."

"You don't think a jury would want to have him lynched?"

"Some might," she said. "Bring him in and see what he can tell you. Any word on what she was doing out there that late?"

Blake shook his head. "No one's talking. My gut says she had a drink or two with a co-worker, and no one wants to admit it because she was underage."

"Figure that out. That won't excuse this guy, but the defense will use it as a mitigating circumstance."

After Det. Blake left, she followed Lt. Hollings to his office. He closed the door and the two of them sat down. "Sorry about the kid," Hollings said. "You know how these young bucks can get."

She pursed her lips. She did indeed know, but she wasn't about to give the police a pass. As a prosecutor, you got burned when you let your guard down. The only thing she'd learned of any use so far, it was best to keep your mouth shut when you didn't have to speak. Silence was power.

Hollings folded his hands in front of him on the desk, tucked his upper lip into his lower, sighed as though in contrition. He said, "This is gone be a tough one."

"What actual evidence do you have?"

"He's admitted he was driving home along that road and said he hit something. He's given us access to his vehicle, and my god, you should see it. Blake's right. There's no way he could've known he didn't hit something. The windshield is all bashed in and the grill is smashed. We have a forensics team on it, and it sounds like they've pulled blood samples and scraps of clothing and what looks like paint—possibly from the bicycle. So it won't take much to establish he hit her. But as far as what he knew when he drove off? That's where a confession comes in."

"How is he?"

"Truthfully? Shaken up."

"Could he be telling the truth?"

"I don't know. The condition the car's in…"

When he trailed off, she asked if he had any photos.

"It'll take just a second." Hollings turned on his computer. "Had he been drinking? That I can't say. Doesn't look good that he called his lawyer before calling us to turn himself in. He's been cooperative, and I have no doubt he regrets ever leaving the house that evening."

"Are you going to be able to get a confession?"

"Not likely. Blake can huff and puff all he wants, or he can be smooth and sympathetic, but Hayward has the money to afford a legal team and the know-how to keep his mouth shut."

"What's he do for a living?"

"Works for some kind of software company."

"Computer programmer?"

"He's a salesman for a company called Data Dare. Small startup."

"Married? Kids?"

"Got a wife, no kids. They've been married going on four years, probably have the baby itch along about now. They closed on a new house a few months ago, and it seems like they have everything together. Financially."

"What does she do?"

"She's loosely employed public relations. Here we go."

He turned the computer screen to face her, and at first she couldn't believe what she saw. The Durango was in the driveway, its entire windshield shattered, a starburst pattern right in front of the driver's line of vision. She couldn't understand how you could even create that kind of damage by hitting a person, but after such an impact, there was no way you could simply drive home. He'd have to drive with his head out the window just to see the road in front of him. The only reasonable explanation was that the man panicked. He must have been drinking, because that's what causes people to panic. He fled home, sobered, and called his lawyer.

Until now, Claire had tried to withhold judgment. She believed most people who came before her in the courtroom were guilty, but that's all they were, guilty cases, statistics to work her way through. Looking at the damaged Durango, the cracks in the bumper, the way the bumper was falling off on the passenger side, the shattered windshield, she suddenly developed an image of a younger Daniel Hayward, entitled, accumulating wealth, taking what he wanted out of life. There were plenty of men like that in her class at law school, and they usually came from a family with money. Nobody had ever told them no and meant it. The next wave of the old white guard, future Republicans (fiscal conservatives, they couldn't give two shits about social issues), wheelers and dealers, always looking to negotiate. They'd negotiate anything—the price of a new car, a grade on an exam, a serious offer from a prestigious law firm—and they more often than not got what they wanted, as if the world somehow rewarded a fathomless belief in oneself.

And now one of those assholes had hit a young woman, driven off, and expected to negotiate his way out of a prison sentence. Throw some cash at a lawyer, hammer home the finer points of the law, raise three children and become a member of the country club. With these men, the past is never dead because the past never happened. Everything was about the present and the future, and it burned her to think that only death itself could tamp down their arrogance. But by the time death came for them, they would have already blazed whatever trail they had to blaze, and they would be tired and self-satisfied and ready for the end. Just her luck, not even death would humble these men. Well. They didn't know Claire Fields. She had the law on her side, and she was tougher than any of them realized. They called them gunners in law school, the nondescript kids who made a break for the top of the class. Claire never had a shot at the top of the class, but she was a gunner in life. Down but not out after her last big mistake, she now had the chance to make a difference and ensure justice was served. Her career and her reputation depended on it.

"Jesus," she said of the photographs.

"I know it," Hollings said. He flipped through a few JPEGs, one angle after another of the brown Durango. A close-up of the bumper. A close-up of the windshield. A wide-angle of the vehicle in front of the house.

"How did he even make it home?"

"Hayward wouldn't say anything, but the lawyer says there's an explanation."

"They better hope it's a good one, if we put these in front of the jury. Your forensics team is looking into it?"

"We're on it. The investigator on site says he found blood and hair on the bumper, nothing on the windshield."

"Could that be the bicycle?"

"Could be. I've been researching collisions like this, but I can't find any precedent, at least not in any database I have access to."

"When are you going out there?"

"We've arranged a pickup at one. It'll take a couple of hours to get him processed, but we hope to start questioning him in late afternoon. You want to be there?"

"Just keep me informed," she said. "Will you print one of those out for me? I want to ask around."

"Will do. Let me know if you find anything."

Claire left the station with the photograph in a yellow envelope. She walked into Old Town Overlook, bought a paper from the rack, and went into the Griddle & Trough, an offbeat restaurant popular with the locals. After she'd sat down and ordered a short stack of blueberry pancakes and a cup of coffee—always with the coffee, her heart was going to explode one day, and she lay awake at night twitching like a junkie coming down from his high, but she needed a ritual—she spread the paper out on the table and hunched forward to see what was happening around town. She knew the troubles of the newspaper industry, exacerbated by the economic downturn and the rise of so-called citizen journalists, and it made her sad. Strange for someone her age, but she liked a daily paper. She liked the comics and the straight coverage and the clean prose. It reminded her of her father, who never went a day without reading at least two newspapers, one local and one national. He vacillated between the *New York Times* and the *Wall Street Journal*, showing no political allegiance to either but just looking for a good deal on the subscription rate; she never could figure out her father's politics, which was probably just as well, because it freed her up to form her own views, which she held close to the vest.

Yet for all her ability to moon over the print news, one look at today's paper and she cursed the day the printing press came into existence. Someone had leaked information about her case: *Person of Interest Comes Forward.* To be fair, JJ Sims had written a clean piece. No hatchet job on the police, the prosecution, or the alleged perpetrator, although he did lay it on a bit thick for the victim—the "mangled remains" of the bicycle, language such as that. Claire leaned back and ground her teeth. This would bolster her case, raise its profile, raise the stakes for her to get a conviction she wasn't at all certain she could get based on the briefing she'd received at the police station, Detective Blake's passion notwithstanding. She would have to give JJ a call, ask him to stop stirring the pot so blatantly. Big scoop for him, she knew, and a big scoop meant a happy readership, and a happy readership meant more eyeballs, more advertising, more revenue.

Like most people in her office, Claire had an uneasy relationship with the press. JJ covered the crime beat for the *Island Packet*, and since Claire handled much of the criminal work for the solicitor's office, the two of them were on good terms. Mostly. She did blame him, partially, for jinxing her in the Michael Baldwin case.

Every time JJ had called her, Claire had said, "Just stay home today, and we'll get a conviction." Then he'd show up and the judge would reschedule for some reason or another. She'd never forget, late in the trial, telling JJ, "What else can possibly go wrong? We'll see our conviction."

Well, she'd gotten the conviction, and then she'd seen it overturned due to bungled evidence. Her relationship with Barry Dewitt in itself should have been irrelevant, but in the way of small-town gossip, they may as well have been pop stars on the cover of *Us Weekly*. Given how fast the Baldwin case tanked, everyone viewed their relationship as an unseemly conflict of interest, especially given that while Barry was spending nights in her condo, his wife had been working nights as a nurse at the local hospital. Claire had no excuse: some people made you feel good, and you wanted to relive that experience, deepen it, devastate your life. One more tally in her line of failed relationships. One more new low.

She'd give JJ credit for this: When the affair had come to light, he'd called her and told her straight up that he was writing about it, that his editor had assigned it to him, that he didn't like it, and that he wanted her to know he was sorry. Unusual for a reporter to apologize for writing the truth, but there it was. She didn't blame JJ, or the newspaper, or Barry Dewitt, or the judge. If she'd learned nothing in her thirty-one years, it was how to take responsibility for her actions.

Today, reading the article about Hayward, she dug her phone out of her purse and dialed JJ Sims.

"Hey there," he said. "I was just thinking of giving you a call."

"I'm sure you were."

"I take it you've read today's paper."

"Who's leaking information to you?"

"You know I can't."

"Yeah, yeah."

"You want to meet up for coffee? Set the record straight?"

"Of course not."

"Well, listen. My editor wants me to keep scratching this. Is it safe to say we reached out to your office and that you've arrested someone?"

"Of course not."

"Have you arrested someone?"

"Arrests aren't my department."

"Have you charged anyone?"

"Not yet."

"But will you?"

"I promise, you won't be the last to know."

"That doesn't help me out with my editor. You know he won't settle for anything less than a complete statement from you, the detectives, the mayor, and everyone in power between here and Columbia."

"Well, he's just going to have to wait this time."

"I'm on your side, Claire."

He didn't have to tell her what he was implying, that not everyone at the paper was on her side, and that she could deal with JJ Sims or be fed to the vultures, who would certainly make this investigation miserable. She said, "JJ. I'll work with you where I can. Look, how about this. I want to make sure justice is served. That was a heinous crime, leaving the poor girl on the side of the road, and we're working with the police to explore every avenue."

"That's garbage," he said. "Come on, Claire."

"I want to see this thing through. You know me."

"That I do."

"Then you know I'm not lying. I really am working with the lead detectives, and I'm going to make sure we play our cards right. Off the record, you know I've got the Baldwin case hanging over me, so I'm not trying to rush this one. You've already scooped us. There is a person of interest. I can't tell you on the record that I've spoken with this person, or what this person has to say, but I can tell you"—she took an intake of breath—"keep scratching whatever source you've got."

"Uh-huh."

"Don't be surprised if you've got a good story for your weekend edition. Tell your editor."

Her pancakes arrived right as she got off the phone. She was playing with fire, she knew, in flirting with the press, making suggestions off the record, encouraging JJ's curiosity. But this Daniel Hayward business was going to be a bad one, and she thought if she could build some goodwill with JJ now, maybe get the news on her side, she might have an easier time with the jury in a few weeks—assuming a few weeks was all it would take to sort this mess out.

7

There were times when Claire still fantasized about being a firefighter. In grade school, when seemingly everyone was interested in what she wanted to be when she grew up, she wanted to fight fires. At the time she was too young to know anything, couldn't understand what such a life would be like, and yet everyone from her parents to teachers to miscellaneous relatives to her friends' parents insisted on knowing what she would do with her life, as if she at seven had some secret self-knowledge that your average thirty-year-old lacked. Today she knew herself well enough to know she never would have even made it through the basic training, that the career was a pie-in-the-sky fiction for her, same as being an astronaut or president was for her elementary school classmates. But this afternoon she sorely wished she were in a different line of work. Sitting around for eight hours with nothing to do before running into a burning building sounded like a dream career compared to negotiating with Henry Somerville, Daniel Hayward's Charleston attorney, a silver fox with a silver tongue and, underneath the polite veneer, mean as a hornet.

No one in her office knew this—in fact, it might be her biggest secret—but she'd had a run-in with Somerville while she was clerking for a district judge in Charleston during law school. As a clerk, her role was little more than unpaid intern (she could have made more money selling coffee at Starbucks), but it was an important line-item on her resume, and thus her future career depended on her using her expensive law degree to write press releases and file papers.

As a big-time defense attorney, Somerville was a fixture in the courtroom. He didn't do TV ads, he didn't chase ambulances, but he caught the high-profile cases, the occasional South of Broad scandals (which never made the news but which Charleston residents surreptitiously followed), the Porter-Gaud graduates, the city council brouhahas, and the odd celebrity who got into some manner of trouble after hours during the filming of a movie (he once represented the esteemed but largely forgotten Quinn Rollins, lovable male lead whose career took a sour turn after one too many cocaine busts, rehab, and the shaky disheveled look he'd worn since the early nineties). Somerville was in his late fifties, tall, in good shape, with thinning gray hair he parted in such a way that he still had the authoritative presence of a man fifteen years his junior. His jaw was sharp and jutted out noticeably when he chewed, as though he were sawing into his food. Thin cheeks with a reddish tint to his pale skin. Lines that followed half a century of diligent shaving. If he weren't a lawyer, he would have made a fine sales director or politician. He hobnobbed. That much was clear, even to Claire. Doubtful he would remember her, but she was sick with apprehension.

As a clerk, one of her tasks had been to gather sentencing recommendations from the prosecution and the defense and deliver them to the judge for consideration. But being twenty-four at the time and having a slew of competing interests in her life, she'd once neglected to turn Somerville's sentencing request over to the judge, so the judge simply went by the prosecution's recommendation and issued a hefty sentence. The difference may have been a few months in the sentence—no life-changing consequence, she'd felt—but that hadn't stopped Somerville from taking time out of his busy lawyer's day to come over to the courthouse to dress her down.

"I mean, really, what were you thinking here?" he'd asked her in front of a large cloud of witnesses, including a judge on break from the bench. "You don't turn that in and what happens? My client can't get a fair sentencing, and we have to go through an arduous appeals process. And for what? Rules matter, Ms.—what was your name?"

"Fields. Claire."

"Ms. Fields. I presume your law professors—where did you go to school?"

"South Carolina."

"Right," said the UVA-educated attorney. "I presume your law professors hammered into you the one rule of our line of work, which is that details matter. You have to be perfect if you want to succeed. Otherwise you go back to the world of administration or go find a job in public relations, something less rigorous and more bubbly."

Claire had stood there, in the courtroom hallway, tears stinging her eyes, and waited for it to be over. When she'd turned it over in her mind over the coming weeks, she'd caught the unapologetic sexism in his comments. *Law is a man's field, because we get the details right. Have you considered going back to secretary school, little lady?*

Somerville hadn't let it drop. When the judge was on break, he'd gone in to ask, "Sandra, is this your clerk? Where do you find these kids? Is it the internet, ruining everything?"

"Henry," the judge—who'd not hired Claire and didn't even know her—cut in mercifully.

"All right, I'm through," he'd said to the judge. To Claire: "But listen, don't ever make a mistake with one of my cases again. You won't find work in this field if you can't do the job right."

The lid had come off her coffee just then, and the cup dropped to the ground and spilled brown liquid everywhere. Somerville sidestepped it in disgust.

He'd taken off then, having no other business in the court but to berate poor Claire, who made sure never to get near one of Henry Somerville's cases again. No one—not the judge nor the other clerks nor the casual bystanders in the hallway—had said a thing. They'd let her find her way to the ladies room to recover her wits. The incident was never spoken of, but it made an impression on her—about her line of work (this was a game for grown-ups, no distractions allowed), and men in particular (alpha personalities must be met with alpha personalities). Now, it was time for her to confront Somerville as a professional, and the question was: Would he remember her? Would he immediately know he had the upper hand in this case? Would he remind her of that? Rumors swirled around Somerville, because, like Claire, he was secretive about his personal life. Kept to himself, networked in crowds that kept their business behind closed doors. No doubt many a mover and shaker could tell a story or two about him, but equally doubtless, said story would never emerge.

8

On the first morning of deliberations between the two sides, Claire woke early and pressed her favorite suit. She showered, spent more time than usual in front of the mirror, curlers in her hair, powder on her face, ruminating sadly on the faint traces of lines at the corners of her eyes she knew would soon enough be full-on crow's feet, the body's inevitable entropy on an exponential climb. She lingered over scratching her dog goodbye before getting into her vehicle and motoring to her office, reminding herself that she had the solicitor's office behind her, that Chuck would come to her rescue if she got into a jam (and trying to suppress the thought that she already had a strike against her, and that Chuck couldn't come to her rescue without jeopardizing her career and her life).

Somerville was already in the office when she arrived, which threw her because he was twenty minutes early. There he was, looking the same as ever, in the conference room with a cup of coffee and his smartphone out, scrolling through messages, a thick file on the table in front of him.

"He's early," the receptionist said. "I didn't know what to do, so I sent him in there."

"No, that's right."

Claire set her stuff on her office desk and was organizing her thoughts, steeling herself, when Chuck poked his head in to say, "You ready for this?"

"I've got everything lined up here."

"Good. Don't be intimidated."

"Not at all."

"Get him, tiger."

Chuck shoved off the door frame and left her there, the nervousness and intimidation rising up. *Get him, tiger.* What was that? He never talked like that. It made her wonder what Chuck knew about this case, about Somerville, or about Claire that he wasn't letting on. It also, strangely, endeared her, perhaps because it reminded her of her father calling her Claire Bear. She would have to call her father this evening. It had been too long, and she felt a stab of worry for him.

"Okay," she said to herself. She picked up the Hayward file, her favorite pen, and her coffee cup.

She opened the conference room door and found Somerville rattling off into his phone. "No, no, no, this is what you tell her. Just tell her to switch the nozzle around and it should work fine." Same booming voice Claire remembered from the Charleston courthouse. She shuddered. He waved and carried on for another minute, meaningless words she felt certain were uttered just to keep her waiting, keep the power in his court. When he finally hung up, he gave an apologetic shrug and said, "My daughter. Trouble with her apartment."

"Ah. Claire Fields," she said.

"Nice to see you," he said, giving nothing away. He extended his hand. "So. Daniel Hayward." Already taking control of the conversation. "I presume you'll want to meet with my client as soon as possible."

"That would be ideal."

"Good, good. We can arrange that. I'm sure we all just want to get this horrible mess behind us. Now as you know, he's been giving his full cooperation to the police, and we understand charges may be necessary but—"

"Let me stop you there," she said. "We've already filed charges against him."

"Yes, manslaughter, and let me just—"

"And we're going to pursue them aggressively," she continued. "I appreciate your client has cooperated with the police, but he made a serious mistake in driving off that night, no matter what he thought he hit, so if you're here to talk about settlement, I've brought—"

"Whoa, whoa, let's just slow down here," he said, reasserting control. "Now, I'm not sure you're giving my client enough credit. He feels awful and wants to do everything he can to assist. I appreciate what you're doing. You've got a job, I've got a job. And our system will decide."

"Our system has rules, which your client clearly broke."

Just for a moment, Somerville's jaw wavered, but he corrected quickly, smiled, and said, "Good. I'm glad you got that message back in your clerking days."

Now it was her turn to waver. Before she could speak, he continued, "When do you want to interview Mr. Hayward?"

"As soon as possible, like you said. This afternoon?"

"I'm sure we could arrange something for tomorrow. Of course I'll be there. You may want to bring Chuck along."

She ignored his last comment. "Fine. So we're clear, you're not ready to plead?"

"I don't think we need to go there just yet."

"We may want to talk more about this tomorrow. I'm not sure his I-hit-a-deer story is going to cut it."

"Why ever not? It's a dangerous highway out there."

"And I don't know how he managed to drive home. Have you seen this morning's paper?"

"I read it online."

"You might have missed the front-page article. Check it out, and maybe we'll talk more tomorrow. What time did you say?"

"How about two?"

"Fine."

"Better make it three-thirty. I've got a late luncheon."

"See you then."

After he left, she returned to her office and crumpled behind her desk. She felt as though she'd been negotiating wearing nothing but underwear, like a slab of beef on display for poking and prodding. So he did remember her. She was proud of herself for not flinching, and for at least drawing that information out of him. She reminded herself once again that she was a grownup now, that she had authority in this case, and that it was a battle she intended to win.

The front page of this morning's *Island Packet* showed the leaked photographs of Daniel's Durango, JJ Sims doing his best to live up to his end and stir the pot on Daniel Hayward. The front of the Durango was smashed, the shattered windshield on full display on the top flap of A1. Everyone in the community would be irate soon enough. The online poison would spew. For now, Claire had enough of a tailwind to grit her teeth and prepare for yet another confrontation with Henry Somerville.

But first: one final interruption. Her phone rang with her secretary saying that Lauren James, the dead girl's sister, was here to see her.

"Did I forget an appointment with her?" Claire asked.

"No, she just walked in."

Claire stared at her open case notes for a moment. Her mind was blank. Print-outs, reports, an empty coffee cup, a screensaver on her machine flashing Bayard County: she couldn't get her bearings, as though she were in a dream, or had woken from a dream with foggy misunderstanding for why she was here, what she was doing with her life. Her neck felt hot.

"Do you want me to send her in?" her secretary said again.

"I, um, sure."

"The conference room is open. She'll be waiting for you there."

She shook the mouse to wake up her screen, took a look at her inbox (empty), and then peered down at herself, took in her favorite suit (now rumpled), and wished for the day to be over. Chuck said he'd already spoken with the family to keep them informed, and while she could appreciate the victim's family for wanting to ensure Claire's office was doing everything possible to mete out justice for Daniel Hayward, she was not a therapist. She could only direct them toward the right people, something she hoped Chuck had already done. Seeing them would be a distraction, and she briefly resented her secretary—a busybody who got the mail out on time but who chatted so often and so loudly that the working attorneys all kept their doors closed to muffle her yak-yak-yakking—for not sending the girl away.

In the conference room, Lauren James was biting at an uneven thumbnail with her other arm draped comfortably over the back of the chair. Claire's first thought was that the girl appeared vaguely simian in that pose, but she modulated her thoughts as the girl came into view. She wore a slinky white shirt and tight jeans (inappropriate for a law office, Claire felt), and she had the brazen yet vulnerable face of a girl in the churning phases of young womanhood. Claire remembered that age well (acne, boys, body image issues) and she felt an unwarranted connection to the girl.

She introduced herself and sat across from Lauren. "Would you like any water? Or coffee?"

"I'm fine," the girl said.

"How can I help you today?"

"I wanted to get an update on Samantha's case."

"Did Chuck already meet with you and your family?"

"He did, but he didn't tell us anything. Just that you were pursuing some lines of inquiry." She said this last phrase with a contempt that reminded Claire not only what a mess young women could be, but also how dangerously smart.

"Well, that's true," she started. "As you know, the police have a person of interest."

"And what does that mean?"

"It means they think they know who was driving the vehicle."

"Good. Have you arrested him?"

"We're bringing him in for questioning tomorrow."

"And then you'll arrest him?"

"If there's probable cause for a crime."

"He hit and killed my sister and drove off. That's not crime enough?"

"Well, as Chuck may or may not have mentioned, we have to proceed carefully. If this man did it, we want to make sure we can prove the crime and convict him. That's the only way justice can be served."

"How long is this going to take?"

"It's hard to say," Claire said. "Depends on if we go to trial, or if he confesses for a plea bargain."

"And what's that get him?"

"A plea bargain? If he confesses, we might negotiate a sentence without going to court."

"But you're not going to let him off."

"No," Claire said. "We're not going to let him off."

She couldn't tell what Lauren wanted from her. Claire's instincts said the girl was hiding something, but people under duress behaved in all different ways. There was no telling what was on this girl's mind.

Claire asked, "How's your family holding up?"

"Terrible. No one's speaking to each other."

"I know it's tough," Claire said, "but all I can tell you right now is to try to be patient, and know that we're doing everything we can to bring the perpetrator to justice." Claire had to be careful here, because she could only say so much, especially given her last trial. She hardly trusted herself with this case, much less had the brash confidence necessary to say a conviction was assured. But she had to offer Lauren something. "I should warn you, too, though, that if there's a trial, we may need you and your family to testify."

"About what?"

"About your sister. Just tell us about her, what she was like. Try to build a sympathetic picture of her."

"Will I have to talk about myself?" Lauren asked.

"Maybe about your relationship with your sister, and about what kind of family you have. Basic things."

Something flashed in Lauren's eyes.

"Is there anything I need to know?" Claire asked. "About you and Samantha? Or about what she did after work that night?"

"No," Lauren said quickly. "She was a great sister." She took a moment to compose herself and then said, "I have to go."

9

That evening Claire was supposed to have dinner with her father, but she called and left him a voicemail to beg off. She felt a twinge of guilt, because the man lived alone and she was his only daughter and his days seemed to revolve around his work for the cable company, which was winding down. She wished he would get remarried or join a social club, and felt badly that she'd not started a family and filled his life with grandchildren. He would have liked that, she thought.

Alone at home, she poured a glass of chardonnay and reviewed her case notes, sketched out her interview with Daniel Hayward. He wouldn't be able to tell her anything about Samantha James. The girl and her family seemed like the paragon of the upwardly mobile of middle America, but something niggled at Claire about Lauren's visit this afternoon. She was hiding something, and whatever it was, she suspected it was a whole lot more interesting than anything Daniel Hayward could tell her.

Claire's immediate challenge was that everyone was crafting a story around Daniel. The media with its photographs of the

Durango's smashed windshield, the James family in their grief, Somerville with whatever angle he'd chosen to pursue. If she were him, the first thing she would want to do is get those photographs excluded, because the spiderweb of glass told the world Daniel was not innocent. No one in any reasonable state of mind could ignore the fractured windshield and drive home. Claire shuddered at what must have happened during the collision, the sickening *smack!* of the Durango slamming into the girl. And to do that to the windshield? She must have been flung into his line of sight, a shadow in the darkness, another *smack!* as he slammed on his brakes, perhaps swerved. She believed Daniel himself also had a story, though what that story might be, she couldn't say. Perhaps he was wracked with guilt, was lying awake every night with a memory of the double smash. She couldn't envision anyone coming to a halt, pausing to gain their bearings, and then deciding to drive off. She couldn't come up with a story to justify it. He might not be a monster, but he'd made a grievous mistake, and was now caught in the gauntlet of the law.

She felt anxious about her interview tomorrow with Daniel, because of Somerville, and her history with him. They had all the same facts, but were writing different stories, and what kept her awake tonight was lack of imagination. She couldn't see what Somerville could say to rationalize his client driving off. It felt too easy to expect a quick plea, but if she were in Somerville's shoes, she wouldn't know what other tack she could take. She looked him up online and found his firm's website, stared at his well-fed face and imagined all the men she'd gone to law school with, men who wanted to join South Carolina's grip-and-grin legal establishment, men like her boss Chuck. She was tired of facing such men as opposing counsel, but a Google News search for him intrigued her. The web was littered with something about his personal life, a scandal related to alleged dog abuse. A trending article on BuzzFeed pointed to the hashtag #dogjustice and people on Twitter calling for Somerville to get canceled. She was savvy enough to recognize a scandal manufactured by the under-employed—and this particular story seemed to be based on a video of him simply playing with his dog in a park—yet she also suspected that Somerville, dog lover or not, had a deficiency latent in his character.

She copied the link and emailed it to JJ.

Thought you'd like to see this if you haven't already stumbled on it.

Then she turned her attention to Judge Kenneth Rhodes. Although a jury would decide the case, the judge would issue the sentencing. He would decide the difference between twenty months suspended and twenty years in prison. She pulled a few of his opinions out of the Westlaw archives to see if he'd ever written anything around mistakes of fact or hit-and-runs or highway incidents. She had the advantage of having met him when she was in law school. South Carolina Law had presented him with some obscure honor that required a speech from the judge (and provided the law school a reason to solicit more donations from its alumni). At a reception, she'd asked him what it was like, being a judge, and he'd been honest with her.

I wasn't prepared for how it would change my life.

In a good way?

Yes and no. It's an honor to serve on the bench. It really is. But it's like being a politician. Everywhere I go, I have to think about security, and I have to think about public perception. A lot of my friends are lawyers from my years in private practice, but now I can't just meet them for dinner at Chili's, because if they show up in my courtroom the next day to argue a case, that's a bias. Even if I try to remain aware of it, and approach each case as objectively as I can, that air of impropriety is always there.

Sounds tough, she said, feeling a little stupid and insensitive.

It can be isolating, and it's definitely a re-alignment, but that's how life goes. You're young, so you can still do anything you want, but you don't have to become a judge to find a lot of doors close on you as you get older. At least that's been my experience. Only thing I really know is that it's a good idea to look for the counter-narrative.

The counter-narrative?

There's always more than one side to a story, or a position, or a case. My job is to understand every side.

So you can find the middle ground.

Well, maybe not middle ground, he said. *The truth sometimes exists on the fringes. Not always. But sometimes.*

I'll keep that in mind, she said. *Maybe I'll see you in court some time.*

Good luck, he said. *And do me a favor? If you ever see me in Chili's, say hello and call me Kenny. Try to pretend I'm not a judge.*

She wasn't certain Judge Rhodes remembered her the first time she appeared in his courtroom, but he always treated her with respect and humility, which made her feel undeserving when she was trapped in the muck of a nasty case. Seven years later, she still thought about counter-narratives and the quest for truth, but her truth today was that she wanted to win the case and put Daniel Hayward behind bars, to find some measure of justice for the James family.

10

Claire expected Somerville would call to reschedule the meeting with Daniel yet again, which he did at eight-fifteen in the morning. Her receptionist patched him through and he said without hello, "Something came up this afternoon. Any chance you could meet Mr. Hayward this morning?"

"What time?"

He paused. "Oh, say ten-thirty? Actually, if we could come over now, that would be ideal."

"Ideal for whom?"

"You're right, let's say ten-thirty."

At ten-forty, Somerville showed up with Daniel in tow, out on a stiff bond but looking fresh and well rested. She met them in her office conference room: Somerville and Hayward on one side of the table, Claire on the other. Claire thought about inviting Chuck in, but felt the need to prove herself. The investigating officers had been unable to interview Hayward without Somerville around, and, from Blake's report, Somerville had clearly coached his client into saying nothing, which meant it was on Claire to coax out a fair plea. That, or a trial.

"Good morning, everyone," she started.

"Good to see you again, Claire," Somerville said. *Claire.* The nerve.

"Hi, Henry," she said. We could all be on a first-name basis here. "Hello, Daniel."

"Good morning," he said, his voice deep yet soft, uncertain. Daniel was a heavyset thirty-something with a chipped front tooth and a bush of brown hair. Hard to tell what he thought of her.

She looked him over for a moment. Not quite what she'd anticipated. She'd expected him to be an overweight frat boy kind of guy, but he was muscular with just a bit of a paunch. His hair had started to thin, the look of a man who wore a baseball cap too often. His jaw was rounded and fleshy and sort of drooped like a sac, and the back of his neck had two triangles of hair that had grown in below the hairline, the man a week late for a much-needed haircut. He wore a suit and tie, which she imagined he wore regularly for his software sales job. Hoofing from town to town, visiting warehouses and manufacturing plants and over-air conditioned office parks, up-selling some piece of software, some app, some business service, some microsite—whatever would help increase productivity and get the revenue machine churning. She knew his type. She had his number. But now her job was to send him to the state penitentiary, where he would be indistinguishable from a pill-pusher or a wife-beater or a drunk driver as easily as a hit-and-run manslaughter perp.

Claire's office was a standard government building, with limited windows and low ceilings and stark lighting in general. The conference room had a nice mahogany table and a tall window through which a shaft of light funneled in. From somewhere, an HVAC unit hummed. She never even noticed it anymore except when guests were in the building. She imagined Somerville's office in Charleston, all hardwoods and tea service from his secretary, and knew he must be thinking: no surprise, this was how government offices worked. Churning air conditioners, grimly bureaucratic employees, basement lighting.

"So," she said. "My name is Claire Fields, and I'm with the solicitor's office. Thank you for coming."

Daniel said nothing.

"I've spoken with your attorney"—she nodded at Somerville—"and I want you to know I appreciate all your cooperation with this investigation. I know this must be difficult for you, and I want you to know I appreciate that. I'm here to discuss the possibility of a plea, which I presume Henry has briefed you on?"

Daniel nodded and kept his eyes low.

"The way this might work is that rather than go to trial, you would sign an acknowledgment that you were driving the vehicle that struck Samantha James and that you knowingly drove off. In exchange, the solicitor's office is prepared to offer a reduced sentence—a felony hit and run rather than manslaughter, which is what you've currently been charged with. Do you understand?"

"This was all a terrible mistake," he said.

"I understand that, and I understand mistakes happen. We all make them. But now we must follow the course of the law."

"The law says try me with manslaughter or settle with a hit and run."

"The law says you've committed a crime."

"That's bullshit." He sat up. Out of the corner of her eye, Claire saw Somerville straighten up himself. Daniel went on, "Whatever I did, it wasn't intentional. It was an accident. The choice you're offering me isn't a choice. You're offering me the chance to say this wasn't an accident."

"I'm sure hitting Samantha was an accident. No one's disputing that. But you decided to drive off."

"I didn't know I'd hit anyone."

"But you knew you hit something. And you didn't pull over to see what it was. The case you're arguing—what Henry will take to court—is that you committed a mistake of fact, that you didn't know what you were doing. The case my office will be bringing to court is that this was no mistake of fact. My office will argue that you willingly drove off, for whatever reason, knowing you may have hit—and possibly killed—someone. Had you been drinking that night?"

"Don't answer that," Somerville said. "Ms. Fields, you're out of line." *Ms. Fields.* She smiled politely at him.

Daniel kept his eyes on the table in front of them. "I want to tell you, I want to make sure you understand, Daniel, that despite what Henry might tell you, your case doesn't look good. Have you seen the newspapers? You're all over the front page. People are speculating that you'd been drinking, and that you drove off to avoid a drunk driving charge. People are calling you a coward, Daniel. Saying you're not a man willing to take responsibility."

"That's enough," Somerville said.

"Are you prepared to fight that?"

"I said that's enough."

"Were you smoking marijuana that night? Have you ever smoked marijuana? Who were you out with? Why were you out with her? Were you sleeping with her? Did your wife know you were meeting with her?"

"Ms. Fields!" Somerville leaned in and put his hand on the table as if to shield his client from her barrage. But she felt her teeth sink in and couldn't let go.

"Answer me, Daniel. We can settle this now, or we can go to trial, but I promise you, if we go to trial, it's going to be bleak."

Daniel looked up and straight at her, eyes steady and clear, and said, "I'm not pleading guilty to a felony hit and run."

"Henry's got my number, if you change your mind."

Daniel said nothing as she stood.

In the hallway, Somerville took her by the elbow. "The hell was that? I should file a complaint, you're slandering my client."

"I'm not saying anything about him. I just want him to know what he's up against."

"He's well aware."

"Is he? Are you?"

Somerville smiled. "Claire, I've been in this business thirty-five years. I'm not in the habit of giving my clients bad advice. One word to the wise, though? Don't tip your hand this early on. Takes all the fun and the challenge out of trying a case."

"Word to the wise yourself?" she replied, steeling her nerves for the last few moments with him. "Overlook is different from Charleston. This is a small, small town, you're not going to just come in here, say your client thought he hit a deer, and send him home with a slap on the wrist. If we go to trial, he's going to serve time. A lot of time. I'm going to make sure of that."

"We'll see," he said. "I hope your courtroom skills are a little more developed than your coffee-handling skills."

"Everybody's young once."

"And everyone makes mistakes. You said so yourself."

Without giving her the chance to reply—not that she had any decent reply in mind, something she would turn over for hours until the perfect zinger occurred to her—Somerville walked out, a spring in his step. He was agile in body and mind for an old guy, and as soon as he rounded the corner, she scurried to the ladies room, where it was déjà vu all over again. She was a clerk, Somerville yelling at her in the courtroom hallway, yet this time she'd won the argument. She was in the right, she was sure of it, yet she felt as though she'd been pummeled. *Everyone makes mistakes.* Yes, she knew that, and she knew Somerville knew as well. Easy for him to call her out. What did it matter if his career took a hit, at his age? For her, she needed the win to stay in her boss's good graces and keep paying on those student loans.

She returned to her office and found Chuck.

"You get a plea agreement?" he asked her.

She shook her head, followed him to his office.

"I wouldn't expect Henry to cave," he said. "He's an arrogant prick, isn't he?"

She laughed. "That he is."

"What's their case? Sticking with the hit-a-deer story?" Chuck nodded to himself. "That's to be expected. Might even be true." He held up a copy of the newspaper, Daniel Hayward's mug shot on A1. "You read the online comments for this?"

"Some of them."

"Nasty business. They're going to have a hard time convincing a jury that Hayward doesn't deserve the electric chair."

She almost felt pity for Daniel, for a moment, sullen and stone-faced behind the bad advice of his defense attorney. But the pity quickly passed.

"Well, keep after him," Chuck said. "First priority is to tell the press we're sticking with manslaughter. Scare him a bit. Let them know we're not messing around. Then let's go after the wife. What's her name—Francine? Where has she been in all of this?"

"From her police statement, she didn't know where Daniel had been. He came home late, but he sometimes goes out with the guys from the office. She was in bed and barely woke up. He didn't say anything to her, just took a shower and came to bed."

"We'll need to subpoena his phone and credit card records. See if he's got any credit cards she doesn't know about."

"You think he was having an affair?"

"It's a possibility. Or maybe he was just out at Wild Wings and had a few too many shots of tequila. Either way, we need to know where he was that evening and what he was doing. Talk to the wait staff. I'm sure the detectives are on it, but in case they're not."

"Got it."

"Who's the investigator?"

"Blake, is the detective."

"That prick."

"Hollings is the lieutenant."

"I'll grab coffee with Hollings. See what we can dig up."

Chuck rubbed his hands together like a kid on his birthday. What excitement was just around the corner? This was a special day for the solicitor's office. Claire almost felt better, but something still nagged her, Somerville too confident for the case he'd signed up for. *One word to the wise, though? Don't tip your hand this early on. Takes all the fun and the challenge out of trying a case.* She needed to figure out what she didn't know so he wouldn't blindside her. She remembered the shame from her last case, how she'd botched it over an unsatisfying affair, and she felt in her bones today that she was not up for this new case. Whatever happened, she felt she would inevitably let someone down.

11

As she sometimes did when she felt caged, she got in the car after work and drove out the wide highway and across the bridge onto Hilton Head Island. Below her, starlight shimmered on the surface of brackish water, the reeds and swamp grasses and low-growth foliage a tangle of shadows. It was a half-hour drive out to the beach, a complete waste of time and gas, but ever since she started driving in high school, it had nearly always helped her clear her head to wend her way out to the ocean, where she would sit on one of the dunes, away from the tourist resorts, and listen to the waves and allow the sea air to erode away her concerns.

On the drive out, she called her father. She'd not actually spoken to him in weeks, just traded texts and left him yesterday's apologetic voicemail for bailing on dinner. A conversation was long overdue.

The phone rang four times before he picked it up, sort of coughed, and said, "Hello?"

"Hey, Dad. How you doing?"

"Well hey, Claire." His voice lifted an octave or two.

"How you doing?" she asked again before he could ask her how she was doing, having no clear answer for him, just needing to hear her father's voice.

"Ah, I'm all right. Bout the same here as always."

"Yeah? I'm sorry about yesterday."

"Oh, that's all right. I understand."

He spoke with a lazy country drawl, which she'd first picked up on when she was in college. She'd found it endearing for a while after leaving home, but now it had come to seem like an affectation. Her father was a kind man, yet the world had not been kind to him. An introverted soul, Larry Fields was not in a position to become anything more than a bit player on the world stage: quiet work, a wife he doubtlessly loved with affection if not passion, and a daughter who was making her own quiet way through the world. Claire had played the dutiful daughter for as long as she could, but now she had her own life, her own concerns.

"Work going all right?" she asked.

"I'm staying busy as I want to be. How about you?"

Work was all he seemed to understand. Getting up early, getting to the job site before everyone else, getting to it. In his own career, he'd gone from project manager to office drone, an elder statesman who was lucky not to have been laid off in the Great Recession, but who would not survive another corporate downsizing.

"Nothing new," she said. Then she said, "Well, I have one case. You heard about the hit and run? The dead girl on Reedy Road?"

"I heard about that on the news."

"That landed on my plate."

"Oh my," he said.

"It's a pretty nasty case," she said, and she began to tell him about the details.

"Was she wearing a helmet?" he asked.

"Yes, Dad."

"Mm."

"It was late at night, and he says he thought he hit a deer."

"Dangerous for a girl to be out at night like that. Especially on a bicycle."

"She had a reflector, and because he drove off, we don't know if he'd been drinking." Claire wanted her father on her side, wanted him to make some comment about what a bastard Daniel Hayward was. She shouldn't be talking about the case at all, with anyone, but tonight she needed her father's support. Just this once.

Instead, he said, again, "Mm."

"You think it was her fault."

"I don't think that," he said. "I just think she put herself in a dangerous situation."

"She was killed, Dad, and she wasn't in the wrong."

"Mm."

Claire drove on. Outside, the last of the day's light bruised the ragged sky, the days noticeably shorter even though it was still technically summer. Fall would come on gradually and then suddenly, like so much else in life. A grown-up time of year, her new favorite season, when the tourists left the Lowcountry and the heat broke and the air turned crisp. Never cold—it was lower South Carolina—but cool enough to wear a light jacket.

Her father broke the silence. "You want to try to reschedule dinner soon?"

"Definitely," she said. "This case is going to keep me busy, though, maybe through Labor Day."

"I understand. You do what you need to do."

"You got any social events coming up? You thought about joining some kind of group? Silver Sneakers at the Y or something?"

"Ah," he grunted.

"I know, Dad, I'm just saying."

"Maybe I will," he said to appease her, but they both knew it for a lie. He was a committed introvert who liked a one-on-one but clammed up in a crowd of three. She worried about him, because his life seemed so dreary without her or her mother there. She wished he would meet someone, go out and mingle, join a club or a church or something, but his life continued to pass, work throughout the week, some project or another over the weekend, until it appeared he would finish out his life, however long that may be, in the same holding pattern he'd been in for years.

"Okay, Dad, well I got to go," she said after a while. "I need to fix some dinner myself."

"Late dinner."

"Well, you know."

"You enjoy."

After an awkward moment of silence, they said their good-byes and Claire drove on. She genuinely hadn't eaten this evening. There was a Wendy's on the way to the beach, which she usually stopped at for a frosty at least. She pulled into the drive-thru and said, "Let me just get the junior bacon combo with Coke."

"You want to up-size that?"

"Not today, thanks."

The box squawked some price, and she wheeled around to pick up her food. New pear trees grew out of the grassy median between the drive-thru and the parking lot.

A station wagon in front of her pulled away, and she gave her money to the cashier.

"Hey, Claire," the cashier said, and chuckled.

She blinked, recognized the woman—she was heavyset, had dark hair stained burgundy, and thick makeup around her eyes—

but struggled to remember her name. Then it came to her. "Hey, Starla. How are you?"

"Nothing much." She and Claire had known each other since the second grade, though they were never close after elementary school. They'd landed in different cliques, but perhaps none of that mattered after high school. As with Wendy at the outlet mall and Barry Dewitt, life in a small town meant you knew people on a hello basis for years, no matter where you and they ended up. And you never knew how life might come around again full circle.

Starla handed Claire her change and her food. "Thanks," she said, and smiled, genuinely happy to see a familiar face and be recognized, and to be reminded of simpler days before the trials of adulthood, careers and affairs and the pressure of getting out of bed in the morning.

She pulled into a space and turned off the engine. She never ate inside because there would be people with their children to interrupt her thoughts. A quiet meal in her car may have looked sad from the outside, but it was a small gift for herself.

The fries were cold by the time she finished them, and she crumpled everything in the sack and tossed it onto the passenger side floor. Then she maneuvered the car back onto the highway and out toward the beach.

The lights and traffic thinned as she moved out of the shopping district and into the more residential beach neighborhoods. She continued several miles to the end of a strip and found a public beach access. It was full dark when she got out, left her phone on the driver's seat, her shoes where the roadside scrub gave way to warm sand. Wind tossed her hair and ruffled her clothes. Beaches were always much cooler than land, and she had fond memories of evenings out here during high school, a sense of freedom at being off the grid. She came out here often on her own, but also came with a small group of friends, as seniors, to roam the sandy stretches and drink wine from plastic cups and yell into the surf. Everything about life in front of them.

From the beach in the daytime, you could see ships moving in a line toward the Savannah harbor, but tonight the ocean was black and empty. She could have been anywhere on the eastern spine of the United States, nothing but shadowed houses, the marshes, the sound, and before her the rippling black sea, the crash of the waves, the spatter of starlight, the ragged cloud in front of the moon. The Daniel Hayward case would test her. She knew this. The crime, the defendant, her career—all raised the stakes, and it would take all her energy to manage her life over the next few weeks. She could have been Samantha James. She could have been killed, and her father left alone. She wished he'd understood. All she wanted was for him to tell her he loved her and that it would be all right. But that slice of truth, apparently, was too much to ask.

12

On the first day of the trial, she was up before her alarm. She fed the dog to shut her up, and then she poured coffee and turned on a lamp in her home office, began to look over the case notes yet again, ran through her opening argument and the rhythm of the day in her mind. She would not go to the office, not before the trial, believing it to be bad luck. It was one of her peculiarities, like the way she insisted on walking up a flight of stairs so that she always ended on her right foot at the top, taking two at a time if necessary to even out the progress. She'd staved off many of her OCD impulses left over from childhood, but the stairway thing lingered, as did the occasional superstition.

When she arrived at the courthouse, the media was already there, the TV van, a few photographers. As she walked across the parking lot and around toward the front entrance, she realized she'd timed her arrival to match Daniel Hayward's. Well ahead of her, he loped up the steps, his lawyer and a paralegal behind him. He wore the same dark blue suit with a white shirt and a yellow tie he'd worn to their plea negotiations, but his face now looked worn out, like his dog had been shot late last night. Claire stopped and held her briefcase close to her chest. It was on her to prove, beyond a reasonable doubt, that this man had knowingly struck another human being on the highway at night and driven off, whether from panic or intoxication or cowardice. The defense would make its case: here was a man on the rise in the community, a respectable citizen who made what the law referred to as a (horrible) *mistake of fact*, believing to have hit a deer rather than a human, to have driven off without realizing the damage he'd inflicted, to have had a moment of sheer hell upon realizing just what he'd done. They might bring up Samantha's missing hour, her negligence for being out so late on a bicycle, and try to paint her as some kind of rebel. Perhaps the kind of girl who would drink wine on a beach and yell into the surf. Not the kind of girl you would want babysitting your children. She shouldn't have been out there, the defense would argue, and Daniel was as much a victim as Samantha. It was an accident, an error, a casualty of life in a society and nothing more.

It was her job to slide into his mind, and reveal it for what it was, mistakes be damned. No one could experience the double-smack of the collision, the shattering of the windshield, and drive away in good conscience. Either Daniel was inebriated beyond cognition, or he'd exhibited a lack of conscience. Claire's responsibility was to Samantha James, whose broken-down parents would be put on the witness stand today. When Daniel Hayward had vanished into the courthouse, and the TV crew set up its reporter and the newspaper photographer had wandered off—none of them taking note of Claire, thanks for small favors—she turned and walked around the building to the side entrance, wobbling in her heels like a girl playing dress-up, which was how she felt.

At the side entrance, as though waiting for her, was a rangy young man with reddish hair and two days of a beard. He looked drunk, slouched up against the outer wall of the courthouse, but he stood confidently and in control as she neared.

She was about to lower her eyes and pass by with a subtle nod when he held up his hand and said, "You the prosecutor?"

She stopped. "I am."

"You gone put this guy away?"

"That's the plan," she said. "Who are you?"

"Name's Charlie."

"Charlie Gibbs? Samantha's boyfriend?"

He nodded.

"I know this must be tough for you," she said, feeling inside like she needed to find a new profession. First the sister showed up not wanting anything in particular but clearly hiding something, and now the boyfriend stood here drunk. Definitely drunk, even if he was able to stand on his own two feet, she could smell beer on his breath, and leaching out of his skin. "Were you planning to sit in on the trial? The front door would be best. I just came over here to avoid the press."

"I'm not in a state to watch the trial," he said. He leaned uncomfortably close, though she wasn't afraid of him. He was thin-boned and on the short side, and she felt, not unreasonably, like she could take him down if it came to it. But she didn't think anything would happen beyond another awkward moment or two before he moved out of her way so she could enter the building.

"That's probably best to stay away," she said.

He reared up slightly. "Why you say that?"

"Well, you've obviously had a few drinks. It's nine in the morning."

"What's it to you?"

"Nothing to me. I sympathize, but the jailer and the other cops who will be there might not be so relaxed."

"I ain't worried about no cops. You just make sure you get a conviction."

With that he pushed away from the wall and lurched toward the parking lot.

"You get you a conviction, and we'll be all right," he said without looking back at her. He raised his hand in a wave as she watched him go.

The side door was heavy, the spring not set correctly, so she was nearly wedged into the doorway as she shoveled her way into the musty building, the stairwell, the wraparound hall. It smelled like an old country church, faintly of mold and age. In the courtroom, the defense had settled at the table, and quite a few spectators had filled the pews. Witnesses, family, friends, members of the bicycling community, a few reporters. Doubtful anyone was here for Daniel Hayward. Perhaps one of the women sitting by herself was his wife, wrestling with the demarcation of their lives into before and after, one foot already out the door. Although there were a few loose ends—Claire knew Lauren James was hiding something, and she sensed she'd not seen the last of scrawny old Charlie Gibbs—she knew from the facts of the case that Daniel Hayward's life had been ruined. She thought of the scandal she'd read about Henry Somerville on BuzzFeed, and she believed she had them both. Her job was to put the final nail in Daniel's coffin, yet she hoped that for his sake, Daniel Hayward had at least one companion left for when he faced his inevitable reckoning. You died alone, but for everything else in life you could ask for help, if you knew how. With this final thought, she walked up to her table with her notes and her briefcase, prepared to argue her case for putting Daniel Hayward in prison for many years.

CANCEL CULTURE

1

Henry Somerville saw the young man with the cell phone, but he didn't register him as a threat. Waterfront Park was filled with young people, a roux of tourists and college students out sunbathing and reading and tossing Frisbees. A quiet, idyllic day in which nothing untoward was happening or, conceivably, could happen. Henry had knocked off for the afternoon, put on a pair of shorts, and brought his dog out for a walk. He currently stood thigh-deep in the park's Pineapple Fountain and had the dog in the water with him. She was a large-eared cocker spaniel he and his wife, or ex-wife, had picked up once their last child had moved out for college. His ex had wanted the breed, yet somehow it had been Henry who was responsible for her now that his wife, or ex-wife, was spending his money on Viking River Cruises across Germany and France, leaving her South of Broad carriage house largely unlived-in. He picked up the dog and tossed her into the middle of the fountain, a high toss, the kind of fun throw he used to do with his children in the pool. The dog sailed in an arc and splashed in the water, submerged for a moment, and then bobbed up and paddled back to the fountain's edge. When she'd clamored out and shook herself off on the lip of the fountain, he picked her up and tossed her again. This had become their ritual on Monday afternoons, for several weeks now, and the dog had never seemed happier, had never followed him around quite so like a puppy, had never sat by his side on the couch while he reviewed cases late into the evening. She'd always been a mercurial, aloof dog, but now they'd bonded. Nothing to it.

The young man across the park wore surfer shorts and flip-flops and a purple t-shirt reading *Original Hipster*. Henry saw the boy walking across the park, and out of the corner of his eye saw—or later believed he saw, memory a fickle, unpredictable thing, as he so well knew—the boy stopped and fiddled with his smart phone. Henry tossed the dog another time and then, sensing the boy was still behind him, turned to see the boy lower his phone from filming position and scuttle away. Later, when the footage appeared on major entertainment-news sites such as BuzzFeed, Henry believed that the head-turn had been his undoing. For just a moment, he stared at the camera slack-jawed, with a cranky, befuddled glare that bespoke a deviant mind—the grainy pictures of a terrorist glancing at a camera as he passed through airport security.

He watched the boy scurry off, and then he grabbed the dog's leash and hooked it to her. She shook herself off once more before the two of them strolled out of the park. No one else took any notice of them. He tried to put the young man out of his mind.

Henry Somerville was anything but unobservant. He had excellent instincts and, like a chess master half-glancing at the board while playing an amateur, could spot a trap from three moves away. He was right to be concerned about the young man with the camera, because that evening the boy—a recent college graduate, unemployed, self-righteous—posted the footage on TikTok and Twitter under the headline "Old Man Torments Dog in the Park" and then forgot about it. Like so many millennial writers—would-be journalists or citizen-journalists or social media mavens—he posted a never-ending stream of garbage. Literally, photos of trash that lingered too long on King Street on a hot afternoon. Or pseudo-artistic shots of shattered glass beside a dumpster. The man with the dog had been a one-off, something unusual that caught the boy's eye. The boy would later regret posting the video, due to the attention and the backlash from the angry civil libertarians on Reddit who hounded him with jabs about Big Brother and the Stasi and the security state, but he atoned by continuing to post more and more videos and photos he believed to be exposés. A miniature Julian Assange or Edward Snowden, but with no actual secrets to shed light on or news to share.

The boy only had a few hundred followers on Twitter, but one of them had been a fellow English major who'd amassed a large following in the slam poetry arena. The slam poet re-tweeted the video with amusement and also forgot about it. One of his followers re-tweeted it, and eventually a writer from BuzzFeed saw it, recognized the look of an aberrant soul cruelly hurling a dog into a fountain, hit re-tweet, and posted the video on the site. From there the video took on a life of its own, received hundreds of thousands of views, enough to inspire the hashtag *#dogjustice*, with calls for Henry's arrest. Some tweeters evidently misunderstood the video so violently they believed Henry had killed the dog, purposefully drowned it like a sack of unwanted puppies in the days before the ASPCA and the Humane Society.

Henry was not on social media and knew nothing of any of this until a news crew showed up on the street in front of his house and a reporter was at his door, peering in the window, calling through the glass, "I'd just like a word!"

His ex-wife's attorney sent him a letter demanding Henry turn over the dog, citing cruelty and emotional abuse and a litany of alleged crimes of the heart. Henry knew the attorney well, had played squash with him in their younger days, and suspected the man enjoyed antagonizing Henry with these threatening letters. Henry certainly would have enjoyed it, the law one long and dull career filled with citations and arguments built around the difference between *may* and *shall*. The truth was objective in black and white, and the sport came from being able to intimidate your antagonists. He picked up losing cases for the sheer challenge of tilting at windmills, and derived enjoyment from the shocked media when he pulled an upset (to say nothing of the shock from genuine upsets).

"I want to sue this kid back into his parents' basement," Henry said to his own occasional attorney, an old law-school chum named Neville Brinson, over an early afternoon bourbon.

"What would that accomplish?" Neville asked. "Hmm? The genie's out of the bottle."

"It would make me feel a hell of a lot better."

"Henry, you want, I can file papers tomorrow morning. Get this kid in court, intimidate his parents into coughing up a settlement out of their 401(k)s, that's just going to bring more bad publicity to you. What would you tell a client in your situation?"

Henry took a long drink and swirled ice in the glass. "Lay low and wait for the storm to pass."

"There you go. What cases you got coming up? Anything to distract you?"

"Hit-and-run culprit down near Hilton Head."

"There you go," Neville said again. "Head down to the beach, do some golfing, give hell to the local prosecutors down there, and when you come back in a few weeks, it'll all be over. There's always some new thing to catch their interest."

"Where's a good hurricane when you need one?" Henry asked.

2

They said North Carolina was a valley of humility between two mountains of conceit, and Henry Somerville had ties to both mountains and basked in his role as the big fish in these small southern ponds. He was a Lowcountry gentleman from a family whose exaggerated pedigree went back to Jamestown and the founding of Virginia. This was to say, the Somervilles were among the original American aristocrats. His grandfather was a South Carolina legislator and had an unsuccessful bid for governor during the Depression, when mistrust of the upper crust was at its highest throughout the country, and not even the conservative state of South Carolina could stave off the working-class desire for progressive leadership—even if that leadership would be considered hard-right by today's standards. So the Somervilles left politics and entered the law. More than one judge, a pair of litigators, and a high-powered corporate attorney who had made it to New York City.

Such was the pedigree of Henry Somerville, a man now estranged from his wife and, apparently, embroiled in an online scandal over his dog. He was tall and had silvering hair combed over Republican style (the hair thinning and graying by the week), a bit of a paunch, squared-off features that made him look like he could have succeeded in a political race for an office higher than a humble Charleston barrister, as he liked to think of himself. Maybe he still might run for something, but he thought it unlikely. He wasn't the politicking type. There are two kinds of lawyers: the analytical and the charismatic. The charismatic wind up in politics, where they spew bluster about the law, while the analytic ones actually write and defend the laws behind the scenes. To those who knew him best, Henry always appeared a little dumbfounded by his success in life. Not that he wasn't a confident man, but that the world was such an unreasonable, unpredictable place, it struck him as strange that a few simple business practices had kept him fed for several decades. *I throw out the fishing line once in a while and reel 'em in*, he once said of how he landed clients. *It's a beautiful thing.*

The truth was Henry had won a couple of high-profile cases early in his career and had been riding off their success ever since. He was batting about five hundred, not embarrassing by any means but also nothing to merit his reputation as a Charleston titan. Such was the way of business, where reputations were largely based on a feeling rather than data. The tide was turning, and he sensed that if he were a younger man, he would have a hard road in front of him, but he was too many pieces ahead for life to deliver a surprise checkmate at this point. Now that he'd weathered the Great Recession, he knew he would retire easy.

So he thought nothing of a call from Cleveland one Monday in July, nor of the man on the line who said he needed to retain a lawyer for his son.

Judy came into his office and said he had a call and the man wanted to speak to Henry directly.

"We've got a process for this," Henry said, surprised that Judy had bothered him with the call. She was an impeccable gate-keeper and knew how to politely decline work from the cranks who didn't understand how this process worked.

"He said his boy's in trouble and he'll only talk with a lawyer about it."

"Does he want to hire a lawyer or get free counseling?"

"Didn't say. His son's near Hilton Head, and it sounds like it could be a lucrative case."

Henry looked at her over the top of his glasses. Cases had been a little light since the incident with the dog, but this was the first indication Judy had offered that she was worried about finances. True, they'd been running on the fumes of minor drug possession and simple assault cases for the past few weeks, and hadn't seen a meaty retainer-level case in a few months, but they weren't hurting for money. Rent on the office was a steal, and while Judy's payroll was not insignificant, it also was not a bank-breaker, even with the specter of government regulations hanging over their heads. Although he wouldn't admit it out loud, this year's Social Security tax cut was a boon for his bottom line, almost mopping up any lost revenue from the dog-fountain video scandal.

"Hell, Judy, if you're worried, pull up a chair and we can talk."

"I googled him while he was talking," she said. "He's the CEO of a hospital system up there."

"Well, hell, patch him through," Henry said. Why not? He'd built his business making cold calls and could certainly bend some rules for one client a year.

"I'll be glad to take it on, Mr. Hayward," he said to the man in Cleveland, once he'd heard the gist of the story. "Has your son already spoken with the police?"

"Not yet," the man said. He sounded brusque and ready to get off the phone. There was some noise in the background, running dishwater perhaps. "He's just told me what's in the news and that he thinks he was the one who hit the girl."

"He isn't sure?"

"I think he's sure, he just doesn't want to admit everything at once. To me, anyway. He'll tell you the whole truth."

"Good. Well, I'll want to drive down there to meet him, and be there when he contacts law enforcement. He'll need to make a statement, but you don't want him saying a word to anyone without a lawyer."

"That's what I told him."

"May I ask how you found me?"

"I asked around," Hayward said. "Your name kept floating up."

"Will you be coming down to meet with Daniel as well?"

The man paused, cleared his throat. "I can't right away," he said. "I'm on the board of a health system going through a merger, and—I just, legally, need to be present until the closing. If, ah, if—"

"I'll take care of Daniel," Henry said. "Find out what happened, where he was, what the circumstances were, and what law enforcement and the local prosecutor have in mind. This is going to be a process, and in these first days, well, we don't know how things will shake out. I'll make sure Daniel is taken care of until we know what the road ahead looks like."

"I appreciate that."

"We might not know much until I can interview any witnesses and take a look at the accident site. Now, I think I should warn you, it could get much worse before it gets better. Depending on what we find out, there's going to be a lot of heated emotions, and the criminal side is only one angle to consider."

"A family's civil suit."

"That's right," Henry said. "It might not hurt to begin thinking about assets, and what's in Daniel's name, and maybe take stock of your family finances."

"Already ahead of you there. You just worry about this first step in the process," Hayward said. "You work on a retainer basis?"

"My rate is $375 an hour, and for this I'll need a $20,000 retainer up front."

The man said nothing. If he was a hospital executive, he knew what attorneys cost, and he also likely knew Henry's fee was the least of his concerns. Bond alone for Daniel Hayward could be in the six figures, of which the family would need the customary ten percent.

"I do have an agreement," Henry went on. "Daniel will have to be my client, even if you'll be paying the bills. He can sign a waiver allowing me to share information with you, but he'll have to do it on his own. No coercion."

"Of course," the man muttered.

The dishwater in the background seemed louder now. Or maybe it was the wind. Maybe the man was in his parking garage, huddled in a corner away from the noise of traffic, thinking about his son a thousand miles away and the danger and damage of the unknown.

"How's Daniel's mother doing? Does she know anything yet?"

"I haven't told her," Hayward said.

"You'll want to have that conversation. I'll drive down to Overlook tomorrow morning to meet with him. Once he comes forward to the police, the media is going to be all over him. You may in fact be getting a few calls from reporters, if the Charleston press catches wind of it."

"Our number's unlisted," Hayward said.

They hung up after a few more pleasantries, and Henry took a look at his Outlook calendar. He had a smattering of court appearances but nothing else that he couldn't take care of on the road. His dog was with his ex-wife, and word of the social media storm surrounding the video of him at the fountain kept trickling up to his office. Although he'd resisted ever joining social media (and wouldn't even use email if he could get away with it), most of his friends and colleagues had succumbed and gleefully asked him about the scandal. They, of course, knew he loved that dog and was no animal abuser, but they got a charge out of the embarrassment, for he'd done everything to eradicate shame from his life. Even the divorce he shrugged off as a natural progression and the mutual decision of two consenting adults (though he was irked by the disparity in the settlement agreement; he'd had his balls handed to him for sure). So there was no reason he couldn't simply take a few weeks, close up the office, and head down to Overlook for a working vacation. Judy, his secretary and paralegal, could manage the phones and the paperwork and call him if anything urgent came up.

A hit and run. Always the hit and run. He thought of his brother, Phil, a landscape worker and alcoholic in recovery, and the unfortunate events last winter. If you asked Henry Somerville what his big dream was, he would look at you with contempt. Big dreams were for the young. He'd set out with some vague ambition when he went to law school, involving money and power and taking his place in the world, but he'd never had a clear plan for leaving his mark. Some people made great art, others ran Fortune 500 companies, others still put passion into causes, lobbied for change, ran for office. Henry Somerville, it seemed, defended hit and run drivers. It was a fallen world, he knew, and he could rationalize it and felt no qualms. Everyone deserved a good defense, and he had nothing to answer for. A psychoanalyst would say he was repressed, that he'd never taken full stock of his upbringing, his domineering father, his weak-willed but conniving mother, or the legend of his family pedigree. But he thought nothing of these things, and would smirk if anyone suggested he take a look at his psyche. His therapy was in cashing the paychecks.

3

A partial list of things Hollywood gets wrong about life as an attorney:

- Lawyers did not fall into the predictable two camps, with the hungry idealists fighting for justice on one hand, and the greedy bloodsuckers draining money from their clients through over-billing and collusion on the other.
- In fact, despite the high hourly rate, many lawyers were hurting for money and business. A mortgage's worth of student loans could easily cut a six-figure paycheck down to a middle manager's salary. Henry was well beyond the age of student loans, had gone through law school when it was still possible to work and pay your way through (Baby Boomers: getting all the good deals, and then inflating costs for the next generation), but he wasn't making the

kind of money he might have if he'd actually tried to build his business into a retail office, or just gone in-house somewhere and risen to a corporation's c-suite.

- Client interaction was a rarity. The exception with Mr. Hayward notwithstanding, paralegals and secretaries signed on clients, did the majority of the prep work, handled most of the phone calls, kept track of schedules and invoices, and generally kept things running—very much the way nurses and administrators kept a doctor's office running, and you only saw a physician for those few crucial moments of diagnosis.
- Life was more bureaucratic than dramatic. File a motion, schedule a deposition, call this person, call that person, fill out this paperwork, don't forget the crucial semicolons in that report, hey Judy what can I bring you for lunch, you're in court tomorrow at three, raise an objection, offer a motion, call the prosecutor, interview witnesses, Judy cancel my one o'clock, renew his life insurance, pay his estimated taxes, go to the dentist. The stuff of Tinsel Town, this was not.
- One case seldom made an impression. Henry had nearly fifty cases on his docket, a steady pipeline of quick afternoons to negotiate plea deals for drug possession and assault, with the occasional high-profile crime that would take a few weeks to negotiate. Although he would be driving down to Overlook tonight to meet with Daniel Hayward, the kid barely registered on his radar.
- A law firm was a business. Henry spent much of his time thinking about marketing and taxes and keeping his inbox clear—not the majesty of the law.
- Most criminal defense cases did not rest on winning over the jury with personality. Most cases are cut and dried— and frankly, most defendants are guilty—and the drama comes from errors in the prosecution or law enforcement. Prosecutors start with the upper hand, a pawn ahead, and the criminal defense attorney's job is to hammer away at procedural questions. If a Breathalyzer was used to test for

drunk driving, when was the last time law enforcement had it serviced? Did a police officer toss away the defendant's keys in a rage rather than filing them as evidence? Was the prosecutor late in filing a motion? Was the court schedule too booked to accommodate a week's worth of defense witnesses? As in a game of chess, Henry's job was to look for weaknesses and to attack with pins and forks to gain the upper hand.

- Most cases settled out of court. Juries are almost an afterthought in the grand scheme of things.
- The law, Henry felt, was actually quite dull. It paid the bills and allowed him to make a good (but not great) living, and it gave him some access inside the local power structure, but he was mostly a cog in the machine, a well-dressed sprocket with a bourbon-soaked, steel-trap mind and nothing much to expend his energies on.

4

What these small-town citizens didn't understand was that South Carolina was hurting. The rest of the state was experiencing stagnation, not recovery, yet business was booming in Overlook, wealthy retirees in their enclaves, homebuilders developing one tract of land after another, tourists who could afford it from across the country vacationing here, attracted to Hilton Head's natural landscape. This was grace unearned, a natural resource people in the rest of the state looked on with a mix of envy and disgust.

Henry Somerville understood this. Sure, he made a fine living defending the overly entitled—money kept coming into his bank accounts, and he was happy to let his retirement accounts grow—but he took a clear-eyed look at human value and economic development, and had little interest in the so-called charms of Overlook. He was here for one reason: business. And his business today—a Tuesday—was to see how bad of a jam Daniel Hayward was in, and to sign him on as a client, assuming the boy's father came through with the retainer.

The Haywards lived in a riparian community called Pine Breeze—meant to evoke a golf course, or, perhaps, but less likely, a furniture polish—in a magisterial plantation-style home custom built from a set of builder's plans. The neighborhood was a blend of Spanish-inspired stucco homes, Lowcountry colonials, presidential estates, and a quad of craftsman bungalows near the clubhouse. In other words, an overwhelming style that would be called "transitional" if the homes were half the price, but as it stood the general architectural guidelines were murky. Henry was not here to judge. He once had designs on retiring to a place like this himself, if his family had held together and the economy had not collapsed and his business wasn't threatened by a viral video scandal. It felt rather nice to stand on Daniel Hayward's brick driveway, which was set back on a circular eyelet of homes, plenty of trees as a buffer between houses so you didn't feel you were under the keen eyes of your neighbors. One of the neighbors had a Trump sign boasting in the front yard, which Henry suspected violated the rules of the homeowners' board. Gates within the gated community.

He rang the bell, and Daniel Hayward answered the door wearing a white t-shirt and overly long gym shorts, bottle of water in his hand. His eyes looked past Henry and combed the neighborhood before he stepped back and asked Henry inside. "I'm sorry I was working out and didn't have time to clean up for you," he said by way of a greeting. "I took the day off of work but was going a little stir-crazy."

"Not a problem," Henry said. He'd dressed rather casually himself in khaki slacks and a blue and white checkered button down with an uncomfortably warm navy blazer, which he would remove as soon as they'd all made their introductions. Fortunately, Daniel kept his house well air conditioned, maybe as low as seventy. Also: dim. The walls were painted the same rich gray as the exterior, with cream trim and crown molding, and the floors were wide planks of dark wood, which gave the house a smothered feeling. Too many walls, too little lighting.

Henry followed Daniel through the entryway, a tight den, and into the kitchen, where Francine was jotting a few notes on a grocery list, purse over her shoulder.

"Sweetie, this is Henry Somerville," Daniel said. "The lawyer Dad lined up."

She finished jotting the line on the list, and then capped her pen and put the list in her purse before focusing her attention on Henry. "Thank you for coming down," she said, and she came over swiftly with her hand extended.

"My pleasure," Henry said.

Francine was buxom and blonde and had enormous, glassy blue eyes and held Henry's gaze with a practiced public relations smile before saying, "I'm off to run a few errands, so I won't be in your way."

"I'd actually like to talk with you a few minutes before I leave," Henry said.

"How long are you here for?" she asked.

He glanced at her husband. "I don't know. Couple of hours?"

"I'll be back in time to see you, then. I won't be gone but an hour or so. Unless you needed me right now?"

"No, go run your errands. Daniel and I have a few things to catch up on."

"I'm sure," she said, and Henry wondered what his client had told her, how much she inferred, and how she might react under the media pressure. He suspected she would be fine, but that you couldn't say the same for their marriage. Therein was the first problem for Henry. A spouse could be a wild card, and if she had grievances, she could lay out incidents that would show Daniel was just the sort of man to feel no remorse about leaving the scene of a crime. Anyone who had been married any length of time had such dirt on their spouse. We were all sinners with secrets. You couldn't live with someone for days, weeks, years, without those secrets emerging. A shouting match, a shove, some act of physical or emotional violence: this was the stuff that tested marriages, strengthened the bond or ripped it asunder.

"We can sit out on the porch," Daniel said when she was gone. "You want anything to drink?"

"I'm all right," Henry said, and he thought it bold when Daniel brought a Belgian IPA with an unreadable name with him out on the screened-in porch. They had two wood-burning fireplaces, one in the den, the second on the porch, TVs over each. A ceiling fan swayed lazily overhead on the porch. Daniel clicked off the TV—weekend sports highlights—and offered Henry a seat.

"Thank you for coming down," Daniel said, and chugged a third of his beer in one sip. "Excuse Francine. She's under a little pressure about all this."

"I'm sure she is. What have you told her?"

"Same thing I'm about to tell you. I was out Thursday night, and on my way home, I hit something, but I didn't know what it was."

"Well, before we get started, I just want to run through a few preliminaries. All I know is what your father and I talked about yesterday. I understand he's willing to pay my retainer, but if I take your case, you are my client, with all the privileges and privacy that affords."

"Got it."

"You can instruct me if you want me to keep your father abreast, but I can't release anything to him without your authorization. I say this because this arrangement is a little unusual. Not unheard of, but unusual. I've got my standard agreement with me, which we can go over, but it basically lays out our working agreement and says you're responsible for the bill. I don't mean to be crass in bringing up money right up front, but I want to make sure you and me and your father all understand the arrangement. This case could become long and messy, and we'll all need to keep our cool."

"I understand," Daniel said. "What do you mean long and messy?"

"Well, you say you hit something. Either you hit the girl, or you didn't. If someone else hit her, you're off the hook. Easy enough to verify whether your car made the impact. But if you did hit her, then there's a whole series of questions: what you knew, whether you'd been drinking, how conscious you were when you drove off, and how much traction this story gets in the media. The prosecutors will be keeping tabs on all those things and weighing what to charge you with. So right now, there are just a number of unknowns, and my job today is to get a handle on some of those unknowns."

"Where do we start?"

"Tell me about that night," Henry said. "We'll go through the whole evening, step by step, but to help me get the broad strokes, you were on your way home, correct?"

"That's right."

"So it's dark, and you're driving home and you hit something. What was the impact like?"

"It wasn't that big. There was definitely a thump and a crunch of something hitting the underside of the car, but I thought it could have been a dog or a deer or even a tree branch in the road. It was just something, but it was dark outside and I couldn't see anything."

"Did you pull over?"

"Of course I stopped and got out, but I didn't see anything."

"You look around? In the foliage?"

"Everywhere. Nothing there."

"Okay. Good. So you were driving along. How fast were you going?"

"I don't know. A few miles over the speed limit?"

"Which was?"

"It's a 35-mile-an-hour zone. I may have been doing forty."

"So you hit something driving at forty miles an hour. Did you pull over right away?"

"Sure. I slammed on the brakes right away."

"So you didn't see anything, and you went home. Wait, before we get there, slow down. Tell me where you were coming from."

"I was out at dinner, with a client." Daniel took another long swig.

"A sales meeting?"

"More like a friendly get-together."

"Just you and the client."

"Just us."

"Male or female?"

"Female."

"Was this anything more than a friendly get-together?"

"What do you mean?"

Henry smiled. "I'm not accusing you of anything, but I think you know what I'm asking."

"No. Jesus. She was just a client."

"Did Francine know you were meeting her?"

"She knew I was meeting a client."

"But did she know you were meeting a woman, alone?"

"She didn't ask."

"Have you told her?"

"Not yet."

"You'll need to do that. Like, tonight. Because it may end up on the front page of the newspaper in a day or two."

Daniel blanched. "How do we stop that?"

"You don't. Believe me, I wish we could, but there's no logic behind what catches fire and what doesn't. All you can do is get in front of it by being honest. Now," Henry said quickly, before giving Hayward a chance to think about the media circus. He didn't know how much Hayward may have researched him before this meeting—or how much his father had known before calling on behalf of his son—but Henry wanted to keep the conversation on Daniel. "Where was this dinner?"

"At Libretto's. It's an Italian place in town."

"Upscale?"

"Modestly."

"What did you order?"

"I had veal scaloppine."

"Appetizer? Dessert?"

"Just coffee after."

"Anything to drink?"

"We split a bottle of wine."

"Red?"

"Yes. A zinfandel. Their house wine, on special."

"How much did you drink?"

"About half the bottle."

"Half the bottle? Or more than half?"

"Maybe sixty-forty. But I wasn't drunk."

"But then you ordered coffee. And you had a heavy meal."

"Exactly."

"Did you meet at the restaurant?"

"I picked her up."

"And drove her home?"

"Yes."

"Where does she live?"

"She lives in an apartment off 46."

"Near the restaurant?"

"A couple miles away."

"So you drove from the restaurant to her apartment. Did you go in?"

"No, I just dropped her at the door."

"Did you walk her up to the door?"

"To the stairs."

"Kiss her goodnight?"

Daniel paused. "On the cheek."

"Anything else?"

"No."

"Okay, so then you got back in the car, and drove straight home?"

"Yes."

"I haven't driven by the accident site yet. How far is it from here?"

"It's about six miles from her house to mine, maybe seven, and the accident was on Reedy Road, about halfway between here and there."

"Any other traffic out?"

"No. You should drive it at night. You'll see what I mean."

"On my agenda for this evening," Henry said. "So, no cars. I came through the front gate today. How do you get through?"

"I've got a sticker on my windshield."

"So it's staffed 24 hours a day? And a guard took a look at your sticker and let you in?"

"Yes."

Henry made a note to check with the security company, to see if the guard noticed any damage to the vehicle. "Did you take a look at your vehicle when you got home? To see if there was any damage?"

"No."

"Why not?"

"It was late, and I was tired. I pulled into the garage, and I did take a look at the front bumper, but didn't see anything obvious. I figured I'd take a closer look the next day, or over the weekend."

"So you came inside and went to bed."

"Yes."

"Francine ask how your meeting went?"

"She was asleep when I got in."

"What time was this?"

"I got home about 11:30."

"What time does she normally go to bed?"

"Ten, ten-thirty at the latest."

"What about the next morning? Over breakfast?"

"We heard it on the local news."

"That there was a hit and run?"

"Yeah, and that the girl died at the scene."

Henry studied him carefully with the next question. "And did you make the connection?"

"Not at first. I know I should have—she died on the same road, at the same time I was on it, but I wasn't feeling all that well, and had really almost forgotten that I hit anything."

"Did Francine ask you about your night?"

"She did, but only as small talk."

"And what did you tell her?"

"Just that the dinner went fine."

"Nothing else?"

"I don't talk much about my work with her."

"When did you make the connection that you may have struck the girl?"

"When she left for the day, Francine came back in and asked what happened to the car. I followed her out to the garage and saw the bumper and then I knew. I mean, I didn't say as much—I told her I hit a deer on the way home—but I knew the damage was more than a dog or a tree limb."

"How did Francine react?"

"She was pissed."

"About the damage?"

"About the expense of repair. We haven't paid the car off yet, and you know how dealers are. It was going to be a thousand dollars."

"But she didn't make the connection about the hit and run?"

"No."

"But you had."

"I just knew."

"And then what?"

"I called in sick to work. I knew I couldn't take the car out, because people would be looking for a damaged vehicle. This sounds bad, but I went back to bed to try to forget about it. I thought maybe I was having a nightmare and needed to wake up again. You ever had such an experience? Where you realize your life is wrecked, and it takes a few moments to settle in?"

Henry understood the feeling well. When he was a younger man, he'd gone into the yard with a chainsaw to try to limb up some of the trees on their property. The chain had slipped and spun around and slammed into his middle finger and nearly taken it off. He'd dropped the chain saw, and had a moment where he knew what he'd done but felt no pain. Then in a rush his leather glove had gone from beige to a brutally dark brown as blood instantly pooled and saturated the entire glove, and a pain unlike anything he'd experienced before or since settled in. He still lacked feeling in the tip of that finger—the middle finger on his right hand—twenty-five years later. From that moment on he'd outsourced his yard work and focused on what he did best. In that respect, it was a revelation: that he was no longer a resilient twenty-one, that he had neither the strength nor the know-how for manual labor, and that life and good health operated on a contingency basis. He was lucky, all things considered. He knew Daniel Hayward had experienced a similar moment of realization before the burst of blood and pain, and he also knew Daniel

Hayward had not been so lucky. The truth hadn't emerged, not yet, but Henry already saw a long road ahead for this young man.

"I slept most of the morning, a really deep sleep, and I woke up after eleven, went downstairs, and saw the car was still damaged. I googled the girl, and you've seen the news reports. People were already calling for my head, and I hadn't even turned myself in to share my side of the story yet. I thought about saying nothing, but I figured they'd be onto me eventually, when I went to get the car repaired."

"That's probably true," Henry said. "Case like this, you really can't hide for long. Not in today's world."

"Right."

"So you called your father, and he called me, and here we are. Okay. Good. Can we take a look at the car?"

"There's something else you should know before we do." Daniel finished his beer and opened the door for Henry. In the kitchen, he tossed the beer into the trash, and he leaned on the counter.

"What is it?"

"It's going to look bad."

Daniel led him into the garage, and Henry took a breath. His case had just gone from a simple week of asking around and an easy settlement, to a lengthy farce battled out in court. The Durango's entire windshield was smashed, several starbursts with spider webs cracking away. Henry's mind shifted from *easy win* to *it's over.* No way Daniel could say he thought he hit a dog or a deer, with this kind of damage. No way, really, he could safely drive this vehicle anywhere. On closer inspection, Henry saw the dented bumper, and when he knelt saw what could be blood and hair clinging to the corners of the headlight. The undercarriage was scuffed up, but no sign of blood beneath. The blood on the bumper wasn't necessarily human, didn't necessarily belong to Samantha James, but regardless Henry knew what it was. And so did Daniel.

Henry let out a sigh as he stood up. Hayward hung back, as though the car was one spark away from exploding, hand to his chin, thumbnail in his mouth. He straightened up.

"I don't know, Daniel." Henry looked back at the wrecked vehicle and shook his head in wonderment. "We've got a long road in front of us."

"What am I supposed to do?"

"Right now, sit tight. I need to get ahold of the prosecutor and law enforcement this afternoon and let them come out here to take a look."

"Can they do that?"

"Legally? You can sit on it. You can leave the car in the garage, and unless they get a lead on you being out there, they can't come in and take a look. But if your client says, hey wait a second, Daniel drove right by there, the police can get a warrant. And they'll keep coming until they find out everyone who drove that road Thursday night."

The garage door opened just then, startling them both. Francine's daytime running lights shined a spotlight on them.

"Plus, there's Francine," Henry said.

"She won't say anything."

Francine got out of the car and looked at them and, without saying anything, pulled a couple of Target bags out of the back seat and went inside.

"She might," Henry said. "I should talk with her. Meanwhile, we'll need to decide what you want to do."

"What do you advise?"

"I have the retainer agreement with me, which I'll need you to sign if you want me to represent you. And if so, my advice as your attorney is, you should take a shower and get dressed before the police get here."

Daniel cursed.

"I'm sorry not to have better news for you."

After a few minutes of pounding silence, Daniel closed his eyes and said, "All right. Go get your agreement and talk to Francine. I'm going to take a shower."

Henry nodded. "You'll be all right. I'll be here with you."

A few moments later, with Daniel upstairs, Henry found Francine in the kitchen, pulling out groceries for tonight's meal. "It's bad, isn't it?" she said.

"It's going to be a long road," Henry said again. He could think of nothing else to say about the situation.

"I knew when I got home Friday and saw that windshield, I knew he'd hit that girl."

"He said he could explain the windshield," Henry said.

She shrugged. "He was upset. You can at least say that much for him."

"I'm sure."

She slammed a few more groceries on the counter: white beans, chicken stock, red bell peppers. Henry recognized in her the outgoing, bubbly personality of a public relations fixer, a college poet or painter who found she did all right in the world of commerce. She had a rock the size of a nickel on her finger, her hair in a practical ponytail, and had on a t-shirt and yoga pants, the evening and weekend wear she'd worn regularly since moving to Overlook. It would be a long night for her. "What's going to happen now?" she asked.

"Now, I've got bad news. You may want to hold off on starting dinner."

He explained he would call the police, and the police would come out and take photos and get an initial statement from her and Daniel tonight. He would have to go in for a longer statement likely tomorrow, and would likely be charged with a hit and run by the end of the week.

"Is he going to jail?"

"I don't know. Once they charge him, they'll arrest and arraign him, so he'll have to spend some time in a holding cell before we can get bail processed and get him home. After that, we'll either reach a plea agreement or go to trial. Whatever happens, this isn't going to be easy, for either of you, no matter what you do. Daniel's going to need support."

"We've been under pressure for a while," she said. "I don't know if I have the support to give him."

"Maybe, before the police come, you can tell me your side of what happened Thursday night?"

"What can I tell you? He was out with a client. I went to bed and didn't hear him come in."

"You didn't wake up at all?"

"I stirred when he got into bed, but I wasn't fully awake, and don't even know what time it was."

"And the next morning? How did he appear?"

"Groggy. He's not a morning person, and he maybe was a little grumpier than usual, but he put on coffee and asked me what my day looked like and said he thought he hit a dog or something on his way home."

"How did he seem?"

"He was upset about it, clearly. He loves animals, and would have a whole litter of dogs if I weren't allergic, but he also seemed to be holding back, like he didn't want to share the gristly details with me, you know?"

"Sure. I'd do the same, if I knew I'd hit a dog."

"But I saw the blood on the bumper, and the windshield, and knew it wasn't a dog. He tried to say he meant deer, but when I heard the story of the girl on NPR..."

"When did you hear the story?"

"On my way to an interview."

"And did you call him?"

"No, I wanted to let it digest for a while. Then I had a busy day and just tried not to think about it, but when I came home and saw the car, I didn't have to ask him anything. I came in and he looked like he'd been beat to death. He asked me to sit down and said he had something to tell me. I told him I thought I already knew, and he started crying. He reached out for me and hugged me and said he didn't know. He thought it was a dog. He was sorry."

"And then what?"

"I told him to turn himself in."

"Without a lawyer?"

"With a lawyer, without a lawyer, I told him not to sit on this, but he wanted to call his father first, and his father said he'd arrange a lawyer and to hold tight."

"You didn't agree with that?"

"The family of that girl deserves to know what happened to her."

"I agree," Henry said.

"So yeah, I disagreed. Daniel sat on it over the weekend, and now here we are on Tuesday, nearly a week later. What's that been like for the family? And how's it going to look when Daniel comes forward? It's been all over every news channel out there. You'd have to be under a rock not to know about it. Only reason he could be sitting on it is he's guilty and was trying not to get caught."

"Well, he's not going to sit on it anymore," Henry said. "I'm going to make some calls, and the police are likely going to be here within an hour, if you needed to take a few minutes to clear your head."

"I think I will," she said. She began putting the groceries away. "Do I need to be here?"

"It would be best."

"I'm not staying the night," she said.

"You don't have to, but it would be best to hang around for a few hours, to get through the initial statements. I'll be here to help field the questions."

"I'm going to line up a place to stay and pack while they interview Daniel." She bore her eyes straight into his and said, coldly, "You're his lawyer, if you want to give him a head's-up."

5

After the police had gone—a modestly friendly showing, in which they'd recorded a statement from Daniel and his wife, examined the vehicle, taken photographs, and grown sterner with every passing moment, concluding with the need for a formal follow-up statement at the station in the morning, an excoriation not to leave town, and a promise from Henry that his client would continue to be cooperative—Henry had left husband and wife to work out the details of the what-next, Francine's bag already packed and Daniel blinkered from the interview, the weight of his crime settling in and his future in doubt. "I'll meet you at the station at ten to nine," Henry told him. "Don't panic yet. The best thing you can do is cooperate by making yourself readily available, but don't say anything to anyone without me present."

He called Daniel's father on his way out of the neighborhood, left a voicemail that he'd signed a client agreement with his son, and that Daniel would be giving a statement to the police in the morning. He couldn't say much more without violating client confidentiality, but the elder Hayward may want to give his son a call this evening.

Then Henry drove out the reverse course of Daniel's trip home last Thursday evening. The late summer dusk made it difficult to find the accident site, but then he saw the bicycle chained to a tree, a wreath and candles and flowers. He pulled onto the side of the road, took note of the overgrown foliage, the way the live oaks sprawled overhead, blocking out light from the emerging stars. It was a straightaway, no curves to hide behind, no hills. The cover of night would be their best defense, and perhaps the scrubby limbs of box elders and young oaks sprawling out from the swampy woods.

He drove into town. Overlook had a central square, but most of the community was built off the main highway leading into Hilton Head, a series of frontage roads and strip malls tucked away behind palmettos and live oaks, a mock-paradise, a retirement theme park. The bistro where Daniel and his client had dinner was in a one-story strip next to an insurance broker and a tax firm. He ordered a glass of zinfandel and a hearty spaghetti with meatballs dish. The restaurant only had a few patrons, which made him wonder how they stayed in business. Granted it was Tuesday, but it was still summer in a tourist town. November would not likely be busier. And like any good Italian restaurant, the serving size was out of control. He imagined a retired New Jersey stockbroker in the kitchen, bored in his retirement and busier than ever losing money hand over fist but living out his lifelong dream of serving his family's signature dishes to strangers. Henry ordered another glass of wine and took his time with the meal, let it digest, ordered a cup of decaf. Business had not picked up, and the quiet space gave him plenty of time to imagine Daniel and the client here, leaning in over wine, a candle in the middle of the table. He could see Daniel placing his hand over the woman's, joking about nothing important, the old rituals of flirting. He was old-fashioned. He still assumed pretty young women in business were biding their time and hunting for a husband, someone with steady employment who would give them babies and let them take time out of work.

Francine had struck him as alien, the cut of her chin mirroring that of a man: a shrewdness, savvy. She saw through the world and had the decisiveness, the self-awareness, the ruthlessness to cut bait and move out on Hayward right before things got bad for him. Whereas, he thought over dinner, his ex-wife had hung on until it was clear he brought nothing to the table of their marriage. She'd left with the bitterness that derives from recognition: of her own foolishness, her naiveté, her stubborn belief that the marriage had been worth pursuing. No, it was those wasted years and wasted energy that had made her so angry— and gleeful now that she had the dog, and that Henry was mired in scandal. At last, the world saw him as he really was, a sponge or a virus, a leech. Henry had no defense, and believed he owed no apology. Let his ex-wife fume. He could fume, too. He knew it was uncharitable of him to think her dull, but she herself brought little to the table in this life. How he'd ended up with her, well, that was in the past and what was done was done. He *cared* about their marriage, but he was a man of action, he would gladly have molded his life to hers, adapted, but she kept everything in until one day she could no longer hold it.

He paid his tab at Libretto's and, two glasses of wine resting comfortably in his blood, he wended his way back to the site of the hit and run. This part of the world was still undeveloped, somehow, so that the darkness beneath the lush foliage was almost glaring, a throwback to the days before electricity, the eighteenth century as easily as the twenty-first. Replace the pavement with dirt and the car with a horse, and he could be a colonial farmer on his way back from town. But they weren't in the eighteenth century. This was not the laconic antebellum south, but rather the information age. Who were this girl's parents to allow her—yes, allow her, nineteen or not—to travel this strip of dark on her bicycle? Henry had two grown children himself, a boy loafing around in Boulder and a girl married to an ex-air force guy who worked for Northrop Grumman in the DC suburbs. They were safely into their twenties, yet if the girl weren't married, Henry would be checking in on her to make sure she wasn't doing anything stupid. He understood from his own bleached memories that young adulthood was the most dangerous time of all, and he had no doubt that his children had both done foolish things, yet he also believed he'd shielded them from life's most depraved possibilities. They may not have realized it, but he made sure they always had a safety net. This darkened highway absolutely did not.

He had a room at a Marriott off the main highway, guarded by leaning palm trees and sweetgum. The room had ants and a hot tub, and he had no interest in trying to set up to work this evening. His phone showed a full inbox—much of the traffic from his secretary, some of it from animal rights cranks around the internet, activity Neville Brinson swore would die down soon. "Just don't engage," his friend said over and over. "Hit delete and you'll never hear from those nut bags again." How easy that was for Neville to say. The world was screwing with Henry Somerville, he was in the right here, yet he was unable to respond to defend himself. This was America, goddammit, not some old East European puppet government behind the Iron Curtain. You couldn't be accused without knowing your accuser, and you had the right to a trial. You had the right to an attorney. The American public, we just want our day in court, we were entitled to it, it was our birthright. Yet there was no trial for Henry, and although Daniel Hayward would have a trial, the online invective would pass a sentence long before whatever judge landed with the case on his (or her) docket. The culture had turned fascist!

The wine was seeping out of Henry's system, so he changed into exercise clothes and found the hotel's gym, a tiny room with two exercise bikes, two treadmills, some free weights, and a rowing machine. Henry's knees were too shot for the treadmill, and the last time he rode an exercise bike long enough to feel the burn, he ended up with an unmentionable rash. Thus he rowed, and although the gym was empty, as he rowed he thought about how he might look to an observer, the hero in a movie, brooding soul and James Bond fit. Henry was not fit. He was not fat, and maintained a nice cut in a suit, but his endurance was shot from too many years of smoking (he'd quit in the late nineties, but his lungs had never fully recovered). His body was loose and doughy, like folds of bread around a bear claw. Yet he pushed himself into the gym every day, believing in the value of ritual and showing up for the game. He sometimes fantasized about writing a book, or giving a TED talk about his life, or maybe just a lectureship now that the College of Charleston was opening a law school. His one piece of advice was that to do well in life, you just had to be better than the next guy. There was the old joke about the two guys camping, and a bear comes into their camp. The first guy starts putting on his shoes, and his friend says, *Are you crazy? You can't outrun a bear.* And the guy replies, *I don't have to. I just have to outrun you.* Henry knew it would be stupid to give an entire lecture or write a book about that joke, but the principle was all a young person needed. Most people in life were lazy. They half-assed things. To succeed, you just had to get up earlier, work harder, do more for less.

On his nightstand at home was a copy of Garry Kasparov's *How Life Imitates Chess,* a book his son had given him last Christmas. The two shared an interest in chess, and found it a safe realm for conversation, considering the growing polarity in their politics. Kasparov, the one-time champion (now retired), had taken to writing about politics and business and had written this primer on strategic decision-making. Henry was unsure whether there was any subtext in the gift. Decision-making was never Henry's weak spot, and he did enjoy a good business book, but his son's sympathies, after the separation, were with his ex-wife, which meant everything was fraught with tension. (The two used to play chess as well as discuss it, but fathers and sons should not play games that test each other's skill at anything.) He'd left the book in Charleston, so after showering he got into bed and turned on the TV to watch SportsCenter. He picked up his phone and checked through his email again, nothing from his family, his children, old friends, nothing but work, work, work and general griping from his secretary. Poor Henry, his sad life. No wonder the Gideons put Bibles in hotel rooms. There was no place more lonesome than a hotel room on a business trip. He plugged the phone in and changed the station to the local news—in time to catch the local news story about Samantha James. Police had reported talking with a person of interest. The reporter left out Hayward's name, but Henry knew the guy had only a few hours left before the media storm.

Before turning off the TV and hitting the light, he emailed Judy and asked her to cancel anything he had on his calendar next week. He needed to gather documents from the prosecution and start interviewing witnesses, which he couldn't do until they formally charged Daniel with a crime. Might be the weekend before the arraignment. The wrecked windshield would be a problem, he knew. He wasn't sure how Daniel even made it home, and he began formulating the terms for a plea agreement. Maybe he could come up with some plausible story. For now, his first step was to get the guy out on bail, and his second step was to start building the case to poke holes in whatever the prosecution would be gathering. Procedural wins: not all that different from chess, where a win more often than not came from one blunder by your opponent, where they kept the window open for you to fork their king and a rook, say, or to trade a bishop for a queen. Your strategy was to look for the blunder. That was how, Henry knew, he would win his case for Daniel Hayward.

6

The week did not go well for Daniel. The police dragged their feet collecting evidence, and formally charged him Friday afternoon. Henry met him at the station, met with the officers on duty, and tried to get his client in front of a judge that afternoon, but nothing doing. The cops wanted Daniel to spend the weekend behind bars, and Henry would be there for the arraignment. It was all procedural at this point, but the process suggested they were going to hit him hard and fast, so Henry extended his stay at the Overlook Marriott for the weekend. He stayed off the internet yet received numerous texts from friends expressing concern over the #dogjustice trending. Instead, he took long walk-jogs on the hotel treadmill, sampled the area restaurants, and watched a couple of baseball games in the evenings, late July a dead time for most of what interested him.

There is little to be said for Daniel's weekend. Still numb to the accident and the nature of the crime and the manner in which the story of his life had been derailed, Daniel went into his jail cell and sat down on the lumpy bunk, leaned his head against the cold wall, and zoned out for forty-eight hours. For another person, the hours might have been interminable, but rather than sheer tedium, Daniel experienced a fog, like battling a flu virus that kept you on the couch for a week. Certain minutes stretched to an hour, but certain hours blinked past, so that time became an unreliable witness to his incarceration, his soul simmering in a stew of guilt and fear, trembling with regret. No, nothing could be said for Daniel right now, but Francine: she was another story. Henry Somerville had observed her practical public relations nature, but she was no dumb cheerleader, no stymied housewife. It took her the week to let her husband's crime settle in, and to make arrangements, but once she'd decided to leave him, she cut ties without a public tear in her eye or a private pang in her heart.

The day Daniel turned himself in, she kissed him lightly before he left with the lawyer, who explained Daniel might not get in front of a judge today, which meant he would be gone until Monday. This suited her fine because then she wouldn't have to explain while packing, could evade anything contentious and remain in the moment with herself. She made a peanut butter and honey sandwich for dinner and ate carrots with hummus on the side. She went to bed early, exhausted from the week, and felt it strange to be clicking off the lights and heading upstairs alone. She often went to bed before Daniel, but left him watching sports in the living room, the din of the television and the lights at the base of the bedroom door a constant reminder that she was not alone. Now the house was quiet, the living room dark. She brushed her teeth and put on a nightgown and settled into the sheets. The house was already cool, and the AC blew more air into the bedroom. If it were winter, perhaps she would have missed the warmth of Daniel's body, the presence of someone beside her, but tonight she rolled onto her side and wedged a pillow between her legs and pulled the sheets to her chin and was asleep before her mind could tick through what tomorrow would look like.

Although they were a month beyond the solstice, the evening blush still lingered past nine, and even at ten, when Francine drifted off, the sky held a faint shiver of twilight. At five the next morning, when dawn's glow began illuminating the day and the birds arose from their nests, a stopwatch began chirping in Daniel and Francine's bedroom. The sound merged with her dream at first, and then continued piercing her slumber until she woke up, disoriented.

Chirp-chirp. Chirp-chirp. Chirp-chirp.

She turned on the bedside lamp and looked around, the sound coming from Daniel's side of the bed. He had a wooden nightstand with a single drawer, which she opened and began rummaging through. He didn't wear a watch, she thought. Did he even own a stopwatch? Where was this coming from?

Chirp-chirp. Chirp-chirp. Chirp-chirp.

Nothing in the drawer. Nothing on the nightstand. Nothing on the floor. She peered into the crevice between the nightstand and the wall but still saw nothing. Then the chirping stopped. She leaned against the nightstand, the lamp burning her eyes, the room quiet now. When she turned off the lamp and finally returned to bed, she couldn't get comfortable. The sheets were wrinkled and still warm with the heat of her body. The windows were gray with twilight, and birds were singing in the backyard.

Chirp-chirp. Chirp-chirp. Chirp-chirp.

7

The day of the arraignment, Henry breakfasted at a joint called the Griddle & Trough. He devoured a plate of biscuits and bacon and three cups of coffee while he read the morning news. Nothing about his client's bond hearing, just run-of-the-mill articles about property values, Lowcountry tourism, the death of a former high school basketball coach, and a referendum on new breathing apparatuses for the local fire department.

Then this girl in tight jeans and a slinky white shirt came in and took a seat at the bar. She might have been twenty, maybe younger. She ordered a coffee to go and looked right at him on her way out. She was much too young for Henry to have any sexual interest in her, impossibly young and vulnerable, a double-edged blade of need and knowledge. He was much too old for a girl like that to take note of, but there it was: a nervous glance his way. She had her tongue in her cheek and kind of rolled her hair in a way that let him know she'd seen him and knew he'd seen her.

Things grew more complex still later in the morning when he saw the same girl at the bail hearing. She sat alone in the back and clenched her jaw and glared at Daniel. He would later learn she was the dead girl's younger sister, eighteen and fresh out of high school. She was supposed to start at USC in a week but she'd taken a semester off to grieve and pour her energy into the trial. Over the coming weeks, she would talk with just about every reporter in South Carolina, organize a bicycle rally in memory of her sister, stand vigil over the site of the accident, candle in hand, every night alongside a rotating crowd of mourners and strangers in solidarity. The kind of publicity that would make

Henry's job all the more difficult, the truth no longer something to clarify but rather something to find in a jigsaw puzzle of facts and innuendo. Although he knew it was impossible, knew he was anonymous until he got out of the car with Daniel Hayward this morning for the obligatory perp walk across the courthouse steps, he wondered if she'd somehow recognized him at the breakfast joint. He would never completely shake the image of this girl, sitting in the back of the courthouse, one foot propped on the seat in front of her, grinding her jaw, biting her nail. Perhaps this sense of—what?—defiance he saw in her would drive his strategy in the trial. He was nothing if not competitive.

Then the hearing began to determine whether Daniel could leave the jailhouse and return home to await the trial. Everyone rose when the judge came in and took his seat, and then waited quietly for him to start the proceeding. Judge Kenneth Rhodes: unusual for him to preside over the arraignment, but Henry welcomed it for it gave him the chance to study in the flesh the man he only knew by reputation. Judge Rhodes was a black man practicing in South Carolina, and it didn't take a law degree to understand the obstacles he'd overcome to get where he now sat. He was from one of those mid-state towns that are little more than dirt-road hamlets, worked his way through Howard University, earned a master of divinity and completed law school at American before returning to practice in Columbia, where he befriended a number of key legislators who eventually saw the wisdom of appointing some diversity to the circuit court. Today he wore big glasses with a faint tint left over from the outdoor sunlight, short white hair and a grumpy, no-nonsense expression. He cleared his throat and called for the prosecution.

Before the prosecutor stood to speak, she glanced around the courtroom. Her eyes danced past Henry, paused, and returned. She smiled for half an instant, and then she stood and requested Daniel remain in custody. She spoke confidently and without notes, and Henry studied her as well. A pretty, sober-faced woman, with bright red hair and just the faint speckle of gray appearing at her temples, and disarming green eyes visible even from Henry's perch, he recognized her but could not immediately place where. The perils of getting older, one of those signs he tried his best to ignore.

"You believe he presents a flight risk?" the judge asked her.

"He's not local, your honor. All his family is in Ohio, and we believe he poses some risk of fleeing the state."

"Some risk is not quantifiable," Judge Rhodes said. "Be precise."

She wobbled a bit on her heels. "We believe there is substantial risk he could use his family connections to leave the state."

"Your honor," Henry boomed a few moments later. "My client has no history with the law. He's been a resident of Bayard County for seven years now. He's married. He owns a house. He has employment. He's fully cooperated with law enforcement in this investigation and offers his full support in allowing the truth to come out. In no way does he pose a flight risk, nor harm to anyone. We request that he be released until the trial."

The judge summarily granted bail, a hefty fifty thousand dollars, and with that Samantha James's sister bolted from the courtroom. Henry watched her go with more curiosity than ever. He would not be able to interview her or the family—there was no way they would let him, the wolf, into their nest—but he nonetheless made a note to ask around. Then the door clopped shut behind her, and everyone in the courtroom exhaled.

8

"Daniel is, I don't know, he's the kind of guy who will give you the shirt off his back," said Karen Sinclair: divorced, sultry, mysterious businesswoman pushing forty, which to Henry Somerville was the smoking hot prime of life. He had no trouble understanding why Daniel Hayward might ask her out to dinner. In fact, Henry intended to ask her out to dinner himself when this was all over. She had a mean smoky eye and managed operations for a local real estate brokerage specializing in land development. It was a brave new world after the bubble burst, with massive transfers of wealth as cash buyers scarfed up properties for pennies on the dollar. Well into the Trump presidency, the tax cuts fueling the upper crust but doing nothing to stimulate the economy, companies everywhere looked up and realized it was no longer business as usual, that they needed to be nimble to compete, and in real estate, that meant having a technological edge. Mobile listings, searchable criteria, clean web design across platforms, and, most important of all, data collection.

They were in her office a few hours after Daniel's arraignment, in a trendy corporate office park on the island. She had a view of the marshes, while her bosses had a view of the sound. Henry was thinking about Samantha's sister bolting out of the courtroom, his mind buzzing with possibilities.

"Big data doesn't mean a thing," Karen explained. "It's just a buzzword, like innovation. Makes for a good magazine headline, but it's absolutely worthless as a concept without the right infrastructure to translate data into something useful. That's what Daniel's company did."

"They gave you the infrastructure?"

"Maybe infrastructure is the wrong word. Framework is a better word. A way to uncover more data at your fingertips than you were aware of."

"Give me a for instance," he said, trying to understand what exactly Hayward's company did—and thus why Karen was his client, and what purpose they had in dining together that evening.

She grimaced like she was trying to justify standardized testing to her ten-year-old. Henry couldn't tell whether she thought he was a dummy for having her explain the obvious, or she was simply reflective and self-conscious about discussing the new world of American business. "Our customers are interested in properties with water," she said quietly. "You know, fishing ponds, rivers. We're building a searchable database so you can go on our website, sign up, and receive alerts any time a property, anywhere in the country, goes on sale that has water. Or that is income-producing. Or whatever. Now, that's one type of data we're able to access and share with prospective buyers, but what we've found is that buyers who are interested in land with water also have a number of characteristics of interest to other businesses. Sporting goods is the obvious choice. What good is a fishing pond without a pole and tackle? There are research firms who pay good money for people with the income to spend on land with water who might also want to buy, say, X, Y, or Z."

"So you're doing market research," Henry said, "and selling it to the big firms, like a credit card company."

"Credit card companies are amazing," Karen said. "We demonize them because of the crash, but they know more about the average American than anyone in our government, than doctors or teachers or even our relatives. They know what we want and what we're going to do months, even years, before we do it."

"And with that knowledge comes responsibility, right?"

"Of course," she said. "But the responsibility is about more than protecting privacy or something like that. The responsibility is to make the world a better place. To make us better."

Henry listened to her speak and tried to suss out whether she'd drunk the technology Kool-Aid, or had begrudgingly learned the lingo of branding the way most of us had learned the lingo of sports. *Get in the game. Let's hustle.* Equally banal and insidious language, but at least it was universally understood. Data metrics terrified him, though he couldn't distinguish the engine from the chrome. Words like *operationalize* and *actionable* sounded busy, but didn't say much.

"All that to sell some land, huh," Henry said.

"We're all in two kinds of business. It's like the proximate cause and the ultimate cause. My proximate business is facilitating land sales, but really I'm a middle manager. I'm in the *information* business. That's what most real estate brokers don't understand about life after the downturn. You can't live by the same rules and expect to get results. Daniel understood that."

"Tell me about Daniel," he said.

"Daniel understands this," she said. "He knows how to talk about where the world is going without making you feel like a dummy, or without giving you anxiety about the future. He's a salesman, right? And he sells you on the future, but even better, he has a vision of the future, and he *sells* you on his vision."

"Which was?"

"It's about the integration of people and data. He believes people are going to look back at these years in American business and ask: how did we do it? How did we make it through this transition where automation and changing demographics and everything around the web—it's all converging, and businesses are rushing to keep up."

Henry thought of his children—the boy in graduate school, with long hair and wearing a bandanna like some writer he admired, and the girl with her arts administration job and her husband working as a defense contractor, re-creating the kind of life their parents and grandparents lived, and he didn't see the world changing all that drastically. He wasn't a fool. The bar association held CLE workshops about how the same disruptions that ruined music and the newspapers would soon be coming for the lawyers, but his balance sheet hadn't wavered in twenty years. He was taking a hit this year because of the cell phone video scandal, but he believed the changes in American culture were largely media hype. Not that he would say this to Karen Sinclair. All he wanted from her was to find out how much Daniel had to drink before the hit and run.

"We split a bottle of wine," she said.

"What kind?"

"Zinfandel, I think. He picked it out."

"Is this the first time you'd had dinner together?"

"First time in the evening, yes."

He narrowed his eyes. He'd not asked Daniel how far the relationship with Karen Sinclair had gone. It might re-frame things a bit if they'd already slept together.

"Was this a business meeting, or a social call?"

"Are you asking whether there was something going on between me and Daniel? No. There was chemistry, but I wasn't going to let him act on it, if he even would have."

"You don't know?"

"It's not something you easily bring up."

"I'm sorry to pry," he said, "but you'll likely be called to testify. If there were anything going on, the prosecution wouldn't let up until it came out."

"There's nothing to come out," she said.

"You sure?"

"Look. Maybe things toed the line, but Daniel put a firm stop to things that evening when he dropped me off. There was nothing more."

She spoke confidently, and seemed unaffected by Daniel's status as a married man. He wondered what she meant by *toed the line*, but then decided it didn't matter. If she'd slept with Daniel, she would keep it under wraps, provided the prosecution hadn't stumbled onto any witnesses. And if they had, if they asked her point blank, she wouldn't be flustered or embarrassed, and would instead make the prosecution appear like the improper party.

"Did either of you recognize anyone in the restaurant that night?" he asked.

"I didn't, but it's a small town. People recognize each other all the time."

"Ever been to that restaurant before?"

"A few times."

"Would the staff recognize you?"

"It's possible, but I doubt it. I'm not one to get to know my waiter."

"Did anyone from your company know you were meeting Daniel?"

"No, I didn't tell anyone."

"Would it be considered odd for you to meet with him?"

"In my role?" She thought for a moment. "No, I have to meet with people all the time. Wining and dining, it's part of my job description. Not really, but it's something I do often enough."

"Do you go out to dinners with other business partners?"

"On occasion."

"I might need to depose one or two of them, just for background evidence."

"To establish what? That I have to go out to dinner with people regularly?"

"To show this was a plausible business dinner, to clear the air," he said. "I know it's uncomfortable, but I don't want the jury getting side-tracked by anything untoward."

She scoffed.

"Who paid the tab? Daniel?"

"With a company credit card," she said.

"Fair enough. One last question before we move on: about how much of your conversation was business related?"

She neither blinked nor colored, but instead came back with, "How am I supposed to measure that?"

"Was it all business?" he pressed. "Or did you talk about personal stuff?"

"We talked about some personal stuff. How's your family? What do you do when you're not working? Just small talk."

"So, what? Eighty-twenty business? Sixty-forty? Fifty-fifty?"

"I'd say sixty-forty."

"And of that forty percent, anything flirtatious? Any joking around that might be misinterpreted?"

"I'm sure anyone could read anything they wanted into it, but it was perfectly innocent," she said.

Henry suspected there was something more there, but she was formidable, and would not flinch under the bright lights of the courtroom. He needed her on their side, and for now she seemed amenable to the notion that it was a horrible accident, that Hayward's driving off was an honest—if tragic—mistake, and that there really was a defense for him.

He asked her if she remembered what time they left the restaurant.

"Oh, it was about closing time. Maybe ten o'clock."

"And he dropped you off at your apartment? Did he come in?"

"He walked me to the door, but he was a perfect gentleman."

"And it was, what, about ten-thirty when he headed home? Did he mention stopping anywhere, or having any other plans? Even if it was just to fill up his tank with gas."

"No, not that I know of," she said. "He did text me, though."

Henry sat up. "When?"

"Not long after dropping me off. Just to say he had a good time."

"Can you show me?"

She already had her hand in her purse to find her phone. A moment later she pulled up a thread of texts:

Running late
No problem!
I enjoyed this evening
Great me too

All could be interpreted several ways, but what worried him was the time stamp. Had Hayward been texting when he hit Samantha? He knew Claire Fields—young, inexperienced, but no fool—would jump on phone records to show negligence. Henry could get in front of this, maybe, but he needed to visit Daniel again to see what other texts the guy may have sent, or phone calls he placed, or scrolling around on the internet rather than paying attention to the dark highway. Meanwhile, photos of the vehicle would be the real challenge. He needed to get a motion in front of the judge to try to get them excluded.

He thanked Karen Sinclair for her time.

"Did you get everything you needed?"

"For now. We'll need a deposition, where I can get a basic statement under oath. We'll likely want you in court as well."

"Sure. When do you think that will be?"

"Depends on the court's timeline, but I imagine in the next few weeks. Do me a favor? Write down what you just told me, and any other details you can think of, while your mind is fresh."

He stood and began packing his yellow notepad back into his briefcase.

"That poor girl," Karen said.

Henry sat back down. "I know," he said, "but the best thing we can do now is to reconstruct the truth—the whole truth—of that night."

"To get Daniel off."

"To make sure he gets a fair hearing, and doesn't go to jail for any longer than he deserves."

"Do you think he deserves to go to jail?"

"I'm not a judge. I can't say what justice is, but I can tell you mistakes happen a lot more frequently than you'd think. I suspect you know how fast it can happen. We've all been there, where one moment, one action, separates us from criminal charges. The question is, do you let grief for the girl weigh stronger than what Daniel may or may not have intended? Do you judge him by feelings or facts?"

9

Henry seldom considered the difference between truth and spin, and considered even less the definition of justice. His job was to checkmate Claire Fields, and despite all the evidence that kept trickling out about Hayward, Henry felt confident the prosecutor would make a number of errors. She was younger than Hayward, in her first job, where she should be filing briefs and helping her bosses plot strategy rather than taking the lead. He'd researched her last week, read the news of her involvement with that police officer in the Baldwin case, and filed it away as something that might give him leverage. If it came to an appeal, he could suggest she'd compromised herself with the entire police department by having one illicit affair, and could not be expected to try an objective case. Then he found her on LinkedIn and recalled where he'd met her at the courthouse years ago, when she was a clerk for Judge Simpson. Clerks always missed a step and damaged cases, Henry thought, women especially, but he'd been especially gruff with her about neglecting the sentencing recommendation because he himself had been mired in his brother's affairs. Everyone had a scandal in the family, and Phil was one scandal after another.

It started when they were children, and the ultimate scandal was simply Phil's birth. The filthiest secret in Henry's life was that he was breastfed until he was four years old. He'd more or less weaned after the first year, a late-night dream feed continuing into his second year. His mother's milk supply had nearly dried up, but it was a comfort to both of them, and helped him sleep through the remainder of the night in whatever strange town or whatever new naval base they lived on. Henry's father spent much of his career on a ship, leaving Henry's mother to struggle with a baby and few possessions and no friends. Then Phil was born before Henry's second birthday, and their mother's milk supply shot up. Henry did not remember this, but his mother, perhaps feeling bad for abandoning her first-born to sustain the second, still allowed him the occasional suckle, which by then he was able to ask for. He'd grown tall enough as a toddler to reach up and grab her breast, and soon developed the language of request: *More? More?*

Henry couldn't pinpoint his first memory at his mother's breast, his early life a patchwork quilt, one base house after another. Hot weather, cold weather, a babysitter named Maureen, Phil a colicky infant who had somehow usurped Henry's place. Once, while temporarily living in a trailer park on the Texas coast, Henry had gone out to play in a diaper and t-shirt and bare feet, and plenty of other toddlers had done the same. Some bully kid had picked Henry up and hung him by the shirt on a fence, and Henry had sat there all morning, seemingly content but inwardly confused and uncertain, two states that would carry him through much of his childhood. His mother, evidently distracted by the ever-wailing Phil, had gone outside and plucked up the first toddler she saw as her own, and it wasn't until lunchtime that she actually paused to examine the boy she'd corralled, and realized this was not the face that presented itself at her breast twice a day. She'd found Henry hanging by the fence, and although Henry had little memory of this moment, she began to weep. She'd always suspected she was a bad wife and mother, the daughter of a staunchly middle-class home and a tyrannical father and a near-mute mother who never shared with her the secrets of housewifery.

Mary mothered by appeasement. She basked in the bond between her and her boys (a miscarriage and a hysterectomy prevented her from having more children after Phil), and she believed that what felt so right, her boys at her breasts, receiving nourishment, could not be wrong. She knew she was supposed to cut them off, but lacked the stomach or heart for it. And then it just continued, Henry taking her breast in the evenings after a day at preschool. By then both of them knew it was unnatural, and by some instinct he refrained from mentioning it to anyone, especially not his father. He simply went into his parents' bedroom late at night, crawled into bed with her and took her breast in his hand. She sat up and obliged by lowering her nightgown and allowing him to drink. By this time Phil, age two, had weaned and had not shown the same proclivity, which was fine by Henry. He enjoyed this private time with his mother, this secret between them, and he believed he was her favorite son after all, younger brother be damned.

His father would return from sea and stay home for two weeks at a clip on leave, and in those times Henry instinctively knew to keep a low profile around his mother. No climbing into bed with the two of them. But she delighted him by finding time together; while their father was in the shower, say, she would come to Henry and offer her breast quickly, and he would nurse vigorously on both sides. He later knew from watching his wife breastfeed (a habit she quickly relinquished for formula), what breastfeeding did to a woman's nipples, and he shuddered to think of his father coming out of the shower, finding his wife with nipples erect, and believing her hot and bothered for the naval officer. Henry had primed his mother for his father, and his father serviced his mother routinely before returning to his ship. Thus the pattern continued until Phil, the fink, caught wind of the illicit nocturnal sessions and used it to his advantage. Jack, home from the ship one day (they were living in Germany then), caught Phil in some act or another. Henry never knew for sure, but suspected Phil had broken a cuckoo clock Jack had purchased in Italy, and in a weak attempt to deflect attention from his misdeed, announced, in his lispy toddler squeak, "Henry breastfeed."

That stopped Jack mid-sentence. "What did you say?"

"Henry. He breastfeed."

"Mary! What is this boy talking about?"

Jack thundered through the tiny house and found his wife, whose first response was denial. "I have no idea what he's talking about."

And then Jack found Henry, held the boy at arm's length, and said, "What's this? Eh? What are you doing with your mother?"

Henry, knowing the jig was up, grew hot in the neck and felt pressure in his chest and said nothing, stared at the ground while his father stared at him for long enough to determine the truth, that Phil (still in trouble for breaking the clock, no escape for that one) was not making up a story, and that Henry knew what he was doing was wrong, and that his wife was likely to blame. Needy, irresponsible, a bad mother. What kind of world had Jack come home to? He sent both boys to bed. Phil, punished but feeling smug, promptly went to their bedroom door to listen, and Henry followed. He couldn't make out what their parents were saying, but he heard plenty of *Jesus, Mary, what were you thinking?* and *This stops tonight.*

Since then, Henry had been on his own. His mother exhibited a coolness toward him, which he later understood to be a mask for longing, but she'd had her orders from her husband and was old-fashioned enough that, the secret once exposed, she quit hiding it and cut him off the breast. Henry, despondent, missed both the taste of his mother's milk and the private time with her, as well as his father's gruff affection. Whenever his father came home off the ship, stinking of diesel fumes, it took a few days to adjust to the new order, Jack and Mary settling into their routine, the boys re-learning who this man was. He was short with them, military-terse, commanding, but he nevertheless loved Henry and Phil as his boys and took pains to spend time with each of them while he was home. After the revelation of the breast, Jack's relationship changed for both of his boys: with Henry for obvious reasons, but also with Phil, in part because Phil had been the messenger and in part because Jack couldn't shake the vision of his wife breastfeeding both their boys. He wasn't angry with them, because they were too young to be conscious of what they were doing (he reserved the anger for his wife, his stupid, selfish wife), but his boys were now alien to him, creatures living in his house, with their private lives and secret relationships, and it made Jack feel like a visitor in his own home. Nuclear family fission.

Phil, too, had not fared well, but it was Henry who felt the blow even when those nocturnal feedings became a dream in his memory. Even after forgetting the specifics, he clammed up and passed the rest of his childhood in secret longing, with the balm that he would one day get out and make his own life, find his own comfort (a comfort his ex-wife provided, until she didn't). He went through the motions and guarded his secret shame, and by the time he finished college, those early years of breastfeeding with his mother were like a different life altogether, something he'd witnessed on television rather than experienced, and he almost persuaded himself it had never happened. He met and married a girl in law school (she was an undergraduate, conservative and ready for a family), and he said nothing to her about his strange family. She of course met Mary and Jack (now retired and working for a logistics company), who welcomed her into the family. The Somervilles had taken their place in Charleston's upper echelons, the naval years merely a tour of duty. Now they had the income and the connections to practice philanthropy, and supported the art museum and the historical society and went to black tie galas twice a year. Henry the budding lawyer and Phil, well, never mind about Phil, the parents were so glad to meet Henry's soon-to-be-wife. No one ever said anything about the tumultuous childhood.

It wasn't until Henry's wife began breastfeeding their own children that changes began happening inside Henry. He no longer remembered the nights with his mother, but something in his subconscious made him exceedingly virile around his wife, her nipples elongated, her areolae chapped from suckling babies, her breasts swollen with milk. He walked around with an erection for several years while his children were young, and then they all grew older, the parents worn out from chasing after the children and ferrying them from one activity to another, the children swept up in their own lives and oblivious to their parents, and above it all the looming expenses of college for the kids and retirement for Henry and his wife, which meant he worked and worked and he reached a ceiling in his practice, him and Judy, making as much money and billing as many hours as was possible. The next step would be to bring in an associate and expand the firm, but he didn't want to do that. He liked where he was, so he continued on, overwrought, wrung out, and then the kids were gone and his marriage had disintegrated and now he was staring down the barrel of old age. That's how life must go for the upwardly mobile, those lucky enough to live in the wide middle of American life. You do your best, you take a few risks, you calculate your success, and life moves on around you, the mortgage gradually shrinks and the IRA gradually balloons and maybe your marriage falls apart or your children turn into assholes, but all you could do late in life was reevaluate your strategy, make a few corrections and try to hang on.

His brother, Phil, did not play that way. He was an innocent, in many ways: a natural weaning at fifteen months, secure as the baby of the family, but after the rift—his father's mistrust, his mother's resentment, his brother's shame—a light had gone off inside Phil, and he later took risks to feel alive. Smoking, staying out late, driving too fast, drinking. In adulthood he renounced his leg up for college and went to work for a homebuilder, learned to install cabinets, so that's what he did: installed cabinets. He was good at it and enjoyed it and the pay was not all that bad, though he did live in West Ashley rather than one of the tonier suburbs. He drove a used Chevy Blazer and got married and divorced in quick succession, and then just wasted a decade in dive bars.

Then came the crash, when no one knew whether the anemic economy was on the mend or whether another shoe might drop. When the housing bubble burst in 2007, Phil's cabinetmaking jobs slowed from fire hose to stream, and when the banks began to fail and credit dried up, new jobs became a trickle. In 2009, the largest company he contracted with went out of business, leaving a half-finished development on the far side of Mount Pleasant and more than a dozen contractors in the lurch. Phil believed he had another hundred homes to install cabinets for in the next three years, but instead he was left with the tab for materials from his last job, advised to get a lawyer and stand in line. He went out and got exceedingly drunk with a painting crew he was friendly with. They bought round after round, marched up King Street as if in defiance of the economy and the bad draw, and they landed in a piano bar that carried them through the remainder of the evening.

Then Phil found his Blazer parked on a side street not far from the college, and stared for some time at a new science center under construction, the college's sprawl unhindered by the Great Recession. Just move some of the endowment from one fund into another, keep lobbying the state legislature not to cut funding, and on the party goes. Phil was not a begrudging man, so it was more a gaze of stupefaction, disbelief he'd reached this point and a slight bemusement that so many years had passed. What had become of his life? What would he do tomorrow? Did he even care? Henry didn't know, but he did know what Phil did next would set the tone for the remainder of his life. He got in his Blazer, put it into gear and somehow see-sawed his way out of the parking space and onto Pitt Street. The most direct route home would be for him to bear right onto Calhoun, cross the James Island Connector, and head up into West Ashley. Or, wend his way over to Coming Street, a north-running egress out of town, until he hit 17 at Spring, which also would have gotten him home to West Ashley—perhaps without a hitch. Perhaps if he had taken those two direct routes, he would have swayed into his home, puked in the trash can in the kitchen, passed out with his shoes on, nursed the next day's hangover, and moved on with his life. Or perhaps he would have drunkenly driven off a bridge and drowned in the Ashley River. No telling.

What did happen, however, was from Pitt Street, he hung a left onto Calhoun heading away from the river. Past Marion Square, he turned up Meeting Street and took it north toward Highway 17. So far so good, but in this part of town people seldom acknowledged the crosswalk, and simply stepped into the street whenever they felt like it. So when Phil hung a left onto Spring and hit the gas, he likely saw nothing but green lights ahead and not the hooded black man walking into his lane. Henry doubted his brother even saw the man at the last minute, likely so fixated on the traffic lights, which is one way drunks keep from getting pulled over. Run a red light, you're toast. Hit an automobile, you're toast. Fall asleep at the wheel, you're toast. But pedestrians? There was no bluff suitable for those wild cards. With a thud, Phil knocked the man into the street and ran him over, sending him into a coma he would never wake from. He would be unplugged from life support in six weeks, a permanent vegetable with no living will and no chance of recovery. By that time, Phil had been charged with reckless driving and hit and run, and Henry had helped him negotiate settlements with the prosecution, the insurance company and, finally, the man's family—all before it became a murder case. Even still, he readied a motion to dismiss any further charges, should some appear, after the family pulled the injured man off his feeding tube and ventilator, alleging it unnecessary and unrelated to the accident with his brother.

The man Phil struck worked in the kitchen of one of the new restaurants on upper King, and had been walking to the nearby Piggly Wiggly for groceries before catching the bus home to North Charleston. He had a wife and grown children and although he was not living large by any means, he had provided a stable home life for his family for twenty years, enough to buy a (modest) house on a (relatively) quiet street. After settling with the insurance company and making good progress with the prosecution, Henry drove out to the victim's house to visit his widow. Her name was Charlotte, and she didn't at all seem surprised to have a white man show up on her doorstep, wearing a button-down shirt and carrying a black leather briefcase.

"Ma'am, I'm here on behalf of Phil Somerville," Henry said. "May I come in?"

She turned away from him but left the door open as she returned to the couch, where she had a stack of thank-you cards, a pen, and a book of stamps. "We've been getting flowers and gifts for a month," she said. "Always another thank you to write."

"It's good that you have a strong support network," he said.

She shook her head, but he couldn't tell whether she was amazed at his brazen entrance into her home or his stupidity when it came to condolences and life and death. Charlotte was quite heavyset and had owl glasses and kept clicking her pen while he talked.

"Let me start by saying how sorry I am for your loss," he said. "I understand Ray passed away a few days ago."

"Gasped his last breath at six o'clock Friday."

"I know how hard that must be."

"Mm hmm."

"Well. Why I'm here. I'm an attorney working for Phil Somerville, who as I'm sure you know has been charged with the hit and run. The law is going to judge him and set out an appropriate punishment, but you as Mr. Warren's next of kin have your own rights in the situation. Are you familiar with civil justice?"

"Can't say I am."

"Phil is in criminal court now. He broke the law, and is being tried accordingly. But victims—or their families—can also take someone to what's called civil court. Do you have representation from a lawyer?"

She shook her head.

"That's fine. If you did, I would need to go through them, but I can tell you, hiring a lawyer and working your way through the courts is expensive. I'm hoping today we can come to an agreement without you having to go through all that."

"What sort of an agreement?"

He set his briefcase on his lap and opened it. "Whatever you must be thinking, Phil feels terrible and wants to make things right." Henry pulled out a one-page contract. "I have an agreement here where he will offer you some settlement money for your loss."

She scoffed. "In exchange for what?"

"This is a good-faith gesture. He wants to atone for his crime." He pulled out two bundles of hundred-dollar bills. "I have here thirty thousand dollars, which should pay for the funeral expenses and any remaining medical expenses." He gauged her reaction, and then he pulled out another bundle and said, "Additionally, there is another twenty thousand for pain and suffering."

She gasped at the sight of the fifty thousand, kept her eyes off Henry for several moments. Then she steadied her gaze and said, "What are you buying me off for?"

"This isn't buying you off."

"What do you want from me?"

"This is a good-faith gesture," he said again. "Now, this piece of paper is a contract where you acknowledge receipt of the money, and by doing so, you agree not to sue Mr. Somerville."

"You're a lawyer?"

"I am."

"How much you think I could get from him if I took him to court?"

"It's tough to say. After legal fees, you might come away with this much or more, but that's a gamble. You might walk away with nothing."

"You're cutting me off at the pass, is that it?"

"We want this resolved, quickly and quietly. Mr. Somerville has a long legal road in front of him, and he wants to make sure that when he gets to the end of that road, it's really the end."

She took off her glasses and rubbed her eyes, stared a few moments at the stack of thank-you cards. He wondered if she were conscious of the disarray in her apartment. It was clear she tried to keep it up: no specks of dust around the framed photographs of family members, the dishes put away in the kitchen, no clutter on the coffee table, but the couch cushions had seen better days, the fabric wearing thin, and the furniture had scuffs and scratches, perhaps from years of a happy family's tumble and play, but it all made him think of a thrift shop's mustiness. Not enough light, no crisp fabrics or showroom furniture. "You know how many of these I've had to write?" she asked of the thank-you cards.

"I don't," he said, and he looked her square in the eyes.

"Going on a hundred. Family, people from church, people Ray worked with going back thirty years, high school friends. Do your people come out with this kind of support? Or do you go straight to the lawyers to settle things with cash or in court?"

"We all grieve, Mrs. Warren."

"But throwing around fifty thousand in cash must make grieving easier."

He said nothing, waiting for her to get off her soapbox and take the money and sign the paper. He knew she wouldn't walk away from that kind of cash. Even if she had designs on hiring an attorney and taking Phil to court, what he'd said was true: there were no guarantees. Henry certainly wouldn't be offering this kind of settlement again.

She put her glasses back on and asked to see the paper.

"I have two copies, for us both to sign," he said, and he handed her a pen.

"This means you won't be coming back here asking for anything else from me?"

"That's right. You'll never see me again."

"Good," she said, and she signed the papers.

On his way out, he hadn't gotten off the stoop when he heard her wail inside, a long scream followed by two short sobs, like the beginning of some message in Morse code. He thought about turning around and knocking to see if there was some way he could comfort her, but he knew he had nothing to give her. Henry had come here to take, to get her signature to protect his brother. Phil would lose his license for six months and be on probation for a year, but the entire incident would eventually go away. He would have to sell his house and move into an apartment, and find a full-time job as a groundskeeper for one of the local plantations. Planting bushes for a living and riding around on a moped did not scream high society, but every family had one, and the Somervilles were no exception. Henry feared he might have a difficult time sleeping after bribing Charlotte Warren with hush money, but he surprised himself by forgetting it easily. That was the way to deal with the morally objectionable: forget about it.

It wasn't until the case of Daniel Hayward that he thought again of his brother's crime, and how quietly it passed compared to Hayward's. Phil's hit and run may have earned a blurb on the *Post & Courier* website, but no one followed up because the victim was black and the perpetrator was poor. Poor and minority crime didn't sell papers the way clean-cut and upwardly mobile white people did. At least, that was the law of media in South Carolina. Henry had paid Charlotte off with fifty thousand of his own money, but with Daniel Hayward, his job was to make money, not dip into his retirement, so his incentive was to make sure this trial went his way—but not too quickly—which meant no settlement ahead of time. He believed he could win it, earn probation for Daniel but skip the felony and the prison sentence. A felony was not an option.

10

Beyond the interview with Karen Sinclair, Henry accomplished little before the trial. When Hayward turned himself in, they held him over the weekend, and Henry was there for the bail hearing: a high price, going for the jugular. The judge, Kenneth Rhodes, was a theological man of a different era, never went out in public without a tie and sport coat. Henry knew him tangentially, same as he knew about everyone worth knowing in the South Carolina legal field, but had never had a case in his courtroom. In the weeks between now and the trial, Henry would research the judge's opinions and try to see how he ruled on hit-and-run cases. Judge Rhodes did not have a reputation as unreasonable, no nickname like "The Hammer," but judges could be unpredictable. No way around it, it caught Henry off guard when the judge dismissed his plea that Daniel Hayward be seen as a local setting up local roots. The gal from the solicitor's office all but called Hayward a carpetbagger, and Judge Rhodes banged his gavel and issued a fifty-thousand-dollar bail as casually as if he requested bacon on a turkey sandwich.

Hayward's father wired the money and Hayward put his house up as bond.

"You all right?" Henry asked his client as they walked down the courthouse steps.

"I just spent a weekend in jail."

"That was dirty of them, but they didn't leave us an option. We'll hit 'em hard now, that's how they're playing it."

"Long as you've got a plan."

Henry let Hayward walk ahead. He saw the solicitor gal leaving the courthouse, and he went over to try to talk sensibly with her.

"We're putting together a plea package now," she said. "Your client wants to come by this week, we can talk numbers."

"Say he'll plead guilty. What are we looking at? Community service, public apology?"

"We're keeping it a felony," she said.

"Well, hold on."

She stopped. "Your client did a heinous thing, and now a young woman is dead."

"He made a mistake. And now you want to ruin his life? To what end?"

"Justice," she said.

He remembered that response a few days later, at the plea negotiation, when the solicitor gal once again tried to play hardball, insisted they accept a felony hit and run or go to trial. Something was personal for her in this case, the animation of a vendetta, so Henry called Chuck Goodall to see what the story was.

"What can I tell you, Henry?" Chuck said. "This case has teeth, and Claire's running with it, same as I would do, and same as you would do if you were on our side."

"Have you been following it?"

"I get reports."

"She asked for no bail, and wouldn't plea to anything but a felony."

"And your point is?"

"Don't you think that's a little excessive? I understand she might be trying to overcome some recent hurdles with her career, but Daniel Hayward shouldn't bear the brunt of whatever she's trying to prove—to you or anyone else."

Chuck was quiet on the other line long enough that Henry wondered if he'd hung up, or lost the connection, or accidentally put him on mute. Then Chuck spoke quietly. "Henry, I can't help you. Claire is very good at her job, and she's got my support on this one. Attacking her or making allegations about what you think you know won't help anything. You want to defend your client? Defend him. Or you want to help him? Urge him to take a plea, because otherwise we're going to send him away for manslaughter, or even homicide."

"On what grounds? There's no proof of intent, nothing but what he says happened."

"We'll see about that," Chuck said, "but right now I need to get back to work."

"I think it's best if we had an open line here."

"Claire's your contact on this one."

Chuck hung up before Henry could push him again.

Coward. Chuck would be up for reelection soon enough, and he didn't have to tell Henry that going easy on a high-profile hit-and-run case would not endear him to the voters of Bayard County. Henry did find it surprising that Chuck trusted the girl to take the lead. She was old enough to know what she didn't know, which meant she was at that vulnerable age where Henry could exploit her shaken confidence. Chuck ought to know better, but perhaps he was getting soft in his older age. Or perhaps he had a thing going with the girl.

The last thing Henry could do in Overlook before the trial was try to interview a few remaining parties. He knew Samantha James's parents would not talk to him without a subpoena, and there was nothing he really wanted to ask them right now. They would offer sobbing, sympathetic testimony at the trial, describe the character of their daughter, how joyful she was, and her bright future. Henry felt for them, he really did. He had a daughter, and even though she was grown and no longer a major part of his everyday life, it would kill him to find out something happened to her. Then why had he taken on this case? Was it money? Greed? No. He believed in the law. As much as he might disdain Claire Fields as a naive upstart, with her talk of *justice*, he did see himself as fighting an important battle in providing a good defense for everyone. He thought of the poor Warrens and the fifty thousand in cash he'd delivered to them. They, too, deserved some form of justice, and he would have respected them had they moved ahead with a lawsuit against his idiot brother. But there were rules, and there were *rules*, and Henry played by the second kind. If it made him a hypocrite, so be it.

He did try the girl's boyfriend, Charlie Gibbs, the one who'd found Samantha on the side of the highway that evening. Henry doubted the kid would have much to say, but he wanted to see how the boy comported himself under pressure, to see how good a witness he would be for the prosecution. Perhaps Gibbs had said or done something, maybe at the crime scene, maybe moved her body, even if just out of the road, something unreported that might call the investigation procedures into question. If the kid was unlikeable, perhaps he would even be a liability to the prosecution, to get him on stage and show Samantha James wasn't the straightforwardly clean cut co-ed reported in the newspapers. Perhaps she was a junkie. You never knew.

Gibbs sold used cars at the pre-owned side of the Toyota dealership. Henry found him wearing a goofy polo shirt tucked into jeans, cramming down a sandwich in the break room. The kid's boss had directed Henry that way, and Henry was glad to find the kid in a moment of vulnerability.

"How you, Charlie?" he asked.

"Who are you?"

Henry introduced himself.

Gibbs chewed open-mouthed for a few moments, took in the lawyer with a cattle-stupid gaze, and then he swallowed and wiped his mouth and took a long drink of a Dr. Pepper. "I got nothing to say to you," he said.

"I haven't asked you anything yet."

"You represent the fella who hit her? You're trying to get him off?"

"I'm trying to establish the facts of the evening."

"Yeah, you're trying to establish your own facts to help that fella, which means I got nothing to say to you."

"How's the family doing?"

Gibbs made a face. "What do you care?"

"I'm just asking," Henry said. "Believe it or not, I know this is a tragic situation, and I know the family must be hurting. That's why I'm here with you, rather than knocking on their door. I know you must be hurting too, but it's different when it's your daughter. That kind of pain is unimaginable."

The air had the ionized commercial sting of halogen lights and merchandise for sale. They say you achieved a new-car smell with formaldehyde, the same chemical you used to process a dead body. The retail economy was a bit like Dr. Frankenstein, trying to create the breath of life but instead feeding a monster. Henry had never worked in sales, had gone straight through college and law school and into practice at a time when there wasn't talk of disruptions in the legal field. Today's young lawyers had to understand retailing, and Henry didn't envy them. Might as well be selling used cars like Gibbs here. Gibbs took a sip of his Dr. Pepper and said nothing.

Henry had what he came for. He was curious to learn how long Gibbs had been dating Samantha, what he was doing the night she was struck, what she did after she clocked out, what happened at the accident scene when Gibbs arrived, but what Henry really needed to know was how sympathetic the boy would appear to a jury. He wasn't an all-American jock out of a TV show, with neatly parted blond hair and a Banana Republic wardrobe. Rather, Charlie Gibbs was high-strung and almost gaunt, like Gumby but a hair-trigger away from crazy. You could see it in the way he was massaging his hand, the way he looked off as if to re-center himself before speaking, a disconnect between the mind and the body. Must be frustrating to go through life that way, slightly off-kilter, seeing the world through a certain lens. Maybe it was a more honest lens, maybe Gibbs was the blind seer, the wise fool, but he lacked the swagger to impress Henry Somerville, and Henry knew a jury would see him as sniveling at best, a liar at worst. Henry would crush him in live testimony, so he would learn what he needed in deposition, with no fear that the prosecution would try to put this kid on the stand.

"How long you been selling cars?" he asked.

Gibbs took another sip of his Dr. Pepper. "Few months."

"You like it?"

"It's all right."

"What's the secret to sales? How do you sell someone a car?"

"I'm on break," Gibbs said. "You want to wait, I'll take you out there and sell you any car you like."

"I'm not in the market right now," Henry said, and he stood up.

"That's the secret," Gibbs said. "Some people want to buy a car, and you sell it to them. Other people who don't, you can't do anything with them."

More wisdom in that statement than Gibbs realized. Henry decided long ago that although he was not a true believing Christian (raised Presbyterian but only went to church for weddings and, more and more these days, funerals), they had it right when it came to original sin. People inevitably let you down, born bad, and there was nothing you could do with them. That's why man invented laws, as a check on human nature.

"I'll see you, Charlie," he said on his way out. "Thanks for your time."

11

The trial was scheduled for the late autumn, around Thanksgiving, so Henry met with Daniel Hayward one more time and then returned to Charleston. Francine had moved out—didn't even have the courtesy to leave her husband a note, it seemed; Daniel came home from his weekend in jail to find her clothes missing and the house empty. Henry could see the house now: smelling musty from lack of life, perhaps a little warm. Quiet. Daniel would have walked in and said, "Hello? Hello?" to one empty room after another until the truth, that queasy knot in his stomach, ruptured. He would have sat on the couch and tee-peed his hands over his mouth and nose, and thought about his life and where everything went wrong. When Henry saw him, Daniel wore the look of a man already condemned, with deep dark eyes and a permanent stoop to his shoulders. Henry knew it wasn't the sentence but the anticipation wearing on him. People were resilient and could adapt when they knew where they were going, but uncertainty could kill a man. Henry made the usual promises— *We'll take care of this, don't fret, I'm just a phone call away*—but then he got in his car and scuttled up the highway, through a tunnel of old oaks and Spanish moss, to his home on the Charleston peninsula.

The first thing that was wrong was the spray paint on the side of his rowhouse, white paint on red brick: *#dogjustice*. He parked in his narrow driveway and stared at it for a moment, and then he set his head on the steering wheel. The neighbors were polite but someone had no doubt already called and left a message on his answering machine, and maybe even called Judy at the office, to see when he would be getting it cleaned up. The paint didn't bother him so much as the question of what next. As with Daniel Hayward, the uncertainty of the future hung over Henry like a guillotine, Henry unable to get out of the stock, the media, he supposed, playing the role of the oppressive state.

Sure enough, here came a little Robespierre now, a cocky young fellow with a big camera slung over his neck, ready to capture a photo of Henry getting out of his car, the paint in the background. It was late in the day and the shadows from the wisteria and crepe myrtle a kaleidoscope on the wall so that with any luck, the vandalism would not show up in a decent photo. Henry considered just putting the car in gear and driving off, and he considered scurrying with his back to the cameraman into his home, but he'd never been one to shy away from conflict. He got out and marched headfirst toward the cameraman, who got his requisite shots before calling out, "Mr. Somerville! A word!"

Henry kept walking without speaking until he reached the little squirt, lunged for the camera, and yanked it from the kid's hands.

"The hell!" the kid yelled, but Henry had already swung it in an arc, building up centripetal force, and slammed it into the sidewalk. The kid yelled again and reached for him, but Henry pulled away and swung the camera again, and this time the strap broke free from the camera and the camera skittered into the gutter.

"Did you paint the side of my house?" Henry asked.

The kid cursed and scrambled for his camera. "No, man, Jesus, what the hell."

He looked up at Henry from his crouch, and for a moment Henry wondered if the kid might lose his cool and come after him. Whatever. Henry was ready. But then the kid just smirked and shook his head.

"You've got problems, man," he said to Henry's back as Henry went inside and poured himself a full glass of scotch, neat.

He knew he'd made the story worse by engaging with the reporter. The photo was likely saved on the SD card, undamaged by Henry's rampage, and now the reporter had a smashed camera to boot. He could already see the headline: *Dog Thrower Throws a Fit.* There would be no end to the story now, but there was nothing to be done. The digital scandal would bleed into the analog world. Death threats would show up in his inbox, at the office. Judy would quit, and his clients, harassed, would find other attorneys. An early retirement was in his future, yet today his blood still simmered from the violence. Whatever happened, it felt good to have taken action, to have engaged, to fight back. He took a sip of his drink and savored the burn in the back of his throat. Then he pulled out his notes for the Daniel Hayward case. He might not have any clients this time next year, if the story with the reporter caught hold, but for now, he had a major case before him, and there was much work to be done.

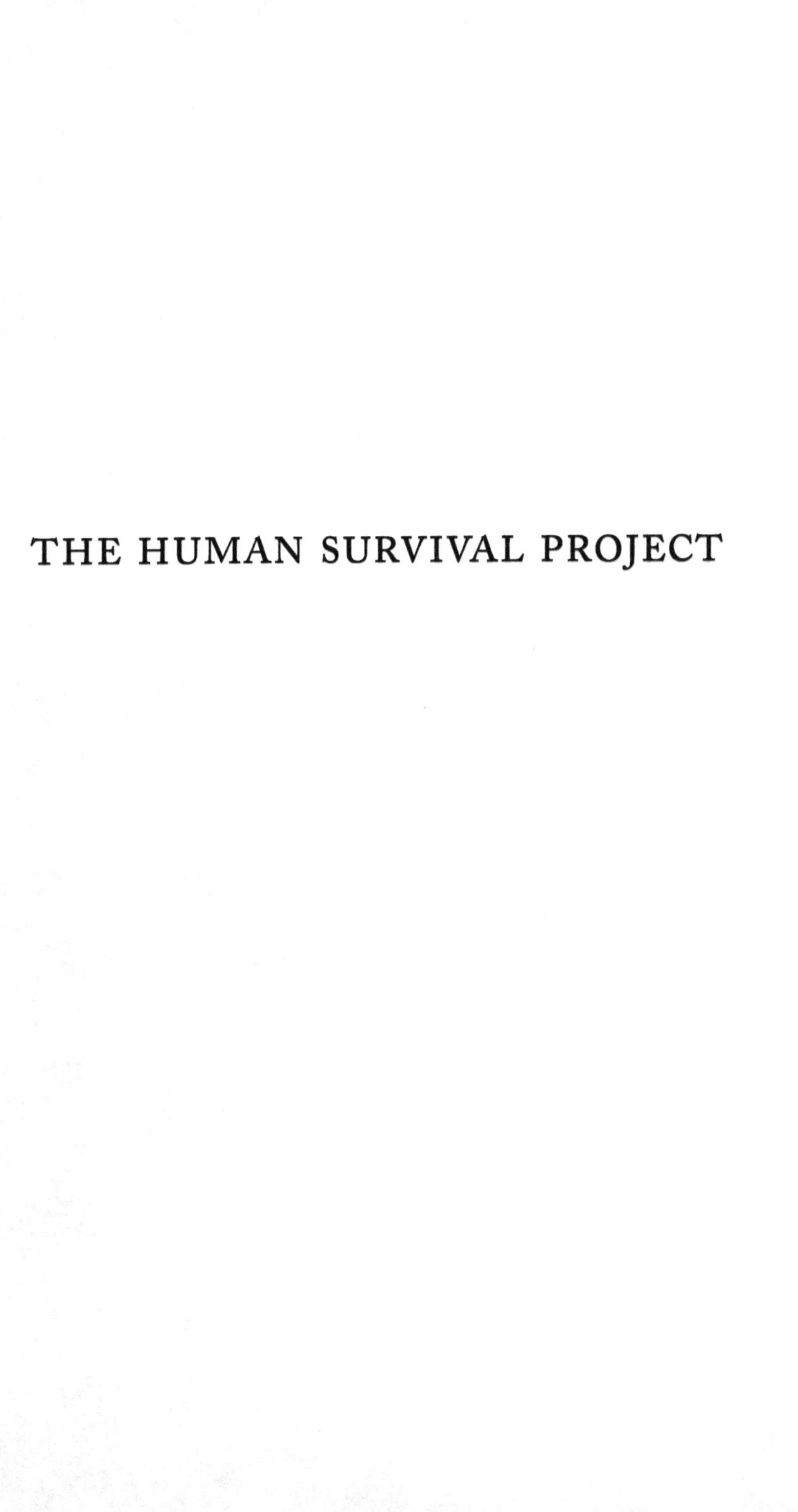

THE HUMAN SURVIVAL PROJECT

1

Destined for greatness: Daniel Hayward believed this of himself throughout a thoroughly unimaginative childhood and an uninspired adolescence and the treadmill decade of his twenties, a belief that, as he crossed into his thirties, had grown difficult to sustain due to a receding hairline, an unfortunate set of talents that had made him well suited for a life in sales but not much else, and an unshakable exhaustion that caused him to avoid work, chores, his wife, and even, on some days, getting out of bed. He'd managed to fake it thus far, one dull day bleeding into the next and the next, but he drank far too much to help him sleep and he couldn't eat and perhaps he made love to his wife more often than he wished in order to assure himself he was not depressed. His wife wanted a baby. He wanted to feel alive again. The house was supposed to help.

Daniel and Francine's house was something to behold. The marketing copy from the builders said everything was *expansive*—the great family room, the kitchen with the island and granite countertops, the private downstairs study—to say nothing of the sloping lawn on the half-acre lot, the well-fertilized Zoysia, the cherry laurel (no cheap privet for him, that blasé builder's bush), the mature trees in the backyard (magnolia, dogwood, even a lemon tree), the pines in the swampy wetlands, the Spanish moss entangled in the limbs of water oaks. Everything was spectacular, everything he'd assumed as his birthright and everything he'd ever dreamed of at his most ambitious. They had an outdoor fireplace made of stone, a screened-in back porch, a mudroom. A mudroom! Best of all, though, for Daniel Hayward, Cleveland native, was that a cold day in Overlook meant fifty degrees. This was vacation every day of his life.

The builders had done a beautiful job, constructed a patio where a man could sit out in an Adirondack chair with a cold beer and enjoy himself, pass half the day without doing anything more than contemplating his empire and reflecting on the meaning of his life, pass your Saturday out there in your bathrobe until you felt like firing up the grill for lunch, maybe go inside for a nap during the hottest part of the day before setting back up for the evening. Yes sir, the only trouble was, when the sun set on you, what were you supposed to do? The porch light shined down on you like a spaceship and attracted more species of moth than Daniel ever knew existed. No sir, a few lights grounded around the patio and you'd have something any man would envy. That's what you wanted out of life, to have exactly what you want, which would set you free. That's what this whole thing amounted to: the rock spinning around the sun, coasting through the Milky Way, drifting in the universe's grand and only exhale, all so one speck of atom dust could smile while nursing his Fat Tire on a pleasant day.

On Saturday, two weeks before the hit and run ruined his life, he had plans to complete the yard: an installation of lights around the stone patio.

"Don't forget we have *Julius Caesar* tonight," Francine told him as he put on his shoes for a trip to Lowe's. "We need to leave around five if you want to eat on the road."

He paused mid-tie, a shoelace in either hand like an offering, and let her words ping around in his mind for a moment, his brain these days an overcrowded junk drawer stuffed with old receipts and half-dead batteries and rubber bands, every thought of use when he needed it but a severe hindrance when all he wanted was his daybook. Yes, somewhere in the back of the drawer was an entry—penciled in, he thought—for the play up in Charleston.

"That's tonight?" As if reiterating would change a thing.

"I planned to turn down dinner with the Kellys."

"That was a good call."

"Ever since their wedding, they've just been, I don't know."

"They're collecting friends. They don't care who we are as long as we helped fill up her dad's country club."

"I don't think it's quite that bad. They did invite us."

"No, and it was a great time. You never actually get much face-time with the bride and groom, so we got to hang out with the whole crowd except the two people we didn't care to see."

"I meant they invited us to dinner tonight."

He finished tying his shoes. He could still purchase the lights, make a plan for the installation, maybe get them in to enjoy tomorrow night. Or, hell, just get them in the ground and enjoy them any night this week. He said, "Are they going to the show?"

"I don't know. I don't think so."

"Then we don't want to do dinner with them," he said. "Right?"

She put her hand to her forehead, her fingers to her temples.

He went on, "They're going to be late and—"

"They were always punctual."

"All right, so they're punctual. But it's Saturday night, it'll take us half an hour to get a table, they'll want dessert. We'll miss the show."

"I guess."

"No, we're doing the right thing. Why don't we go a little earlier? We'll pick up a quick sandwich in town. It'll take us half an hour, plenty of time to get our seats. Do you know what time the play will be over?"

"It's a few hours. Maybe ten?"

"Jesus," he said.

"I know, but we haven't been back to Charleston in a while."

"No, it'll be good to see the city again," he said, "even if it's just for this thing. Next time, though, we should plan to make a day of it, maybe spend the night, catch up with some other people. Not the Kellys."

"I'd like that," she said.

He clamped his teeth. Was now the time to say: Let's make a day of it? Let's spend tonight? Was he meant to arrange something for the two of them? The theater was pretext, he knew, an excuse for romance in their quest to make a baby, yet he'd had ambitions for his day, to put aside thoughts of clients and his company, try not to think about the end of the world and humanity, and simply enjoy their new home. Why buy a place if you were simply going to leave it for the weekend? He said, "All right, I'm off here. I want to get a few things done before we go. You want to go to Lowe's with me?"

"Do you want me to go with you?" she asked.

"I always like your company." After a moment, he said, "Come on. Get your shoes."

So it would be the two of them.

2

The play was uninspired. "Why is it," Francine asked, "that theater people insist on being 'creative' with Shakespeare? Is there something so wrong with the play that you have to junk it up?"

"I don't know. I kind of liked it."

They were walking back to their car from the campus. The night was hot, and shadows of streetlamps cast palm-front hatchmarks on the brick sidewalks. You could hear college students yelling up and down King Street, students who, until recently, Daniel believed he could still relate to but now, with a decade on some of those students, he felt irritated by their smug confidence.

"It was gaudy and overdone," she went on, "and they changed the order of scenes around for no reason."

He laughed. "Well, I didn't notice it."

"You never took Nan's Shakespeare class. Seriously, have you ever noticed that? No one ever does just straight Shakespeare."

He thought but did not say that perhaps the problem was they kept attending performances, something he could do without. Tonight's summer Shakespeare took an Orwellian, futurist-America take on *Julius Caesar*, in which the president was assassinated by a rogue militia concerned about government expansion and the unchecked powers of the state. The tragedy of revolution was that to maintain a peaceful society after a coup, you had to resort to the same tactics as the oppressor you overthrew. It was clearly an intellectualized take on the resistance to Trump, Democratic in-fighting, and the culture of digital spying that defined the 21st century. Nevertheless, Daniel thought the production was nicely done, plus it was action-packed and had strobe lights and drumbeats. In truth he lacked an interest in literature for literature's sake, instead caring more for historical trends, material he could glean and apply to his own life. The theater, the symphony, the art museum: none of it really *moved* him, but he liked to be in a position to do these things once in a while, to afford them, to please his wife, to be able to look in the mirror and say he was a cultured man. This was the truth as well: he felt ashamed, when he thought too deeply, about his lack of ability to follow a sonata, or appreciate a book for its story, or distinguish between art and kitsch, the grand and the gauche.

Francine, however, seemed born with the ability to appreciate the arts, although he suspected her private education had something to do with it. She came from a family with high expectations of their daughter, both that she would achieve much and live a life of glamour, and that her husband would provide an income commensurate with the income her father provided their mother. Daniel was on his way to such an income, and he was proud of having scooped up the college belle, a well-bred and large-breasted blonde whose lack of real-world experience helped maintain her smooth skin and relaxed nature. She was ostensibly a freelance copywriter, but ever since they'd moved to Overlook from Charleston, this meant she had one weekly column in the local paper, occasional proofreading from a local PR agency, and a food blog where she posted recipes and photographs of every meal.

They had parked on Coming Street several blocks north of the campus, near a house where he once lived. This was below the roughest section of town, so there was no reason for concern even when a homeless man shuffled out of an alleyway. He may even have been sober. Nonetheless, Francine tightened her grip on his hand, and he had to pull her to keep moving up the street. Safely locked in their car, she clenched the handle on the door and the emergency brake as he steered them through the city's borderline rough streets. Stopped at an intersection, she closed her eyes, for outside a nearby club a line of black men and women stood with hoods and sagging pants (for the men) and provocative skirts and flaunted cleavage (for the women), while bass thumped from inside the club.

"How did we get to be so suburban soft?" he asked when they were on the highway out of town.

"I just don't feel safe there anymore."

"We survived four years of college."

"I know."

"I lived right there for a year."

"I know."

"We're turning into our parents."

"I know."

"I won't let anything happen to you."

She took his hand and squeezed.

Back at their house, it was past midnight, and she quickly went through the rituals of scrubbing off her makeup, pulling her contact lenses out, changing into old and unattractive sleepwear. He poured a glass of whiskey and turned on the television to one of the late shows, which he ignored while he pulled out his phone and sent a flirtatious text to a client he was on the verge of an affair with. She didn't respond, but then she seldom did. Therein was the allure.

3

Daniel and Francine's courtship began in earnest the spring of senior year in college, three years after their long conversation at the Philosophy Club oyster roast on Sullivan's Island. Daniel had been flashing his eyes toward every blonde he passed on campus until he finally spied Francine walking into the Starbucks beside the theater building and felt the instant shock of familiarity. He jogged across Calhoun and entered the store, which was small but had a little back terrace where he was certain he would find her. But it was empty. He returned inside and scanned the same six faces yet saw no Francine. The heavy stone of disappointment was just starting to settle in his gut when she walked out from behind the coffee bar with her hair pulled up, wearing a green apron and carrying a cup of ice water. The hairs stood up on his arm. Would she recognize him? Be happy to see him? And was she single?

When Francine saw him standing there, her mind fired back to the night on the beach, to how kind and warm and funny he'd been, and how she regretted leaving him to get in the car with her boyfriend at the time, a loser of the first order. She'd regretted it then, and thought of him over the years, in low moments. Now here he was, harried from the jog across Calhoun and looking at her like Lloyd Dobler from *Say Anything*, might as well have been holding up a boombox blasting Peter Gabriel. She took in a breath and promptly spilled a glass of water all over the counter.

"Well hey," he said. "Uh, I was just, uh, coming in for a cup of coffee."

She picked up her cup and tossed it in the trash and was looking around for a towel or something to clean up the water. Her colleague had already brought over a mop and muttered, "I got it." Francine wiped her hands on her apron and looked again at Daniel, who stood there expectantly, and she blinked and said, "Sorry? Oh! Coffee. Right. What size?"

"How have you been?" he asked as she poured a dark roast.

"Good. Um, you know. Um." She knew she sounded like an idiot, but it wasn't until she dropped the coffee cup that she paused a moment, her back to Daniel, to collect herself.

"Jesus, Francine," her colleague said. "You all right?"

"Just can't get it together today," she said.

She grabbed another cup and filled it perfectly and set it on the counter in front of Daniel, who asked, "Am I making you nervous?"

"They pay me to spill drinks. If I don't drop something every minute, they'll dock my pay."

"You should call in sick today and come out to lunch with me."

"But I'm already here," she said, already thinking that sounded like a fine idea. She'd run out of time finishing a project at the library and had not eaten.

"So what? Not like they can't handle the rush." The coffee shop had emptied completely. "Let's go get a burrito and catch up."

She looked over at her colleague, and then back at Daniel, and wondered if she would be fired for ducking out of work. Her pants were wet from the spilled coffee and she smelled like French roast.

He took her hand across the counter—he took her hand!—and said, "Don't worry about your job. Let's go have some fun."

She was surprised by the joy she felt in pulling off her apron and walking around the back of the bar and out to meet him. They might have been married already, so comfortable did she feel with him, so relaxed and lighthearted that she was unaware of the cage she was putting herself into.

4

The excitement of a college love behind them, the story of Daniel and Francine's marriage was, for the most part, dull, and the few sparks of the unusual were shamefully, and unfortunately, American. After Daniel's epic, multi-year pursuit, they dated several years while Francine pursued her master's in English. They married at twenty-five and slowly moved into their careers. Francine had entered graduate school with the vague notion of earning a doctorate and transitioning from student to professor. She loved learning and enjoyed the classroom but had little sense of how to make a career in academia. Her father owned a line of beachwear stores. His was the language of operating profit and estimated taxes and supply chains and tourist boosterism. She had little understanding of his business beyond money came in, merchandise went out, and hurricanes were to be respected out of fear. Her mother stayed at home with four daughters, the stair-step girls of whom Francine was number three, complete with middle child syndrome. She studied philosophy and English in college and for a while thought of herself as a poet. She failed to get into an MFA program and instead remained in Charleston for her master's in literary studies. She ripped her way through the postmodern canon, had a brief flirtation with a visiting DeLillo scholar who was giving a talk on simulacra and the War on Terror. Then she had another degree and at twenty-four was once again faced with carving out a life for herself. Daniel, still mooning over her, had been working as a software sales rep (cloud solutions for warehousing and distribution companies in the Carolinas), but he now found an opportunity to work for a tech startup: still in sales, but with more interesting clientele.

He told Francine he was moving to Overlook—a town he'd visited and fallen in love with, the antithesis of Cleveland, the "mistake on the lake"—and he wanted her to join him and to get married. "It's the perfect time, now that you've finished your degree," he said.

"What would I do down there?"

"What would you do if you stayed here?"

She had no answer. In her strain to finish her master's thesis, she'd decided to wait a year before applying for Ph.D. programs, and had so far done nothing to move in that direction. No letters of recommendation, no publications, no papers she could even prepare for publication. Mediocre GRE scores, no research passion, no teaching certificate. She wasn't even writing poems, or reading poetry, these days. She had adopted a golden retriever and was excited to take the dog to the park, and she liked watching obscure movies through Netflix, and she truly did love Daniel, had been won over by his dogged persistence and his natural charm and his confidence in dealing with people. Francine felt high-strung by comparison. Maybe she could get her teaching certificate (what were the requirements for that, again?) and settle into a pleasant groove near Hilton Head Island. Overlook was a non-entity, with low pressure, where you could make a modest living and go through your days without trying to impress people with your knowledge of world events, or eating at Beard Award restaurants, or attempting to intellectualize every facet of human existence: the Lacanian theory behind her love for her dog, the panoptical gaze of grocery store cashiers, violence and the sacred at the dinner table. (It didn't take much to convince her that she was not cut out for scholarship, or what passed for scholarship today.) Her oldest sister had gone through medical school and was saving babies—literally saving babies—in her residency as an obstetrician, while her next oldest sister was working for Deloitte in New York, doing God knows what, telling businesses how to operate or something, while her younger sister married straight out of UVA with honors and had become a near-perfect homemaker. No, a life off the grid in Overlook sounded just transgressive enough to satisfy her ego, an easy out to save face for her floundering twenties, so she married Daniel the next year and began thinking about babies.

That too became one more place of failure to round out her twenties. As a co-ed, she'd been staggeringly dishonest with herself about what she wanted from life: independence, she would have said. To remain a free spirit. To make an impact on the world. She would have said all of those things when her subconscious had other ideas. Buried in her psyche, a story about her life was already written, a story about marriage and children and raising a family. A story she was on her way toward living when she married Daniel, but which derailed once the challenges of conception began. Years later, when she began writing YA novels under her maiden name, she found solace in her power to manipulate her characters and sculpt the story herself.

Daniel, meanwhile, was suffering his own private agony: boredom with what passed for real life in twenty-first century America. He'd spent his college years buried in the past, studying great men and thinking about Cold War foreign policy. Of the two, he was the one meant for life as a professor—that, or a plum position at a think tank. He wrestled with ideas and kept up with the news and was unsurprised when the situation in Iraq deteriorated. *Those assholes have read Thucydides, but it's like they skipped all of modern history,* he railed to anyone who would listen in 2003, 2004, 2005. *France, Russia, China, Cuba: name one country other than the U.S. that had a successful revolution that didn't immediately devolve into guerrilla warfare and an eventual dictatorship.* But like Francine, he graduated with limited ambitions other than to find a job and enjoy the beach and avoid going back to Ohio to work for his father or one of his father's cronies.

Sales was a safe fallback in America, and with a well-proof-read resume and a few weeks of knocking on doors, Daniel found his first job, which involved making lots of phone calls, reading dull technical reports, and making routine visits to warehouses and factories around the state. In the two years on this job, he learned several things about himself and the world, among them:

- No one cared about history. People loved to learn some neat factoid (*Did you know Napoleon Bonaparte invented Chicken Marengo while fighting the Austrians?*) but had little use for the application of history's lessons to current events. If you tried to engage someone in such a discussion, there was a fifty-fifty chance they would bring out the old saw: "Those who don't understand history are doomed to repeat it." *What does that even mean?* he wanted to shout.

- He was good at sales and enjoyed making money. If you couldn't be saving babies like Francine's sister, you might as well settle for doing something you're good at and that brings in enough income to buy what you want to buy when you want to buy it. One advantage of living today was that immediate gratification was as much a requisite as running water, practically a utility in modern life.

- Much of South Carolina, however, was no place for grat-ification. Greenville-Spartanburg and Columbia and Charleston had enough going for them that you could feel like you were part of the world, but they were in many ways unbearably conservative, cloistered backwaters with merely a sheen of cosmopolitanism. The rest of the state, the small towns and decrepit crossroads, had any number of minor factories (run by robots), or distribution centers (fifty-foot high mazes of brown boxes), with the same earnest good old boy at the helm. Overweight, balding, divorced, a pack of Camel Lights in his breast pocket. Pleasant enough to be around for ten minutes, a torture to spend the day with, and a nightmare vision of one possible future in this life.

- You didn't have to be that guy. You could still achieve a kind of greatness in the way you lived, and what you made from the opportunities and experiences at hand. He had no future selling warehouse management software—the company was too big, too global, the corporate ladder too fragmented—but getting involved in a startup would mean as the company grew he would be among the founding employees, grandfathered into the executive level. He might even be able to retire by forty if things went well enough.

5

By the time of the accident, they'd been married seven years and were living the model lives of the upwardly mobile. They owned a Keurig and a first-generation Nest thermostat and a trashcan with a motion-sensor lid and a house big enough for a family of five to live comfortably. They had a French press, and a four-slot toaster, and a cabinet full of red KitchenAid mixers, blenders, and food processers. They had a Roomba! Surely children were just around the corner, so they were enjoying what they thought were their final seasons of freedom.

On summer nights, Daniel cooked a pasta dishes that they enjoyed al fresco on the back patio.

"This looks lovely," she said on one of those nights.

"Chicken scampi with lemon cream sauce," he said when he set the dish in front of her. "I was able to use the first lemons from the new tree."

It was mid-June, before the hottest of weather struck. The days were long so that even with dinner at eight, twilight was still half an hour away. "I had to swing by the grocery before I got too far," he said by way of apology for the delay.

"That's fine. I've got nowhere to be." She took a sip of chardonnay.

"That new Piggly Wiggly still has a few kinks to work out. It took me forever to find everything."

"You should have gone to the Publix," she told him.

"That's all the way out on 278."

"Well, you spent the time either way."

"Anyway," he said after a bite. "Tastes good to me."

"It's very good."

"I didn't realize until I was unloading the groceries that I accidentally bought kosher salt," he confessed. She was finicky about her groceries, he knew.

She chuckled.

"What?"

"Nothing."

"No, what? The salt?"

"There's a difference."

"You've got a whole pantry full of different salts," he said, laughing. "Iodized, kosher, sea salt. I can't keep it all straight, and it's all sodium chloride, isn't it?"

"Yes, but kosher salt has bigger crystals than regular salt."

"I thought that was the sea salt?"

"It is. The sea salt has big crystals, kosher salt has medium, and table salt has the smallest."

"So what's the difference?"

She shrugged.

"There's no difference," he said, returning to the scampi. They were both grinning at this point. "There's not," he said a moment later. "Okay, I get that sea salt has big fat flakes, but it's all dissolved in the liquid. It doesn't matter."

She shrugged again.

"Why do they call it kosher salt? What makes it kosher?"

"I don't know."

"I thought you were supposed to know these things."

"Honey, we both know this isn't my strong suit. You'll have to ask my father."

"Lord, that'll go over well."

"He might be glad you're taking an interest. I never did."

Like his own Christian childhood, Francine's Jewish upbringing was in name only, or so she liked to contend. Her mother may have been indifferent, but her father insisted on all the Byzantine rituals that Daniel could never completely figure out. He knew her father was never happier than when the family came together for the Passover Seder and he could play the patriarch, the one time a year his wife ceded authority. They'd welcomed Daniel into the family, and if there was any reluctance they hid it well and paid for a traditional Jewish wedding for Daniel and Francine, which Daniel had to explain to his own parents, stoic Midwesterners who seemed incapable of understanding the sensitivities of an interfaith marriage. Her family was all talk-talk-talk, break the glass, whereas his family relied on subtext and innuendo to convey meaning. Somewhere in college, Daniel had lost patience with indirection, which he viewed as weakness, and he appreciated Francine and her family's ability to spit it out, whatever it was. Yet his protestant reticence reared itself on matters of family. His mother had said more than once something along the lines of, "If you decide to have children, and if you decide to have them baptized, we hope you'll do it at St. Paul's. This will always be home, you know." "Yeah, Mom, we'll see," he'd say, every time, knowing already that any children they had would not be raised in his parents' church, and believing in his heart that science carried the day and that religion had served its purpose.

When they finished the scampi, he cleared their plates and brought out the bottle of wine to refill their glasses. "I'm fine," she said.

"You sure?"

"I'm happy to sit out here with you."

He filled his glass with a few ounces more than he needed, to kill the bottle. The strain of trying to get pregnant was in front of them, when they would both quit drinking and he would take up exercise in a way he hadn't done since he was a freshman in college and walked across town nearly every day with his roommate to go to the gym. Fresh squeezed orange juice with ginger, almonds, oysters, all the foods that allegedly increased your sperm count. He felt little panic, being a man and having no timeline, but over the coming year Francine would grow edgy, and he would begin to appreciate his parents' stoicism, their ability to communicate without having to communicate. It was a conservative life of ritual, perhaps not all that different from Francine's family. He would learn, in their efforts to conceive, that ritual went a long way toward keeping you grounded. But tonight, that was all in the future. Tonight, he enjoyed a full glass of wine on their patio, Francine's hand over his, the stars emerging as the twilight cooled and night settled in.

Later they went upstairs and made love, his head in a fog from the wine, and he fell asleep without reflection, hardly conscious of her as she went to the bathroom and then put on a t-shirt and shorts, dead to the world when she snuggled up against him beneath the covers. He woke in the night and glanced over at the clock, but couldn't read the time. The numbers glowed green, and the green light emanated throughout the room: the chair with the never-ending pile of laundry, the trinkets and knick-knacks Francine kept on her dresser, the smoke detector plugged into the ceiling. He was still naked beside her but lacked the energy to get dressed. Before he drifted off again, he thought about his life and what he'd achieved—a wife, a house, a steady income—and what he would still like to do. He still believed there was some greatness in his future, something he would do or stature he would achieve, but his imagination failed him as to what it might be. Some great thing, was all, and he fell asleep again without any answers.

6

It was difficult, for a layperson, to understand what exactly his company in Overlook did. Data Dare Inc. (a Latin redundancy translating to *the gifts to give*) was the brainchild of one Marcus Van Bergen, a former sales colleague of Daniel's who went into business with Walter Cox, CFO, and Ellen Briggs, CIO. Daniel had not been offered a voting partnership but was one of three other founding employees to receive a plum salary with stock options, and his primary role was to serve as the lead sales guy. "This thing's going to sell itself," Marcus said over drinks at the start of it all, "so we're going to need you to do more than sales. This is all-hands-on-deck, true business collaboration, from product offerings to consulting to the furniture we buy for the office. Put whatever you want on your business card," he added. "Someone should be called Chief Imagination Officer. Ellen, you want that?"

"Information, imagination, it's all the same, right?"

"Love it," Marcus said. "And Daniel, what do you think? Chief Connections Officer?"

"Whatever you say, boss."

"Ha! Get bent."

They clicked glasses and the company was established. Daniel and Marcus had come out of software sales, while Marcus had known Ellen and Walter since college and poached them from successful roles in the Fortune 500. Marcus could do that, Daniel knew. He didn't belong in the business world, at least not in the southeast. Marcus was a lanky rubber band of a man gone prematurely bald but with a neat red beard that squared his face, and, because he was now an entrepreneur and lived in a climate that seldom dipped below sixty degrees, his daily uniform was a pair of Birkenstocks, tan or olive green Duck Head shorts, and a button-down safari shirt, all of which made him look like a knotty-limbed zookeeper rather than a tech visionary. But he had a master's in economics from George Mason University, where he was a Mercatus Fellow and fell under the wing of a handful of futurists whose ideas and worldview convinced him: (1) to invest in cryonics so that some future generation could bring him back to life in the form of a brain emulation, (2) the wealth gap was about to get bigger as "doers" became commoditized and "makers" reaped all the rewards, and (3) big data was his golden ticket to life as a maker. True, the term *big data* became a media catchphrase when it became clear to the rest of America that our lives were being digitally archived and analyzed and repackaged for marketers. Marcus was rather fond of the word *dataveillance*, a more accurate expression of what he saw happening, which was nothing less than the shift of old-school espionage tricks into the corporate realm. Surveillance relied on images, observations, and informants, whereas dataveillance was about analyzing trends in the paper trail, or the metadata stamp of 1's and 0's.

Their company's biggest coup—the one that made Daniel's eyes light up and gave him a reason to get out of bed in the morning—was a pro bono research institute Marcus hooked up with through one of his old graduate school professors. The Human Survival Project, or HSP, brought together futurists, psychologists, statisticians, evolutionary biologists, geologists, astrophysicists, paleontologists, economists, and other researchers all interested in the field of human extinction. Some saw the tech singularity around the corner, when artificial intelligence and human-machine interfaces would render old-school analog humanity as obsolete as an 8-track tape or a rotary telephone. How would we get along with our digital overlords, they wondered. Would we be like zoo animals, kept around for amusement, or would we be deemed a threat to annihilate a la *The Terminator?* Other researchers were less concerned about whether we would survive the singularity—so named because, the argument went, the pace of technological change was climbing exponentially and would soon shoot up toward infinity such that it was impossible to foresee what lay beyond that singular asymptote—but rather, what do computer-augmented humans do next?

"There's a strong case that we're currently living in a simu-lated world," the head researcher said when the Data Dare team visited the HSP headquarters in Boston.

"I'm sorry, what?" Daniel asked.

Four of them—Marcus, Ellen, Daniel, and a British researcher named Quirk—sat in plush leather chairs in a fifth-story atrium with glass walls and a Hollywood view of the Charles River and the foliage-front of MIT.

"The idea is that some time in the future, after this singu-larity—although I don't really like the term 'singularity,' as such—

we will develop the ability to run historical simulations." He nodded to Daniel. "You said you were a history major. Imagine not just reading about some historical event, but being able to run an actual flesh-and-blood simulation of a Civil War battle."

"Like virtual reality?" Daniel asked.

"Something like that. The medium might not exist yet, but, yes, you could immerse yourself in the world, or just watch it from the outside, like television, or *The Sims*. And as we know, once you do something once, chances are you're going to replicate it. In the case of technology, replication means millions, if not billions, of times. You make one iPhone, it's fun and successful, and suddenly you have a planet of them."

"You think everyone on the planet is going to be running Civil War simulations."

"Why not? We'll probably have figured out how to live forever, so you have to give future generations something to do. Ancestral simulations sound like great fun. Get to know your great-granddad Benjamin Quirk, eh?"

"What does that have to do with us living in one of these simulations?" Daniel asked.

"Well, at this point, it's just a matter of probability. If you make a billion simulations, what are the odds that you're in the 'original' world? Next to zero. So if we ever make one simulation, you can guarantee we're all living in one of the many billion simulations that will be created."

Marcus grinned at the prospect and asked Quirk what were the odds we'd create a computer simulation.

"You know, this is all a bit speculative, and I should add I'm not the one who has proposed this theory, and I don't know if I would say I even endorse it."

"We're not the press here," Marcus said. "We're not going to put this in the *New York Times*. We're just here to learn what all goes on here so we can best help you with your research. Now come on, what are the odds we're in a simulation right now?"

Quirk shook his head. "Some of my colleagues put it at one in five. The idea being that we might never get to the computer processing power necessary to run these kinds of simulations, or we might quit on ethical grounds (though I doubt it), or we might blow ourselves up, or just never figure it out. You have those four possibilities, or…"

"Or we create a simulation," Marcus finished, "in which case we're some teenage history geek's science experiment."

"Do you really think people will one day want to just make up a world?" Daniel asked. "Without taking responsibility for the ethics inside it?"

"Look, most of us here are scientists. We all have some kind of moral grounding, and we talk over lunch about the ethical frameworks of our research, but at the end of the day, we're too damn excited about that next discovery to worry too much about it. You're in the information business. We're in the knowledge business, and in our world, Eve has already bitten from the apple. We've already been cast out of the garden, so our best hope is to gain even more knowledge to stay ahead of whatever's out there. Who knows? There's a super volcano under Yellowstone that could kill us all next week, or maybe there's an asteroid with our name on it. If we stick around long enough, this planet is done for, even if we don't do ourselves in with climate change or nuclear warfare. Whether it's a singularity a generation or two down the line, or another million years, if humans are going to survive, we have to keep innovating and think about where in the cosmos we might go."

"Brain emulations!" Marcus said, and Daniel was starting to wish he'd stayed home. Gone to Home Depot to buy a bag of Milorganite to help the grass through late summer.

"That's one possibility," the researcher went on. "We create a giant server, download our brains, and blast off into the Milky Way. But to your point," he said to Ellen, "maybe there's an answer somewhere in the past. You go back to study ancient civilizations, they're not primitive. Their societies might have collapsed before they could really get somewhere, by our terms, but the Greeks or the Persians—any one of them could have stumbled onto the steam engine and launched themselves into the future. The sole reason the Industrial Revolution occurred when it did was we had some form of stable society that allowed our population to boom. Any scientist will tell you that every great invention had more than one inventor behind it. Someone just got it into product development first, but very few ideas are one-of-a-kind. That's the value of studying the past, is to watch for good ideas that just didn't germinate. Maybe the person was killed in the Holocaust, or got hit by a bus, or just couldn't put all the pieces together. There's a job for a company like yours in the future: creating simulations and mining the data for good ideas that were discarded."

"Exactly," Marcus said, as though he would personally be around to see the business proposition through. "And Daniel can tell you about that. You were a history major, weren't you?"

"What? Yeah," Daniel said slowly. "But what you're talking about, that doesn't tackle the ethics of creating simulations. You're talking about souls who love and know loss, and you're manipulating them."

"I'm doing no such thing," Quirk said. "I told you, I'm not necessarily endorsing this idea, but what I will say, again, is that if we ever create one of these simulations, we're most certainly living in one. And what does that say about our own souls? Or our own creator? I wouldn't be too quick to judge the morality of some kid who created you out of thin air and can hit delete any time he wanted."

7

"He actually said that," Daniel said later, at dinner with Karen Sinclair at Libretto's, less than two hours before he would hit and kill Samantha James on Reedy Road. "He actually told me not to insult my creator."

"That's blasphemy," Karen said. As she swallowed a bite of pasta, he thought about what he was going to do tonight. He'd picked up a vibe from Karen and no longer trusted himself around her. Until recently, he'd believed himself comfortably tethered, far past thoughts of other women—married for too long, cognizant of the business relationship between him and Karen, conscious of his weight, which had ballooned in the two years on the job with Data Dare—but he could no longer deny the body had its own mysterious way of working. He felt a tingle at the sound of her voice, behind the dactylic *blasphemy* was a long itch followed by two quick scratches. *Come do me.*

He took a gulp of wine and said, "Those guys are operating on a different plane altogether. I always thought Marcus was cerebral—which he is, don't get me wrong."

"But he's selling software rather than saving humanity," she finished.

He took another long sip of wine.

"I know I shouldn't ask about it," she said, "but what do you think is going on with him and Ellen?"

"Who, Marcus? I don't know. What do you mean?"

"I mean, I always thought they were a couple."

"You did, huh?"

"Jeez, Daniel, you're supposed to be helping me with information, and I have to tell you what's going on in your shop? She and I are in a wine and design class together, and last time I saw her, she seemed, I don't know, off. A little squirrelly, like she'd been caught coming out of someone's motel room. Did she have her own room while you all were up there?"

"I don't know anything about that," he said.

At this Karen put her foot against Daniel's. It could have been an accident of readjustment, but he knew it wasn't and that if he weren't careful, he soon might end up in the wrong motel room himself. The only question was whether he could shut it down before the genie came out of the bottle. Later, he would feel shame that Francine was nowhere in his mind tonight—not a fond anchor, not a nagging guilt, just an absence—but the wine had gone to his head, and to his crotch, and all he could think about was the fluid way that Karen Sinclair moved her head as she ate, and the unreserved and watery gaze she held him with as she talked.

8

Francine wanted a baby that never came. What had she been thinking in college, when life had endless possibilities spread out before her like a sea with no horizon? One of a quartet of sisters, a mezzo-soprano with a keen eye for image and a love of stories, Francine wrote her way through high school, wore neckties to be provocative, fell in with the theater crowd, did everything she could to gain a voice at the dinner table, to pull her father away from the headache of payroll and accounts reconciliation (the rewards of owning his own business and living out the American dream, all the more American for his Israeli heritage), and in college she fell in with a musician—a cellist, mind you, not some shaggy tramp of a drummer. She never worried about money, never even understood it, for her father was too kind-hearted to allow any of his girls—and that's what he called him, *his girls*, a proud moniker from a man outnumbered—to go hungry. When she called up with an overdrafted bank account, he simply asked her how much she needed, and when she said, truthfully, "I don't know," he offered her five hundred. Happy days of dazzling discussion, close readings of Elizabeth Bishop and John Berryman, reflections on the nature of reality and the ethos of doubt, and then she was a senior facing the next big thing.

The cellist was long gone when Daniel Hayward showed up in her life as one possibility. He was handsome, and confident, and pleasantly obtuse about much of the world, but Francine was clear with him: she too had her ambitions. She might join him in his quest for greatness, as his partner, but she foresaw a life of scholarship, toiling away as a poet in obscurity, which required a master of fine arts and a lucky break that never came. The luck all went to Daniel, it seemed, so she found herself married and moving into a tremendous house and losing sight of why she ever wanted to be an artist. She would later call her college self a dilettante, with a roll of her eyes. This would be much later, after Daniel, when she found success as a young adult author, on book tour, doing the marketing shuffle, business-minded and cynical about the artist-nobody-reads. But between her flamboyantly artistic college years and her ROI-conscious publication years, there was Daniel. The love of her life, it seemed.

What they didn't tell you was that having a baby at thirty was a different animal from having a baby at twenty-two. Her youngest sister, Lydia, almost like a rebellion against the free-spirited Francine, had found a mate, married him, and had two babies already with a house in the suburbs of Greenville. Francine had scoffed at that—joked with Daniel about how her sister had not even gotten the chance to live her own life, and what would happen when her sister woke up thirty-five and furious that she didn't know who she was or what she wanted out of life—but the joke was on Francine. Poor Francine, who a few years later, on the other side of thirty, wanted nothing more than a baby but appeared to be barren. At least that was how she felt every month when the stick came back negative yet again, despite all the scheduling and the timing and the romantic evenings and the different positions and the holding up her feet after sex to keep the semen in: all of it was a farce! Meanwhile, Lydia at twenty-eight and juggling two babies younger than three, had a seventy thousand a year shoe sales business on Etsy. One more thing Francine didn't understand. She took a modest comfort in knowing her older sisters were no happier than she, Jamie working all hours and lacking any semblance of a social life, and Ruth having broken off a recent engagement to a fine man to pursue an affair with a married one.

When she and Daniel first started trying for a baby, eighteen months ago, Francine had no cause to believe the world was against her. She'd been thirty-two, beautiful, and successful in her own way. Daniel's career was on the rise, and she was finding enough freelance work to feel like she was contributing to the family, and she assumed pregnancy would work the same way, that she would stop taking birth control and after a couple of months she would be picking out colors for the nursery. The first month, when her period came, no big deal. She wasn't expecting it on the first shot. The second month, it started to hurt a little. After all, she'd timed their love-making for when she was ovulating, but still, she told herself, no big deal. She'd been on birth control for a decade, so it might take some time to settle out. At the end of the sixth month, Daniel could hear her peeing on the stick, and would hear the telltale thump when it hit the trash can in disappointment, a single line on the readout mocking her. Why this, the single line on the pregnancy test? She prayed regularly for the first time since she was a teenager, and felt her God had forsaken her, just as she'd forsaken Him during her heathen years. All those months—more than a hundred—she'd taken the birth control pill religiously to avoid pregnancy, and now she felt like she was having payback.

At nine months—long enough to have grown and birthed a baby—she had an appointment with her OB-GYN, who told her these things can take time, a baby will come, everything looked good. "Give it another six months," the doctor said. "It could be stress. It might be good if you both stopped drinking. Consider taking a vacation."

"But we already live in paradise," Francine said.

"The change of scenery is what's important."

Francine got dressed again. Even though she didn't work out of an office, she still liked to dress professionally, in dark pants and button-down blouses, and today she wore the pair of mint earrings Daniel had gotten her for her birthday. She felt them dangling from her earlobes, swinging when she turned her head toward the doctor. It helped to focus on something small and tactile, because she felt her body had betrayed her and everything below her waist was once again a mystery.

"You'll be all right," the doctor was saying. "And if nothing happens in another few months, we can start some testing, but I have a feeling you'll have good news before the new year."

That, too, had been a joke, because in January they crossed the one-year mark of trying with no results, and she could feel Daniel growing frustrated with her. He'd given up drinking, or said he had, but she could sense his stress and dissatisfaction in the way he made love, no longer a joy but rather a mechanical chore to get through before going back to watch a ball game downstairs, leaving Francine to lie in bed with her feet propped on a pillow, to cry and pray alone.

Daniel was still a good man. She recognized that, even if he sometimes failed to treat her with kindness. Or, not a lack of kindness, but rather a lack of attention, a frustration at the situation between them.

One night at dinner he cracked open a third beer and she gave him a look.

"What?"

"You know what."

"A second beer won't hurt anything."

"You remember what Tom and Katie said." Tom and Katie were older friends in the neighborhood who swore the secret to having a child once you were on the other side of thirty was simply to quit drinking, as if God rewarded teetotaling with a bounty of children.

"They got lucky," he said. "That's all it is. It's just statistics."

"You know what the statistics say about children born to women over 35. How the rate of birth defects spikes."

"Stop reading the internet," he said before taking a long swig of his beer. "We're not that old. We've got plenty of time."

In February, they visited a fertility specialist for testing, and found out Daniel's count was plentiful. He had an overabundance, was fertile, fecund, exuberant with sperm, so the problem lay with her. The doctor said her blood tests came back normal, prescribed her a low dose of Clomid, and said the next steps, which they could begin any time, would be a few rounds of intrauterine insemination, followed by discussion of in vitro fertilization. Neither she nor Daniel spoke as they left the doctor, stopped by Target to fill the prescription, and went home to their spacious, hollow home. Daniel was overly kind to her that evening, cooked her dinner, asked if she wanted to make love, which she did not. She could hardly stand his condescending gaze, eyes that said, *I'm bringing everything to the table here.* He chattered on about his work, a client up in Boston that would require a business trip. "The Human Survival Project," he said. "They're researching the end of the world."

"Great," she mumbled.

"Hey, I know it was a tough day. I know it was. If I could wave a wand to fix it, I would."

"But you can't."

"But I can't."

"Maybe it's just as well," she said. "If the world is coming to an end, maybe it's better that we don't bring a child into it."

"Hey, that's not true."

"You just said it. Natural disasters, nuclear bombs, accelerating technology, the human race is on its last days."

"No, no, these guys are researching possibilities. It doesn't mean anything's going to pass. It's just like insurance. Buying car insurance doesn't mean you're going to get in a wreck, right?"

"Whatever. I have a headache."

"Francine." He put a hand over hers to keep her at the dinner table. She indulged him, hoping against hope he might have some miraculous comment that would make her feel better. "We'll get there. We just have to take the long view."

"Thirty-five is coming fast."

She was obsessed with her age, as if her clock would start winding down the moment she crossed into middle age. "And lots of people have children older than that," he said.

"This isn't helping."

"I'm sorry," he said. "Hey, why don't we take a long weekend somewhere, when I get back? We can go to the Bahamas or something."

"We live in paradise," she said, same as she'd told her OB.

"So we'll go to Ontario. Isn't there a Shakespeare festival up there you've talked about going to? The place doesn't matter. It's about taking a break, you and me."

"I'll think about it," she said, and she went up to bed.

What she wanted was for him to read her mind, to follow her up and keep talking to her, draw her out of what was fast approaching a depression, make her feel something, warm her up, impregnate her. Take care of her.

Instead, she listened to him clear the table and wash dishes, and then she heard the TV click on to the day's sports highlights. She fell asleep soon after, and didn't wake up when he came to bed.

That was how it was from February through July. The Clomid changed nothing. She felt the same, continued timing her ovulations, continued making love with Daniel in the same distant way. It was less frequent now, less urgent, and neither of them mentioned the next step with the fertility treatments. It was a spring and summer of stalemate, where neither spouse knew how to break the lines. Daniel seemed unable to reach her, unable to find whatever fire in his belly would inspire him to take charge and manage the schedule of their ovulations (for they weren't simply *her* ovulations, not in this endeavor; it was *her* body, *her* failure, she felt, but this was a joint task). And Francine? Her neurochemistry had gone awry. Perhaps it was the medication or the year of disappointment, but she felt as though walking through water, where it was a struggle to wake every morning. Her freelance work nearly dried up, and she spent long hours at the library, laptop open, surfing the internet and checking her email as though salvation were one unread message in her inbox away. She sometimes drove over to the island for lunch, and more than once had considered jerking the wheel and spinning off into the water. She could see it: the flat water of the sound rising up, the splash on the windshield, the gradual darkness as the car sank lower and lower and filled with cold seawater. The only other thing that could have broken the stalemate was a baby, but of course every month, like clockwork, her period arrived, and she resigned herself to waiting out the next cycle.

Daniel went on his business trip to the Human Survival Project headquarters, and he returned on a Tuesday with his mind abuzz over the metaphysical possibilities. He seemed evasive to her, and he kept bringing up the idea that life was nothing more than a computer simulation.

"How does that even work?" she asked one night in exasperation. "I don't know about you, but I know I have a consciousness. I'm not some simulation."

"No, no, we would all be simulated consciousnesses."

"But how could anyone have access to my mind? I get that we might all be programmed animals, but I think, therefore I exist. I'm not just some made-up being."

"I'm not saying I've got all the answers, I'm just telling you what they're researching," Daniel said. "I thought you'd find it interesting."

It was all coming back to her, those college classes on human nature and epistemology. Abstract analytics had never been her strong suit. She was a *no-ideas-but-in-things* poet, and even though she hadn't written a poem in years, or even read a book of poetry, she was still that gal at heart.

She said, "I guess I just don't like the idea of it. What would be the point of living if life were just a construct of some other person's imagination?"

"How would you say that's any different from religion?"

"I don't share your people's belief in an old man God conjuring up the world in seven days. That's never made any sense to me," she said, and even as she said it, she felt a twinge of guilt, for this was exactly the God she'd been praying to all these nights for a baby.

"Well, I can't help you if you're not open to the discussion," he said to shut things down.

"You always do this."

"Do what?"

"You always try to start some conversation about your work, and about the way the world is changing and how you and Marcus and the team are doing all these great things to get ahead, and when I raise any point of skepticism, you always just shut down. Can't I have an opinion? Can't you, for once, just let me put my head in the sand about the end of humanity, and take my side?"

"It's not about taking sides," he said. "It's just a conversation."

"No, this is a trial, and I feel like I'm in the defendant's seat."

"You're not on trial for anything," he said, but he said it kindly, apologetically, knowing full well they were no longer talking about his work and the Human Survival Project. They both intuited that there are some things you can't say, some bridges you can't cross—especially in a marriage—and they quietly retreated from this No Man's Land.

"I've got a few more business meetings this week, so I won't be home for dinner on Thursday."

"That's fine," she said. "I'll make some pasta for myself. Are you around this weekend?"

"All weekend's free."

"Good."

They'd never taken that trip, and he hadn't even brought it up once the travel season opened. She'd been hoping he might just surprise her with two tickets to the Stratford Shakespeare Festival, but he'd buried himself in his business this year, worked long hours, sixty, seventy hours a week. She would have applauded it, his industriousness and the way they were saving money, if they'd had anything to save for, but there it was. The money was worthless, empty materialism.

She opened a glass of wine that night, after they'd cooled off, and said, simply, "I'll stop if anything happens."

"No, no, you deserve a glass now and again."

"You want any?"

"Sure." He accepted a glass like Adam accepting the illicit fruit in the garden, guiltily but with a sense of mischievous pleasure at breaking the rules. Human nature.

She drank several glasses that night, and the night after, and on the Thursday night of the hit and run. She went to bed early that evening, thoroughly drunk from three glasses of Riesling, read a few pages of a paperback novel, and turned out the light. She thought nothing of Daniel's business meeting, figured he and Marcus went out afterward for a few beers. Maybe her husband could let off some steam, and maybe—maybe—Marcus might have some words of wisdom. She doubted it. Daniel's boss was a bachelor and relished that lifestyle, so although Marcus was the older man, Daniel in many ways was the more mature. She went to sleep believing this her last night of stalemate in this protracted war between her and her husband. The grenade pin had already been pulled, the timer set, and tomorrow she would come out of the trenches in surrender and look for the next thing.

9

Daniel was sensitive to his wife's thoughts as they tried for a baby, the excitement, the need, the schedules, the dread, the disappointment, the perseverance, the inferiority, the panic. He tried to stay with her at every step, went into the room at the fertility doctor's with the magazine and the cup, was prepared for the bad news to fall on his shoulders, held her in the night and told her it would be all right. The truth, however, was that he was exhausted. They were no longer the same people as when they met in college. Like the fabled ship that over time is rebuilt plank by plank with new lumber and picks up a completely new crew: is it still the same ship? In the ten years they'd known each other, their cells had reproduced many times over, and while they each had one continuous train of thoughts and experiences that led them from A to Z, point Z was so far removed from point A that, had they met today, he suspected they might not even connect. He'd felt the thunderbolt in college, fresh out of an all-boys high school and overwhelmed by the sunny South. Now he had a career and confidence, and less tolerance for what he perceived as her neuroses. This cut both ways: he knew she, too, had grown into herself and might find him ill-mannered and materialistic, always fiddling with the bank accounts, always chewing on his fingernails.

Such is the nature of a marriage. Time passes, you evolve, you grow comfortable, you forget to keep the mystery and the surprise, and then one day you look at each other and realize this is good, but it's not great, and you can't figure out how to fix it. Time lashes on.

After the regrettable trip to Charleston to see *Julius Caesar*, Daniel had taken the trip to Boston to tour the facilities of the Human Survival Project, and he'd come home swirling over the ideas he'd encountered. He'd not felt such energy since he was in college: the significance of their work astounded him. Here he was, schlepping around with software sales literature, trying to help businesses improve their margins through data analysis, and his new client, meanwhile, was literally working to save the human race. If he ever had a child, that child's future would depend on the work they were doing at HSP. That's what he'd tried to convey to Francine Tuesday evening, when the discussion devolved into bickering, the subtext being that if the human race was doomed, maybe it was a good thing they couldn't conceive. He didn't believe that, but he also couldn't shake the suspicion that their lives were much more fragile than he'd previously believed, and that the structures around them, in America, were nothing but a Potemkin village put on for show.

Karen Sinclair understood him. There was little else to be said of their short-lived flirtation. As a client, she kept in regular contact with him, and she had an old-fashioned appreciation for a long, cocktail-infused business lunch. He was forthright with his wife about these lunches, how he and Karen would split a bottle of wine or enjoy a few bourbon cocktails (she drank hers neat, whereas he preferred Coke and ice), after which he would have to take the rest of the day off to recuperate. His job was sales, but even he found it difficult to keep up with Karen's energy and wit. She was firm, vibrant, and had long and wavy ash-blond hair with penetrating, watery eyes that simultaneously gave too much of herself away while making herself a complete mystery. He knew her marriage ended more miserably than most. From what Daniel gathered, her husband, for no clear reason, decided he no longer loved her and walked out one night never to return. The blow was doubled because Karen was already in her thirties, left with neither husband nor child and a racing clock against which she might never recover. The ex-husband remarried quickly and now had a mess of children, it seemed, which left Daniel baffled. You never knew about people in their private lives, but Karen seemed to him worthy in every way: beautiful, intelligent, the kind of woman you wanted to spend time with not only because she was intrinsically interesting but because she made you feel good about yourself.

So here he was, a few hours before the hit and run changed everything, out with Karen Sinclair and pretending everything was ordinary. "I'm sure Trump will be reelected," she said, her foot still resting against his. They'd drained the bottle of Zinfandel and still not indicated what would happen after he dropped her off, what dinner might mean for their relationship.

"You think?"

"I can't stand him, but yeah. You think anything about Ukraine or Russia or all these indictments is going to change people's minds? I have family in the upstate, and they all have an entirely different narrative about what's going on."

"I don't know. I think the people who voted for him, all those manufacturing guys up in Michigan? They see him for what he is."

"Maybe some of them, but what do they care? They knew he wasn't going to build them a literal factory, and they like that he's standing up to Mexico and China. And who's going to do anything better? I like Warren, but people don't want a woman running things."

He was silent for a moment before saying, "I could get on board with Warren. I voted for Hillary, so I don't know."

"They're going to eat themselves alive," she said, without tipping her hand to which way she leaned, politically. "You just watch."

"Uh huh."

While Francine dozed at home, Daniel polished off another glass of wine. He wasn't quite drunk—he weighed over two hundred pounds and had eaten enough carbs to sop up most of the Zinfandel in his belly—but he was buzzing past the point of wanting to take Karen Sinclair home and toss her onto a flat surface. One glass of wine ago, maybe, but now he was starting to get tired and believed he'd be unable to perform. The sadness of adulthood washed over him, and he understood the way affairs worked: one mistake after another, until, somewhere along the way, with neither intention nor initiation, it simply became your life. He could still right the course. Steady the ship. One indiscreet moment followed by freedom.

He paid the check with his corporate credit card, and waited for her while she went to the restroom. The restaurant had emptied out so they were one of the last tables. One of the waiters was sweeping the carpet; another rolling silverware; the hostess sat at the front and played with her iPhone. He hadn't recognized anyone except the staff, and he trusted waiters were discreet about who they served, should Daniel ever return with his wife. He ate one of the complimentary mints and said, "Let's do it," when Karen asked if he was ready.

"Have a good night," the hostess said on their way out.

"You too," Daniel said. He stopped for a toothpick and then shuffled after Karen.

They said little on the ride home. She asked if he had any more business trips coming up, and he told her no, he was home-bound for a while, and then they listened to a few classic rock hits in what turned out to be comfortable silence. Karen lived in a tony apartment complex fortified by gray Hardie Plank siding and chemical-green shrubbery. He suspected she'd once lived in a fine house with that bastard husband, and had downsized after the split. He didn't pry for details. None of his business, for one, and with anyone much older than thirty, he'd learned, you had to be careful what you asked about. In your twenties, you can make all kinds of mistakes, date the wrong person, flunk out of college, drink too much, and you can still rebound and become successful. In your thirties, you run out of second chances, and he was starting to see more and more people sliding into middle age with genuine baggage: exes who were abusive, children to care for, the kind of career missteps you didn't come back from. To ask for details was to risk invading some truly personal territory, and you had to be on very good terms with someone to enter that space. Some people would volunteer the truth of their lives, but those were the kind of people who tended to live with too many cats, and might be better off on some form of medication.

He and Karen had a good time, and were able to flirt and talk business and keep each other company without dredging up any skeletons, and he aimed to keep it that way when he found a visitor's parking space and turned off the car. His mind fuzzy with wine and his moral bearing wavering like a compass needle too close to a magnet. He took a deep breath. He wasn't on a runaway train. The answer was sheer willpower. Making the right choice today, and tomorrow, and every day after.

"I'll walk you to your door," he said.

"The perfect gentleman," she said as she grabbed her purse from the floor.

They were both tipsy and leaned on each other for support. "You working tomorrow?" he asked.

"Bright and early, unfortunately."

"Mmm."

They stood on her stoop, and she swayed in his arms, leaned in and gave him a hug. She although she wasn't much more than half his weight, she wobbled and nearly pulled him into the wall. "You'll have to hold me up," she said.

"I've got you," he said, and he held her fiercely.

Before he could make any decision about what to do next, she leaned back and tilted her head up and kissed him then, open-mouthed, and her mouth tasted sweet like wintergreen. He inhaled, and blinked, and felt conscious of the nearby streetlights shining on them, and considered the possibility of a dog-walker watching them, a neighbor.

He pulled away and saw she still had her eyes closed, and she seemed on the verge of collapse in front of him, the wine evidently taking over. How easy it would be to make that mistake. Until that night, he'd never believed there was a single moment in life that you couldn't come back from. Life was a series of moments, a series of decisions that accumulated and gradually brought your true self into being.

She was waiting for him to take the next step.

He helped her with the door, and she looked back as she stepped into her foyer and turned on a light.

"Night, Karen," he said, and she smiled with understanding.

"Night," she said.

He took another long breath after she'd closed the door, and then he looked around the parking lot to see if anyone was out. He walked with purpose back to his Durango and got in and sat for a few minutes before turning on the engine. He turned back to Karen's apartment and saw the living room light was on, the shade illuminated, and he saw himself walking back over there and knocking on her door and wrecking his life for the third time. Then he turned on the engine, backed out of the space, and headed for home, congratulating himself on making a good decision and getting his life back on the winning track.

He thought about that kiss as he turned onto the main highway and cruised back toward Overlook. He enjoyed this, the special privilege of living in a small town where you could ramble around slowly with a light buzz, something he associated with the farm country of Ohio and Indiana, or Kentucky hayseeds with a cooler of beer in the bed of a pickup truck. He wiped his lips with his sleeve and thought about Karen, delicately drunk, the way her red hair fell over the sides of her face and shadowed the sharp angles of her cheekbones, her blazing green eyes. He also thought of Francine waiting for him at home, and all they'd been through and their efforts to make a baby. Francine was still beautiful. She'd changed some over the years, so incrementally he'd not even noticed, yet when he thought about her now, he realized he'd married a girl and lived with a woman, whose curves and overall confidence crushed him with love. In the swirl of his thoughts, he made a left onto Reedy Road, swung the car wide and almost missed the turn. He shook his head and aimed for the center of his lane, and then as the trees rose up around him to hide the moonlight, and the darkness was punctured only by his scuffy headlights, he retreated again to his thoughts, to Francine. Making the right decision, even when impaired with several glasses of wine, thrilled him, and he wished, as he did on occasion, that he could propose all over again to Francine, express how much he loved her anew. He barely paid attention when his phone buzzed, and he pulled it out of his pocket on autopilot, swiped the screen and saw a text from Karen: *I enjoyed this evening.* He jotted out a reply, a few quick words: *Great me too.* She was still his client, and he wondered what she would make of tonight in the morning.

He was sliding his phone into his pocket when the collision happened. It was a sound more than anything else, a *whoomp* and a *crack*, and he jerked the steering wheel and slammed on the brakes, came to a halt.

His mind was foggy, and he only wanted to be at home, to slide under the covers with Francine and make love to his wife. He could see her curves and feel her warmth. In his mirrors, he saw nothing but blackness, so he put the Durango in park and opened the door and walked around the vehicle.

He saw nothing: he would go over this moment in his memory for the rest of his life, the contingencies, and he always reached the same conclusion: his mind was clear, and he genuinely saw nothing. No skid marks, no bicycle, no body. The side of the Durango was scratched up, but he assumed it had been a deer, or a tree limb that had snapped and was dangling back there over the road.

He looked again but, again, saw nothing, so he climbed back into the Durango and headed home.

10

Wine takes its time as it courses through your blood. When he left the restaurant, he was buzzing slightly but could have passed any field sobriety test. When he left Karen Sinclair's apartment, he was tipsy and likely should not have gotten behind the wheel, but he'd driven under worse circumstances, and it was eleven o'clock on a Thursday in Overlook. No one was out. By the time he arrived home and shut off the car, the wine had gone to his head completely so that he was downright drunk. Fortunately, Francine had already gone to bed and could therefore not berate him for driving home, and he bobbed and weaved his way through their downstairs, poured a glass of water, and drank it all before pouring another to take up to bed with him. He remembered to pull out his contacts—a hard lesson he'd learned a few years back—and slid out of his clothes and brushed his teeth, wiped his lips one more time with a washcloth. Then he went to bed already knowing tomorrow would be miserable. Overnight, he went through the phases of an impending hangover: he passed out, blacked out, and then slept a dreamless sleep for a few hours. At around four, he woke as though he'd been shocked into life. His heart throbbed in his chest, and he lay there trying futilely to go back to sleep, knowing he was awake for the duration. He kept his eyes closed and his head still, but nonetheless felt the slow pulse of the hangover headache come over him, and at six-thirty his alarm went off.

All morning, through a shower and a light, forced breakfast and the email he sent to Marcus to say he'd be working from home today, he thought of the aborted kiss with Karen Sinclair, and of the disaster he'd averted, and it wasn't until Francine asked what happened to his car that he remembered the drive home. "Oh," he said. "I hit a deer or something."

"Jesus. Was it all right?"

"It must have been. I stopped and got out but didn't see it. It could have been a tree limb, I don't know. I'll take it in to a body shop this weekend."

"Good luck with it." She shook her head. "I'm off to a library for a few hours. You all right?"

"Yeah, just getting too old for these late-night sales dinners."

"Take care of yourself," she said.

Sitting at the breakfast table, he held her hand tightly and leaned against her body, and she squeezed his shoulder, kissed the top of his head, and left him to stew in his hangover. Even then he thought nothing about the accident and kept his mind on Karen Sinclair, and what a disaster for his marriage it would have been to carry that night one step further. Around ten he fell asleep on the couch and dozed fitfully until around one, when he turned on the TV and started making lunch. Fried eggs and bacon and biscuits and a banana with a pot of coffee: the works. The TV was on Fox in the background, just white noise, and it slowly dawned on him that the news was on and that a reporter was standing out on Reedy Road next to a crime scene, a hit and run and a dead bicyclist.

In the eighth grade, he'd flunked his first quarter of algebra. It made no sense to him, the leap from basic arithmetic to abstract equations. It made no sense, it made no sense, and suddenly it clicked. In a moment everything slid into focus, and he'd aced every math exam since then.

Watching the news report was like that moment in the eighth grade: it made no sense (he'd just driven that strip), it made no sense (he'd hit a deer), and then it clicked (no, he'd hit a bicyclist, a young woman, and she was dead).

He turned off the burners and the oven, left his half-cooked food and picked up his phone and googled the hit and run. The local newspapers had little more information, just that girl's name had not been released, and that authorities were asking for any witnesses to come forward. He thought of the kiss with Karen Sinclair, and he realized he had not escaped, that he was still on a downward trajectory, and in fact would be bottoming out much lower than he ever would have believed possible. He wasn't thinking straight when he went to the garage to look at the damaged Durango, saw the dented and the cracked headlight and the scratch marks running across the passenger door. He leaned in closer to examine it and saw blood and hair in the cracks of the headlight. He looked under the car and saw nothing but the dusty, rusty undercarriage, but the dried blood—brown, sticky—was all the evidence he needed. Then he had a rarely used four iron in his hand, an iron from his nearby bag, and then he was swinging the club repeatedly into the Durango.

Smashed the windshield, dented the hood, shattered the headlight.

He would feel it in his arms later, the bruises from the recoil, but for now all he could feel was a constriction in his chest, like a being squeezed in a vise, and he couldn't breathe. Then he was on the garage floor, amid shattered glass, the golf club skittered beneath the Durango, the concrete cold against his cheek. He lay there a long time, maybe dozed, and kept telling himself, *This is not my life. This is not my life.*

But he'd crossed the threshold, passed through the event horizon, hit bedrock. When he managed to sit up, he put the golf club away and went back inside. Again, he googled the hit and run, and saw no updates: no witnesses (yet), no culprits (yet). Just a string of nasty commentary already beginning to build.

Francine was still out, so he picked up the telephone and called the one person he knew who knew about secrets and how to work around them. He called his father and said, "Dad, I think I'm in some trouble here."

From his manicured haven of local executives in the Cleveland suburbs, his father listened to Daniel explain the story. While Daniel had many things in common with his father—ambition, intelligence, shrewdness—he lacked a measure of focus and street smarts. George kept himself in shape as a competitive swimmer when he was a teenager, and at sixty could go into any gym and out-lift, out-run, out-last almost any younger man, a tortoise-and-hare game to be the last man standing. Daniel's mother was perhaps the one person on earth who truly understood her husband's motives, that when he wanted to finance a grocery store and shopping complex complete with a doc-in-the-box retail location in some poor food desert, he cared little about the under-served population but instead saw the dollar signs of an untapped market. And if his business ventures aligned with the social good? Manna from heaven.

Daniel could picture his father's office, the stacks of medical files and financial reports, the cherry wood shelves one earns the right to with a high six-figure salary. The one sign of his father's humanity was in a framed photograph, perhaps his favorite relic from his family years, of George and his father and Daniel and Alexis in elementary school, out on a quarter-mile track, crouched in a sprinter's start. It had been a crisp day, and they all wore hats and long sleeves, but you could see it on all their faces, the grit to win. That had been a good day, and George had believed then his children would be fine. Alexis was the one who surprised everyone in the family: followed in her father's foot-steps, attained a medical degree at Northwestern and landed as a researcher out in California. Daniel was never quite so put together. He talked a big game, made solid B's throughout high school, and for some reason chose a small liberal arts college in South Carolina. "What's the draw?" George had asked. "Why don't you want to stay in state, save a little money, or at least aim for a school with better name recognition. If you've got to go south, what about Duke?"

"The girls," Daniel had replied. "You know what the ratio is down there? Five to one. There's girls all over the place."

Sure enough, Daniel had found a wife and, despite his efforts, he'd also landed a good job, but he'd grown doughy from too much beer and too many late nights of partying. No surprise the Data Dare team had let him join but denied him partnership. George put up an outraged front on his son's behalf at Thanksgiving— *What do you mean they didn't give you a partnership stake?*—but he knew his son would eventually be eaten alive in the business world. It said a lot about Marcus's business instincts, as well, the ruthless using of Daniel. George had been tempted to invest a little money in the company himself, but wanted his son to enjoy his own life.

And now this: the hit and run. It was the call every parent expects no matter how wonderful their snowflake is. George could hear it in his son's voice: "Dad, I think I'm in some trouble here."

Trouble was right. As father and son talked, each googled hit and run laws in South Carolina, and each felt sick to discover Daniel could face twenty-five years. His father doubted anyone actually served that much time, but this would not be an easy problem to fix. It was slowly dawning on Daniel that no matter what happened, his life would always be divided into then and now. By the end of this first call, George had calmed his son down, told him to lie low through the weekend while George hired representation. That was the first rule a good businessman takes to heart. Don't sign anything, don't make any agreements, don't even let a piece of paper out of your office unless it has a lawyer's blessing. Only when he told Daniel's mother would George drop the brash, tough-as-nails approach to the world and break down in sobs. Despite the cold utilitarian mind he'd honed, he still held a primal fire for his children.

Today, he repeated his warning for Daniel to lie low. "A few hours, or even a few days won't change anything. We need to get in front of this and get your story straight."

"Dad, I don't have a story. All I have is what I told you."

"What you told me is enough. You have a version of what happened, but it would be a tactical mistake to assume anyone will accept it at face value. We have to play this right."

"I don't know if I can."

"You don't have a choice," his father told him.

11

When Francine came home—an afternoon out: lunch with a friend, yoga in the afternoon, Target to pick up *just a few things*—he sat at the table with his heart quivering, breathing shallowly, waiting for the first confrontation of many. She carried a few bags in with her from the garage and set them on the counter, and he waited for her to take note of him, to pause and focus, so he could take some measure of control of the conversation. Instead she turned around and went back to the garage and returned with more bags and looked at him and smiled and said, "I know. I know! But I needed some new yoga pants, and then Kim's having a baby shower in a couple of weeks, so I splurged." She started unpacking a few items she'd bought for her friend's shower: a onesie with flamingos on it, a baby board book, a package of diapers. "I know it's too much, but I thought, 'Hey, no one's going to give her diapers, because everyone wants to buy clothes.' Because look at this outfit!" She paused and sighed and went back to unpacking the Target bags. "I had to get her the outfit, of course, and then of course the book, because you can never have too many of those. Anyway, while I was there I ran into Laura from the gym. Did I tell you about her? She's at the front desk? Her son is apparently getting married. He's all of a year out of high school, so she's mortified."

Here Francine paused and looked at him, leaning back in his chair, trying to hold it together.

"Honey, are you all right?"

His voice cracked, and he had to clear his throat twice before her name would come out. "Francine, I need to talk to you about something."

That moment. The moment she paused to look at him, and saw everything come into focus: the bashed-up car, the accident in the news, his hangover this morning. She knew what he was about to say yet she was not ready to hear it. Here she was unpacking gifts for her friend's baby shower. She wanted a baby herself, she wanted the diapers and the board books and the onesies, the whole mess of trouble a baby brings, she wanted it all with her husband. Daniel was a good man and would make a fine father. If they had a boy, Daniel would raise him into a man, and if they had a daughter, she would steal his heart, and either way Francine couldn't love him more because they would be a family. They could have—would have—been a family.

What else is there to say? She knew what was coming and knew it would change everything. Had already changed everything. There was no rewinding back to when she was innocently unpacking her wares. There was only forward now. Her first thought was that she wished she could hide out in someone else's life, for just a little while, but that was an impossibility.

She was trapped here, in this life, so she walked over and sat down across from him and said, "Go on."

12

Her first night alone in the house, with Daniel in jail for the weekend, Francine went to bed early and was awoken by the mysterious alarm clock. On Saturday she set to packing and texted a friend to arrange a place to stay.

OMG! I heard the news!
Yeah, it's been a shock.
How r u holding up?

How indeed. She thought about herself in college, how she'd rebelled against her family's conservative strain, the capitalist instincts of her father and the homemaking skills of her mother, and felt as though she had years of runway to allow her life to fall into order. There was no one she could blame save herself for being dishonest about what she wanted her story to be. Years of graduate school proving something to someone, years of trying for a baby some form of punishment, and now this. She knew enough, at this point, to know she would not come back from the events of this week, and she would never lose the cynical cast of mind that settled in her first weekend alone. She would stay with her friend for a few days, and then move to be near her family in Myrtle Beach. Say what you will about them, they rallied for her. Her father would arrange an attorney to negotiate the divorce before Daniel had even been sentenced. He found her work in a local PR firm and then, miraculously, gave her space to adapt to her new life.

But that first weekend was an ordeal. She never returned to sleep after the chirping alarm clock Saturday morning, and she spent all day Saturday packing. That evening, she drank an entire bottle of wine, too much for her even at the height of her drinking years in college, and she read about the accident. She'd heard plenty: from the local news, from the flurry of texts, from Daniel's solemn accounting of the evening. Now she wanted to see it herself.

News outlets had broken the story—*Person of interest comes forward*—and she couldn't reconcile the commentary about this man who'd killed this girl with the boy she'd chosen to marry after college, the man she'd been sharing her life with for the better part of a decade. *Coward. Let him hang. I've got a better idea.* She quickly scrolled over to Facebook where, however unlikely, Daniel's friends had shown the tact not to post anything on his wall. His last status update was from a week ago: *Just got back from an amazing trip to Boston! I love my job!* She seldom used social media but appreciated it for the photos. She clicked through photos of her husband on Facebook, where a grainy image stopped her, a photo from nearly twenty years ago he'd uploaded for some reason, Daniel maybe in junior high, his sister still in elementary school, still in awe of her big brother. They were dressed up and standing in front of the columns of the Jefferson Memorial in Washington, the two siblings framed amid a throng of their extended family, all holding bubble wands and having a good time. Their father wore a khaki suit and a bow tie and a safari hat, and the photo caught him mid-blow, lips puckered out, bubbles trickling out in front of his face. To a bystander, he would look like an archaeologist from the twenties—austere, but with a zany Hollywood flair—and you would never know what a deeply unhappy man he was at heart. Center stage in the photograph, Daniel and his sister wore hip shades, Daniel in a yellow tie and blue blazer, with an affectation of too-cool-for-school but enjoying a transparent good time. Beside him, his sister wore a blue sundress and held the wand up in performance, all manner of trick bubbles no doubt just beyond the picture's edge. Francine was shocked to discover the sheer joy on her husband's face, and see how much he'd aged. In this photo from his teenage years, he appeared much as he did when she'd met him: leaner, jovial, a shining light. It pained her to think she, too, was sinking into frumpy middle age.

She copied the photo to her laptop and stared at it, enlarged, and drank another glass of wine and thought about her husband, and the turns his life had taken post-college: the promise of greatness, how brilliant he was, how he'd sorely he'd settled for good enough for her sake, so she could dally as a proofreader while they waited for a baby to come. Time had left its mark on them both, morphed them each into someone new, but Daniel was still tenderhearted. She knew this about him, and she knew he would need a friend. That was why she'd contacted his old roommate, earlier this week, when Daniel had first delivered the news. *Francine, I need to talk to you about something.* He'd laid out the story for her, and then she'd told him she needed time to process it all. She already knew she would be leaving him, although she didn't admit it to herself for a day. She'd called Jay that evening as a parting gift to her husband. She knew it was impossible that an old friend could fill the void she'd be leaving, but she was leaving nonetheless. She'd seen photos of Samantha James, and she knew her husband was guilty of something reprehensible, unforgivable. If anyone asked, she would have been forced to admit she still loved him, but, staring at the old photograph from Daniel's childhood, she also knew she would never forgive him. Her head swirling with wine, she set her head on the desk, broke down, and wept.

13

The trial, when it finally arrived, passed in a blur. Over the five months since the accident, Daniel's life had indeed bottomed out. Francine moved in with a friend, a graphic designer she'd worked with on occasion through the public relations firm, and she'd agreed to meet with him only once, and only in a public place.

"Nothing happened with Karen Sinclair," he said that afternoon in the back of a crowded Starbucks, the din of screaming music and the screeching of the barista's steaming wand drowning out his thoughts.

"I don't care," she said.

"I just want you to know. She's my client, and, okay, maybe it wasn't the best move to meet her for dinner by myself like that, but there was nothing going on between us."

"Daniel. I believe you, but I don't care."

"The accident was an accident. I didn't see her, I would never have driven off."

"I believe you," she said again.

"So what is it? Everything's falling apart, and I just need you," he confessed. "I need someone who still believes in me, and you're the only one."

She shook her head. "You don't get it, do you? You never did. It's not about the accident, and it's not about the client."

"What is it then? The baby?"

"You don't *listen*. You've put me behind your work and all the things going on in your life for months now."

"Really? This is the conversation you want to have? Now?"

"I'm a coward, all right? I'm a shitty wife for leaving you, but this is what I'm talking about. You always get so defensive, it's like you can't see me right in front of you and hear what I'm saying."

"What are you saying?" he said quietly.

"I'm saying this—thing—this isn't working, and it hasn't for a long time. You could have let me in, when you found out what you'd done, but instead you treated it like you've treated everything else in our marriage. You let your father hire that lawyer, and you kept me out, and I don't have the energy to try to keep breaking through this wall."

"What did you want me to do? I needed a lawyer. I'm in deep shit here, Francine."

"I know, and I wish you well. But I was supposed to be your partner, not your pet cat. You can't just scratch me on the head a few times a day and expect that to be enough."

"I'm sorry I couldn't give you enough," he said.

And then he said other things, terrible things, unspeakable things, while she sat across from him, bravely and gracefully, and let him berate her for several minutes, years of pent-up aggression and judgment flogging her for her deficiencies as a wife and would-be mother. When he sputtered out of words and quit hollering, like a wind-up toy whose last gear had turned, Daniel stopped talking and licked his lips and darted his eyes around the room as if to reorient himself. She took one final calm sip of her coffee and opened her mouth to speak one parting zinger, but nothing came. She closed her lips and left without a word.

Daniel watched her go, knowing he'd chased her away, recognizing his problem but unsure how he'd allowed himself to become this man. He'd made several life-wrecking mistakes this year, and perhaps he would have been able to come back from one of them. But the distance he'd built between himself and his wife, the affair, the hit and run—it was all too much.

His final meeting with Marcus had gone no better. "Just until this passes over," Marcus said, with Ellen also at the table as a witness. "If there's anything we can do, as far as helping you with your finances."

"I'm fine," Daniel said. "I understand."

"Once the trial is over, of course, we'll want you back in action, but, you know, our local clients will have seen the news, and there's a chance everyone else might google you."

"Of course," Daniel said.

He no longer got dressed through September, October. Just binge-watched Netflix and drank himself into a stupor every night. He grew a beard so that he doubted anyone at the grocery would recognize him, yet he was so miserable he almost wished he'd not gotten out on bond, had instead been sentenced immediately. It might seem that he felt no remorse—certainly, the online trolls expressed just that opinion—but he thought of little else beyond Samantha James. He searched for her, read the blogs and the news articles, stared at the photo of her that ran in all the press. Young, innocent, beautiful, dead. He'd needed Francine to know there was nothing with Karen Sinclair, because he'd needed his wife to know she was still his, in his heart, and that he needed her now as the only thing good and true in his life. He needed the comfort that goodness, which was beyond him now, a killer, a sinner, still existed somewhere in the world. Perhaps it did still exist with Francine, and for that she had to leave him. He'd long known he was selfish, and rather useless to this world. Until July, there was no reason he shouldn't be on this planet, but there had never been any reason why he should have been on the planet, either. Now the scales had tipped against him, and actually thought about ending it, but lacked the spine. It was all a terrible mistake, his whole life an error, flawed code written into a tiny thread of the universe.

His family had been no help, either. His father arranged the lawyer, and called him weekly, and apologized that his mother was too distraught to talk to him. "You know how she gets, but we'll come down before the trial."

"You don't have to do that," Daniel said.

"We want to be there."

"It's actually easier if I go it alone."

"I understand," George told his son. "We're coming down anyway."

They did come, for the trial, invaded Daniel's home and slept in the guest bedroom and stocked the house with piles of frozen meat from Sam's Club. They made themselves at home and somehow infantilized Daniel in his own house, *his* house, the dream home that was something to behold. His mother was ashen, and the first thing she did when they arrived was hug her son and cling to him. Then she passed the two weeks in a funk, showering but not putting on makeup until the family left for the trial. Daniel had worked so hard to get out, had done well enough at St. Ignatius to get a modest scholarship at the College of Charleston, had never asked his parents for a dime since then. His father had transferred Daniel's remaining college fund of forty thousand dollars into an account and left it to Daniel to make his way in the world, which he'd done until now. Now, his parents barged in and couldn't even let him take responsibility for his mistake and attend the trial on his own. They had to be there, for moral support. It had been called *affluenza*, the way today's well-to-do young had been smothered by their parents and had become unable to make decisions and be held accountable.

Meanwhile, the one relative Daniel would have appreciated seeing was his sister. Alexis didn't speak to him for weeks after the accident, refused to return any emails or texts, but when she finally called, she didn't make it past hello before she broke down sobbing out in California. "No, no, it's fine," he told her. "I know this is a burden for everyone, so don't feel guilty about not calling, or staying away." Then, "Of course you don't need to be here. Mom and Dad are here, and they're suffocating me." Then, "You know how they are." After getting off the phone with his sister, he lay on the bed. He stayed in the bedroom most of the time, unable to face his parents, because he blamed himself for the exhaustion on their faces. They looked old to him now, which he knew was a byproduct of time rather than trouble, but still he felt responsible for keeping them from the golden years of evening sitcoms, where every problem was resolved in half an hour. There would be no resolution, no matter the verdict. Daniel was a guilty man and a lost soul, and whether he was in prison or a free citizen, he would always be a man who'd killed a girl and driven off.

14

The trial lasted three days, and served as an apotheosis for all the rage that had been simmering in the community since the summer. Thanks to all the media coverage, Henry Somerville asked to move the trial to a different jurisdiction, a request Judge Rhodes denied. "We've got a solid defense," Somerville told Daniel and his parents in Daniel's living room the week before the trial began. "If I had to wager, I'd say it'll be a misdemeanor conviction with a suspended sentence, based on how these cases typically go, but of course it'll be up to the judge. The media situation isn't helping anyone, especially with that windshield."

"That was after the accident."

"I know, but I'm not the one we have to sell the story to."

Claire Fields had a solid first day, laying out in detail the way the crime happened, and that Daniel was the culprit beyond a shadow of a doubt. In her telling, with her key witnesses and experts (the waiter, Karen Sinclair, the detectives, the medical examiner), Daniel drank too much wine, got on the highway, hit Samantha James while driving too fast, and waited several days to turn himself in, when it would be impossible to test how inebriated he'd been on the highway. Worse, Karen unearthed the text message he'd sent her somewhere on the ten-minute drive between her apartment and his house. Given she'd sent the message several minutes after he left, and that Samantha's body was found seven minutes away from her house, there was a fair chance he struck Samantha right as he looked at his phone to send a text.

The second day, Somerville made some in-roads by demolishing the prosecution's character witnesses—the boyfriend, the sister—a performance so frightening the lawyer truly earned his extravagant fee. As Daniel watched Somerville dredge up secrets about Samantha's sister and make innuendos about Charlie Gibbs, he sunk in his seat and stared at a spot on the table.

After a midday recess, Claire Fields declined to call any other witnesses, instead hunkered with the family in a meeting room. None of them emerged until just before the trial resumed, and Henry Somerville began calling his own witnesses: Marcus Van Bergen (who testified to Daniel's character and his rising status as a pillar of the community), an independent private detective (who confirmed it was possible, maybe not probable, but possible that Daniel could indeed have stopped and looked for a body and seen nothing on that dark stretch of highway), a series of experts who illustrated how difficult it was to see bicyclists at night, the rate of such accidents, and, in a cruel turn for the family, how even a glass of wine would have impaired Samantha's riding such that she could have weaved into the road and smacked right into Daniel. By the end of the day Tuesday, even Daniel was convinced he might not be totally in the wrong, and his attorney had somehow saved him from total damnation.

Then Judge Rhodes declared the jury would deliberate in the morning before announcing the verdict.

On the way out of the courthouse, it annoyed Daniel that his attorney turned on his phone and stopped to check his messages while Daniel walked to the car and got into the passenger, hoping no one from the media, or the James family, would spot him. The lemon-colored Lowcountry light pierced the branches of live oaks and palm trees in the courthouse parking lot. Even in late fall, it felt like summer here, and he knew his family in Cleveland would be facing a steely sky, mist, and the onset of seasonal affective disorder. Difficult to imagine life on the South Carolina coast could be anything but copacetic, but here he was, and here came Somerville with a distracted look on his face. "I have to make a quick phone call. You all right?"

"Yeah. Just ready to get home."

"We'll head out in a second. Neville," he said into the phone. He listened for a few moments, said, "Uh huh, uh huh." Then, "When would that be?" Then, "Can't I just make a donation to an animal rescue and be done with it?" Then, "Twenty-five hundred bucks? For a camera? Jesus, Neville." Then, "No, I get it. Hey, no, that's great news. If that's what I need to do, I'll be there."

When he hung up, he appeared much cheerier.

"Good news?" Daniel asked him.

"On one front. But right now we need to focus on taking care of you."

15

The Hayward family stayed in that night, ordered pizza. No one seemed hungry and no one had much to say about the trial. Daniel recognized the attorney's strategy, to discredit the character witnesses and create an alternative story in which he, Daniel, was a good citizen and a decent human being who shared the blame with the victim, but of course it was wrong, a story built on a lie that discounted his own drinking, his own cellphone distraction. After his parents had gone to bed, he booted up his laptop and Skyped with his sister.

"I heard about today," she said. "Mom called, pretty shaken up."

"The lawyer did his thing."

"You all right with it?"

"What am I supposed to do about it? Dad hired him to defend me, and as he's said all along, his job is to chip away at the prosecution's case. That means discrediting witnesses, challenging procedures, doing everything he can to end this thing with a not-guilty verdict or a mistrial. In a few months, it'll all be over and forgotten, so what does it matter what he said today?"

"But that girl's sister. It sounded like her parents didn't even know."

"They were going to find out eventually." He took a breath and thought again of Somerville's long cross-examination of two innocent kids trying their best to grieve. "Why's it my fault if she wanted to take the stand and hold court under oath?"

"What would you do if someone killed me in a hit and run?"

"We wouldn't even get to trial," he said.

"Be serious."

"I am. You remember that guy you brought home—"

"I remember," she said.

When Daniel was home from college, he'd come in from something, groceries maybe, and found Alexis shut in her bedroom with a scrawny guy she was studying math with. They were both in the ninth grade, and the guy was probably harmless, probably nothing was happening, but the audacity of it—Daniel grabbed him by the collar and carted him down the steps and threw him out onto the front lawn without a word and slammed the door. She'd not spoken to him for the rest of his vacation, but he'd never heard about the guy—nor any boyfriend for Alexis—since.

"Well there you go," he said.

"Look, all I'm saying is—"

"All I'm saying," he interrupted, "is that I get it, but what's done is done. It's all up to the jury now, and there's no use apologizing for a few hurt feelings in court. That won't bring the girl back."

He had a catch in his throat, and she said, "Daniel."

"I've got to go, Alexis," he said.

"Call me tomorrow."

The night dragged out from there, a fever dream in which, after falling asleep fast and deep, Daniel woke several times, like a drunkard expecting the onset of his next hangover. First, at midnight, when he believed the haze of light at his window might in fact portend the first glimmer of dawn, but it was only starlight and the illuminant moon. He thought of where his life might have gone wrong, because something surely led him to this, some chain of events with a first cause. He thought it might have been his parents: too stern, stalwart yet libertarian in their sensibilities so that he chased the dream of freedom to an entrepreneurial venture in Overlook. He thought back on his childhood in Cleveland, the way he and boys in the neighborhood had the run of the streets in summer, perhaps the last generation to go out and be expected home when the street lights winked on but not before. No tethers, no leashes. He thought of his neighbors, and the spread of ages: younger, older, some in elementary school, others driving and dating, all pushed together by proximity and circumstance, boredom alleviated by hanging around. Maybe one of them had a Game Boy or a Super Nintendo at the house, but the wonders of the internet were a marvel of the future.

He drifted off and woke again around three, this time aching and with clotted sinuses. You know you're getting old when you wake up feeling hung over but have had nothing to drink the night before. He reached for a glass of water on his nightstand and drank it down and stared at the clock, and then he lay back and tried to empty his mind. But the reckoning was already here: the vision of his drive home on Reedy Road, the thump of hitting Samantha, the way his headlights beamed into the darkness as he came to a stop. He'd left his headlights on, he remembered that, and he remembered leaving the keys in the ignition and the car beeping at him obnoxiously as he got out to investigate what he'd hit. He remembered the taillights shining, and the roadside foliage wreathed in an overnight fog, but he could not remember a body or a silhouette or anything that would allude to a person on the highway. He wondered if it were possible that it had all been a misunderstanding, that perhaps he had in fact hit a deer and some other reckless driver had hit the girl. But no: the police had inspected his car, they took blood samples, DNA evidence the prosecutor introduced as an exhibit on the first day of the trial. No, he'd hit her all right, and if he were found guilty, he was ready to serve whatever time they gave him. He had killed someone through his own negligence, and whether it was chance or fate, he was responsible and would always have to live with that.

With this last stage of acceptance, he slept once again and woke a final time at six-thirty, his usual hour. He'd showered and made the bed and was on the stairs before it occurred to him that today was the final day of ambiguity. If found guilty, he wouldn't be sentenced right away, perhaps not until after the holidays and the new year, but he would be living on borrowed time before being remanded into custody. He would be forced to face his family every day—for he knew his mother, at least, would not be leaving—with the knowledge that he was a convicted crim-inal. He would have to clean up the house and arrange for his mortgage and probably find a renter. And he would have to settle his affairs with Francine. He'd heard nothing from her since she walked out on him in the coffee shop. Perhaps she'd contacted a divorce attorney, or perhaps she was waiting for the trial to end.

Regardless of how today would change his life, he thought of Samantha James and her body broken like a bird, her light extinguished, and he felt remorse and knew there would be no mercy. Jesus may love him, a sinner, but to the rest of the world and to himself, he was unforgivable. He told his parents he wanted to drive to the courthouse by himself, to think and reflect. The weather was fair, even though it was the end of November. You seldom had a truly cold snap in Overlook but even still, the sun coasting out of the morning clouds and the sixty-degree air seemed to mock him as paradise lost. Henry Somerville and the sheriff stood in the courthouse parking lot when Daniel arrived, both sipping coffee like maintenance workers on break, long-time colleagues who had a job to do. Daniel waved at Somerville when he got out of his car—a Ford Focus, a used trade-in for the Durango.

"Morning, Daniel," Somerville said, and he extended a hand for a firm shake. "Ready?"

Daniel both of their hands and said, "As I'll be."

The sheriff hitched his pants and straightened his belt and the three of them took the long walk to the courthouse, saying nothing, and Daniel already felt like a man condemned. Put the cuffs on him now, he was already imprisoned in his head. On the steps, the sheriff saw Charlie Gibbs first. The boy wore a hooded sweatshirt and ratty jeans and scuttled toward them with a rifle in his hand. Everyone thinks of fight or flight, that neurological response to danger, and everyone has visions of pandemonium, chaos, screams and shrieks, but when confronted with the unthinkable, our natural tendency is to freeze up in uncertainty. It takes a moment for the mind to register anomalous information, and only after a pause does the body jolt itself out of its conscious, rational mode and into something instinctive. The length of that pause determines life or death, and Daniel Hayward paused long enough to register that this would be his final moment.

The sheriff's instincts kicked in first. He dropped his coffee on the steps and yelled as he reached for his pistol as Charlie Gibbs raised the rifle, took aim squarely at Daniel, and fired.

A MULTI-LEVEL MARKETING OPPORTUNITY

1

It started one day while Charlie Gibbs was sitting glumly in the break room of the dealership. A colleague named Spencer, who had brought in his own Subaru for service with a weeping head gasket, looked over at him and said, "You look like a man who works out."

Charlie Gibbs did not look like a man who worked out. Rangy, pimple-faced, stoop-shouldered and slightly bow-legged, Charlie Gibbs hadn't set foot in a weight room since his ninth grade gym class, where he successfully bench pressed the forty-five-pound bar, once hit fifty sit-ups in a minute, and had a surprising knack for pull-ups, which impressed the football players who could lift 300 pounds but not their suspended body mass. Nonetheless, like most awkward, self-loathing individuals, Charlie Gibbs was open to flattery. "What makes you say that?"

"Just the cut of your build, my man."

Charlie looked down at himself.

"Look at you. What do you bench, about 180?"

"Ha!"

"I'm just joshing with you. You look like more of a runner than weight lifter. You got those long limbs like a gazelle."

"I'm not a runner," Charlie said.

"Well, you look like you could be. You into sports at all?"

"Not really."

"Nah, me neither," Spencer said, and he looked away. He was a few years older than Charlie, had a rake of thinning hair and a narrow face with a crooked smile, eyebrows spaced a little too far apart. He looked like a man who joined his college cheer-leading team ironically, a half cock away from the cool crowd. They were both salesmen for Davis Brothers Auto-Max, the used car arm of a local chain of dealerships spread out on the highway between the interstate and Hilton Head Island. Charlie didn't know him all that well—didn't know any of his colleagues all that well—but Spencer seemed all right. Kept to himself, earned decent commissions, spread the wealth when there was slow foot traffic and Spencer was the only one customers seemed to be approaching.

Charlie had a few minutes left of his break, and he watched *Live! with Kelly* as she introduced her new co-host to replace Regis Philbin. The two of them bantered on mute, smiled their plastic smiles, and manufactured energy like marionettes dancing to behind-the-scenes strings.

He'd almost put his colleague out of mind when Spencer leaned back, clicked his pen a few times, and asked, "You know anything about old Subarus?"

"What do you want to know?"

"Wondering what I can get for my Forester."

"Well, you know we don't get them too often, and they sell quick."

"The shop guys are probably charging me two grand to fix the head gasket."

"That happens," Charlie said. "It's a poor design, but once you get it fixed, it'll run another hundred thousand miles."

"Damn thing was made in Japan. I thought Japanese manu-facturing was supposed to be better than that."

"I don't know."

"I had an uncle," Spencer went on, "he swore you should always buy Japanese. This was back in the eighties, before Toyota and Honda really took over, but he always said Japanese cars were where it's at. He blamed it on the unions. Said Americans had gotten soft and lazy. You believe that?"

Charlie shrugged.

"So here I bought this Subaru manufactured in Japan. Not Indiana. Japan. And the damn head gasket starts weeping. I bought her before I started selling cars. Didn't realize all of them crapped out at a hundred thousand miles, and now I think I just want to unload her." Spencer clicked a pen again, and Charlie wondered what he was getting at. Charlie had been on the receiving end of enough hustles that he recognized a sales pitch coming, even if he was helpless to change the conversation. "What would you sell me if I were in the market for a new car?" Spencer asked.

"Well, I don't know. What would you sell yourself?"

"Hell, Charlie, I don't know. That's why I'm asking you."

"Depends on what kind you're looking for, I guess" Charlie said.

"Creature comforts. Leather seats, nav. system, all that stuff."

"You looking for a car or SUV or what?"

"Doesn't matter. What you got?"

"Everything," Charlie said, but he was tired of the conversation. He had nothing to offer. You didn't have to sell cars for long before you could spot the difference between a tire kicker and a serious buyer, and a customer like Spencer was passing the time. No one shopped for a car without knowing almost exactly what they wanted, and when they couldn't get what they wanted for the price they could pay, Charlie helped them feel good about settling. Or at least, his job was to make them feel good about settling. The best he could muster was to keep them from hating themselves until they got off the lot. Maybe they all went home and discovered they'd been ripped off and sent negative vibes his way. Maybe that was the source of his anxiety.

Spencer must have sensed his overtures were a non-starter, because he shifted gears once again and said, "The reason I ask about working out, I've been working out some myself lately. Now I know I'm not bulked up like Hulk Hogan, but I'd never trust someone who promised me the world. You know those late-night ads for body potion or home gyms? Scams. Just like you wouldn't trust a car dealer who said here's a beautiful car with all the features, nine ninety-nine. We know sales is about knowing the product, finding out what your customer needs, and matching the two up. Am I right?"

"I guess so," Charlie said.

"What do you mean, you guess so? How long you been working here?"

"About a year."

"I see the scoreboard in there. You do all right," Spencer said.

"Thanks."

"My question for you, then, is, what if you could do more?"

"We only get so many customers."

"I'm not talking about selling cars." Spencer leaned in and clicked his pen a few more times. "You know I've gained ten pounds of muscle mass this year? I might not look it, but I'm solid."

"Uh huh."

Spencer leaned back, kept on with the clicking. "Know how I did it? Ribo-Flavor."

"Does that have something to do with our dealership?"

"No, man, what's wrong with you? Ribo-Flavor. It's a protein shake. Don't tell me you've never heard of it? Man, I thought you were savvy over there."

Spencer went on to explain the virtues of the Ribo-Flavor Ultra Protein & Vitamin Shake, which came in three delicious flavors (chocolate, vanilla, peanut butter), involved one easy scoop of powder you mixed with water ("straight out of the tap, man"), and gave you all the protein and energy you needed to rebuild muscle after a workout.

"What happens, man, is when you lift or whatever, your muscles tear. If you don't have protein to help them rebuild, then you just get—BLAH!—atrophy. But if you have protein, it's like a little road crew giving you mass, and mass is power. It's a virtuous cycle."

"My break's over," Charlie said.

2

It took Charlie an embarrassing number of days to understand Spencer was selling Ribo-Flavor powder, and that he was inviting Charlie to join him in a sales venture. Charlie was not friends with his co-workers, had found the job a little more than a year ago when, fresh out of high school and searching for a job, any job, he blanketed the retail strip with applications and got his first callback from the sales manager at Davis Brothers Auto-Max, who indicated Charlie could make a pile of money if he was willing to put in the hours and play by the rules. Charlie quickly learned he had three types of colleagues: (1) the fresh faces, of which he was one, dudes between eighteen and twenty-five who lacked academic credentials but who also lacked fear and would approach a stranger with a friendly smile; (2) the corporate stooges, seasoned and ambitious salespeople looking to rise up the ranks into management or jump ship for better commissions at a rival chain of dealers; and (3) the second-career burnouts, many of whom were divorced or alcoholic or both, who had failed spectacularly in some previous endeavor and, in at least one case, had a felony conviction under their belt. Charlie had found his people. He learned not to be afraid when talking to customers, although his sales manager did tell him he hesitated too much when walking up to someone. "It's like you're trying to gauge whether they actually wanted to be sold a car," his manager said. "Of course they want to be sold a car. Why else would they be here?"

No one had ever heard of *just looking*, apparently. Window shopping did not exist in the realm of used cars.

Spencer was one of the fresh faces, who might be sliding into corporate stooge if he stayed on a few more years. Management posted sales figures on a wall in the office, and Spencer's numbers were always near the top. High margins, plenty of add-ons, a born salesman. Throughout September, trying to keep his focus off his memories of Samantha and the hit and run, Charlie watched Spencer at work, took note of how the man was at ease with everyone, and slowly tried to mirror his colleague's body language. His own name rose up on the board, never to the top but not on the bottom with the newest hires either.

"Killing it, Gibbs," Spencer said one day when he found Charlie in front of the sales numbers. "Hey, why don't you stick around after you get off this evening? I'm grabbing a drink with Jackson over at the Pearl. Got a business proposition for you."

Jackson was a mechanic who never talked with anyone but who had somehow earned the respect of everyone in the dealership. Customers lined up with repeat business and kept the shop's operating profit well in the black. But Jackson understood sales and, as Charlie discovered that night at a table in the back of the Pearl Tavern, he'd taken Spencer up on selling Ribo-Flavor shake mix.

"It's all about diversifying your income streams," Spencer said. "Jackson, how much money you make last month working on cars?"

"I'm on salary. About three grand."

"And what about selling Ribo-Flavor?"

Jackson shrugged over his beer and said, "Maybe a few hundred?"

Spencer slapped the table. "You keep that up, man, you'll be making more money selling protein powder than you do working on cars."

"Who buys this stuff?" Charlie asked.

"I go to a large church," Jackson said. "I just took out an ad in the Sunday bulletin."

"But you don't have to have that kind of a network," Spencer said quickly. "Take me. I'm not from Overlook, I don't go to church, I don't know hardly anyone outside the dealership. It's just about leveraging the contacts you do have. High school friends, or anybody."

In the used car world, you had colleagues, fellow salesmen who worked for the company. In the protein and vitamin shake world of Ribo-Flavor, you were a consultant and had a mentor who brought you in. "Like your Jedi master," Spencer said. "I'm your Obi-Wan Kenobi. I got my Yoda, a guy I know from the Army. He's the one who gave me the hookup, and now I'm giving it to you, Luke Skywalker."

Independent consultant or not, Charlie had to sign a contract to buy the first bulk shipment of Ribo-Flavor, five grand in installments over the first year. "But you'll make twice that even just starting out. Plus, recruit a few consultants of your own, there's no limit." The five thousand included a folder full of sales literature, much like the materials he got from Davis Brothers. One-pagers with titles like "Overcoming No!" and "Finding Your Network!" They were big on social media, even listed out a schedule of Facebook posts so all you had to do was plug and play and wait for the money to roll in.

The first few weeks, it was more of a trickle. Charlie followed the instructions, sent an email to everyone he knew along with an order form, and a friend from high school actually did buy a few cans of powder. "What the hell, Charlie, I'm glad to see you've got a new venture," his friend said. The literature from Ribo-Flavor said Charlie should file him into a new category, from sales prospect to confirmed customer, which meant there were a series of follow-up emails and other communications touting the benefits of Ribo-Flavor, offering gym partnerships and meet-ups, and suggesting his friend join him as a consultant. Charlie never heard from him again, and didn't make any more sales to people he knew. Ribo-Flavor did set up an affiliate website for him ($200 value – free!), and he made a few more sales through the website, probably earning three hundred dollars his first month in business.

Much of the Ribo-Flavor sales literature centered on taking advantage of his social media contacts. Unlike many of his peers from school, Charlie was not social media savvy. Gals he graduated with had Instagram accounts with thousands of followers (mostly, they shared pictures of their dogs). Others had snarky Tumblrs with obscene, even sacrilegious, nom de plumes (think JeezusDick94). And Charlie? He'd befriended on Facebook most of the kids he knew from grade school, put up a few posts last year about selling cars, got no results, and gave up. Now, he took the bold step of trying to sell Ribo-Flavor to those he hadn't already alienated when he began selling cars. A sampling of his posts:

- Looking to bulk up this winter? Ribo-Flavor can help. Never underestimate the power of complex vitamins.
- Could you carve out 30 minutes a day to create a residual income stream? I run my Ribo-Flavor business from my smart phone – and you could too. Let's talk.
- I'm so excited about my life choices this year. The best thing I ever did was say yes to Ribo-Flavor. Want to learn more? Send me an email.
- In the past two months, I've converted 10 pounds of fat to pure muscle mass, and I can bench 225+. Want to lose your training wheels? Give me a shout.
- My mother always told me not to talk religion and politics, so forget about the primaries. Let's talk about fitness. Have you heard about Ribo-Flavor? You need to be in the know!
- One year ago, I was in a rough place. But now I've got a steady income and a tight body the ladies love. Send me a message and I'll fill you in on the secret.
- Today only! I've got one case of Ribo-Flavor to give away at my cost. No pressure, but this is a no-risk sales venture for one of my closest friends. Call if you're interested.
- Looking to bulk up this year? Join me for a live chat where I'll fill you in on what you need to know.

Benching 225 had been a lie. Charlie was skinny and undisciplined, so he stuck with 25s and the bar, but what he lacked in strength he made up for in enthusiasm at the gym. Bodyweight squats, biceps curls, triceps kickbacks, plank-to-press, jumping rope. He stayed away from the deadlifts and the power rack and so never had to reveal his weakness.

No one showed up for Charlie's live chat, and very few of his friends called or emailed him, though he did get a few well wishes from distant relatives and one long-lost elementary school friend whose life appeared sadder and more desperate than Charlie's at his worst. On the positive side, he made friends with strangers around the country, other Ribo-Flavor sales consultants who connected with him and liked his posts, and together they, led by Spencer, created a dude-group echo chamber, sharing each other's posts and competing over scant customers and new recruits. In Charlie's second month, sales flat-lined at three hundred dollars—enough to make his monthly inventory payment but not enough to turn a profit—so it was during the third month that the bottom fell out. When his monthly accounting statement came in from Ribo-Flavor headquarters in Delray Beach, Florida, instead of a check he would receive a bill for $275 to cover five cases of protein shakes, which were currently in a stack in his living room. That would be the first in a slow slide toward insolvency, but the day before the bill came in the mail, he still held out hope, like Robert E. Lee before Pickett's Charge at Gettysburg, that all his wildest dreams might come true.

It was in this state of denial that he ran into Sam's sister, Lauren, in the greeting card aisle at Target.

3

The last time Charlie Gibbs saw Samantha's family was after her funeral in the summer. Of course it had rained, yet the afternoon thunderstorm had not kept away a crowd of her parents' friends (the former soccer moms and the neighbors and church friends who had served on committees with the Jameses), plus a legion of Sam's friends and acquaintances, as well as people Charlie was certain had no connection to her whatsoever: bicyclist grandstanders outraged by the situation. Although the town was overwhelmingly conservative, Overlook had a strong contingent of mostly young bicyclists with an unflagging commitment to environmentalism. They somehow managed, with no apparent cognitive dissonance, to believe in strong government oversight when it came to protecting the natural world while still maintaining the libertarian's view of freedom when it came to traversing the land on two wheels. God gave them the natural world to enjoy but not manipulate or degrade the way automobiles sullied the planet. To them, Charlie Gibbs, car salesman extraordinaire, was the enemy. To Charlie Gibbs, Sam's lover, they knew nothing of her and were here simply to get their politics in the newspaper.

Which they did: photographers from the newspaper and the local Fox station lingered by the curb in front of the Presbyterian church, but they took as many discreet photographs of the James family as they did of the bikers who rallied on the curb in demonstration afterward. (What did they want? Justice! When did they want it? Justice!)

Charlie attended the funeral by himself. His mother had to work but sent flowers and asked him repeatedly to give the Jameses her condolences. He had no other family in town, his father having absconded to greener pastures years ago. Charlie seldom saw the man but still had a collection of birthday gifts from him over the years: a baseball glove, a pocketknife, and, the last when Charlie was twelve, a .22 rifle. His father had taken him out to a range to show him how to use it, and he'd been patient when Charlie nearly shot himself in the foot trying to operate the gun. At the end of the session, Charlie had attained some small measure of competence, the best he would ever get. He assumed there might be a hunting trip, or maybe a shotgun in his future, but his father had never showed up. Charlie had been left without a male role model from then on. He had his mother, a grandmother in Savannah, and an aunt outside Charleston. All these women!

You might think they would have prepared him for the world of girls and dating, or at least the hardscrabble world in general, but he graduated high school with a girlfriend he'd not slept with, a few gamer friends, and no plan for college, a working class guy in a town full of tourist BMWs. He and Samantha James had been friends and then dated casually, perhaps out of convenience if nothing else. She was a kind-hearted introvert without the self-confidence to understand she could date any boy she wanted, but instead hung around the boy from her geography class who made her laugh.

Her family had money: her father a c-level executive who worked four days a week in Charlotte, her mother volunteered at the church and shuttled Lauren, the alpha girl with the million appointments and three failed driving tests under her belt, from one meet to the next. The family had been polite to Charlie when he and Sam were senior sweethearts. They invited him to dinner on occasion, paid for an elegant photo shoot during the prom, and waited patiently for Sam to grow tired of him when she left for college. She had a scholarship to South Carolina, and the family fully expected her to go on to graduate school, do something great, and marry someone exceptional along the way. Instead, she'd continued dating Charlie through her freshman year, came home every other weekend, and shared little with her parents about her life in Columbia. Her parents fretted in the evenings, muttered in bed in the dark about what she saw in Charlie and why she was having trouble launching herself out of the nest. "Don't get me wrong, I love seeing her," Sam's mother said.

"Of course," her father replied.

"But I just don't think it's healthy."

"Maybe I should talk to her. Stop by and take her to lunch on my way back from Charlotte next week."

"I think that's a great idea."

But he never did. Sam's father, Gary, was an old-fashioned Midwestern boy who believed in giving his children autonomy, which, if asked, he would explain meant allowing them to take responsibility for themselves and their affairs. He controlled many of the financial strings of his daughter's world—fed her bank account, indulged her when she came home to Overlook, fully intended to co-sign with her on a condo when she grad-uated—but lacked any connection to her emotional life. She would grow out of the boy, or the boy would have to grow into her. Gary knew his daughter, knew she had a practical mind and an attachment to nice things. The boy was selling used cars. She would figure out his income would never do. Give it time.

Meanwhile, in the year after high school, Charlie moved from his mother's house to a room above her garage—a token step toward independence, for which he paid her two hundred a month—got a job selling certified used cars at the Davis Brothers Auto-Max, and took the SATs. The night Sam was killed, he had a burning secret to tell her, which was this: although he'd been accepted to South Carolina and had filled out most of his paperwork, he'd missed an application deadline for a government loan, which meant he couldn't start until the spring. He thought he'd checked everything off his list, but some form had slipped through the cracks, he didn't understand it. He'd found out while she was in Michigan with her parents, visiting family, and he wanted to tell her in person to gauge her reaction. He had reason to fear Sam might be coming home from Michigan to break up with him—all that time alone with her family, no good could come from that, and the way she kept her distance on the phone, what was *that* about?—so on the night she was struck by Daniel Hayward's Durango, Charlie Gibbs paced and tried to come up with arguments for why they needed to stay together:

- Because we love each other.
- Because we make each other laugh.
- Because it's us against the world, and we can't let the world win.
- Because what will you do without me. (Scratch that.)
- Because what will I do without you.

Sam texted to let him know they'd arrived in Savannah, and that she'd see him after work. She got off at eleven, so he was expecting her at a quarter after. When she didn't call or text right at eleven, he thought perhaps she was working late. Then it was eleven-thirty and he hadn't heard from her, and he began to panic, fearing the worst. Perhaps she really was going to break up with him. Perhaps she'd met someone else, a coworker, say. Perhaps she was at said coworker's place *right now*, banging some line cook like there's no tomorrow. He snuck into his mother's house and made a sandwich and thought about the possibilities, and when he still hadn't heard from Sam at quarter to twelve, he got in his car and went out looking for her.

4

The funeral was a week later, a Friday at noon. Charlie sat in the third row of pews, behind the reserved seats, and Sam's parents nodded to him but failed to invite him to join them in the front. Why would he be on their minds? They'd lost one of their two daughters. He was a painful reminder, the split fingernail you get on your way to work but can't deal with until you got home in the evening. Sam's sister, Lauren, sat between her parents, and Charlie kept his eyes on the family rather than the pastor during the service. Gary and Beth held their composure but Lauren, two years younger than Sam, a turbulent seventeen, wept the entire time. She was so different from her sister: outgoing where Sam had been reserved, into makeup and clothes where Sam had been a tomboy, her mother's daughter where Sam had taken after their father.

Charlie lingered after the service, knew he should say something to the family, *I'm sorry for your loss,* but the words failed him. He jammed his hands in his pants pockets and waited for the family to take notice of him, which they eventually had to do once the church began to empty of their friends and colleagues and neighbors, and Gary said to him, "Thank you for coming, Charlie."

"Yes, sir. I'm sorry. My mother—she wanted to be here, but had to work all day."

Gary nodded.

"She sent flowers, I think, from both of us."

"Tell her we appreciate her thinking of us," Beth stepped in to say. Gary and Charlie were both about to leave it at that, when Beth added, "If you're going home to an empty house, you're welcome to join us for dinner this evening."

Of course he had to accept, and of course it was a disaster.

As he was the only guest, the Jameses tiptoed around family business, made a few gracious overtures, and then everyone collectively seemed to realize what a terrible idea it had been to invite Charlie over. He could sense the gloom even before Beth, making an effort to keep her upper lip stiff, apologized for not having anything prepared.

"Oh, it's fine," he told her. "I can actually go."

"No, no, do stay."

"Mom, let him go if he wants," Lauren said.

"Where are you off to?" her mother asked, and she glided over to intercept Lauren.

"I'm going upstairs."

"But we were just about to figure out dinner."

"I'm not hungry," she said.

Beth leaned in and said, "We have a guest tonight."

"You invited him. What's he to me?"

"We can talk about it later. Please just behave for us tonight. For me."

Lauren sulked back into the family room while her mother darted into the powder room to dab her eyes.

Charlie hated that he lacked the grace to extricate himself, hated the family for inviting him into this situation, hated Sam for riding her bicycle on the highway that night when he would have picked her up, and hated himself for being a Gibbs, poor son of divorced, working class parents, a man who didn't belong in this home, with its sterile décor, the matchy-match of the wall hangings to the paint to the rugs, the whole thing a bogus display of the nouveau riche. Where were the family pictures? The knick-knacks they bought on vacation? Even if they didn't go to Myrtle Beach, surely they went to Florida, or Nantucket, or Vail. Where were the little souvenirs the girls forced the parents to buy? Charlie's house was filled with such bric-a-brac. He'd never before noticed its absence, but without Sam here to add her sparkle of life, he saw how dreary and boringly upper middle class her house truly was. This too, he hated.

Dinner meant takeout from a local Mexican restaurant, no cooking for anyone on such a day, and after painfully gathering everyone's order, Beth trudged out to pick it up. Gary put on Fox News while Lauren pulled out her smart phone and began pinging friends on Facebook chat. Charlie sat on the couch and feigned interest while the talking heads chattered about the weather and gave a rundown of the next news hour. Gary had no interest in conversing, because to focus on the people in front of him would mean reflecting on Sam's absence, and he couldn't go there. Not yet. The following days and months would nearly kill him as he clung to memories of his daughter, his eldest still the tiny and vulnerable package of sugar they'd brought home from the hospital two decades ago, back when he was just getting his first gray hairs, before he'd settled into the pugnacious features of the middle-aged executive. Beth had her own grief, but she'd always been one to lick her wounds in private. When they'd suffered wounds together in the past, Beth had found the reserve to tend to him, to ask how everyone was doing, but with Sam's death, she couldn't muster a word. Perhaps that was why she invited Charlie to dinner, to add that one extra body to help deflect the family's grief, to keep themselves in the public sphere for a few more hours. Once Charlie was gone and it was just the Jameses with their grief, the night would become unbearable.

So Gary tuned out completely, flipped back and forth between Fox News (an explanation of how the tax bill would help the country finally heal from the wound of Hillary's emails), and SportsCenter (baseball highlights and the upcoming football season preview, rankings of college coaches and yet another athlete brain injury).

Beth returned with three bags of food, and Charlie was the only one to help her set out plates and set the table. When all the food was presented, she said, "It's here when everyone's ready," and then she returned to the kitchen to natter. "Go on and start, Charlie," she said, "Go on. Lauren. Dinner."

"Did you get any guacamole?" Lauren asked, rifling through the bags.

"Umm. Should I have?" Beth said.

"It's only the best part."

"I didn't think you liked guacamole."

"Mom, that was Sam."

"Oh."

"She was the picky eater, remember? No cheese, no guac, no sausage."

"I guess you're right."

Lauren went on, "She always said, 'Pigs are smart.' She couldn't stand the thought of grinding up their flesh."

"Lauren."

"That's what sausage is! We always argued about it. Meat tastes great, but if you want to eat it, you have to accept an animal's got to die. I always thought she didn't have the courage of her convictions. Didn't want to kill the poor pig, but didn't mind a cattle prod going into a cow's brain so we could eat steak."

"Lauren!"

"Lauren, that's enough," Gary said.

"Whatever. At least you got the green salsa."

Beth opened her mouth as if to say something but then seemed to forget whatever she had in mind.

Gary filled a plate of tacos and said to Charlie, "Help yourself."

"Yes, please, eat," Beth said.

Gary brought the remote over to the table and continued watching TV while he nibbled at a few tacos. He added the Weather Channel to the rotation, muttered, "Looks like a week of rain coming up."

"Oh, that's too bad," Beth said as she filled her own plate with tacos.

Charlie and Lauren said nothing. Charlie sat next to her and tried to think of something to say, his own grief simmering quietly while hers remained on display as a rolling boil. It felt good to eat something. He'd not eaten much since the accident, his own house quiet and the hours long. He understood this might be his last meal with the Jameses, no reason for him to be invited back, little reason he might want to return. After an otherwise silent dinner, after Gary returned to the couch and Charlie, urged by Beth, joined him while Beth and Lauren cleared the table and gingerly broached the subject of what next regarding Sam.

"The police are just moving so slow," Lauren said. "I mean, you think they would have pulled some paint samples and have an idea of what kind of car they're looking for."

"Maybe they do," Beth said.

"And they can't communicate that with us? We have a right to know who might have killed Sam."

"Actually, I hear there is a person of interest who's come forward. My yoga instructor is a police officer, and she mentioned it at the funeral. Said it was just rumors right now, but she thinks someone might be turning himself in, if he hasn't already."

"Good. He's a monster and should be thrown away."

"We don't know the full facts yet," Beth said.

Lauren stopped with the dishes, put her hands on the counter. "No one does this. No one drives away when you hit and murder someone."

"Well, maybe his lights were dim. You know, cars these days."

"And he wouldn't hear it? He wouldn't feel the collision? Why are you defending him?"

In truth, Beth had no idea why she was making theoretical excuses for the abstract killer of her daughter. She was feeling combative toward Lauren and didn't know why. Misdirected pain in losing Sam, upset that Lauren was seventeen and could say what Beth could not, the world was on fire and they still had to do the dishes. Lauren: beautiful, lean, soft-skinned, and a seething stew of emotional turmoil. She could act out and have the rest of the world chalk it up to being a teenager, whereas Beth—frumpy, wrinkled, doughy—had to uphold old notions of decency. Still, while it hurt her to see her daughter in pain, she recognized Lauren's angst and picked at it, passive aggressively, perhaps covering up for the way she'd lived her own life, in which she was no longer confident.

"I don't know, honey," she said. "I'm just trying to think what would possess someone to drive away. All I can think is he didn't know what he was doing."

"Don't be naive. He knew full well what he was doing, and he didn't want to get caught. If he's turning himself in, it's just because he thinks he'll get a lighter sentence. We can't let that happen."

"We'll see," Beth muttered again.

"We'll see," her daughter echoed. "What you mean is, you're not planning to do anything. Nothing but wither away here and pretend like everything's normal. Let's order out tacos! Let's put on Fox News! Let's blame dim headlights for someone killing my sister. My sister!"

From his perch on the couch in the family room, Charlie listened as the discussion grew heated. He sensed Gary had tuned out completely, zonked into TV land, and he wished he were anywhere else. He grew more and more morose, knew he'd had no business accepting Beth's hasty invitation for dinner, yet here he was, and what he had to contribute to the conversation, too late, was a comment: "You're right about the lights," he said, and the women quit bickering in the kitchen to stare at him.

"What are you talking about?" Lauren asked.

"The lights. Most new cars have dim bulbs, so a lot of people around here drive with their fog lights on all the time."

Mother and daughter were silent for a moment, nothing but the steady drone of a blonde anchor on TV and her leading questions about Medicaid expansion to a plaster-haired state representative. Then Lauren turned to her mother and asked, "Why is he still here?" She turned back to Charlie. "Why are you still here?" Her mother shushed her, but she went on, "You're not part of this family. I don't know why you came over. We tolerated you because of Sam, but you don't belong here. Sam didn't even love you. She was seeing someone else. Why don't you get out and let us grieve in peace?"

5

Why are you still here? Charlie had been asking himself this since he graduated from high school. Everyone else seemed to have big plans. The high school cap and gown ceremony had plenty of talk about the future and what his generation could and would do in the world—big things!—yet he'd remained in town, moved fifty feet from where he'd grown up, found a job he didn't like, and had limited aspirations for anything beyond the hump between adolescence and adulthood.

Sam had been his way out.

Grace, she called herself, in college. Samantha Grace James, always Sam, now Grace, one more American trying to reinvent herself, or perhaps just a lost college student experimenting with different masks of adulthood. Charlie failed to understand what was happening in her head but had the sense not to probe into hidden corners of her psyche. A nineteen-year-old girl in 21st century America was a complicated organism. The rush of adolescent hormones had begun to taper but the country at large was patronizing toward women younger than twenty-five. Perhaps the same was true of young men, but young men lacked the focus and drive of young women, so the world's slights went unnoticed. You never heard about young men changing their names—except maybe a shortening, Mike not Michael, Dave not David—but names meant something different to women. Even Charlie Gibbs could intuit this. He tried not to think about what future might be in store for him and Sam (or Grace). Whatever her name, he loved her, of course, but he also loved the possibilities he saw when he was around her. He clung to that potential and let everything else slide. When she was around, there was no need to ask why he was still here, or, for that matter, why he was here at all. She gave him purpose, she made him feel like he belonged in the world. When he came home with her to the James house, in their gated community, he was conscious of being a rube—not knowing which way to set the fork and knife at the table, not understanding world events, not being in college—but he'd been enough for Sam, which was all that mattered.

Now someone had taken her away: had smacked their car into her and driven off, leaving Sam to bleed to death internally, sending Charlie back to being a nobody, with no companion and no future. Lauren was right: the person of interest was a monster. Lauren would grieve in her own way, through angry letters to the newspaper and lobbying state and local representatives for change, and organizing bicycle rallies and candlelit vigils. She would find meaning within crowds, a balm within politics. She went to rallies with the local bicyclist league, followed the news of Daniel Hayward's arrest, seethed hatred and acted with zeal and spent late nights researching him and his family and his lawyer and the law. By the time Charlie ran into her, months later, in the greeting card aisle at Target, Lauren had transformed her life into a single-minded pursuit. In the interim, Charlie Gibbs had only stewed.

The night of the funeral, after Lauren told him to get out and let the family grieve in peace, after stiff and unpleasant goodbyes and his furtive exit, Charlie went home to his room above his mother's garage, and couldn't sleep. Along with Sam, he'd lost his self-esteem, and self-respect, and the bulwark of optimism that made him feel okay about being a used car salesman with just a high school diploma. If a person of interest had come forward, then the hammer of justice had been cocked, a bullet with the man's name on it, and Charlie Gibbs made a vow that he would see it through. He would guarantee the world was not a random, meaningless place. There were no accidents. People made choices and they had to live with them.

After sweating in bed for a long time, Charlie crept into his mother's house, snagged a glass and filled it with vodka from her liquor cabinet and returned to his cave, where he drank the vodka and thought about this life until he was drunk and no longer thought about his life and went to bed, saving unanswered questions for another day.

6

Samantha Grace James had the unique ability to make those around her shine. Her parents first noticed it when she was still a baby, her personality innate, the biological lightning strike a jackpot for them, for she was a happy baby. Laughter and squeals brought life into their house. When the second baby, Lauren, arrived, her father took Sam out for doughnuts and tried to make her feel special even though Lauren had snatched their mother's attention. Lauren was a colicky, angry baby with dark hair and dark eyes and a ruddy face and an easy scream. Sam watched her baby sister with perplexity, intrigued by this menace to her idyllic life. The two sisters carried on like that, fixed at birth, Sam the easygoing leader and Lauren the wild child in constant need of attention and affirmation.

Those personalities flipped in middle school, when Sam began developing extreme anxiety, doubtless a result of the neurochemical swirl of hormones but also the economic downturn, partisan bickering in the news, and the rise of ISIS all taking its toll. She'd been born into the world post-9/11, a state of endless war abroad and a boom at home, and by the time she grew conscious of a world outside her home, the economic world was crashing. On the news, traders looked in horror as indices fell, and her parents stayed up late having long conversations she did not understand. ISIS was the threat of her middle school years, and then the Trump MAGA wars divided her high school years. Between the pressure of school and grades and testing and aggressive parents and college marketing and the general consensus that if you don't have your life's specialty worked out by the time you hit high school you were basically a goner—all that, too, took its toll, even for a comparatively mellow teenager like Sam. She couldn't sleep and the fatigue affected her grades, which created a death spiral that led to her mother seeking counseling from the best doctor, who had no appointments available for six months.

As it turned out, Beth knew the psychiatrist, Dr. Roth, through some charitable fundraising she had done recently, and she believed the doctor would see her daughter and help her if she could only get him on the phone, but the receptionist was insistent that she call back in six months. Never one to back down from a battle, Beth paid to run a background check on Dr. Roth and discovered his private cell number.

"How did you get this number?" he asked. "My wife, my children, a few friends, that's all. No one has this number."

"So you'll see Samantha?" Beth pressed, until the doctor finally gave in.

"She'll grow out of it," was the best he could offer, though he did prescribe a light dose of Paxil, nothing she would even notice but that might help as a placebo.

She remained on a half-dose of Paxil through high school and into college, and checked in with Dr. Roth twice a year.

"Mm hmm, mm hmm," he said to her philosophic concerns over neurochemical adjustment, whether her personality was actually hers or belonged to her medication, but at the end of their sessions he inevitably gave her a renewed prescription and told her it was her choice whether she filled it. There are two types of people in the world: those who follow the rules and those who don't. Sam followed the rules, and felt that a prescription was a doctor's order, so she took the drug as prescribed without fail, and it leveled her moods and allowed her to flourish.

After her death, when a friend created a private message board and memory blog in her honor, her high school friends wrote in to say they would miss her mordant sarcasm and her general levity. She had wit and could ironically hang with the best of them, but it was never the kind of sarcasm that belied cruelty or low self-esteem. She was nobody's fool, would scrunch up her nose when her teachers handed out an unfair assignment or issued contradictory statements, yet she somehow was able to take the long view as the kids shunted through the education-industrial complex, the freedoms of adulthood the shining beacon toward which they were all heading. Before adulthood proper: college. When she arrived on the South Carolina campus, she abruptly changed her name to Grace. She'd always liked her middle name, not only for its sound but for its biblical connotations. She'd been raised in the Episcopal church, that most waspish of denominations, and secretly saw herself as an instrument of the Lord. Grandiose, yes, but like many theologically confused young people, she'd found purpose in some higher power with the authority to forgive. She'd never been seriously hurt by anyone, had never been wronged nor wronged someone, so Sam's (Grace's) conception of forgiveness was limited to everyday banalities: an irritation, a slight, a spat. Yet if you had asked her what her values were, she would have cited the New Testament virtues of loving one's enemy and forgiving others their trespasses.

She read the four gospels for the first time in their entirety during the summer between high school and college, when she first started working as a hostess at Tokyo and had plenty of time on her hands. She and her girlfriends geeked out over books, and

Sam would read anything with a good story: *The Fault in Our Stars*, *Harry Potter*, and she had a soft spot for Agatha Christie's Miss Marple. Still, she had a bookshelf filled with summer reading for honors English, everything from the Brontë sisters (loved them) to *Madame Bovary* (no sympathy for her) to *Beloved* (could there be a more perfect book?), yet had a thirst for more. She was stunned to find, in the books of Matthew, Mark, Luke, and John, Jesus the man: scruffy, impoverished, ill-tempered. He was a revolutionary who comforted her soul and gave her the courage of her convictions. Though it must be said: she seldom spoke of her theological interests. Overlook was predominantly Christian in theory and went through the motions, but she suspected no one else she knew felt it in her bones quite so acutely. She tried to discuss it with Charlie, who in some ways reminded her of Jesus: thin and delicate as a bird, a gentle soul.

"I haven't been to church since I was in elementary school," was all he said.

"But did you ever *feel* it when you were there? Like someone was actually watching over you?"

"I guess. I don't really remember."

"How can you not have an opinion about these things? This is your soul we're talking about."

"I mean, I went to church as a kid, but after my dad left, my mom and I only went on holidays, or when I visited my grandparents."

"Do you believe in God? In the afterlife?" she asked him.

"I guess."

"You guess."

"I mean, yes, but it's not like I think about it that much," he said.

"What if you died tomorrow? What if a piano fell out of the sky and crushed you? Do you feel like you're right with the Lord and would go to heaven?"

"I think so."

"Jesus, Charlie, what am I going to do with you?"

To Charlie, Sam was earthy and athletic, a kind soul, sure, but not preachy by any means. No, she wasn't a Jesus freak or anything. She may have read the bible but she was always reading, when she wasn't listening to music.

Music: there was her other sweeping interest. Her friend Margaret wrote on the message board that Sam was her concert buddy, always up for a trip to a festival or up to Charleston to the nearest record shop (a record shop!). They liked Foster the People and Imagine Dragons and Jenny Lewis and, somewhat embarrassingly for Margaret, Lana del Ray. In fact, Margaret had dragged out "Summertime Sadness," anthem of their middle school years, whose tone captured the watery sound of loss. Margaret was not a bicyclist, nor particularly athletic, but she synced up with Sam's sister at one of the candlelight vigils and thereafter went to all the weekend rallies, coming home from Columbia, where she and Sam (Grace) had been enrolled. No, Margaret never got used to calling her friend by her new name, but Sam never minded, never said, "No, my name is Grace now." Instead, she threw her arm around Margaret and smiled and gave her a friendly shake. Oh, Margaret missed her friend all right, she wrote on the message board. She was having problems in school, actually, and was thinking of transferring to the local satellite campus for a semester or two.

The University of South Carolina was an urban campus and melded with downtown, yet even in such a public and populated place, where anonymity should have been guaranteed, Sam's presence was felt and missed. Friends recalled her as a team player in rugby. She had the enthusiasm of a leader who has stared clearly at the world and, like the messenger in Plato's allegory of the cave, returned to offer a pep talk on the long view. How will we win? *By being stronger! Faster!* What will we do? *Train harder! Longer!* What makes us better? *Teamwork!* She could lead the rah-rah charge before a game and afterward, at someone's house party, sing fight songs while standing on furniture, beer in hand, sober in mind, happy in spirit. Meanwhile she was bored with her college classes. She went through the hoops to get her A, but felt cheated when she learned the university curriculum was no different from high school. One of her professors recalled being disarmed by her clear thinking. He was young and green and not much older than his students, so a simple *What is the point of this essay?* from Sam (Grace) made him rethink his career, shocking given that he was on the tenure track. No, she had an effect on people, and they remembered her, that much was clear.

Charlie stayed up late throughout the fall after her death, rereading the message boards and thinking about the past year together. Even after she left for college, she returned home to see him, and she worked at Tokyo during the holidays. The restaurant was open on Christmas, and although she took the holiday off with her family, she always went in on the 26th. "It's Boxing Day," she said. "We box up all the leftovers and send them off to the needy." In the middle of Sam's freshman year, the restaurant held an after-hours holiday party on the day after Christmas. Sam invited Charlie, and he was her designated driver (she didn't own a car, and he always had something spiffy in the driveway, thanks to his work), so she drank sake and red wine and grew flushed in the face and on the ride home insisted Charlie take her to his place for the night. "What are my parents going to do?" she asked. "I'm an adult. I can make my own decisions." He thought she was buzzed even though she was drunk, and he was buzzed himself, and weaved the car into his driveway and escorted her up to his above-garage apartment where, for the first time, they made awkward love, both of them virgins and doing their best to pretend they knew what they were doing. *We got this!* she said at one point. *Yeah, baby!* he replied.

Yes, they really said that. Blame the wine.

In the morning, she had no regrets about their night together but she certainly regretted her choice to end the night with a sake bomb, all that alcohol swirled in her blood and she was probably still drunk when he drove her home and parked at the edge of the neighborhood. "I'll walk the rest," she said. "See if I can sneak in the back door."

"I thought you said you were an adult."

She leered at him, slapped her hand on his shoulder, and said he was a really sweet person. "I'll see you, Charlie," she said.

There ensued a honeymoon period where they got together a few times a month. Call it what it was: for Charlie, at least, some animal emerged. Men change after sex. One might compare it to a butterfly breaking free of its cocoon, if the butterfly had swagger. He called her up without fear, he took off his clothes with confidence, he assaulted her with hickeys, and he guided them through all manner of acrobatics in bed. And for her part? Sam was no downy innocent, she had her own biological urges, but she also compartmentalized her life and indulged him as one box, while her studies fell in another box and her rugby training yet another. Whereas men go from rough and tumble boys to tortured adolescents to confident adults—one cocoon, one emergence—women went through a series of phases. Sam's anxiety at thirteen was a manifestation of her body's rapid chemical development, and she emerged at fifteen a young woman with a delightful sense of humor and sharp insights and general good cheer. But she entered another transition as a freshman in college—changed her name, segmented her life, became somewhat unmoored in her sense of self—and while her friends still recognized her as the warm and together girl she'd always been, they also took note of the subtle ways she held herself back. She no longer gave herself over to the world, eyes dewy and wide, but rather squinted and studied her surroundings, perhaps with bemusement or perhaps with skepticism. One tragedy is the world never saw her next incarnation materialize. What great things might she have done in life once she reconciled the compartments? True, she may have become just another body in a sea of ordinariness, but she also may have changed the world.

The summer after her freshman year, she returned home to Overlook, nested inside herself, and picked back up with Tokyo. She brought Charlie a bamboo plant she'd found at a flea market, and he'd put it in water and set it on his dresser before taking her to bed. She saw him frequently, to her parents' chagrin, but it was on off days. Their work schedules failed to coincide, and he grew frustrated by her distance and the way he, too, was kept outside her soul, at bay. She was introverted by nature, and when she was not working, she needed a certain amount of down time, which she never received at home with her parents and sister, Lauren especially an overly vocal theatrical type who believed all the oxygen in the room was for her dramatic monologues about her life and her opinions of the world. Their parents indulged her and urged her to consider moving to New York one day to start a career. Did they actually believe she would make it? Sam wondered. Or were they merely entertaining her so as not to stifle her? Would it be better for them to offer some old-fashioned Midwestern realism, a flint-eyed look at the world and Lauren's future in it? Same couldn't say, but rather than listen to her sister drone on in that voice of theater people, enunciating too carefully in a non-accent and projecting throughout the house, she took long jogs, four and five and six miles at a clip. She ran with headphones and streamed music through her phone and thus knew every time Charlie called her. On these jogs she invariably hit *ignore*, but once, on an unreasonably hot afternoon when Charlie called a third time during her hour-long outing, she swiped to answer just in time to hear him yell, *Pick up your phone!* and then back-peddle when he realized she had, in fact, answered.

"What do you want, Charlie?"

"Just saying hi."

"Hi. I'm running."

"You're always running."

"Well, I want to stay in shape for fall rugby."

"I had the afternoon off. Thought we might go out to the beach."

"Nah, I'm tired and sweaty."

"I never see you."

"We just went out."

"Over the weekend," he said.

"Well."

In the ensuing silence she could feel him trying to decide how far to probe into her melancholy. Would he ask: *What's happening to us?* Or: *Do you still love me?* Or: *Is there someone else?* (I don't know. I don't know. No.) She had no answers and was languishing in the summer heat and dwelling on her life, its compartments, and the way she and Charlie were not always as simpatico as they once were. Where before there'd been an almost electrical current between them, now he felt warm and stale and had the perennial vacuum and Armor All scent of the car dealership. He was not an interesting person, and although she was no snob and had little truck with cosmopolitan know-it-alls, she wanted something more from a relationship beyond screwing around. Call it what it was: perhaps in the beginning they had been making love, but now it was an athletic event, an entertainment, profane and, when it came down to it, rather dull. She was bored with him and bored with her family and bored with Overlook and uncertain how to regain her footing. Perhaps her anxiety medication needed to be readjusted, or perhaps, beneath the friendly sarcasm and congeniality and the team player mantras, she had a secret dark sliver to her heart that made her want to ignore Charlie and let him sweat on the other end of the line. *Answer your phone!*

"So I guess I'll see you when I see you," he was saying, and for a moment she almost stopped him, poor needy Charlie, a wet dog you almost couldn't help but take home, but she held her tongue and let him hang up.

Charlie, too, sensed something amiss that summer, and felt as though he were attempting to scale an eight-foot wall. He could sense what was on the other side but couldn't see it. The shadows grew long after the solstice. The heat and humidity settled in and Overlook set to marinating. Sweat on the small of your back and your temples from dawn to dusk. He and Sam simmered, occasionally went out and continued kissing but neither was in the mood for sex in this heat, and with the flame of physicality guttering, even Charlie sensed he and Sam had little to say in the dispassionate moments. They came from different worlds, and while that had mattered little as seniors in high school, the differences between them grew more and more pronounced. He could feel her on the verge of breaking up with him, and he considered whether he should preemptively break up with her, rip off the bandage and take control of the situation. Instead, he remained inert, worked longer hours at the car dealership, put on a plastic smile and talked to buyers about scotch guarding their fabrics, heated seat upgrades, extended warranty plans, and why he could only give them $2,200 for their trade-in. He was never at the top of the sales ranks, but he also was never at the bottom. He made enough to fly under the radar, a non-being with no Rolodex of leads.

Then Sam and her mother went on their trip to Michigan. The last time Charlie saw her, Sam had come over and spent half the night with him. In a panic, he'd gone out and bought salmon and lemon and pasta and a pinot grigio from an actual wine shop rather than just the local Publix, and had cooked a not-bad dinner for her for which, he felt, she rewarded him by making love, actual love, and lying with him under a light sheet, dozing, for several hours. But around three she slunk out of the bed and began to get dressed. At first he thought she was just using the bathroom, and then he assumed she was cold and said he could turn the overhead fan off or dial down the window unit, but she told him she had to go.

"God, what time is it?"

"Don't worry about it," she said.

"How are you getting home? You can't ride your bike this late."

"I'll be fine."

"Let me drive you." He sat up and leaned over his knees. She lay a hand on his shoulder and told him not to worry, she'd be fine. "I'll worry about you," he said.

"I'll send you a message when I get home."

And she was gone. Just like that: out the door, to her bicycle, to ride home under moonlight. True to her word, she texted to say *I'm home* but nothing more, and then she was gone for a week, and then she was killed. It was only a couple of miles to her house, and she made the ride regularly, no big deal, and the truth was that night she felt immense relief when she trudged out to her bicycle. For the first time all summer, she felt free, and the freedom came, she knew, because she'd accepted it was over with Charlie. No regrets, but it was time to move on. Her mother likely wanted to tell her on the plane ride to Michigan that Charlie was going nowhere and perhaps Sam would do well to broaden her horizon. Well, now she could cut off that conversation, which would force her mother to find something else to nag her about, or, worse, find something actually of interest to say. She was tired on the ride home, yes, but the moon was nearly full, just beginning to wane, and the stars lit up the sky and the road and the entire coastal plain so that it could have been dusk rather than full dark. The night had cooled and a breeze tousled her hair and she stood on the pedals and thought again about her life and basked in her liberation. It would require one more conversation with Charlie, which she knew must be in person after she returned from Michigan, but she had time to organize her thoughts and perhaps feel out a few friends for their advice on how to end it quickly and securely.

Charlie watched her walk out the door and then returned to bed with a cobwebbed mind and the beginnings of a bad wine hangover, and even still he knew in his gut it was over. Had he been able to persuade her to stay, he believed she might have woken up and seen him and the world in a new light, but instead he woke the next morning and saw himself in a new light. The bamboo she'd given him at the beginning of the summer had turned yellow and was beginning to rot in the mason jar of water on his dresser. He'd read somewhere that the key to self-healing was to take care of a plant, and then take care of a pet, and then consider entering a relationship. Learn to care for one thing at a time, and after a year, you were prepared for human commitment. He'd failed the first test, he let his plant die, and he was afraid to pick up a dog. Old Charlie: can't do anything right, just like his namesake from the *Peanuts* comic strip. He was a wet noodle, soft and flavorless, empty calories.

7

Michigan: a sea change for Sam in the heart of America. The idea was a last chance for her to see her grandfather while he was still lucid, his slide into dementia happening rapidly. The doctors said he might live on for several more years, but his memory would not hold out. It started when she was still in high school, his slipped memory and his tendency to repeat himself, small missteps the family blamed on his refusal to get a hearing aid. They only visited him and Sam's grandmother once or twice a year, for Memorial Day and Thanksgiving, and it was easy for Sam and Lauren to misread their grandfather's decline as the simple doddering of your average elderly. Their parents discussed Jack's decline often, and what Barbara might do when he was gone. Sam's mother grieved for her grandfather even though the man was still here, dying one stage at a time, memory and consciousness evaporating like a splash of water on hot pavement, or erasing like chalk, leaving only the residual dust of personality and bodily functions in their wake. The body was a meat sack: respiration, circulation, digestion, input, output, life but not quite life. Small things continued to clue them in during Sam's freshman year. They received two Christmas cards from Jack and Barbara, each written by Jack, each saying nearly the same thing, one postmarked three days after the next. Barbara hired a home aid worker to come in three days a week to help Jack with daily tasks and give her time to do the shopping and a few moments alone to think. She put on a brave face to the world, and only hinted to Sam's mother the difficulty of living with a man whose memory was in decline. "Like living with a toddler all over again," she said once on the phone.

By mid-summer, it was clear Barbara needed more help than an occasional caregiver could offer, and it was agreed within the family, somehow, that Jack would try out an assisted living facility. Temporary, of course, just a few days or weeks to give Barbara some relief, and Beth and Sam would come up for a week to help her scout out a place. Besides, Sam was only home for a few more weeks and it would be nice for her and Beth to spend some quality time together. Sam was of the generation of girls who were very good friends with their mothers, who admired their parents, and now that Sam knew her relationship with Charlie was over, she was free to enjoy herself with her mother. They laughed and flirted and cried over her grandfather, who kept mistaking Sam for Beth as a young woman. They found a homey facility that prided itself on its faith-based nonprofit status and its vibrant social connections, got him situated, and kept Barbara company during those first nights she was alone without a husband in half a century.

"He's a good man," Barbara said to Sam one evening over dinner, her jaw quivering. "I got a good one." She put a hand over Sam's and looked her in the eye and said, "You'll find someone like that, and when you do, you'll know."

"Did you know Dad was the one?" Sam asked her mother later that evening, over a glass of wine, after Barbara had gone to bed.

"I suppose, though maybe not at first. We were all focused on having fun as a group, in college, and somehow Gary and I just kept finding ourselves alone, and, well. I sometimes think he orchestrated it ahead of time, but that could be me being paranoid. It was just so strange the way our friends fell away, and after a few months of that, I couldn't resist him. He somehow became my best friend."

Her mother quit then and stared off with a wistful smile. Sam had heard some version of that story from both her mother and her father at different points of her life, and she knew enough to know there was more to it—more, and less, as with everything significant in life—but also knew whatever mystery lay at the heart of her parents' marriage, it would remain an untold story. Time moved on, and she had a vision of herself one day, perhaps married with her own daughter, visiting Beth to help Gary settle into an assisted living facility, or, worse, a funeral, and it made her sad to think of her parents aging like that and the responsibilities of living that would be heaped on her, as they were now heaped on her mother. She could change her name to Grace and start a new life after college in any other city or town in America, but it was still her life, and she must live it. There was no escape. This insight—the way time moves and generations replay themselves and none of us is the center of the world for long—was significant and precocious and one of the last epiphanies Sam would have in her too-short life. She returned to Overlook with her mother the following week, and returned to Tokyo for the evening shift after their plane landed. Her father was out when Beth and Sam arrived home, and Sam set her suitcase in her bedroom and changed her clothes and told her mother she was off to work.

"I don't know how you have the energy," Beth said, clearly exhausted herself and ready to take a nap on the couch. "You sure you're up for it? That was a long flight after a long trip."

"I'm scheduled to close."

"But if you needed to take the night off."

"Mom, they'll fire me."

Beth shook her head. "We wouldn't have to tell your father, is all."

"I'll see you in the morning," Sam said, and she walked out and hopped on her bicycle and pedaled off to the restaurant.

It was a slow night, a weeknight, and she spent much of the evening on her phone at the hostess stand, scrolling through Facebook and Instagram. Charlie had texted her often while she was in Michigan and, out of politeness, she'd replied. He was looking forward to seeing her, he said. Did she want to plan a date night? Those messages she ignored, but he knew when she was coming home and asked her repeatedly to stop by his place, just for a few minutes, just to say hello, after she got off work.

"I can pick you up, if you want," he said.

"I have my bike."

"It can fit in my trunk."

"I'll see how I'm feeling."

She worried he might show up while she was on her shift, but he had the sense to stay home and wait for her, and somewhere in the final hour she actually did make up her mind that tonight was it: she would ride over there, tell him it was over, and then scoot home and be in bed before midnight. Charlie felt the vibrations and knew what was coming, which may explain why he was in no rush to go out and find her when she didn't arrive right after her shift. It was why he went down to make a snack in his mother's kitchen while she lay dead on the highway, why it took him time to work up the nerve to go after her. He never expected to find her on the roadside. Rather, he believed she'd simply given up and gone home, and that he would have to try to talk his way into their gated community, park in her driveway, toss rocks at her window and negotiate with her from the swampy bushes behind her house. He may not have been the brightest headlight on the car lot, but he knew what was coming even if he wasn't ready to confront it.

What if Sam really was seeing someone else? What if Lauren was speaking the truth that day after the funeral, and there was another boy in her life? When news leaked about the missing hour between the time Sam clocked out and the time Charlie found her on the road, he couldn't help but wonder. Perhaps the man was that line cook at Tokyo, a couple years older than Charlie and Sam, the guy with sandy hair and a winning smile he'd seen her eyeing once. One more thing Charlie had ignored all summer. What would the relationship have looked like?

Originally from Hawaii, the cook—call him Walter—mysteriously appeared in Overlook earlier this summer, perhaps for the golf. You can't account for human chemistry, and work in a restaurant can get dull. You need the banter among co-workers to keep the shifts humming. It wouldn't have taken much, a few flirtatious comments between them. Maybe he put a hand to the small of her back in passing through the drink station. Maybe they sat on the patio during one of their breaks, where she probed Walter about his prior life.

"Why would you leave Hawaii to come here?"

"Have you ever been to Hawaii?" he asked.

"I went with my parents one summer in high school."

"And?"

"And it was lovely. The sun. The water. The fresh fruit. I've never been so relaxed."

"You can't go through life like that."

"I could."

"Well, I couldn't. I needed to experience something other than the island I grew up on, so I came east for school."

That still didn't explain how he meandered his way to Overlook, but she was having too good a time with him for a full-on interrogation.

Her mother, however, interrogated her one afternoon when the two of them ran into Walter in the Target parking lot. It was just a friendly hello, but he introduced himself to Beth unbidden, the way a proper adult would.

"He seems nice," her mother said.

"He is," Sam replied, simultaneously hoping her mother would drop it and that she would ask for more details

Her mother obliged. "Tell me more."

The two laughed conspiratorially all the way into the store as Sam shared the few details she knew. "He's the one you should be bringing home for dinner," her mother said as they pulled out a cart.

"Mm," Sam said. She knew her parents didn't think much of Charlie and would prefer she find a new beau. Someone upwardly mobile, with conservative capitalist values and the drive and capabilities to one day own a house in a gated community. Say what you would about Charlie, a house like her parents' wasn't in the cards for him.

Another time, she and Walter had a few drinks after work. He drove her a few blocks into town, for a change in venue. It wasn't a date, she felt, just two friends winding down after work. Split an appetizer? Sure.

"Let me drive you home," he said.

"I can ride."

"What's wrong with you? It's on my way."

"You don't know what's on the way."

He made a face, at once mocking and self-effacing, and she laughed and accepted a ride. It wasn't until they parked in front of her house, and she said, "Well," and he leaned in to kiss her, and they made out for several moments—then she realized she was in trouble.

The next day, during a slow moment at work, he caught up with her and said he had a good time last night. "Me too," she said.

"But we may have taken it too far. You still have your boyfriend, right?"

She wished she could say no, but she paused for too long.

"When you break up with him, we should go out again."

There was the first piece of grit in the system. She pursed her lips and went back to the floor, and the longer she thought about it that night—as she tried to keep water glasses full and tables cleared and orders moving, never enough support from her colleagues—the more she found Walter just a bit arrogant, a bit smug. Who was this Hawaiian to come in and say *when you break up with him?*

But of course he was right. You couldn't fight human chemistry.

When she got back from Michigan with her mother, she knew she needed to have a conversation with Charlie, but she also had a shift at Tokyo.

After clocking out, she found Walter behind the restaurant, hosing down kitchen mats. A tunnel of white light from the back door lit the alleyway, and she took a moment to admire the cut of Walter before her. Muscular, loose, a five o'clock shadow. Independent like a cowboy on the range.

He smiled when he saw her. "I'm heading out," she said. "I, um, I'm breaking up with Charlie tonight."

Walter nodded. He shut off the water and started winding the hose onto the reel. "How do you feel about it?"

"Good. Scared."

"I'm sorry to hear it," he said. "Not like that," he added. "I'm sorry because I know it's not an easy thing to do."

"Ripping off a Band-Aid, right?"

"Basically."

He leaned against the wall beside her and pulled out a pack of cigarettes, and from the pack he extracted a joint. "You want to smoke this with me? Calm your nerves?"

"Sure."

First time for her, and she coughed hysterically from her first puff. Walter said nothing as he took his own drag and held the smoke in for a moment. They finished the joint together and she felt as though they were already a couple. She felt at ease with him and wanted to stay there forever, but after a few final moments, he said he should get back.

She walked around the building and unchained her bicycle, thinking here she goes to break up with Charlie. If her mother could see her now. If people only knew. Young, friendly Samantha James, not as innocent as people thought she was. She'd not rebelled like this in high school, which was maybe a problem now, because she felt unequipped to navigate the world. Charlie. Walter. Her parents. College. Life.

Did she smoke enough to get high before she rode out onto the highway that night? Enough to impair her judgment and contribute to the accident? Did any of this—Walter, the dilemma, the joint—happen at all?

Who can say.

When Charlie thought about it, Walter was the only man who could be in her life, and he could see it play out like this. Earlier in the summer, Walter had left town to visit his family. Charlie showed up at Tokyo and had a Coca-Cola and a sushi roll on the patio. On her break, Sam had come out to join him, where they had almost nothing to talk about. If they were more experienced in life, they both would have understood the relationship had run its course, and they were being too polite to end it. Sam may have known it then. If Charlie knew it, he buried it because, regardless of how he felt around Sam, he needed the relationship to work. It was a comfort to him, something steady in his otherwise go-nowhere life.

So they sat on the patio and said little, and then one of her colleagues came out and sat near them. Sam waved to her, and the girl said, "Hey, good news. Walter's back."

Sam sat up straight. "Today?"

"Yeah. He's here now."

She slid her chair back and, without even looking Charlie's way, she ran inside to say hello to her friend.

Charlie watched her go in, and then he looked at Sam's coworker, who had lit a cigarette at a nearby table. The gal shrugged, and then she offered Charlie a cigarette. He accepted it and the light, and then he waited for Sam to return.

"He's started his shift, so he won't be able to talk long," the gal said. "I'm sure she'll be back in a moment."

She shrugged again, and Charlie finished the cigarette. Then he put a ten-dollar bill under his glass and walked away.

He wasn't sure if Sam ever came back to find him, and the next time they talked she gave a half-hearted apology for abandoning him. The next week she was on the plane to Michigan, and the week after that she was dead.

The rest is silence.

What we know for sure—what we *know*—is that on a Thursday night in July, Samantha James clocked out at ten. We assume that around eleven she climbed onto her bicycle and began pedaling toward Charlie Gibbs's house ready to have The Talk. She'd made this ride plenty during the summer, knew the roads and the rhythms of traffic and how to edge over into the scrub off the asphalt when lights approached. She wore a helmet and had a flashing taillight and believed herself protected. She crossed the six lanes of Highway 278 without an incident, but on Reedy Road, on a clear straightaway—granted, it was dark from the limbs of water oaks masking the waning moon and the bright stars, a shadowy tunnel of road—a Durango came around the bend behind her. Maybe she edged off the road, quit pedaling and held her breath while she waited for the car to coast by her. They always did, and she only grew nervous if there was oncoming traffic, in which case the passing car might cut it close and she would feel the wind. Or, worse, they would tailgate her, as though willing her to get out of their way already, and hover behind her, revving the engine, ready to pass, and wait until the oncoming traffic was clear. It was stressful for sure, being an eco-conscious bicyclist, but tonight there was no one out. The Durango would pass and she would be alone again with the night to prepare her thoughts.

The vehicle approached fast, yet she never turned to look back at it. She knew the driver could see her and would move over. He would pass momentarily and she would watch his red taillights shrink. Then she hit a rock and her handlebars wavered. She squeezed the brakes and wobbled and felt herself about to tip over and braced for the impending crash—not with the car, the car she knew would pass safely, but hitting the dirt and the scuffs on her hands and perhaps a sprained wrist—and there was a short moment where she heard the Durango and understood not only was she wobbling from the rock but the vehicle was too close, the lights too bright, the speed too fast, but she lacked the time to even consider it had been a mistake to come this way or to think about her life and her family and her future and all she would miss. There was no time for any of that, just a spark of panic in her brain before the collision and then everything went dark.

8

Charlie Gibbs stewed into the fall. As the Daniel Hayward trial approached and his Ribo-Flavor sales had flat-lined to become a liability, he wanted—needed—information from Lauren. Was Sam really seeing someone else? Was she about to break up with him for Walter the line cook? He hadn't seen Lauren—hadn't seen any of the Jameses—since the unfortunate dinner when she'd kicked him out and told him to let the family grieve in peace, but then he saw her in the greeting card aisle at Target and approached her as though meeting an old friend. She was holding one of those cards with a vintage photo of elderly women looking sassy, and she neither put it down nor put it in her basket when Charlie rounded the corner and said hello.

"Hey, Charlie," she said.

He jammed his hands into his pockets and asked her what was going on.

"Just shopping. It's my mom's birthday this weekend."

"Tell her I said happy birthday. Hey, I've been keeping up with the news, on the trial."

"Oh yeah," she said flatly.

"Do y'all know who that guy is?"

"Who, Daniel Hayward? Nope."

"I was just wondering. It's a small town, and I'd never heard of him. Wasn't sure if maybe your parents had run into him."

"Nope," she said again.

Lauren looked the same but different somehow, in the season since she'd last seen her. She had her hair in a ponytail and wasn't wearing as much makeup as she ordinarily did, and maybe it was the cooler weather but her cheeks seemed somehow worn, perhaps dried out from the wind, and her skin was on the pale side, but you could tell she was Sam's sister. They had the same body frame, athletic, and some of the same physical features: a minor crookedness in the mouth, full lips, a nearly imperceptible smattering of freckles over her nose. He felt a lump in his throat remembering how Sam had appeared (and with the memory, her smell and her warmth and her humor), and he remembered how Sam's lips and freckles appeared close up, eyes wide, skin fresh. At the same time, Lauren appeared slightly muted. It could have been the fluorescent lights of retail, but he felt like he was looking at her through a dull lens filter. She wore an unflattering striped shirt and jeans, and although he knew part of her flatness was due to not wanting to see him, he also thought she seemed a little sickly, marginally undercooked.

He pressed on. "Are you nervous about the trial?" She was scheduled to testify, whereas Charlie was on standby.

"I'm ready to speak for Sam."

"Have you met with the prosecutor yet?"

"She's been briefing us all along."

"Oh."

She finally looked up at him with interest and asked, "Have you met with her yet?"

"We met over the summer so she could take a statement," he said. "She took a deposition and said she probably wanted me to testify about Sam. I don't know what to say."

"It's pretty straightforward, isn't it? Sam was heading to your house, and when she didn't show up, you went out looking for her. You didn't see anything, did you?"

He shook his head.

"Then you're mostly to confirm the timeline."

"What about you?"

"I'm there to give Sam a human face and show the jury she was flesh and blood."

"I get it," he said although he didn't. Then he said, "I thought about coming to one of your rallies."

"You should."

"I wasn't sure if you'd want me there."

"Of course," she said, and the flatness returned. "We have them every week."

"Are you getting any response?"

"What is it you think will happen?" she asked. "If you've been following the news, you know the town council hasn't acknowledged us, and that even if we complete our petition, there's no money in the town or the county or the state to pay for bike lanes. You're seeing our response every time you see us in the news. We're trying to send a message, Charlie. Are you getting the message?"

"I am, sure."

"Then we're getting the best response we're going to get. People know we're here, they remember Sam, and they won't tolerate another driver like Daniel Hayward. That's all we're going to get."

"I didn't mean to stir you up," he said.

"You asked."

"Well. Good luck, I guess."

"Come out if you want. Next rally is Friday night."

"Maybe I'll see you there," he said.

She was already looking at another greeting card. He moved on to the pharmacy aisles and picked up what he came in for, deodorant and ear swabs and shampoo, necessities he inevitably ran out of at the same time. He paused in the aisle with the protein shakes and vitamins, just to see what was here. Nothing like Ribo-Flavor on the market, just your standard chocolate and vanilla powders promising muscle tone. He wondered how Muscle Milk and the rest of them got their products into Target, because that would be a coup. He thought about trying to track down the store manager, but then he thought he might need to have some literature and, hell, he only had one box of Ribo-Flavor in his trunk in case the manager wanted to buy it right away, and the manager might want his whole supply.

No, he'd come back for the manager, but there was Lauren. Was he friends with her on Facebook? Did she know about his venture? He couldn't be sure. Sam would have understood the value of Ribo-Flavor, would have appreciated the energy boost before she went out on the field. If Lauren were into athletics— and even if she weren't, if she just needed some muscle tone for, whatever, moving theater sets around—she might need a little pick-me-up. And there were her biker friends, of course, at the rallies.

He found her in the baby section. She was studying some kind of plastic cap, and it wouldn't occur to him until much later to wonder why she was in this section of the store. At the time, she simply looked up at him and said quickly, "Oh. You're still here."

"Yeah, I found what I needed." He lamely held up his shampoo and deodorant and cotton swabs. He steeled himself. "Hey, listen, I wanted to ask you. About Sam. After the funeral, you said—"

"Forget about it."

"I mean, I just want to know."

"I spoke out of turn," she said.

"So there wasn't anyone else?"

She put the cap back on the shelf and was looking down the aisle when she said, "No. No one else."

Why believe her? Why not press her on the point? But he lacked the courage. After an awkward silence, he changed the subject. "I also wanted to talk to you about something else."

"Oh yeah?"

"You know I'm selling cars at Davis Brothers Auto-Max, and, uh, I have this colleague, well, several colleagues, actually, and we, uh, you know, work out and stuff together."

She squinted and blinked as he blundered to the point.

"It's a great opportunity, actually," he rambled on, "where you can make a little money selling shakes directly, or you can get your friends on board, like if you have some bicycle friends, and if they sell to their friends and family, you get a commission."

Lauren stood there with her basket in one hand, empty save for a greeting card for her mother, and a breast pump part in her other hand, and she patiently listened to his pitch for Ribo-Flavor all the way to the end.

"So what do you think?" he finished.

She set the breast pump part back on the hook and smiled and stared at him for long enough that he wondered if he had a zit that needed to be popped or something hanging from his nose.

Then finally she laughed.

"What?"

"This is a pyramid scheme, you dumbass."

"What do you mean?"

"Pyramid scheme. Where some snake-oil salesman has a product, and recruits other people to sell it, and they have to recruit other people, and all the money goes to the top until the whole thing falls apart. That's what brought down Bernie Madoff. Don't you pay attention to the news?"

"No, no," he said, growing hot and flustered, "you make money here. I'm selling shakes directly. There's just this other opportunity for you to sell shakes as well."

"And you get a cut, right? Just like whoever recruited you gets a cut of what you sell?"

"Well," he drifted off. "I bought the shakes from him, so I guess he does get, you know, a commission."

"And how many have you sold?"

"Well," he started but couldn't finish.

"Exactly," she said, and she gave him a pitying smile. "You can only sell so much of that stuff, and it won't work if everyone's a seller and no one is a buyer. That's why it's a scheme. You're at the bottom of the pyramid."

"So you're not interested?" he asked.

"Hey, Charlie, I'm sorry to give you the bad news, I really am." And she actually seemed to mean it. "But, no, I don't think this is going to work."

"Well, thanks anyway."

"Maybe I'll see you at the rally Friday," she said as a peace offering. "Sam probably would want you there. I think she really did love you."

"Really? I thought we were about to break up."

"I don't know about that," she said.

He thought again about pressing the point. Then he let it drop. "Thanks for telling me."

"I'll see you, Charlie," she said.

At his car, he put his purchases in the trunk and took a long look at the big box of Ribo-Flavor powder, four gallon-sized tubs plus a few half-cup samples and pre-mixed shakes.

He couldn't understand why his sales hadn't caught fire—he'd shared the messages on his social media page like the literature recommended, and he had friends, after all, maybe not a thousand like some people, but definitely upward of three hundred—and wondered if there was something in his personality. He knew he lacked the charm or the pheromones to convince people to buy what he was selling, and he experienced a bitter moment for having been played the fool. Spencer had called it a multi-level marketing opportunity, and Charlie was at a loss to understand how something could sound so successful yet be so empty. Spencer still worked at the dealership, with his smug sales record and his friendly good-old-boy demeanor. And that haircut! That powdery Republican pompadour that would endear him to your grandmother. The fiend! The worst of it was, Charlie would return to the dealership and smile and make out like things were just grand between them, and like an oversized student loan on an unfinished college degree, his debt from the Ribo-Flavor would dog him with no recourse.

9

He skipped Lauren's weekly rally for Sam. Instead, he picked up an extra shift at the dealership to catch the Friday night crowd. They were mostly browsing, buyers hoping to take a look at the inventory without some sales vulture pouncing on them, no intention of making a purchase for a few months if ever. Well, Charlie was here to accost them with a friendly *how ya doing*. In the off-hours, which could be interminable on a car lot if the weather was bad, he scrolled through his newsfeed on his phone, un-followed Spencer and the other guys selling Ribo-Flavor, and looked up Lauren. His own page still said he was in a relationship with Sam, her page not yet archived as a zombie, posts of sorrow littering her timeline for the past several months. Although the social media giant had policies for the dead in place, many users who shuffled off this mortal coil left a languishing cyber-trail. It would take well into the new year before the powers that be at Facebook would shut her page down, kicking the grievers to the curb and putting an end to several very long seasons of drama.

Lauren's page, meanwhile, was a hotbed of activity, posts and shares and images ranging from cryptic "look at me" commentary (*People better watch out today, because I'm not going to take much more of this*) to sappy lines from poets (*Find ecstasy in life; the mere sense of living is joy enough*) to updates about her sister's trial, which would be held next week. The legal system moved at a glacial pace, it seemed, which gave commentators bountiful opportunity to dig up every unpleasant fact, every untoward photograph, every driving mishap in Daniel Hayward's record. Charlie was astonished by the trove of content available about the man's life, and the more he read the angrier he got. Daniel had received several reckless driving charges in the past few years, no indication that he'd ever driven under the influence, but he was evidently a poor, distracted driver. Yet, somehow, the case was still under discussion. Charlie must admit he'd only been remotely cognizant that Daniel Hayward was in jail, or out on bond, and would stand trial, soon. He'd not followed the litany of proceedings: arraignment, the discovery, the motion to move the trial to a neighboring jurisdiction, the objection being excessive media coverage, and now finally the trial itself. Over the summer the prosecution had contacted him and taken a deposition and said they wanted him to testify. He'd loved Sam, they said, and could give her a human face. He had a voice. He had stories to tell. He'd found her, after all. He'd had to hold her bleeding and lifeless while he waited for help. He'd had to call 911.

Lauren's rally tonight would be the last before the trial, which could be over in a matter of days, or it could end with a mistrial and be reconvened later, or the trial could end and the sentencing could be postponed until after the holidays. Any number of things could drag this out, yet Lauren and her cohorts were out in force as though this were it, the final push for—what? The jury would be sequestered. The judge would be impartial. But if it was cathartic to the protesters…Charlie clicked on one of her photos and began skimming through all her recent uploads. Paranoia washed over him about what Facebook might be tracking, and whether Lauren would know who had visited her page. Would she even think twice about it? After all, he'd just seen her this week, and therefore had a legitimate reason to look her up (*directions to the rally!* he could say) and, anyway, she probably looked up all sorts of information on people, sexual or otherwise. Who was she to judge?

But he was in public and could not remain in his private mind for long before browsers came into the dealership, a father-daughter combo, and he slid off his seat, scurried to the bathroom, and locked himself in a stall to continue his obsession in peace. He thought about whether he should go to the entire trial, even though the prosecution only needed him for the one morning (twenty minutes at most, said Claire Fields). He knew he could sit with the family and show his support for the cause, and wondered how it would look if he stayed away? Had they already forgotten him? Relegated him to the ash-heap of their daughter's latent history? And would his testimony remind the Jameses about that night, the call he'd been the one to make, the way he'd woken Gary and stuttered through the bad news, so that Gary came to an eventual understanding of what Charlie was telling him, and his wife in the background kept asking, what's happening, what's happening? Was he of any use to anyone, Charlie Gibbs, or merely a blight, a vestige of happier days?

After a long time, one of his colleagues came looking for him, banged on the door coming into the bathroom and said, "Hello? Hey, Charlie? You in here?"

But Charlie was too far down the rabbit hole to offer a reply.

10

The newspapers covered the trial more thoroughly than the rest of the media. It was scheduled for three days: Monday,

Tuesday, Wednesday. After opening statements, the prosecution would begin calling its witnesses, and Charlie was on the docket for Tuesday morning. Monday, he skipped work, unable to face his colleague Spencer, now understanding he'd been swindled. Instead, he had a breakfast cocktail of vodka and grapefruit juice and showed up at the courthouse in no shape to follow the trial. He accosted the prosecutor, Claire, telling her, "You get a conviction, and we'll be all right." He couldn't have explained what he meant, only that he felt a hole in his heart that he felt a conviction might cure.

That evening, after a long nap, he read about the day online. Eight women and four men made up the jury, and Daniel Hayward stood accused of leaving the scene of the accident. Claire Fields wore a sharp black skirt suit with a kind of faint gloss to it that said dry-clean only. She carried a large black bag that doubled as her purse and that carried a case file and a legal pad, all of which she left with her table as she stood to give her opening argument.

"Ladies and gentlemen," she said, making eye contact with each member of the jury individually.

She was in no rush. Now was the time for establishing rapport, not simply blundering through her comments. She was neither vicious nor unjust but rather was here to air out the truth of that July night.

"We will prove," she said, "without a shadow of a doubt, that Daniel Hayward was on his way home when he struck Samantha James on Reedy Road and drove off, leaving her to die alone on the side of the highway. She was riding home from work, a college kid trying to make her way in the world. She had on a helmet and white clothing and had not just a reflector but a flashing light on her bicycle. The road was straight and the night was clear, so that anyone driving the speed limit and soberly watching the road would have seen her. In a few moments, you'll hear from the defense. They'll say it was dark. They'll ask why she was out on the road that night. They'll say Mr. Hayward believed he hit a deer, and that he's been fully cooperative. We're not here to debate Mr. Hayward's intentions or his good will. We're here to find the truth, and to carry out the law accordingly. And the truth is simple: Mr. Hayward hit Samantha James, and he drove off. She was nineteen years old, and she died alone in the night."

True to her word, the defense attorney, a blustering and coughing mustachioed man with rapidly graying hair, stood up and argued why the truth was always more complicated. "I don't need to tell you all this. You all have experienced it yourselves, the words that come out wrong, the idea that just won't convey. You'll see much evidence pointing toward Daniel's guilt, yes, but what Ms. Fields did not tell you is that she isn't interested in trying this as a simple hit and run. Ms. Fields is going to try to portray my client as a philandering alcoholic and a menace to society. She's going to play for your sympathies and portray him as no less than the devil, when in fact my client is already in hell. He understands a young woman has died, and you'll find he is not some demon out to wreck the world. I'm sure we can all agree there's a difference between some maniac aiming for a bicyclist and someone driving home after a long day who makes a mistake, unwittingly, and immediately takes responsibility. The truth hinges on more than the sequence of events that night. The truth hinges on character and motivation, and by the end of this trial, you will know fully the truth of Daniel Hayward."

And so it began. The prosecution's initial batch of testimonies established the who-what-where-when: that Daniel Hayward was at the restaurant with Karen Sinclair, that he had wine with dinner, that he dropped her off before driving home along Reedy Road. A guard from one of the nearby neighborhoods testified that he remembered seeing Daniel's Durango speeding by and that a few moments later he heard what sounded like an impact. "Why didn't you investigate to see what had happened? Or call the police?" Henry Somerville asked.

"Well, you hear all kinds of things from a guardhouse. It wasn't like a car accident, with shattered glass and horns and whatnot. He could have just driven off the road."

"I see. So you don't actually know that the speeding car you saw was the one that hit Samantha James?"

"Who else would have done it?"

"But you didn't see the accident itself?"

"No," the man conceded.

Then came a waiter at the restaurant to say Daniel and Karen had consumed an entire bottle of wine.

"Is that a normal amount, would you say?" Claire asked.

"Objection," Henry cut in.

"Rephrase the question," Judge Rhodes said.

"Do your patrons commonly order wine by the bottle for two?"

"It happens on occasion."

"But is it common? Does it happen every shift?"

"Most, bottles go to parties of three or more. Two people usually order by the glass."

The first day ended with a toxicologist whose sole purpose was to say that, no, there was no way to determine what Daniel's blood-alcohol level could have been the night of the accident, but that if Daniel had stopped, it could have been tested.

"So if a person were drunk and didn't want anyone to find out, he might wait a few days before turning himself in?" she asked.

"Objection!"

"Sustained."

"No further questions," she said.

"Defense has no questions, your honor."

"All right, let's stop here for the day," the judge said. "We'll reconvene tomorrow at nine."

The online news article ran a photo of Daniel Hayward waddling up the steps of the courthouse, looking like a boy who just had a bully step on his sandcastle. Charlie stared at that clip, in the dark, the bluish screen of his laptop pulsing late into the evening. He hated the man: his fat self, his loose tic, his baggy coat and his tight shirt. One could look at this photo and see a man haunted by the knowledge of what he'd done, repentant but unable to atone, but Charlie Gibbs saw a smug fucker who surely believed he would soon close this unpleasant chapter of his life and move on to a long, warm, well-fed life. Charlie Gibbs saw his father and every other person who had cut ties and dusted his hands from his obligations.

The next morning Charlie arrived at the courthouse at 8:30, wearing his ill-fitting suit, his tie tight at the throat and his feet sore from where the edges of his loafers cut into his ankles.

He met Claire in an alcove outside the courtroom, along with the James family and an expert medical witness to declare Sam's death from blunt force trauma. Gary and Beth and Lauren each gave him a curt hello, and Gary leaned in to shake Charlie's hand. "Thanks for being here today," he said. He'd put on weight in the last few months, and seemed generally at a loss for what to do with himself. He was not one of those men who, after the death of a child, becomes a crusader against the cause but rather the walking dead. Beth and Lauren, meanwhile, ignored Charlie completely as they compared notes about the day ahead.

"Okay," Claire said, "thank you all for being here today. Like we talked about, just try to relax and tell your stories. The defense will be asking you yes-no questions. He might not have anything to ask, but if he does, the main thing is don't let him fluster you. That's his job, whereas our job is to tell the jury about Sam. You ready?"

The heat in the courtroom was on too high, which may have felt good if they lived somewhere that actually suffered a winter. Here in Overlook, they could open the windows through December and remain temperate, so Charlie was sweating and uncomfortable while the medical expert explained in graphic detail the bodily trauma of Sam's death, how the impact splintered bones and triggered internal bleeding, the shock of which could have stopped her heart instantly. Otherwise, the contusions in her brain and the resulting hemorrhage would have killed her within minutes, meaning that, yes, she could have been alive by the side of the road. It was highly unlikely she would have been conscious, but it was impossible to speculate. Charlie grew faint and felt a thin film of sweat on his back and his arms and his ears clotted as though plugged up, and he focused on the back of the bench in front of him, the grains in the oak, and it reminded him of a church pew from long ago. He breathed in through his nose, out through his mouth, and was about to leave the courtroom for some water when Claire said, "No further questions."

The defense attorney declined to cross-examine, so Claire, from her table, called Charlie Gibbs. She turned toward him and caught his eye and smiled. He kept his gaze on the witness stand and approached and took a seat. The judge appeared to be about seventy and wore large glasses with square lenses and a thin gold frame, the type that hung low over his cheeks so that they appeared to take up his entire face. Behind the glasses his eyes were dark and deep in their sockets, and were inscrutable. Eyeing him, Charlie could believe the judge was thinking, *Let's hear what you have to say, fella,* or *I wonder what the Griddle & Trough's lunch special is today.*

"Raise your right hand," the bailiff was saying, and Charlie followed the instructions, still refusing to look out on the wider courtroom. Salesman or not, he wasn't meant for life in the public view.

When the bailiff stepped away, he caught one glimpse of the defense—the smug attorney, the fat killer—before meeting Claire's eye. She wore the same type of suit she'd worn yesterday, a hugging dark gray that accentuated her hips and lengthened her legs.

"Mr. Gibbs, for the record, will you please tell us about your relationship with Sam?" she asked.

"Sure," he said.

"Into the microphone, please," said Judge Rhodes.

"Sure," Charlie said again. "Uh, Sam and I were dating."

"For how long?"

"About a year and a half."

"Since high school?" Claire prodded.

"That's right. We'd known each other for a long time, but started dating when we were seniors."

"Was it serious?"

"I guess."

"Did you love her?"

"Yes, yes I did."

"Tell us about her."

Charlie could feel he was flubbing it. Claire had prepped him on some talking points, a short outline of things to be sure to mention, but his mind had emptied in front of everyone, so that she had to eke it out of him: Sam was a special girl, kind-hearted, funny, universally beloved, smart, on her way to do great things. There was no mention of her occasional insecurity or Charlie's shortcomings as a suitable mate. Twenty minutes brushed by quickly, and by the end Claire was smiling and nodding and giving off vibes that he'd said the right things, appropriately drawn the scene of the accident, skirted around the true horror while giving the jury a picture of the viciousness, the heartlessness, of Daniel Hayward's actions.

"Anything else you'd like to add?" Claire asked.

Charlie sat for a moment, comfortable now, loosened up, and he took a moment to think before clasping his hands and forming a steeple with his index fingers. He pointed in Hayward's direction and said, "That man is a coward and a crook, and he deserves the worst punishment you can give him."

"Objection!"

"Sustained. The jury will ignore that last statement. Anything else, Ms. Fields?"

"No, your honor."

She'd already turned to her table and was picking up her next folder. Charlie was unable to tell if he'd gone too far and, like a puppy who'd displeased its new master while still trying to figure out the rules, he was eager to atone.

"Your witness," the judge said to the defense.

Charlie's eyes settled on Henry Somerville for the first time today, watched the man walk to the center of the courtroom, hands behind his back, like an overeducated English teacher considering a tough question from one of his students, before asking Charlie, almost like an afterthought, "Were you and Sam having sex?"

"Objection," Claire shouted. "Immaterial."

"I'll rephrase," Somerville said. "What I want to know is how serious your relationship with Sam was."

"Like I told Claire—Ms. Fields—we'd been dating for a long time."

"Yes, and you said you loved her?"

"That's right."

"Did you intend to marry her?"

"That hadn't come up."

"Had you thought about it?"

"Well," Charlie started.

"Yes or no, Mr. Gibbs. Had you thought about marriage?"

"No."

"So you'd describe your relationship as more casual."

"That's not what I said."

"But you weren't planning to marry her."

"Objection," Claire said.

"Where is this going, counselor?" the judge asked.

"What I'm getting at is this: you've just given us a portrait of Samantha James, and I'm trying to show the full picture of this relationship." Somerville turned back to Charlie and said, kinder, "I remember high school. They called it puppy love back in my day. Some people did marry their high school sweethearts, but plenty of us moved on. Were you planning to move on from Sam?"

"No."

"But you weren't planning to marry her?"

"Not yet, no."

"Yet she was riding over to your house after work that evening. Was she planning to spend the night?"

He kept his eyes away from the Jameses and shook his head.

"Please state your answer."

"Yes."

"Did she do that often?"

"No, not often."

"Had you had anything to drink that night?"

"I had a beer with dinner."

"Do you often drink over dinner?"

"Sometimes."

"What about Sam? Did she ever drink?"

"Sometimes."

"But you both are underage. How did you get your drinks? Do you have a fake ID?"

"No."

"Did someone buy them for you?"

"Occasionally?"

"Really? Who?"

"Our parents."

"Your parents buy you alcohol?"

"My mother keeps it around the house."

"What about Sam's parents?"

"They have wine."

"Have they ever given you wine?"

"Yes."

"And Sam? Did they ever give her wine?"

"Yes."

"Were the two of you planning to have some drinks when she got to your house?"

"Maybe."

"Did you ever have drinks at your house?"

"Sometimes."

"Drinks that your mother bought?"

"Sometimes."

"Did Sam ever bring drinks over?"

"Occasionally."

"What did she bring?"

"Sometimes a bottle of wine, or vodka."

"Where did she get it?"

"Objection!"

"Overruled."

"Where did she get the wine, or the vodka, that she would bring to your house?"

"At work, usually."

"At Tokyo?"

"Yes."

"Did she ever drink on the job?"

"I don't know."

"Had you ever smelled alcohol on her breath when she came over after work?"

"I don't remember."

"Think for a moment. You're under oath, so again, had you ever smelled alcohol on her breath, or suspected she'd had a drink at work?"

"Yes."

"Did she ever seem intoxicated when she came over?"

"No, she never got drunk."

"But she did have a drink at work before coming over, on occasion?"

"Yes."

"Did she have any wine or vodka the night she was killed?"

"She didn't have any with her."

"So you didn't find any bottles on Reedy Road and put them in your car before the ambulance arrived?"

"No."

"And you obviously don't know whether she'd been drinking at work that night."

Charlie was silent.

"Did you know she clocked out at ten o'clock, but didn't start riding toward your house until eleven?"

"I did."

"Do you know what she did in that missing hour?"

Charlie didn't answer.

"Do you know who she was with?"

Charlie didn't answer.

"Do you know if she was seeing anyone she worked with?"

"Objection," Claire cut in. "This has no bearing."

"Let me rephrase," Henry said. "Did Samantha tell you she had any plans after work that night?"

"No."

"She didn't call you up and explain what she was doing?"

"No."

"So you don't know whether she spent that hour at the bar, having a few drinks, before she rode her bicycle toward your house?"

"Objection."

"Sustained. We get the picture," the judge said.

Somerville twirled about the courtroom again as if lost in deep thought. Then he said, "I want to go back to this question of how well you knew Sam. I'm wondering if you actually knew her as well as you say you did. Did you, or do you, for instance, get along with her parents?"

"We get along fine."

"Have you kept up with them these past few months?"

"No, but—"

"Did they approve of your relationship?"

"Well, I'm sure—"

"Or do you think they may have been conspiring with Sam to end your relationship?"

"I don't see why."

Charlie was confused and off-balance, and barely noticed when Somerville picked up a sheaf of paper and said he wanted to enter into evidence an exhibit of Sam's cell phone records, recorded from the phone they found on her body.

"Will you read this transcript, between the two red lines?" Somerville asked, handing Charlie the papers.

"Objection. Immaterial."

"Your honor, the prosecution has painted a picture of an innocent victim run down by a maniac, and I'm trying to show this story is not so cut and dried. Both the victim and my client are more complex than the prosecution would have you believe. We're all human here."

Charlie skimmed the paper and his mind left his body and the courtroom altogether, same as it had when the medical expert had been testifying about the blood and gore of the crime scene. Charlie's voice faltered as he read the conversation between Sam and another number, clearly her sister, where they joked about Charlie and his neediness and his lack of a future selling cars. "You don't want to end up with some skeezy dude in a plaid blazer," one of Lauren's messages said, to which Sam replied, "Imagine Mom's face at the holidays."

It was cruel, and Charlie was completely gone when he looked up.

"Do you still believe you knew Sam?" Somerville asked quietly.

"I know what I know," Charlie sputtered out.

"*He's an embarrassment*," Somerville echoed, a line Charlie still could not believe Sam would utter. "*He's smothering me*. Is it possible Sam was more complex than you knew?"

"Answer the question," the judge prompted after a moment.

"What was the question?" Charlie asked.

"Is it possible Sam was more complex than you thought? Is it possible you never really knew her?"

"I know what I know," Charlie said again.

"But is it possible you're mistaken?" Somerville pressed. "Is it possible?"

"Yes," he said quietly.

"No further questions."

"Ms. Fields?" the judge said.

She stood, shuffled a few papers, and said, "Just a few clarifying questions, your honor. Charlie, I appreciate your time here, and we're almost through. Can you tell me, did Sam ever say to you she'd had a few drinks before riding over to your house?"

"No, she never said anything."

"So you don't know for certain she'd ever had a drink."

"Objection. Leading the witness."

"I withdraw the question, your honor. Do you know, for certain, whether Sam had ever had a drink and then gotten on her bicycle?"

"No."

"Or behind the wheel."

"She didn't drive."

"Thank you, Charlie. Nothing further."

She returned to her seat, and Charlie sat stunned and waited for the next round.

But the judge told him, coldly, "You can go, Mr. Gibbs," and, not knowing whether to return to his seat or where he should go, he strode out of the courtroom and into the nearest bathroom, locked himself in a stall, and threw up.

11

While Charlie hunkered in a restroom stall, Somerville was even more brutal with his cross-examination of Lauren. Claire, mindful both of the need to ensure justice for the James family and to keep her career on the rocks, guided Lauren through a heart-rending account of her sister's life, and when she finished, Claire said, "Thank you, Ms. James. I know this has been tough for you, but we appreciate your sharing this information."

Claire likely assumed Somerville would pass on cross-examination. It was a dangerous game to confront character witnesses, because you didn't want to lose the jury's sympathy and come off like a bully. But by the look on Claire Fields's face when Somerville thanked the judge, stood, and buttoned his jacket, everyone in the courtroom understood she was dreading what the defense attorney was about to unleash. What had she missed in her interviews with the James family? What skeletons had Henry Somerville uncovered?

"Now, Ms. James," he started, "I want to echo Ms. Fields in thanking you for being here today. I'll try to keep this as brief as I can. To start with, will you tell the jury: would you describe your parents as good parents?"

"Of course," she said quickly.

"Caring, attentive?"

"Yes."

"I ask because that's the picture the prosecution is painting today. Your sister is the beautiful daughter of a happy family. Everyone clean-cut like TV characters. So you would agree that they raised your sister the same way they raised you, to be a happy, productive member of society?"

"Yes."

"Earlier, when Charlie Gibbs was on the stand, he admitted Samantha was a bit of a drinker."

"Objection!"

"I'll rephrase, your honor. Mr. Gibbs admitted that Samantha, although she was underage, would drink with him on occasion, sometimes before she even left work. Did you know about this?"

"No."

"And it doesn't sound like your sister, the girl your parents raised."

"Of course not."

"Now Mr. Gibbs seemed authentic to me," Somerville said. I didn't have any reason to believe he was lying, but that's for the jury to decide. What I'd ask, however, is if you ever saw Samantha drinking?"

"No," Lauren said quickly.

"Not once? Not a few sips of wine around the holidays?"

"Well, maybe."

"Where was this?"

"Well, at the house, our parents would have wine with dinner, for special occasions."

"And let Samantha have a glass?"

Lauren nodded.

"So that's a yes?"

"Yes, but it was only a small glass, and only once."

"What about you? Did your parents ever let you have wine?"

"No."

"Have you ever had alcohol?"

"I've tasted it."

"At your house?"

She nodded again. "Yes."

"Were your parents around?"

"They were in the other room. It was a sip of Sam's wine."

"Did your sister have a drinking problem?"

"No."

"Did she drink outside the home?"

"Not that I know of."

"Had you ever seen her with a hangover?" When Lauren didn't answer, he said, "Well, let me ask you this. Do you have a boyfriend?"

"I'm sorry?"

"A steady boyfriend. Do you have one?"

"No," she said.

"Have you recently been in a relationship?"

"Objection. Where is this going?"

"I presume you have a point, counselor?" the judge said.

"I do, your honor. Just a few more questions should wrap us up."

"Overruled, for now."

"Ms. James, have you recently been in a relationship?"

"I was, a few months ago, but we broke up."

"Can you be more specific?"

"We broke up in August."

"Did you love him?"

"No."

"Do you still see him, on occasion? Ever run into him?"

"No."

"Okay, so you had a boyfriend you didn't love, and you broke up. You broke up with him?"

"Yes."

"I don't mean to pry into your personal life, and I just have a few more questions. I know this is trying. But to recap what we've discussed so far, your parents raised you and Samantha both as virtuous young ladies. Samantha may have had a few glasses of wine on occasion, but there was no reason to doubt she was anything but the innocent young woman whose face has appeared in all the newspapers, is that right?"

"That's right."

"Now, my last question." Somerville looked Lauren dead in the eyes and seemed appropriately apologetic for delving into such unseemly territory, a burden placed on him in the name of justice, and he asked, "How many months pregnant are you?"

The courtroom erupted then, with Claire shouting objections, Judge Rhodes banging his gavel, and the startled audience murmuring. From there, Somerville proceeded to eviscerate Lauren—and by extension, Samantha—the same way he'd punished Charlie Gibbs for being a character witness. In the end, Somerville somehow maintained the high ground as the white knight investigating the sordid truth, while Lauren was shown to be nothing less than a tramp who fooled around with a boy and then broke it off with him before she found out she was pregnant. No one in her family knew, yet, although she was four and a half months along. Looking at her on the stand, you could see it: her swelled breasts, her tired eyes, her radiant skin, the bump in her abdomen. Somerville kept her on the stand long enough for the jurors, conservative and Christian, to judge her and her family for this unfortunate turn of events.

Charlie got drunk before he could read the news of the trial, but he gathered the gist of Somerville's cross-examination, and he pitied Lauren as much as he pitied himself. Some commenters online called Somerville a brute, and accused him of smearing Sam's good name, but the net effect appeared to be a loss for Claire. He wished he could ask her why she hadn't thought of Somerville's gambit about the drinking. It was true Sam occasionally had a glass of wine at the end of a shift, but Charlie always picked her up on those nights. She never rode her bicycle home drunk, but he'd not gotten the chance to explain that to the defense attorney nor to Claire. His mind reeled with scores of other points he wanted to make: that so what if he failed to understand Sam completely, that had nothing to do with the crime at hand. Yet Somerville had somehow wrangled a distorted truth out of Charlie, and now the jury's vision was clouded. His only minor solace came from what he read happened after he left the courtroom. Claire's next witness had been Lauren, who gave an impassioned plea for justice for her sister, only to be taken apart by Henry Somerville so completely that the family must be wrecked.

Why are you still here? she'd asked him the night of the funeral. *This is a pyramid scheme, you dumbass,* she'd told him last week in Target. He thought about those comments and he thought about what he read tonight in the news about Lauren's testimony. He believed her when she told him the other day that Sam had not, in fact, been seeing anyone else. But what *had* Sam been doing during that hour? *Had* she been drinking? Was the defense attorney right, that perhaps he'd never really known Sam? And where did he go from here? He thought about his life, and the more he thought and the later it grew, the more he saw what a profound effect Sam's death had made on his life. Not only the loss, but the trial, and the way Somerville had disillusioned him so completely that he could no longer distinguish between his corporeal self, his skin and blood and bones, and whatever spirit or soul lurked within him. In his agitation, he saw himself as an automaton ping-ponging his way through life according to the serves and strokes of forces beyond his control. He was no man, he had no mind, no free will. He served at the pleasure of those in power, men like Henry Somerville or the judge or the killer himself. Not just Charlie: Claire, Lauren, Sam.

As the night dragged on, he stalked message boards and read the commentary. Most of the world online was on Sam's side, but there was a hollow glee to their commentary, something self-serving, the way a populist politician will get on the stump and decry the fat cats for their excess, all the while earning more and more coin for their next campaign. It was all a racket! The whole world was a lie! He understood what justice meant, and saw that after today's debacle, Sam would not be redeemed. Her death had been unjust, and unjustified, but her killer would walk thanks to the wheeling and dealing and clever wordplay of his attorney. The rest of the night became a blur of blue-screened rage and stinging eyes, and the next morning Charlie found himself in front of the courthouse, in his pickup truck, his old .22 rifle, the gift from his father, in the passenger seat. The morning was crisp, in the mid-fifties, but sunny. If the Bermuda grass had not all gone dormant the color of coleslaw, you might think it was a beautiful May day. May Day. He chewed on his nails with his knee propped up against the steering wheel, and he watched from across the parking lot as the small-town courthouse came to life: the maintenance workers trudging in followed sometime later by sashaying suits and official looking administrators. A courthouse is an odd place, where the public and private sectors clash like armies, the humble bureaucrats on one side with laws and procedures backing them up, and on the other side the business leaders with deep pockets of entitlement.

Charlie watched it all, and he watched as the killer's lawyer pulled up and stood with the sheriff, and then the killer arrived and met the two of them in front of the courthouse and began walking toward the steps. On the first day of the trial, the news media had been here with cameras and reporters eager to catch a glimpse of the killer, but the novelty must have worn off because other than a few stray pieces of litter, no one and nothing was here to greet the killer and his lawyer. No one except Charlie Gibbs. He bit a final clip off a hangnail and then he snatched his rifle out of the passenger seat and opened the door and shuffled up to the steps, arriving at the same time as the killer. He stopped and cocked the rifle, and both Somerville and the killer took notice at the same moment: they stopped mid-step, their eyes widened, and they paused for just one split-second too long in indecision, and in that moment of weakness, Charlie Gibbs raised the rifle to his shoulder, took aim, and fired.

12

In the months leading up to and after the trial, during idle pockets at work, while our envelope manufacturing client brainstormed ways of revamping their business, and at night while my wife slept soundly beside me, and in the shower while hot water drummed my chest red, I continued to reflect on this story: what Daniel must have been thinking, what the victim's family must have been going through, how the attorneys were approaching the case. There was something voyeuristic about my interest in the trial, the way I'd come to know Claire Fields and Henry Somerville in my head, my thoughts about what they were thinking as they went through the trial, the truth beyond the headlines. I wanted to find something more to Daniel's story than what lay on the surface, yet I now believe that my interest in the trial, like all voyeurism, was just another form of escapism. You watch others to refract your own life and live out your own fantasies of what could be, and Daniel has come to seem like my double. His marriage could have been my marriage, his mistake could have been my mistake, and his judgment could therefore be my judgment.

Each day the commentary grew more vicious until it reached an apotheosis on the day of the verdict, the day Charlie Gibbs fired his gun toward Daniel. The news media, so clearly elated by the drama, swirled around the victim's family, who gave impassioned statements and analysis. The sister in particular seemed to be riding a wave and sought out the spotlight with intention in a way almost dishonest. Then it was over, and everything slid into the past. Memory, history, consciousness. The present was a moving target, everything else a construction. Historical archives and the human imagination were the only proof that anything beyond the now ever existed. This was what made us human: the invention of history, the invention of time, the invention of consciousness. Awareness of the self. The ability to create and follow a story. In other words, people had imaginations, and it was imagination alone that allowed me, finally, to look inward and understand the drama around Daniel Hayward. Wittgenstein said that which one cannot name must be passed over in silence. Silence seemed unjust for everyone involved in this tragedy, a resignation. All I have are the facts. James Baldwin once wrote that "all art is a kind of confession, more or less oblique." This was my story as much as Daniel's, and if I wanted to know more about him, to find some meaning in all of this, I would have to invent the story myself.

13

Of course Charlie Gibbs missed. He was incompetent to the bone and had not fired a rifle since his father left when he was thirteen. Therefore, his aim was wild and the bullet struck the steps and spat chips of concrete onto Daniel's pants. The sheriff pulled his sidearm and was able, in the interim between Charlie's shot and cocking the weapon for a second shot, to rush over and subdue the boy. Henry Somerville and Daniel Hayward snapped to attention and also rushed over. Somerville snatched the rifle and used the length of it to fend Daniel away so that the sheriff could turn Charlie over against the sidewalk, pin him screaming and face-down, and cuff his hands behind his back. Attempted manslaughter: an offense relegated to a couple inches in the newspaper's B section by the time of his own trial, the drama of Samantha James long forgotten and Charlie an unhinged used car salesman, unworthy of national news, it seemed.

After the shakeup, Daniel sat on one of the steps and put his head in his hands, stared at the concrete between his shoes. More police officers came out of the courthouse, along with the press and a few bystanders, and Henry Somerville fought off the media with a series of statements about the unfortunate turn of events and thanks to the grace of God that no one was injured. Meanwhile, a photographer snapped a photo of Daniel that perfectly caught the spirit of the man and the day: Daniel crumpled in a heap on the steps of the courthouse, the building of justice with its Greek revival columns towering in the background, as though he were about to face a pantheon of angry deities who would negotiate his future. His body's shadow rippled down the steps in front of him, and beside him you could see the chip in the pavement from the gunshot. A fractured man, mere inches from death, collapsed in defeat from or atonement for the year's events. The photo would accompany the bold-type headline on tomorrow's front page, announcing a verdict for the trial of the autumn. It might have been a local-yokel paper, but its news still carried weight, still captured a record of our shared humanity.

Somerville leaned down toward his client and asked if he wanted to petition for a delay in the trial. It should be no problem; Daniel could request a visit to the hospital to check for stress injuries from dodging the bullet. But no: Daniel wanted to get the verdict over with. He followed his lawyer into the courtroom, and after everyone settled and Judge Rhodes banged the gavel to call the day to order, he asked if the defendant had any final statements before the jury deliberated. Daniel stood and said, "I think about Samantha every day. This was all a terrible mistake, and I'm sorry." The judge nodded and then dismissed the jury. They returned in less than an hour with a decision. The foreman handed Daniel's fate to the bailiff, who handed the note to the judge. "Will the defendant please rise?" he asked, and Daniel, tragic figure or cowardly criminal, stood again to hear his fate.

THE JUDGE

Good morning. I have reviewed the file on this unfortunate case several times over the holidays, and now we have reached the time for sentencing. A few words are in order, both out of respect for the victim, and to acknowledge the defendant's final words, that this was all a terrible mistake. Mistakes do happen in this life, yet we also live in a fallen world where humans take action freely and are responsible for the consequences. The jury has found Daniel Hayward guilty for failure to stop at an accident resulting in the death of a person, Samantha James. The law stipulates a range of sentencing guidelines, under the South Carolina code, section 56-5-1210, which says that because of the death, the defendant is guilty of, quote, "a felony and, upon conviction, must be imprisoned not less than one year nor more than twenty-five years and fined not less than ten thousand dollars nor more than twenty-five thousand dollars."

Now, my job as the presiding judge is to weigh the evidence and the conviction and, most of all, the defendant's character to determine where in the range of one year to twenty-five years would be an appropriate sentence. Has the defendant accepted responsibility for his actions? Has he demonstrated remorse? And what degree of responsibility and remorse separates a one-year sentence from a ten-year sentence from a twenty-five-year sentence? If I were Pontius Pilate, I could throw the question to the people and abdicate my responsibility, but I don't have that luxury.

We began down this road in July, when the defendant turned himself in, was arraigned, and then released on bond. The defense soon petitioned the court for a change of venue, arguing that due to extensive media coverage, he could not receive a fair trial in Overlook. I do cite the media as being unseemly, but their coverage, by and large, revealed the facts for what they are. Twelve average citizens have acknowledged their duty to judge the defendant based on the facts of the case as they heard them in this courtroom. The jurors gave up three days of their lives to listen patiently as the prosecution and the defense unearthed the facts and called up the character witnesses, and the jurors listened while the counselors issued motions and threw barbs at each other, all for the sake of winning.

The defendant was afforded every accommodation due to him by the law, including months to prepare for the trial, representation by highly experienced counsel, and the opportunity to share not only the facts of the night in question—the what, where, when, and how of the accident—but also, perhaps most importantly, the why. All of human life remains a mystery, but especially the realm of crime and punishment. Why do people behave as they do? Why did the defendant leave the scene? We may never know the truth of those moments last July, but the character witnesses and the defendant's presence in the courtroom suggest he is no deviant, but an ordinary man who made an egregious error, came forward, and has stood trial for that error.

But we should also acknowledge Samantha James, the victim who was unable to come forward and offer testimony. She was not afforded the chance to plead her case, and while the voices of her family and friends have been admirable, they are mere avatars. By all accounts Samantha was a joyful young woman trying to make her mark on the world without taking a toll on our resources. Just as we will never know what went on inside Mr. Hayward's head the moment of the accident, we will also never know what the world would be like if Samantha James were still here.

I was admitted to the bar nearly forty-five years ago, and during my tenure practicing law and judging cases, I have often asked myself how things might be different: what if this person had taken a right turn instead of a left? Or if they had left home a few moments earlier or later? It's difficult to go through this long life without feeling like everything boils down to chance occurrences. If the good Lord has a plan for us—and I believe He does—it remains a mystery, leaving us right where we started, with the task of finding certain justice in an uncertain world.

In Daniel Hayward's case, the facts have been aired, and they have pointed to one conclusion, and the jury has found him guilty. So, Mr. Hayward, will you and your counsel please stand.

It is the judgment of this court that the defendant, Daniel Hayward, is hereby committed to the South Carolina Department of Corrections to be imprisoned for ten years, with five years suspended. The defendant shall surrender immediately for service of the sentence at the institution designated by the Department of Corrections. Upon release from imprisonment, the defendant shall be placed on probation for four years and shall serve five hundred hours of community service speaking to groups such as Mothers Against Drunk Driving, Students Against Destructive Decisions, and other comparable organizations. Finally, in accordance with the law, the defendant shall pay a fine of ten thousand dollars, due in full immediately.

Mr. Hayward, you have a right to appeal any findings of the jury as well as the sentence of this court. That completes this matter.

✦ ✦ ✦

Such were the words of Judge Rhodes in January, after which Daniel was remanded into custody, taken to the local detention center, and held for three days before being transferred to a facility of the state department of corrections. I never heard from Francine again, nor did I expect to, nor have I visited Daniel in prison. Although I think of him often, what would be the point?

We created a turnaround plan for the envelope manufacturer, which entailed them hiring a slew of software engineers and kids fresh out of VCU's brand school to help the company morph into an integrated marketing firm. By the new year I was knee-deep in project management, allowing the entire cast of this drama—Claire Fields, Henry Somerville, Judge Rhodes, the James family, the Haywards—to recede into memory, like a social media melodrama that flares bright and then gutters away. I woke up at five every day and was on my email by six, arranging a video shoot here, working with a web vendor there. We don't have a process in America to let dying industries simply close their doors. Instead, like old age for human beings, a business's twilight years are a whirlwind of activity that keeps people like me afloat.

I sometimes think about the work I do, which is not dissimilar from the work Daniel did, which if I'm honest is not all that much different from selling used cars like Charlie Gibbs. I make more money than Charlie did, and my company has a hip office in Richmond's Scott's Addition, a big brick building that used to be a tobacco warehouse, with open rafters and tall windows and a general aesthetic that marries our town's Old South heritage with the 21st century creative class. There's a certain respectability to my world that you don't associate with used car salesmen, but we're all just trying to make a buck, and deep down we know which project (or car) is a lemon. Sometimes an envelope manufacturer is just an envelope manufacturer. They might print direct mailers, but that didn't make them a direct mail organization, any more than a 2005 Hyundai could pass for a Lexus.

Meanwhile, the story of Daniel Hayward continued to gnaw at me: the mystery of what happened, the character of my old friend, the menace of the pitchfork mob online, and what it all meant for my own life.

In the spring, nearly a year after the trial, I visited Overlook to help my parents clean up a few things to get ready to sell their house. I would be there for three days, in the quiet and small house of my upbringing, my parents quietly cold toward each other, a step-change in age, skulking around the old ranch house. People I no longer knew now that I myself was sliding into middle age, and I admit I had another agenda for visiting beyond helping them sort through my childhood cassette tapes and karate trophies and sell unwanted furniture. In the weeks leading up to the visit, I'd gotten a message to Judge Rhodes, who, surprisingly, agreed to join me for a cup of coffee on Friday morning. "I'm mostly retired now," he wrote in an email, "but I'd be glad to meet with you." He suggested the Griddle & Trough and asked if I knew it. "I look forward to it," he said.

I'd told him I was a one-time English major who was thinking about writing a book about Daniel. This was not strictly untrue, but I had neither the time nor the temperament for Literature anymore. In college I'd taken a short fiction class, and while I never had trouble sliding in to the heads of characters unlike myself, I never knew what to do with them. Consulting 101: Know your business. Know your customer. Know your customer's business. A fiction writer has one thing in common with a business consultant, in that both of our professions rely on the imagination. How do we know another human being? What are they thinking? What do they want out of life? What it is it like to be someone else, to possess another's consciousness? And the question I could never get past in college: What will they do next?

Perhaps these are unanswerable questions, in the end.

As for Judge Rhodes, someone should write his story, though I wouldn't know where to start and might not be the right writer to tell it, too captivated by his *story* to get at the ordinary truth of the man. He was a black judge in the South, which meant his life had great depth but was fraught with clichés and misunderstandings. Born on a dirt road in Mathews, South Carolina, he left his family and his kin, caught a bus to Washington, D.C., to attend Howard University for four years in the early sixties, his family's first college graduate, and then he continued on with his studies to earn a divinity degree before becoming a lawyer. He returned to South Carolina, the native son, to become one of only a few African American circuit court judges in the state's history—quite a legacy, quite a long march from the country hamlet to his seat on the bench. Who was this man, what was it like to be him, and what did he think about the world?

These were questions I never asked, because I only met him one time, for less than an hour, over coffee, at the Griddle & Trough. I never knew him well enough to know what impression, if any, the Hayward trial had made on his consciousness, and in our short discussion that day, we never got around to discussing the role of justice to society at large. Was he an arbiter of the truth in an age of fake news? What did he think of the assault on facts? Was objectivity even an option in today's world? I doubt it.

That day of our meeting, Judge Rhodes wore civilian clothes: creased gray pants, a checkered blue button-down, a smile that said *retired middle manager.* "So you're writing a book, huh?" he said when we sat in a booth together.

"Well, maybe, if I can ever find the time."

"I sometimes think I might like to write myself, now that I'm retired."

"I bet you've got some good stories to tell," I said. "I appreciate you meeting me."

"Of course, glad to do it. You want something to eat, or just coffee?"

"I'm good with just coffee," I said.

He put the menus back in the rack behind the condiments. "You been here?"

"Many times," I said. "I grew up in Overlook."

"Ah, so these are your old stomping grounds."

"This place wasn't open when I was in high school, but it's good to come home to."

"The owner is a friend of mine," he said. "We go back a ways. He had his own law firm for decades and sold it four or five years ago and decided to open a diner. Not my idea of a relaxing retirement, but to each their own."

"Lot of work for sure," I said.

"You got that right. I don't think he takes but one day a week off, probably working longer hours as a cook back there than he ever did in his law practice, but I suspect he's happier for it."

"Because it's something he wants to do rather than has to do?"

"And there's no pressure here. Worst thing that happens is he goes out of business, but he doesn't have to worry about paying his daughter's private school tuition, and he doesn't have to schmooze for clients. That really is the worst. So tell me what you're working on."

"I don't know exactly. Do you remember the Daniel Hayward hit and run case?"

"Very well."

"Daniel was my college roommate."

"Ah." He folded his hands in front of him and sat back.

"You know, I've got mixed feelings about the whole thing. I'm just hung up on how there are these moments in life you can't come back from, and how one quick mistake changes an otherwise good person's life."

"Uh-huh."

"I take it you don't necessarily feel the same kind of sympathy?"

He stirred his coffee absently for a moment. "Well, I think most people that end up in my courtroom deserve to be there."

"Really?"

"Yes, most people on trial are guilty, and the rest is just horse-trading."

"That kind of surprises me."

"You thought I might be on the side of the disenfranchised?"

"Not necessarily."

"Look, when I was in college, I did the marches, and I recognize our system still has amazing flaws. Mandatory sentencing, for instance. I have a drug addict come in front of my court, and it's strike three for him and I have to send him to prison for twenty years—is that fair? I don't think so. That's the legislature taking judgment out of my hands and drawing a box and saying everything fits neatly inside that box. I can't think of anything more foolish, but that doesn't mean the drug addict isn't guilty of possession. He most certainly is, if he shows up in my courtroom. You don't like it?"

"No, I guess I was just expecting a little more room for…" but I couldn't say why I was here.

"You're looking for a Hollywood ending," he said. "The defense attorney gives an impassioned plea, and the jury, out of the goodness of their hearts, sets a wrongly accused man free. Sometimes that happens. Juries are made of people."

"But most people aren't wrongly accused."

"Life in a courtroom is a lot more prosaic than you might think. So you want to write a book about your friend Daniel, huh."

"Maybe a novel, fictional version of him."

"He your main character?"

"I don't know yet."

"You don't know?"

"I'm a business consultant," I admitted. "I don't really know what I'm doing. I was thinking about writing a morality play. Just try to show everyone's truth and let the reader decide what to think."

"That's one approach," he said, and he held up his hands. "Hey, I'm not the expert."

"Well, neither am I. But I tell you, you do know the law, and you know about crime and punishment."

"I do," he said.

"Maybe you could just tell me a little about what it's like to be a judge."

"What do you want to know?"

"I don't know. Anything. Everything. In my day job, I have one window on the world, so I'd love to hear about how you view your work. For me, I don't think about what I do in special terms. It's all mechanical, but some people I work with have these fully fleshed-out theories of American business and capitalism. I guess I'm wondering if you ever think philosophically about what you're doing, about justice and mercy and why people behave the way they do, or is it just a job like making widgets?"

He gave a heavy sigh.

"Sorry to be all over the place."

"No, it's fine. It's been a long time since I've put much thought into the philosophy of the law. Like you were saying, it's what I do. But no, I would say I still do put a great deal of thought into why people behave the way they do, and what would be an appropriate punishment. Take your friend's case. I have no doubt that he hit the girl that night, and I can still remember his righteous lawyer trying to imply the girl was the one riding home drunk.

That was a low blow, and it might be the reason I remember the case so well. I also suspect Hayward was drunk. Now, I'm sure he regrets it, and I might even believe he honestly was able to talk himself into believing he might have hit a deer, but alone in the dark, you know what you've done. You can't hide from the truth, any more than you can hide from God. My job is to facilitate bringing the truth to light."

"I read your speech at the sentencing."

He laughed and shook his head.

"It was good," I said. "I was surprised at the biblical echoes in your writing."

"Well, I believe we're on this earth for a reason, and my faith probably does filter into the other areas of my life."

"I saw you had a master's in divinity. How does that part of your life, your faith, mesh with your job as a judge?"

"I believe in original sin. It's no longer a popular stance, because we're supposed to have transcended all that. We're all free and on a level playing field, and we can reinvent ourselves to escape the past."

"You remember what Faulkner said about the past."

"It's not even past. I think about that often. Most of the people I sentence would ascribe to that philosophy. I'm not even talking about whatever they did to land in my courtroom. I mean the old past, their parents or their grandparents, and on back. You know how I ended up where I am? I was lucky. I had two parents who instilled in me values of hard work and the love of God. I didn't always appreciate it at the time, but that had a profound effect on me. Even still, despite having a successful life and being in the position I am, I recognize I'm a fallen man. We all fall short in the eyes of God, and it has nothing to do with how we live our lives and everything to do with events before our time. This is maybe more than you were looking for, but I think about that every day."

"Original sin."

"The bite of the apple. I sentence people within the range permitted by the law, but that law is a human convention, and quakes before the other law."

"How do you reconcile the two?"

"They don't always conflict. Jesus said love God, and love your neighbor, but what does that mean? I interpret it to mean living every day with humility. Hubris is self-love, so the opposite of hubris—love of another—means admitting you don't have all the answers, that you could be wrong, and that you must act according to the will of the Lord, as you understand it."

"And what does that mean about mercy? You can't do that, as a judge."

"Well, there's a difference between mercy and clemency. I could have sentenced your friend to one year suspended and satisfied the letter of the South Carolina code, but would that have been a mercy? He would have been free to go home that afternoon, but he would also have to live with being a killer—just as he's had to live with it in prison. Mercy is something I can't grant. The girl he hit—her family could forgive, which might have been a kind of mercy. But true mercy comes from above."

I knew my bible well enough to know what Judge Rhodes was saying was open to debate. I was no theologian. I had no master's of divinity. But I recognized in him the same conservative strand I see in my grandfather and his generation. These are people who still believe in miracles and the divine, whereas in my generation, technology has taken much of the mystery out of the world. I'd come here perhaps looking for wisdom, and maybe *we're all sinners* and *don't get a big head* are all that pass for wisdom in this life, yet I couldn't shake the feeling that I was missing something, that there was more to experience and justice and life and time and death than a few platitudes, but there it was. Anyone you put on a pedestal, for whatever reason, will let you down as soon as you realize they're human.

After some more chatter, mostly about Overlook politics, and a little more about the owner of the Griddle & Trough—whose life had its own tragic dimensions that I won't go into here—I thanked him and told him I didn't want to take up any more of his time.

"I hope you got what you need," he said. "I'm afraid I didn't have much to offer you. Truth is, being a judge for so long, I've lost the ability to see it with any kind of wonder. Maybe you were right up front, it is just a job."

I thanked him again and picked up the ticket.

"Let me pay for it," he said.

"It's on me. Not often I get to have coffee with a real live judge."

On our way out the door he asked what kind of business consulting I did. "I've always wondered what exactly that means."

He stood there in the sweltering day while I sputtered a few words about helping businesses figure out what they do best, and compared it to therapy. Finally I stopped and said, "I think it means whatever the consultant wants it to mean."

"I should tell my grandson. He calls himself a 'radio entrepreneur,' but I have no idea what that means. I just know he's living at home and gets free albums in the mail."

"He'll make more money if he can find a way to call himself a consultant," I said, and the judge chuckled.

"All right, young man, go write your book," he said.

I shook his hand, and wondered yet again what he was thinking. Who *was* he behind the grandfatherly persona? What did he think about the world? What kind of man was created by a lifetime of heavy thinking and clear-eyed reflection he practiced every day from the bench? Where did he get the vision you needed to listen to testimony in a case like Daniel Hayward's hit and run, hear the heart-wrenching stories from the family, hear the shades of nuance from the defense, cut through the rhetoric and find the facts and weigh the facts against the law? In other words, how do you exercise judgment? In some ways, though I knew he would object to the language, it was like playing God on earth. I believed he did have the power to extend mercy, but that in his world, mercy on earth was a mirage. Guilty or innocent, free or in prison, we were all sinners.

I got in my car and turned the AC on high, and I watched him lumber to his own car, put his sunglasses on, and drive off west down the highway. I sat there for a long time and thought of Daniel Hayward, and how bored I was with my own life, with my job and with Kate. I still think about the life that could have been, the many directions I could have taken if I had not gone into business, if I had not married so young, if I had thought to pursue a different kind of life. But what would I have done? Moved to New York to become an unimportant writer in Brooklyn? Returned to Overlook to sell real estate or get into land development? The town had changed since my high school years. My old high school had been demolished and my friends had scattered across the country. Faulkner was wrong. Sometimes the past really is past, even if we don't want to recognize the present for what it is. And so, with more questions than answers, I left the judge at the diner and headed up I-95, toward home, where I got back to work.

Jon Sealy is also the author of *The Whiskey Baron*, *The Edge of America*, and *So You Want to Be a Novelist*. A South Carolina native, he lives in Richmond, Virginia.

www.ingramcontent.com/pod-product-compliance
Lightning Source LLC
Chambersburg PA
CBHW051645180726
48284CB00006B/1874